T0165823

Murder Most Divine

Murder Most Divine

ECCLESIASTICAL TALES OF UNHOLY CRIMES

Edited by

RALPH McINERNY AND MARTIN H. GREENBERG

CUMBERLAND HOUSE
NASHVILLE, TENNESSEE

Published by Cumberland House Publishing, Inc., 431 Harding Industrial Drive, Nashville, TN 37211

Cover design: Gore Studio, Inc.
Text design: Mary Sanford

Library of Congress Cataloging-in-Publication Data
Murder most divine : ecclesiastical tales of unholy crimes / edited by Ralph McInerny
    and Martin H. Greenberg.
        p. cm.
    ISBN 1-58182-121-2 (alk. paper)
        1. Detective and mystery stories, American. 2. Clergy--Fiction. I. McInerny,
    Ralph M.
    PS374.D4 M857 2000
    813'.0872083522--dc21

                                                                    00-064421

1 2 3 4 5 6 7—05 04 03 02 01 00

Contents

Introduction

RALPH MCINERNY

No literary genre exhibits art's dependence on a moral point of reference more strikingly than the murder mystery. To take the life of another is wrong; the murderer must be discovered and suitably punished. That is the rock bottom assumption of the murder mystery. In an age when commonly shared moral beliefs are increasingly atrophying, the murder mystery continues in popularity, perhaps as the last refuge of the reader who wants to see good triumph and evil punished, at least on the printed page.

Was G. K. Chesterton's Father Brown the first clerical sleuth? I do not know. Given Chesterton's accomplishment in the five collections of stories featuring his engaging priest, Father Brown might have been the last as well. Few writers would be willing to risk comparison with the works of one of the consummate stylists of the English language. When it was proposed to me that I should launch a series of mysteries featuring a priest, I reacted as one would to any sacrilegious suggestion. Get thou behind me, agent. Presume to rival Chesterton's Father Brown? It is tough enough being compared with lesser lights. But I was young and foolhardy then and overcame my reluctance. I have just finished the twentieth of my Father Dowling mysteries, *Triple Pursuit*. It is not that I survived the comparison with Chesterton—only a few reviewers were irresponsible enough to make it—but that I and many other writers came to see that in a morally disintegrating society, any appeal to what had once been the common morality is more easily made through a clerical or religious figure whose confidence in the moral law was bolstered by their religious faith.

The nun or priest or monk represents right and wrong more dramatically than an officer of the law or ordinary private detective. A master detective need not be a moral paragon; since Sherlock Holmes, it is the convention to invest the great man with flaws, though flaws unrelated to the skills needed for detecting. Severer demands are put on the man of the cloth or cowl and the woman with a veil. Writers, themselves unsympathetic with religious beliefs, are drawn to such figures in order to look for chinks in the armor of representatives of religion. Finding celibacy incredible, a writer's imagination may teem with images of sexual repression. "State of Grace" is one such story; "Holy Living and Holy Dying" another. The former, a hardboiled story in which everyone is corrupt, including the sleuth, displays an unsure grasp of the ins and outs of clerical life, but not only readers who are similarly ill-informed can enjoy it. The bishop's basement is equipped with all the instruments of torture with which Hollywood has furnished the Inquisition; a Bible said to have belonged to Saint Thomas More is sold for a hundred dollars! The latter, "Holy Living and Holy Dying," one of the better written stories in this collection, somehow surmounts its reliance on cliches of this variant on the genre—the confessional, the supposed celibate having recourse to prostitutes—and makes the improbable plausible. There is little detecting done in either—events simply disclose themselves.

The eighteen stories brought together in this collection are not, of course, homogenous. The role of the cleric or religious varies from story to story. There are four stories that have a religious woman as principal figure, but some are modern and some are medieval. In several of the stories, it is the cleric who is the criminal rather than the sleuth. Andrew Greeley's story conveys something of the confusion felt by some clerics as to what it is they represent, but by and large, whether seen as the basis for a charge of hypocrisy or as the filter through which events are assessed, the requirements of Christianity are unambiguously assumed in most of these stories.

Unlike natural kinds, literary genres and their subdivisions can be shuffled and reorganized in various ways. Thus, the stories in this collection can be divided into the medieval and the modern. They can be separated into those that feature religious women and those that feature male clerics—priests, bishops, monks. They can be divided into those that approach the world of religious belief from the outside and those that move from within. And they could be divided into those that are marked by rather elementary mistakes about Christianity and Church lore and those that are sure. The medieval ones could be divided into those that contain embarrassing ignorance of Latin and those that do not. And the familiar subcategories of the mystery could be invoked—hardboiled vs. softboiled. Two of the stories ascend into almost mystical fantasy.

Given these various possibilities for grouping the stories, any taxonomy chosen would be more or less arbitrary. So it is that the stories are presented in an alphabetic order based on the surnames of the authors. I would like to say at least a word or two about all the stories, but considerably more about some of them. Readers will of course agree or disagree with my preferences, and that is as it should be. The stories were not gathered to represent any *a priori* attitude of my own, and the hope is that those who do not share my predilections will find here ample opportunity to indulge their own delights.

Stories set in the Middle Ages inhabit a world where Christian belief is taken to be universal and murder is unlikely to be thought of as just what you would expect from a believer. "The Monk's Tale" is perhaps the most successful use of the medieval setting by the stories in this collection. We are in England in the fourteenth century; the story is told in a chronicle that a penitent friar keeps for his superior—he is under a cloud for having gone off to war despite his clerical status, and for having taken a brother with him who was killed, leaving their parents bereft of children —the problem is the death of an abbot. Our friar is the assistant in such matters of Sir John the coroner, and off they go. The monastic life is described with authority but the story never becomes learned display. The transposition into this setting of the conventions of the detective story is adroitly handled.

Medieval mystery stories seem to have a recurrent component of their own—murder by poisoning, the poison garnered from the monastery herb garden. At least this is true of both "The Witch's Tale" and "The

Monk's Tale." "Conventual Spirit" is set in the convent of the Parclete, founded by Peter Abelard, with Heloise as abbess. Mysterious muddy footprints visible within the walls each morning lead the nuns to some-times sniggering speculation as to which of them might be having a night visitor. Detection makes clear that one of the nuns is going out at night, and leaving the muddy footprints on her return. In the final scene, the nun whose curiosity has uncovered this much receives sage advice from Heloise the abbess. The sleepwalking nun is espied dancing in the nude on a moonlit hill and Heloise gives the younger nun a quasi-psychiatric explanation. One would have liked more of Heloise, endowed with her historical gifts of high intelligence and self-effacing passion. "When Your Breath Freezes" is written on the assumption that the religious life is somehow pathological. The setting, for unexplained reasons, is Alaska; the narrator's presence in the convent is curiously unjustified, the ending gothic.

"Brother Orchid"—was this made into a movie starring Edward G. Robinson?—is set in the 1930s, its slang is hopelessly dated, but still it somehow engages the reader and holds his interest right through to the surprising and satisfying ending. Of all the authors represented here, Andrew Greeley knows most about the priesthood. His story is adroitly constructed and engagingly narrated by a priest—or is he a bishop? This is never made quite clear—who unsurprisingly holds most of the author's progressive views. In an effort to deal with a penitent who wants absolu-tion before he kills someone, Bishop [or Father] Ryan finally, against his bent, has recourse to the old catechism explanation of mortal sin. A sur-prising yet perfectly plausible ending puts this story at the head of the class.

"Mea Culpa" will be the favorite of many readers, I think. The char-acter of the narrator is well-rounded, and if the adults, particularly the stepfather, are often grotesques, the story moves with unhurried sureness toward its denouement. The use of the confessional is particularly effec-tive. "The Second Commandment" is a long and subtle story which is in many ways the most religious in this collection. The ending may have the look of a contrivance, but waiving that, the story has the most elaborate architecture of any in this collection.

And so I come to "Murder Mysteries." It would be easy to ridicule the theology of the story—an angel is murdered, its body found with blood all over the floor. Of course angels don't have bodies and they couldn't die if they wanted to, let alone be murdered. Somehow such metaphysical niceties cease to matter. The story begins in the City of the Angels, Los Angeles, and employs the device of a stranger telling a somewhat amoral young man a story involving angels, through the course of which we eventually learn he is one. The narrated story is set in heaven prior to the creation and angels are depicted as busy designing the world God will bring into being. They are trying to get the hang of death, and this is what leads to the murdered angel. The antagonists are God and Satan and the fallen angel on the park bench in Los Angeles, who tells the story,—no mute Milton he, however inglorious—sided with Satan. The revolt against God is based on the charge that He causes everything necessarily and yet holds agents accountable. How revolt would be possible if freedom is absent is a bit of a problem, but the story's imaginative range and success in writing about angels and heaven in juxtaposition with a seedy and decadent Los Angeles, makes this reader forgive all its faults.

It is sometimes said that Chesterton deliberately created an anti-Sherlock Holmes character with Father Brown. Holmes proceeds with all the impersonal objectivity of the scientific method. Brown steps into the shoes of the unknown perpetrator and is thereby able sympathetically to discern which of the suspects is guilty. "The Wrong Shape" is from the first collection of Father Brown stories, *The Innocence of Father Brown*, and has been chosen in the hope that it is relatively less known than the others. Of my own Father Dowling story, I will say only that my character began to feature in shorter fiction more than a decade after first appearing in print. I write a Father Dowling story for each issue of *Catholic Dossier*, a magazine I edit. This is one of them.

Recently I was in Melbourne at an academic meeting where we speakers were given a dinner by Archbishop Eric D'Arcy, substituting for the ordinary, Archbishop George Pell, who was in Rome. Before we went in to table, a short, bearded priest came up to me and studied me with smiling eyes. "I am Father Dowling," he announced. And so he was. He had an armful of my novels which I was delighted to sign for him. But I had the odd feeling that he was the fictional and my own Father Dowling the real one. Authorial fantasy, of course. But doubtless all the authors of stories in this collection harbor a similar certainty. Our common hope is that the reader will share it, if only for an hour or two.

Murder Most
Divine

niceties cease to matter. The story begins in the City of the Angels, Los Angeles, and employs the device of a stranger telling a somewhat amoral young man a story involving angels, through the course of which we eventually learn he is one. The narrated story is set in heaven prior to the creation and angels are depicted as busy designing the world God will bring into being. They are trying to get the hang of death, and this is what leads to the murdered angel. The antagonists are God and Satan and the fallen angel on the park bench in Los Angeles, who tells the story,—no mute Milton he, however inglorious—sided with Satan. The revolt against God is based on the charge that He causes everything necessarily and yet holds agents accountable. How revolt would be possible if freedom is absent is a bit of a problem, but the story's imaginative range and success in writing about angels and heaven in juxtaposition with a seedy and decadent Los Angeles, makes this reader forgive all its faults.

It is sometimes said that Chesterton deliberately created an anti-Sherlock Holmes character with Father Brown. Holmes proceeds with all the impersonal objectivity of the scientific method. Brown steps into the shoes of the unknown perpetrator and is thereby able sympathetically to discern which of the suspects is guilty. "The Wrong Shape" is from the first collection of Father Brown stories, *The Innocence of Father Brown,* and has been chosen in the hope that it is relatively less known than the others. Of my own Father Dowling story, I will say only that my character began to feature in shorter fiction more than a decade after first appearing in print. I write a Father Dowling story for each issue of *Catholic Dossier,* a magazine I edit. This is one of them.

Recently I was in Melbourne at an academic meeting where we speakers were given a dinner by Archbishop Eric D'Arcy, substituting for the ordinary, Archbishop George Pell, who was in Rome. Before we went in to table, a short, bearded priest came up to me and studied me with smiling eyes. "I am Father Dowling," he announced. And so he was. He had an armful of my novels which I was delighted to sign for him. But I had the odd feeling that he was the fictional and my own Father Dowling the real one. Authorial fantasy, of course. But doubtless all the authors of stories in this collection harbor a similar certainty. Our common hope is that the reader will share it, if only for an hour or two.

The Second Commandment

Charlotte Armstrong

Halley was sure glad the damn fog had rolled up and was billowing off over the mountains. Hey, if you looked southwest, you could even see a couple of stars. Lucky. They might have to hang around, maybe till morning.

And it was a little too quiet out here. Not much traffic on California Route 1; on a night like this there had better not be. The sea kept booming; it always did. The men shouted once in a while at their work, but they knew their business. They'd have her up on the road, and pretty quick.

Hey, here's my chance, thought Halley, to get all the stuff down, like they keep telling me. So the young sheriff's deputy opened the back door of his official car and leaned over to let the dome light fall on his paperwork. The husband was sitting inside, and quiet.

"May I please have your name again, sir?" Halley used the polite official drone.

"Hugh Macroy." The other's voice, even in exhaustion, had a timbre and a promise of richness. A singer, maybe? Young Halley's ear had caught this possibility when he had first answered the call. He never had seen the man—at least, not too well. Now the lighting was weird—red lights flashing on the equipment, for instance.

"Address?" Halley asked, after he had checked the spelling.

"382 Scott—no, I'm sorry. 1501 South Columbo."

"That's in Santa Carla, sir? Right out of L.A?"

"Yes." The man was holding his head at the temples, between thumb and two middle fingers. Poor old guy, he didn't hardly remember where he lived. But Halley, who knew better than to indulge in emotions of his own over one of these routine tragedies, figured himself lucky the fellow wasn't cracking up.

"Your age, sir?"

"Forty-five."

(Check. Kind of an old-looking guy.) "Occupation?"

"I am the pastor at St. Andrew's."

Halley became a little more respectful, if possible, because—well, hell, you were supposed to be. "Just you and your wife in the car, sir? En route from Carmel, didn't you say? To Santa Carla?

"We had expected to stay the night in San Luis Obispo."

"I see. Your wife's name, please?"

"Sarah. Sarah Bright."

Halley wrote down *Sara.* "*Her* age, please?"

"Fifty-five."

(Huh!) "Housewife, sir, would you say?"

"I suppose so." The man was very calm—too beat, probably, thought Halley, to be anything else. Although Halley had heard some who carried on and cried and sometimes words kept coming out of them like a damn broken faucet.

"And how long you been married?" the deputy sheriff continued politely.

"I think it has been two days, if today is Wednesday." Now, in the syllables, the voice keened softly.

"Any chil—"(Oh oh!) "Excuse me, sir."

"There is Sarah's daughter in San Luis Obispo. Mrs. Geoffrey Minter. She should be told about this as soon as may be. She will have been worrying."

"Yes, sir," said Halley, reacting a little crisply, not only to the tone but to the grammar. "If you've got her address or phone, I can get her notified right now."

The man dictated an address and a phone number as if he were reading them from a list he could see. Halley could tell his attention had gone away from what he was saying.

Halley thanked him and called in from the front seat. "Okay. They'll call her, sir. We probably won't be here too long now," he told the silent figure and drew himself away, shutting the car doors gently.

He strolled on strong legs to the brink. He could hear the heavy water slamming into rock forty feet below. (Always did.) The night sky was clearing all the way overhead now. There was even a pale moon.

Some honeymoon, thought Halley. But he wasn't going to say anything. It had occurred to him that this one might not be routine, not exactly, and that Halley had better watch his step, and be at all times absolutely correct.

"How's it going?" be inquired cheerfully of the toilers.

They had a strong light playing on her as she came up in the basket. She was dead, all right.

Macroy got out of the car and looked down at her and maybe he prayed or something. Halley didn't wait too long before he touched the clergyman's arm.

"They'll take her now, sir. If you'll just come with me?"

The man turned obediently.

Halley put him into the back seat of the official car and got in to drive.

As the deputy steered skillfully onto the pavement, Macroy said, "You're very kind. I don't think I could drive—not just now." His voice sounded shaky, but it was still singsongy.

"That's all right, sir," said Halley. But he thought, Don't he know his car's got to stay put and get checked out, for godsake? That kind of voice—Halley didn't exactly trust it. Sounded old-timey to him. Or some kind of phony.

On the highway, that narrow stretch along the curving cliffs, Halley scooted along steadily and safely toward the place where this man must go. By the book. And that was how Halley was going, you bet—by the book. It might not be a routine case at all.

So forget the sight of Sarah Bright Macroy, aged fifty-five, in her final stillness. And how she'd looked as if she had about four chins where the crepey skin fell off her jawbone. And thick in the waist, but with those puny legs some old biddies get, sticking out like sticks, with knots in them, and her shoes gone so that the feet turned outward like a couple of fins, all gnarled and bunioned. Um boy, some honeymoon! Halley couldn't figure it.

So swiftly, decisively, youthfully, he drove the official car, watching the guy from the back of his head in case he got excited or anything. But he didn't.

He just sat there, quiet, stunned.

Sheriff's Captain Horace Burns was a sharp-nosed man of forty-seven and there was a universal opinion (which included his own) that you had to get up early in the morning to fool him. His office had seen about as much wear as he had, but Burns kept it in stern order, and it was a place where people behaved themselves.

Burns had felt satisfied with Halley, who sat up straight in the hard chair by the door with his young face poker-smooth. His report had been clear and concise. His mien was proper. The Captain's attention was on this preacher. He saw a good-looking man, about his own age, lean and well set up, his face aquiline but rugged enough not to be "pretty." He also saw the pallor on the skin and the glaze of shock in the dark eyes—which, of course, were to be expected.

Macroy, as invited, was telling the story in his own words, and the Captain, listening, didn't fiddle with anything. His hands were at rest. He listened like a cat.

"So we left Carmel early this afternoon," Macroy was saying. "We had driven up on 101. We thought we'd come down along the ocean, having no idea that the fog was going to roll in the way it did."

Behind him a clerk was taking it down. Macroy didn't seem to be aware of that.

"But it did," said that voice, and woe was in it. "As thick a fog as I've ever experienced. We had passed Big Sur. You can't, you know, get through the mountains and change routes."

"You're stuck with it," the Captain said agreeably.

"Yes. Well, it was very slow going and very tiring. We were so much delayed that the sun went down, although you could hardly tell."

"You stopped," Burns prodded, thinking that the voice sounded like a preacher's, all right. "About what time?"

"I don't know. There was a sudden rift and I was able to see the wide place to our right. On the ocean side. A scenic point, I imagine." The Captain nodded. "Well, it looked possible to take the car off the highway there, so I—so I did. I had been so tense for such a long time that I was very glad to stop driving. Then Sarah wished to get out of the car, and I—"

"Why?"

"Beg pardon?"

"Why did she wish to get out of the car?" The Captain used the official drone. When the minister didn't answer, Burns said, "It has to be included in your statement."

"Yes," said Macroy. He glanced at the clerk. "She needed to—"

When he got stuck, Halley's face was careful not to ripple.

"Answer a call of nature," droned the Captain. "Has to be on record. That's right, Reverend?"

Macroy said with sober sadness, "Yes. I took the flashlight and got out to make sure there was enough margin between us and the edge." He stared over the Captain's head, seeing visions. "The light didn't accomplish much," he went on, "except to create a kind of blank white wall, about three feet before me. But I could check the ground. So I helped her out. I gave her the light and cautioned her. She promised not to go too far. I, of course, got back behind the wheel."

He hesitated.

The Captain said, "Car lights on, were they?"

"Yes.

"She went around behind the car?"

"Yes."

"Go on. Full details, please. You're doing fine."

"I was comforting my right shoulder with a little massage," said the minister with a touch of bitterness, "when I thought I heard her cry out."

"Motor off, was it?" The Captain's calm insistence held him.

"Yes. It was very quiet. Except for the surf. When I heard, or thought I heard—I listened, but there was no other cry. In a short while, I called to her. There was no answer. I couldn't—couldn't, of course, see anything. I called again. And again. Finally, I got out."

"And what did you do?" said the Captain.

"The flashlight," he said, "was there."

"Oh, was it? The light on, I mean?"

"Yes." Macroy seemed to wait for and rely on these questions. "It was lying on the ground, pointing to sea. I picked it up. I began to call and range the whole—the whole—well, it was a sort of platform, you might say, a sort of triangular plateau. I shuffled over all of it—between the pavement and the brink—and she wasn't—"

"Take your time," said the Captain.

But the minister lifted his head and spoke more rapidly. "At last, and I don't know when, a car came along. Mercifully it stopped. The driver offered me a ride. But I couldn't leave her." The anguished music was back in the voice. "How could I leave her?"

"He didn't get out? The driver of the car?" said Burns, again coming to the rescue.

"No. No. I begged him to send some help. Then I just kept on ranging and calling and—hoping and waiting, until help came." Macroy sank back.

"He called in, all right," Burns said in his flat tone. "Hung up without giving his name. But he can be found, I think, any time we need him."

Macroy was staring at the Captain with total incomprehension. He said, "I would like to thank him—yes, I would like to someday." Not now, wept his voice. Not yet.

"Can be arranged." Burns leaned back. "Just a couple of questions, Mr. Macroy. Was it your wife's suggestion that you stop the car?"

"I beg your pardon?"

"Did she ask you to stop? Or was it your idea?"

"Oh, I'm sorry. I wasn't following. No, it was my—well, you see, I knew she was in distress. But it was I who saw the opportunity."

"I see," said the Captain. "And you got back in the car for reasons of—er—privacy?"

"Values," said Macroy with sudden hollowness. "How ridiculous! In that dangerous spot. I knew how dangerous it was. I shouldn't have let her. I shouldn't."

The Captain, had he been a cat, would have had his ears up, and his tail, curled, would have stirred lazily.

"I will always—" Macroy was as good as weeping now. "Always regret." His eyes closed.

"You were only a few miles from low ground," said the Captain calmly. "You didn't know that?"

Macroy had his face in his hands and he rocked his whole body in the negative.

The Captain, when his continued listening was obviously proving unprofitable, said for the record, "You didn't know. Well, sir, I guess that's about all, for now."

"Where have they brought her?" Macroy dropped his hands.

"I—er—wouldn't go over to the funeral parlor. No point. You realize there's got to be an autopsy?" Macroy said nothing. "Now, we aren't holding you, but you're a lot of miles from home, so I think what you'd better do, Reverend, is go over to the motel and rest there for the night. We'll need your signature on your statement, for one thing. In the morning will do." The Captain stood up.

"Thank you," said Macroy. "Yes. I couldn't leave."

"Did you push your wife?" said the Captain conversationally.

Macroy's face could be no paler. "No," he said with wondering restraint. "I told you."

"The motel," said the Captain in exactly the same conversational manner, "is almost straight across the highway, a little to your left."

Macroy ducked his head in farewell, said nothing, and walked to the door. Halley jumped up and politely opened it for him.

"Halley." Burns was mild but Halley turned quickly and let the door close itself behind the minister.

"Yes, sir."

"This one is going to splash," said Burns glumly. "So watch yourself."

"Yes, sir. Did he do it, sir?" My master will know, of course, Halley's face said.

"Whether he did or not, we're going to be able to say we went looking for every damn crumb of evidence there ain't going to be." This was, however crossly said, a palsy-walsy kind of thing for Burns to be saying.

"You saw the woman, sir?" The Captain stared sourly but Halley went on. It bubbled out of him. "I can't help thinking—some honeymoon! I mean—"

The Captain grunted, "Yeah, and he's a pretty good-looking Joe. Well," he added with a warning glare, "keep your little old baby face *shut.*"

"Yes, *sir.*"

"Thing of it is," said the Captain less belligerently, "there was this opportunity. But if he did it, he don't *know* why. And he can't believe it, so he don't really know it at all. Don't think that can't happen."

Halley marveled respectfully.

"You get on over to the funeral parlor, and when the daughter shows bring her by."

Burns turned to instruct the clerk. Damn vultures, he thought. The damn press was out there. Well, *they* didn't have to go by the book, but they'd get precious little out of him.

Saul Zeigler, aged twenty-two, was standing with Carstairs in the hallway of the low building. Zeigler was a local, just out of college, working for peanuts and green as grass. He deferred to the older man, who was semi-retired these days but still picked up occasional plums for the big L.A. paper. Carstairs, with his connections, had already been on the phone to Santa Carla. Zeigler was impressed.

When they saw a man come out of the Captain's office alone, Carstairs moved in before Zeigler could get his own wits going. The hall was a barren length, with institutional green walls, a worn linoleum floor, and three naked light bulbs strung in a line overhead. The tall thin man looked ghastly.

"Reverend Macroy?" Carstairs was saying. "Excuse me. Terrible tragedy. Could we talk a minute?" Carstairs did not wait for permission. "Your bride was Sarah Bright? That's right, isn't it, sir?"

"Yes."

"My name is Carstairs," said Carstairs, forcing the manly handshake. "I'm that necessary evil, the newspaperman. But it's always best to get the facts from the ones who were there. Better all around."

Smooth, thought Zeigler, as Carstairs kept boring in.

"Sarah Bright was the widow of Herman Bright? Bright Electronics?"

"Yes.

"A very successful enterprise, I understand."

"Yes, I—yes."

"I understand you'd moved into her mansion on South Columbo?" Carstairs was chatty-sounding.

"Her house," said Macroy wearily.

"About how long had you two been courting, Reverend?" Carstairs became the old buddy.

Zeigler thought the drawn face winced, but the man said quietly, "We met about six months ago."

"She was an older woman?"

"Older than I," said Macroy. "If you would excuse me, please, I am not feeling up to an interview. I would like to get over to the motel now and be alone."

Carstairs brushed this off as if it had never been spoken. "Bright died four years ago, wasn't it? And your first wife died when?"

The minister put out one hand and braced himself on the wall. "Nine years ago," he said patiently.

"You and Sarah Bright got married Monday?"

"Yes. In the morning."

"And took off for a honeymoon trip?" Carstairs had shouldered around to face Macroy, who seemed driven closer to the wall.

"Yes. Yes. May I please—" Macroy pleaded.

"I'm very sorry," said Carstairs, "I know this is a very bad time." But his feet in their battered alligator shoes didn't move. "If you could just run over what happened, just briefly? I certainly want to get it absolutely straight, absolutely correct."

"We left Carmel early this afternoon." The minister put his free palm over one eye. "I took the scenic route because I thought she would enjoy—"

"Bum choice this time of year, wasn't it?" said Carstairs in a genial way.

The minister took his hand down and moved until his shoulders touched the wall. He was blinking, as if there was something going on that he couldn't understand. His silence was thunderous.

Zeigler found himself pushing in to say respectfully, "I understand, sir, that the whole coastline was closed in tight. Worst fog in years. Pretty bad, was it?"

"Yes," said Macroy, but he was looking at the older man and a hostility had sprung up, as invisible but as unmistakable as a gust of wind. The dazed look was beginning to lift from the dark eyes, like mist being blown away.

Carstairs said blandly, "Now, you stopped, sir? Why was that?"

Macroy didn't answer.

"I'm trying to find out how this terrible thing could have happened," said Carstairs, all innocent patience. "Why you stopped, for instance? What I mean, there couldn't have been a whole lot of scenery to see, not in that fog and after dark." Now his innocence was cruel and he was defensively hostile. Zeigler could feel it on his own skin.

Macroy said, "No." His voice had gone flat.

"Why did you get out of the car? Or, I should say, why did the lady get out? By herself, did she? Didn't have a little lover's spat, I'm sure. Then why did she get out?"

Carstairs was bullying now, and young Zeigler discovered that *he* couldn't take it. So he tugged at the bigger man. "She hadda go," he said deep in his skinny young throat, "and you know it, so why badger the poor guy? Lay off!"

"So okay," said Carstairs, "but you tell me how in hell she could have *fallen* off that damn cliff?"

"Maybe you don't understand women," said Zeigler fiercely.

Carstairs laughed. Then Zeigler saw the minister's face. He stood there, leaning against the wall, having made no move to escape. On his face there was such a look of loathing and sorrow and bewilderment—

"People are always interested," said Carstairs cheerily, turning back on his prey. "Do you happen to know what Mrs. Bright—excuse me, Mrs. Macroy—was worth?"

Macroy shook his head slightly. His lips were drawn back. He looked like a death's-head. Abruptly he thrust himself from the wall. "Let me pass."

"Why, certainly. Certainly." Carstairs played surprise that his courtesy could possibly be questioned. "Thank you very much, sir," he called after Macroy, who walked away from them. Then he said to Zeigler, "And how do you like them velvet tonsils? I'll *bet* he knows. The merry widow was worth millions, kiddo. So maybe she *did* have to go. Right?"

Zeigler didn't dare open his mouth.

Then, at the far end of the hall, the street doors burst open and a woman and two men entered. The woman came first, weeping violently, her head down, a handkerchief over her mouth.

Macroy saw her and said, "Eunice. I'm so sorry, my dear. So sorry." The music was back in his voice.

But the woman dropped the handkerchief and lifted red-rimmed furious eyes. She was about thirty, already thickening at the middle, no beauty at best, and now ugly in hysteria. "I don't want to talk to you!" she shrieked, recoiling. "I never want to see you again, ever!"

A dapper man with dark-rimmed eyeglasses put his arm around her. "Come now, Eunice. Hush up, sweetheart."

"All *I* know," the woman screamed, "is that my darling mother was just fine until she had to marry *him,* and now she's all smashed up and dead and broken!" She wailed and hit out at the air.

Captain Burns was there as if he had flown in. He didn't care for scenes. He and Halley took hold of the woman between them, but she cried out to her husband, "You *tell* him. He's *not* going to live in my mother's house and have all my mother's lovely things."

Burns said, "You'll come with me now, Mrs. Minter." And she went.

But Geoffrey Minter lingered to say to Macroy in a high, cold, uninflected voice, "You'd better not try to talk to Eunice just now. She's very upset."

The understatement of the year, thought Zeigler.

Macroy said, "Geoffrey, believe me—"

But Geoffrey said, "By the way, Eunice wants *me* to take charge of the funeral. I certainly hope you aren't going to raise any objections."

"No," said Macroy, staggering. "No. None at all." He walked away, curving erratically to brace himself against the wall at every few strides.

Zeigler said, "He's never going to make it across the damn road."

"So be his guide," said Carstairs. "You and your bleeding heart. But what you get you bring back to Papa. I'll cover the loved ones."

Young Zeigler went sailing after the minister. Carstairs was waylaying the son-in-law. Zeigler heard Minter's high voice saying, "I don't know the legal position. No new will has been drawn, not since the marriage. We'll find out." He, too, seemed furious in his own tight way.

Zeigler took the Reverend Macroy's arm and began to lead him.

† † †

The arm he held was tense and deeply trembling and it accepted his hand only by default, but Zeigler got them safely across the highway and into the motel office. Zeigler explained to the woman there—"tragic accident"—"no luggage"—"Sheriff's Captain suggested—"

The woman was awed and a little frightened. It was Zeigler who took the key. He knew the place and guided Macroy into the inner court, found the numbered door, unlocked it, switched on a light, glanced around at the lifeless luxury.

He didn't know whether he was now alone with a heartbroken bridegroom or with a murderer. It was his job to find out, if he could. He said, "Looks all right, sir. Now how about I call up and have somebody bring some hot coffee? Maybe a sandwich? You probably ought to eat."

A funny thing was happening to Zeigler's voice. It was getting musical. Damn it, whichever this man was, he was suffering, or Zeigler was a monkey's uncle.

But the minister rejected music. "No, thank you. Nothing." He remained motionless, outside the room. There were hooded lights close to the ground along the flowered borders of this courtyard and they sent shadows upward to patch that stony face with black. Zeigler looked where the man was looking—at three high, scraggly palm tops, grotesque against the clearing sky—between them and the stars, some wispy remembrances of that deadly fog still scudded.

"Come in," coaxed Zeigler. "I'll be glad to stick around a little bit if you'd like—"

"I'd rather be alone."

It was time for Zeigler to insist solicitously. But he heard himself. Saying, "Okay. I don't blame you." As he turned away, Zeigler said to himself in disgust, and almost audibly, "But I'm one hell of a newspaperman."

Macroy said, "And I'm one hell of a clergyman."

He didn't seem to know that he had spoken. He was standing perfectly still, his hands clenched at his sides. Up there the palm fronds against that ambiguous sky were like a witch's hands, bent at the knuckles, with too many taloned fingers dripping down.

The moment had an eerie importance, as if this were some kind of rite. To placate the evil mist now departing? Or a rite of passage?

A goose walked over Zeigler's grave.

Then the Reverend Macroy went into the room and closed the door.

† † †

Carstairs pounced. "What did you get?"

"Nothing. Not a word," said Zeigler, lying instinctively. "Shocked stupid, poor guy."

"How stupid can you get for more than a million bucks?" said Carstairs. "Especially if you're untouchable."

"What?" said Zeigler.

"I just got off the phone with his Bishop." Carstairs looked disgusted. "Whaddaya know? Your buddy is a Lamb of God or something and pure as the driven snow."

"What did he ever do to you?" asked Zeigler curiously.

"What did I do to him, for God's sake?" Carstairs' eyes looked hot. "So I don't live in the Dark Ages! I got to get back on the phone."

Zeigler wondered who was guilty of what. He honestly didn't know.

† † †

The Bishop, whose name was Roger Everard, came as soon as he could, which was at about ten o'clock the following morning. "I don't think it's wise, Hugh," he said soothingly as he pulled up his trouser legs to sit down and gazed compassionately at this unshaven face, so drawn with suffering. "I don't think you should make any such decision, and certainly not so precipitously. It's not wise at this time."

"But I *cannot*—" said Macroy.

"Surely you understand," said Everard, who often had a brisk executive way of speaking, "that these people are only doing what is their obligation according to law. Nobody seriously imagines, my dear fellow, that this was anything but an accident. And you must not feel abandoned, either. After all, you should realize that the members of your congregation can scarcely rally around when they don't even know where you are. Now, now—" the Bishop didn't pat him on the head, but he might has well have "—there are certain things that must be done and I'm here to do them."

"I am not—" said Macroy "—good enough for the job."

"You have had a terrible shock," said the Bishop didactically, "a grievous loss, and a very bad night. I beg you to be guided by me. Will you be guided by me?"

The Bishop had already tried praying aloud, but when he had seen that the praying was only increasing Macroy's distress he had cut it short. "You know," he continued, leaving God temporarily unmentioned, "that I am perfectly sure of your complete innocence, that I entirely understand, that I mourn your dear wife with you, and that I want only to be helpful and do what is best. You know that, do you not?"

"I know," groaned Macroy.

"Well, now. Here is what I advise. First, you must make yourself presentable. I believe that your suitcase is now available. Then, since you are not to be in charge—and after all, Hugh, Sarah *isn't here*—you must come home."

"Where is home?" Macroy said. "I gave up the apartment. And I cannot go to Sarah's house."

"Home with me, of course," said the Bishop triumphantly. "Now, I have brought along young Price. His father used to do my legal work and the son has more or less inherited. Freddy may not be the churchman his father was, but he is trained and intelligent and surely he can be helpful in this unfamiliar thicket. There must be an inquest, you see. I want you to talk to him, and then you must talk to the Sheriff's man, but I should imagine only briefly. And, Hugh, I want you to brace yourself to your tasks. I shall drive you by your church and you will go to your office long enough to cancel or rearrange your appointments and delegate your responsibilities. You must be strong and you must not be afraid, for remember—" and the Bishop went into scripture.

When he had finished, the face was looking somewhat less strained. The Bishop patted Macroy on a shoulder and then trotted back across the road to see whether there was any other way in which he could be helpful. A very busy man himself, the Bishop had had to cancel several appointments but he didn't begrudge his time and effort in this emergency. Obviously, poor Macroy was devastated, and the Bishop must and would take over.

✝   ✝   ✝

Frederick Price, a busy young man in his middle thirties, ready and willing to be useful, came swinging into the court of the motel carrying the Reverend Macroy's suitcase, which had been taken from Macroy's car. The car was now parked behind the Sheriff's office, still subject to examinations of some technical kind.

Price knocked on the proper door and went in, introduced himself, and offered the minister his possessions. He saw the strain and the fatigue, of course, and was not surprised. He didn't believe this man was guilty of any crime. He guessed him to be a sensitive type and thought the whole thing, especially the red tape, was a rotten shame under the circumstances. But Price was well acquainted with red tape.

As Macroy opened the suitcase and took out his shaving kit and a clean shirt, Price said, "I've been talking to Burns and the others. The inquest is set for Friday morning. I don't think we'll have any trouble at all, sir. I'll be with you. You'll be all right, sir, so don't worry. It's only a formality. As a matter of fact, there is no evidence of *any* kind."

"Evidence?" said Macroy vaguely. He went into the bathroom to shave, leaving the door open.

"Oh, by the way," sang out Price loudly enough to be heard over the buzz of the electric shaver, "they found that motorist. The one who came by?" Price was practicing lay psychology. He'd better not pour it on too thick or too soon—not all that he had found out. Chat a little. Engage the mind. Distract the sorrow. Un-numb the man, if he could. "Captain Burns was pretty clever," he continued. "As soon as that call came in last night, he guessed from where. So right away he calls a man—Robbins is his name—the man who runs the first all-night gas station you hit once you're off the cliffs. He asked this Robbins to take a look and see if anyone had just been using the phone booth, and if possible to get the license number on his car. But the gas-station man did even better, because the fellow had used his credit card."

Price got up and ambled toward the bathroom, not sure he was being heard. Macroy seemed to be avoiding the sight of himself in the mirror while he shaved. "Name was Mitchell Simmons."

"I beg your pardon?"

"The man who stopped out there on California One." Price understood Macroy's fragmented attention.

"He was very kind," murmured Macroy.

"What he was," said Price, "was very drunk. Oh, he corroborates what you say, of course. He's a salesman. Admits he was in high spirits, to coin a pun, and in the mood to pick up waifs and strays. Which is a risk, you know."

"It is?"

"Matter of fact," said Price cheerily, "it was one of his strays who phoned the Sheriffs office. Your kind friend was in no condition to dial, I guess."

The minister turned his clean-shaven face and it was full of pain.

Price said quietly, "I'm sorry. Didn't mean to say he wasn't kind. Look, I've got some further details. I suppose you'll want to know—er—just how she died. Burns will tell you. Or I can, if you like."

"Thank you," said Macroy. He came back into the bedroom and started to unbutton his rumpled shirt. "Yes?"

She broke her neck on the rocks," said Price. "So it was instantaneous, if that's any comfort. No pain at all."

Macroy's face was still.

"She—well, you see—" Price was remembering uncomfortably that it may have taken very little time to fall forty feet, but it had taken some. "She was washed to and fro until she was—" Price didn't have the heart to say how battered. "Well, soaking wet, for one thing. The coroner says that her bladder was empty, but that has no meaning. With death—"

Macroy sat down abruptly and put his hands over his, face. "Go on, he said.

"That—part of it," said Price. "It's a little unfortunate that it has to be brought out, but I think I can assure you that it will all be handled in good taste. I think, by the way—" he changed the subject gladly "—that Minter has cooled off considerably. He made a few poorly chosen remarks last night—about her estate, I mean—but he's thought twice about it and he'll be more circumspect in the future."

Macroy was shaking his head. "I don't want her money. I won't have anything to do with Sarah's money. That wasn't what she was worth."

Price was unable to keep from sighing his relief "That's fine," he said innocently. "Now please don't worry about Friday's inquest, sir. I'll be there, right by your side all the time. The thing is to give your testimony as quietly as possible and try to—I could coach you a little, perhaps. I've been through this before, you know."

"Thank you. Have they—finished with her?" Macroy took his hands down and seemed stiffly controlled. He didn't look at Freddy Price.

"The body will be released in time to be flown to Santa Carla for services on Saturday. Mrs. Minter wants the services there—because of her mother's friends. I'm sure—" Price stuck. The fact was, he couldn't be sure that Macroy was going to be welcome at his wife's funeral.

Macroy stood up and reached for his clean shirt.

"As for this inquest, that has to be, you know—" said the young man "—it *will* be an ordeal. Why should I lie to you?"

Macroy looked at him curiously.

"But there's nothing to worry about, really," said Price heartily. "The important thing is to get you completely in the clear."

"Is it?" said Macroy monotonously.

In the car later on, the Bishop excused himself and began to work on some papers. Price was riding next to the Bishop's driver. Macroy sat silent in a rear corner.

When they pulled up before St. Andrew's the Bishop noticed that Macroy was looking at it as if he had never seen it before. "Come," said Everard briskly, "run in. Your secretary will be there, I assume. Just make your arrangements as quickly as possible."

Price looked around. "You clergymen sound as if you're in the old ratrace, just like everybody else."

"Too true," sighed the Bishop.

Macroy got out and walked through the arch and across the flagstones and then into his office. Miss Maria Pinero, aged forty, leaped up and cried out, "Oh, Mr. Macroy! Oh, Mr. Macroy!" She had heard all about it on the air.

✝ ✝ ✝

In the car, Price said to the Bishop, "It's still a little hard to figure how she could have fallen. They didn't find a thing, sir. They can't even be sure just where she went over. Too many people messed around out there while they were getting her up the cliff. But there's nothing for *him* to worry about, that's for sure."

"I see," said the Bishop, looking sternly over the tops of his spectacles. "Guide him, Freddy, will you? He's in a sad state, I'm afraid."

"Do you think, sir," said Freddy Price, "I could possibly ask him to tone down his voice? It might sound—well, just a bit theatrical."

The Bishop's brows moved. "Bring it to his attention. That is, if you can get his attention." The Bishop sighed deeply. "No relatives. Nobody who can reach him on that needed human level. Well—"

† † †

"I'll take care of everything," Miss Pinero was saying. "Of course I will. I understand just how you feel. It seems so cruel. To get out, just to stretch her legs after a long, long drive—" She began to weep.

Miss Pinero was not an unhandsome woman, but something about her did not appeal to men. As a matter of fact, Miss Pinero did not like men, either. But the Reverend Macroy was different. So kind, so clean and gentle—and so distant. She would do almost anything for him. She had been so happy that he wouldn't be lonely any more.

"But God knows, doesn't He," she wept, "and we must believe that it is, somehow, for the best?" Carried away by her own noble piety—for it was her loss, too—she snatched up his right hand. Macroy snatched it away.

She looked up at him with tear-dimmed vision. She had never so much as touched him before, but surely he must know that taking his hand would have been like kissing the hem of his garment.

"I must leave now." He sounded strange.

"I'll be here," she cried, "and whatever you ask—"

"Forgive me," he said hoarsely.

He walked away. She knew that he staggered as he turned a corner, and her heart skipped. He sounded as if he couldn't bear to think of what she had almost done. Neither could she. Miss Pinero trembled. She wished it hadn't happened. She wished that Sarah Bright was still alive. Maria had felt so deliciously safe, and free to go on worshiping him.

The newspapers gave the story considerable space. After all, it had every-thing. They cautiously asked no questions, but they inevitably raised them. How could the elderly bride have fallen? There were some blithe spirits in the city who took to collecting the assorted circumlocutions having to do with the poor woman's reason for going off alone into the foggy dark. There was one columnist, based in the East, who—supposing that, of course, there was no such thing in Southern California as a reli-gious group that was *not* led by some crackpot—was open to a suit at law. The Bishop considered it wiser to ignore him.

Macroy did not read the newspapers.

On Friday the inquest came rather crisply to the verdict of Death from Accidental Causes.

Halley, telling how he had been the first to see a body down below, was a model of professional objectivity. The medical part was couched in decently euphemistic language. Eunice Minter had not attended at all. Geoffrey Minter said that, as far as he knew, Mrs. Sarah Bright Macroy had been a happy bride. He exuded honorable fairness. Freddy Price was pleased on the whole with Macroy's behavior.

The minister, however, looked beaten and crushed. His voice was low and sad and tired. Everything droned along properly. When the coroner, who was a straightforward country type, said bluntly, "You got back into the car for reasons of leaving her alone to do what she had to do?" Macroy answered, his voice dead against the dead silence of the room, "I thought, at the time, that it was the courteous thing to do."

A soft sigh ran across the ranks of those present.

"So you have no idea how she came to fall?" pressed the coroner.

"No, sir."

And the coroner thought to himself, Well, the truth is, me neither.

But when Price spoke finally, to inform the world in a quiet and mat-ter-of-fact manner that the Reverend Macroy firmly and irrevocably refused to have any part of the Bright money, that did it.

Price got the minister through the swarming cameras and away with an air of "Aw, come on, boys, knock it off" jaunty enough to arouse nobody's aggressions. But afterward, as they drove back to the Bishop's house, young Price for the life of him could think of nothing to chatter about. Freddy would have enjoyed hashing it all over; he'd done his job.

But this man was a type he didn't understand. So Freddy made do with the car radio.

The Bishop's spacious residence was well staffed—Macroy had every creature comfort. But the Bishop was simply too busy to spend many hours or even an adequate number of minutes with his haunted guest, who from time to time renewed his plea for a release from his vocation.

The Bishop, refusing to consider this, continued to advise patience, pending a future clarity. But, he said, obviously someone else would have to take over the Sunday services at St. Andrew's. The Bishop had resolved to do it himself.

But he did think that if Macroy, with the help of God, could find the fortitude, he also ought to be there. This martyred innocence, thought the Bishop (who *had* read the papers), had its rights, but also its duties. A man, he mused, must stand up to adversity.

On Saturday, at two o'clock, the funeral of Sarah Bright Macroy was well attended. The Minters and their two teenage children sat invisibly in a veiled alcove. But those of Macroy's congregation who had had the temerity to come spotted him and nudged each other when he arrived a trifle late and sat down quietly at the very back of the chapel.

He did not join the family at any time, even afterward. Nor did he speak to any of his own people. When it was over, he vanished.

He had looked like a ghost. It was a little—well, odd.

On Sunday the Bishop, at the last minute, found himself unable to conduct the nine-thirty service, which had to be canceled. (Although the organist played.) In consequence, at eleven o'clock, St. Andrew's had all its folding chairs in its aisles.

Macroy, in his robe, was up there, inconspicuously, at the congregation's right or contra-pulpit side, where, when he was sitting down, he was actually invisible to most. When they all stood, it was noticed that he did not sing the hymns. But he did repeat with them the Lord's Prayer, although his voice, which they were accustomed to hear leading, so richly and musically, the recitation of the ancient words, seemed much subdued.

Then the Bishop, who had never himself dwelt on some of the circumstances, and did not for one instant suppose that anyone *here* could do less than understand their essential pathos, made an unfortunate choice of words in the pastoral prayer.

"Oh, God," he prayed in his slight rasp, "Who, even in fog and darkness, seest all, be Thou his comfort; station him upon the rocks of his faith and Thy loving kindness, that he may stand up—"

The ripple ran, gasping from some of the listeners, yet not so much sound as movement, swinging the whole congregation like grass, before it ceased and all sat stiffly in a silence like plush.

The Bishop sat down, a bit pinkly. He could not see Macroy very well. Macroy did not seem to have taken any notice. In fact, Macroy had been moving, looking, acting like an automaton. The Bishop was very much worried about him, and he now bemoaned his own innocence, which had tripped him up, on occasion, before. When it was time, he preached an old sermon that was sound, although perhaps a little less than electrifying.

Then there they were, standing together in the narthex, as was the custom at St. Andrew's, Macroy a tall black pole beside the little black-robed beetle-bodied Bishop.

Now the people split into two groups, sheep from goats. Half of them simply went scurrying away, the women contriving to look harassed, as if they were concerned for a child or had something on the stove at home, the men just getting out of there. The other half lined up, to speak first to the Bishop and gush over the honor of his appearance in their pulpit. Then they each turned righteously to Macroy and said phrases like "So sorry to hear" and "Deepest sympathy" or a hearty "Anything I can do."

About twenty of them had gone by, like a series of coded Western Union messages, when Macroy put both hands over his face and burst into loud and anguished sobs.

The Bishop rallied around immediately and some of the older men shouldered through to his assistance. They took—almost carried—Macroy to his own office, where, Macroy having been put down in his chair, the Bishop firmly shut the door on everybody else. He sat down himself, and used his handkerchief, struggling to conquer his disapproval of a public exhibition of this sort. By the time the Bishop had recovered his normal attitude of compassionate understanding, Macroy had stopped making those distressing and unmanly noises.

"Well, I was wrong," the Bishop announced good-naturedly. "I ought not to have urged you to come here and I am sorry for that. You are still in shock. But I want you to remember that *they* are also in shock, in a way."

The Bishop was thinking of the reaction to his boner. He was not going to quote what he had inadvertently said, since if Macroy had missed it the Bishop would accept this mercy. Still, he felt that he ought to be somewhat blunt—it might be helpful.

"I'll tell you something, Macroy," he said. "You've got a fat-cat suburban bunch in this church, with economic status and—may the Lord help them all—middle-class notions of propriety. My dear fellow, they can't help it if they don't know what to say to you, when it has probably never crossed their minds that the minister or his wife might sometimes have to go to the bathroom."

Then the Bishop sighed. "This is especially difficult for them, but they'll stand by you—you'll see. I'm sure that you can understand them as well or better than I."

"It's not that I don't understand them," said Macroy. "It's that I can't love them." He had put his head down on his desk like a child.

"Oh, come now—"

"I cannot," said Macroy. "So I must give it up. Because I cannot do it."

"I think," said the Bishop in a moment, "that you most certainly can't—that is, not yet. You must have time. You must have rest. Now, I shall arrange for substitutes here. Don't worry about it."

"Don't you still understand?" said Macroy drearily.

"Of course I do! Of course I do! It was simply too much for you."

"Yes. Yes, if you say so."

"Then, if the coast is clear, we had better go home." The Bishop thought that this might become a serious breakdown. Poor tortured soul.

†   †   †

That evening the Bishop bustled from his study into his living room, where Macroy was sitting disconsolately idle.

"Now," the Bishop said in his raspy voice, "you know that you are very welcome in this house. There is plenty of room. The cooking is not bad. Everything here is yours. However, I'm afraid that I shall have to be

out of town for a day or two beginning tomorrow and I don't like to leave
you all alone in your present state, so I'm going to ask you to do something for me, Hugh. Will you promise?"

"Yes," said Macroy listlessly.

"Will you talk to a Dr. Leone tomorrow?"

"A doctor?"

"He's a psychiatrist whom I've known for years. There have been
occasions— He is excellent in his profession. He can give you a full hour
tomorrow, beginning at one o'clock. I have set up the appointment and I
think it is wise—very wise—that you keep it. He can help you through
this very bad time."

"What?" said Macroy strangely. "Isn't God enough?"

"Ah ah," said the Bishop, shaking a finger, "you must not despise the
scientist. In his own way he is also a seeker after the truth. And God
knows that you need some human help. That's why I simply cannot leave
you here alone—don't you see? Yet I should go, I must. So will you please
be guided by me and do as I suggest?"

"Yes, I will," said Macroy apathetically.

† † †

"She died when you were twenty-five?" Doctor Leone said. He had
observed the harsh lines on this face relax in memories of childhood, and
he began to forgive himself for his own faulty technique. Well, he had to
push this one. Otherwise the man would still be sitting as an owl by day,
and there wasn't time. The doctor already knew that he would never see
this man again.

"You were the only child?" he continued. "You must have adored her."

"I didn't pray to her, if that's what you mean," said Macroy with a faint
touch of humor. "I loved my mother very much. But she wasn't perfect."

"How not?"

"Oh, she wasn't always—well, she didn't love everyone. She had a
sharp tongue sometimes." But the voice was as tender as a smile.

"Didn't always love you, for instance?" the doctor said lightly.

"Of course she loved me. Always. I was her son." This was unimpas-
sioned.

"Tell me about your father."

"He was a machinist, a hard-working man. A reader and a student by
night. Very solid and kind and encouraging."

"You were how old when he died?"

"He died when I was twenty-seven—suddenly and afar."

The doctor listened closely to the way the voice caressed a phrase. "He loved you, of course. And you loved him."

"He was my father," the minister said with a faint wonder.

The doctor was beginning to wonder, Is he putting me on? He said with a smile, "Just background—all that we have time for today. Now tell me about your first wife. Was it a happy marriage?"

"It was," said Macroy. "Emily was my young love, very dainty and sweet. A cherishable girl." The doctor heard the thin and singing overtone.

"You had no children?"

"No. We were sad about that. Emily, I suppose, was always frail."

"After she died, what did you do?"

"Went on, of course."

The doctor continued to suspend judgment. "Now, this second marriage. What did you feel for Sarah?"

"She was a lovely, lively spirit," said the minister. "We could talk. Oh, how we could talk." He fell silent.

"And you loved her?"

"Not with the same kind of love," said Macroy, faintly chiding, "since we weren't young any more. We were very—compatible I believe is the accepted word."

Putting me on? He must be, thought the doctor. "And her money was no object," he said cheerily.

"The love of money is the root, Doctor."

"All right. I know my questions may sound stupid to you," said Leone. "They sound pretty stupid to me, as a matter of fact." He leaned back. Leone never took notes. He was trained to dictate, in ten minutes, the gist of fifty. "Now, I'm going to become rather inquisitive," he announced, "unless you know that you not only can but should speak frankly to me."

Macroy said gently, "I understand." But he said no more.

Going to make me push, thought the doctor. All right. "Tell me about your honeymoon."

"I see," said Macroy. "You want to know—whether the marriage was consummated? Will that phrase do?"

"It will do."

"No, it was not," said Macroy. "Although it would have been sooner or later, I think. She was—so warm-hearted and so lovable a presence. But you see, we had understood, quite well."

"You had both understood," said the doctor, more statement than question.

"I told you that we could talk," said Macroy, catching the latent doubt. "And that meant about anything and everything. That was our joy. As for—after all, in my case, Doctor, it had been nine years. I was a Minister of the Gospel."

"Did you try with Sarah and fail?" the doctor said easily.

"No."

"There wasn't a disillusion of any kind in the intimacy?"

"No. No. We enjoyed. We enjoyed. I can't be the only man in the world to have known that kind of joy." Macroy's face contorted and he became silent.

"Which you have lost," the doctor said softly.

"Which I have lost. Yes. Thank you." The man's head bent.

"So the very suggestion that you—yourself—might have thrown all this violently away. It must have been very painful to you."

"Yes."

"Knowing that you wouldn't, couldn't, didn't—there's still that sense of guilt, isn't there?"

"Yes."

"Surely you recognize that very common reaction to sudden death— to any death, in fact." The doctor wasn't having any more nonsense. "You have surely seen it, in your field, many times. People who compulsively wish that they had done what they had not done and so on?"

"Oh, yes, of course. But am I not guilty for letting her venture alone on that cliff?"

"It was the natural thing."

"It is the human convention." The voice was dreary and again it ceased.

The doctor waited, but time flew. So he said, "Every one of us must take his time to mourn his dead. But Bishop Everard tells me that you wish to give up the ministry, now. Why, Mr. Macroy?"

Macroy sighed deeply. "I am thinking about the silly but seemingly inevitable snickering, because of the circumstances."

The doctor hesitated. "The—er—circumstances do make an anecdote for thoughtless people. That must be very hard for you to endure."

"Oh, my poor Sarah."

"Then is this a factor?"

"I will say," said Macroy, "that I don't altogether understand that snickering. And why is it inevitable? If I may speak frankly to you, Doctor—"

Leone thought that there was a glint of life and challenge in the eyes.

"Surely," said Macroy, "every one of us knows his body's necessities, and furthermore knows that the rest of us have them, too. Yet all of man's necessities are not as funny as all that. Men don't think it funny, for instance, that they must eat."

"The whole toilet thing," said the doctor, "is too ancient and deep-rooted to be fully understood. It may be that the unpleasantness is too plain a reminder of our animal status."

"We laugh at what we hate so much to admit?" Macroy said quickly.

"Possibly." The doctor blinked.

"'Tis a pity," Macroy said in mourning.

"Why," said the doctor, who was beginning to feel that *he* had fallen into some trap, "is it that a man like you, who can look with this much detachment at human inconsistencies, cannot transcend an unimportant and temporary embarrassment? Surely you ought not to be driven out of a life's work just because of—"

"I didn't say those were my reasons."

"I'm sorry. Of course you didn't. What are your reasons?" The doctor was sunny.

"I cannot continue," said Macroy slowly, "because there are too many people I cannot love."

"Could you—er—amplify?"

"I mean that I felt so much anger. Fury. I hated them. I despised them. I wanted to hit them, shake them, scream at them, even hurt them back."

"In particular?"

"It began—" said Macroy. "No, I think that when the police officer asked me whether I had pushed Sarah to her death—oh, it hurt, of course it did, but I remembered that he might be compelled by the nature of his duties to ask me such a thing. But then there was a newspaperman. And when to him Sarah's death meant somewhat less than the death of a dog would have meant to a man who never cared for dogs, that's when I found myself so angry. I hated and I still do hate that man. From then on, I have seemed to be hating, hating—"

The doctor was lying low, rejoicing in this flow.

"Sarah's own child, for instance," Macroy went on, "who was so cruel in her own pain. Oh, I know she was not herself. But I had better not go near her. I would want to make her suffer. Don't you see? Of all the contemptible—I want revenge. Yes, I do. That young lawyer who missed the point. I know he meant no harm, but I just couldn't—I even loathe my poor secretary for making some kind of idol out of me. But I'd known and understood and borne that for years. Even if she is wrong to do that, I shouldn't suddenly loathe her for it. Yet I find I do. And I loathe the cowards and the hypocrites and the snickerers—they all disgust me. There seems to be no way that I can bring myself to love them. I simply cannot do it."

"You cannot love?" droned the doctor hypnotically.

"Even the Bishop, who is a good man. When he refuses—oh, in all good heart—to hear the truth I keep trying to tell him, sometimes I must hang on desperately to keep from shouting at him. Isn't that a dreadful thing?"

"That you can't love?" said the doctor. "Of course it is a dreadful thing. When your young love died so many years ago, perhaps—"

"No. *No!*" Macroy groaned. "You don't seem to understand. Listen to me. I was commanded to love. I was committed to love. And I thought I could, I thought I did. But if I *cannot do it,* then I have no business preaching in His Name."

"I beg your pardon?" The doctor's thoughts were jolted.

"In the Name of Jesus Christ."

"Oh, yes. I see."

"No, you don't! You don't even know what I'm talking about!"

The doctor got his breath and said gently, "I see this. You have a very deep conviction of having failed."

"Indeed," said Macroy, "and I am failing right now. I would like, for instance, to hit you in the mouth—although I *know* you are only trying to help me." The minister put both hands over his face and began to cry bitterly.

The doctor waited it out, and then he said that they wouldn't talk about it any more today.

When the Bishop returned to town, he had a conference with Dr. Leone.

"He's had a traumatic experience," the doctor said, "that has stirred up some very deep guilt feelings, and, in projection, an almost unmanageable hostility that he never knew was there. I doubt he is as sophisticated as he thinks he is—in his understanding of the human psyche, I mean. He does need help, sir. He isn't really aware of the demons we all harbor. It's going to take a lot of digging to get at the root."

"Hm. A lot of digging, you say?"

"And I am not the man," said Leone. "I doubt that he and I can ever establish the necessary rapport. Furthermore, my fees—"

"I know." The Bishop was much distressed. "But what is to be done, I wonder. He isn't fit, you imply, to go on with his tasks?"

"You know he isn't."

"Oh, me," the Bishop sighed. "And he has nobody, nowhere to be taken in. Since I—" the Bishop shook his head sadly "—am not the man, either. You don't think this—this disturbance will simply go away? If he has shelter? And time to himself?"

"May I suggest," said Leone smoothly, "that the state hospitals are excellent? Very high-class in this state. And even the maximum fee is not too high."

"Well, as to that, there is what amounts to a Disability Fund. I should also suppose that the Minters, who are very rich people—" the Bishop was thinking out loud "—even if the marriage has to be declared invalid. But wouldn't it be cruel?" The Bishop blinked his eyes, hard. "Am I old-fashioned to think it would be cruel?"

"Yes, you are," said the doctor kindly. "He needs exactly what he can get in such a place—the shelter, the time, the trained attention. As far as time goes, it may be the quickest way to restore him."

"I see. I see." The Bishop sighed again. "How could it be done?"

"He would have to commit himself," said Leone gently.

"He would do so, I think," said the Bishop, "if I were to advise him to. It is a fearful—yet if there is no better alternative—"

"The truth is," said Leone fondly, "you have neither the free time nor the training, sir."

"We shall see," said the Bishop, who intended to wrestle it out in prayer. "We shall see."

Two years later, Saul Zeigler approached the entrance with due caution. He had stuck a card reading PRESS in his windshield, anticipating argument since he wasn't expected, but to his surprise there was no gate, no guard, and no questions were asked. He drove slowly into the spacious grounds, found the administration building, parked, locked his car, and hunted down a certain Dr. Norman.

"Nope," said the doctor, a sandy-colored man who constantly smoked a pipe, "there is no story. And you won't write any. Absolutely not. Otherwise, how've you been?"

"Fine, fine," said Zeigler, who was up-and-coming these days and gambling that he could become a highly paid feature writer. He'd had some bylines. "Just insane, eh?"

The doctor grinned cheerfully. "Not my terminology."

"Put it this way: you're not letting him out?"

"Uh uh."

"Will you ever?"

"We hope so."

"When?"

The doctor shrugged.

"Well, I suppose I can always make do with what I've heard," said Zeigler impudently.

"Saul," said the doctor, "your dad was my old buddy and if I'd been the dandling type I probably would have dandled you. So you won't do this to me. Skip it. Go see Milly. She'll have a fit if you don't drop in to say hello."

"So would I," Zeigler said absent-mindedly. "Tell me, *did* he murder his wife?" There was no answer. "What set him off, then?"

"I'm not going to discuss a case with you or anybody else but the staff," said the doctor, "and you know it. So come on, boy, forget it."

"So how come I hear what I hear?" coaxed Zeigler.

"What do you hear?"

"You mean this is an instance of smoke without even one itty-bitty spark of fire? Not even one *semi*-miraculous cure?"

The doctor snorted. "Miraculous! Rubbish! And you're not going to work up any sensational story about him or this hospital. I can't help it if millions of idiots still want to believe in miraculous cures. But they're not coming down on us like a swarm of locusts. So forget it."

"I've met Macroy before, you know," said Zeigler, leaning back.

"Is that so?"

"Yep. On the night it happened."

"And what was your impression?"

"If I tell you," said Zeigler, "will you, just for the hell of it and off the record, tell *me* what goes on here?"

The doctor smoked contemplatively.

"Religion and psychiatry," said Zeigler, letting out his vocabulary and speaking solemnly, "have been approaching each other recently, wouldn't you agree, Doctor—in at least an exploratory manner? Supposing that you had, here, a clue to that growing relationship. Is that necessarily a 'sensational' story?"

"Oh no, you don't," said the doctor. "For one thing, he isn't preaching religion."

"How do you know?"

"I know."

Zeigler said, "You won't even let me talk to him, I take it."

"I didn't say so. If we understand each other—"

"Well, it was a long drive and it shouldn't be a total loss. Besides, I'm personally dying of curiosity. My impression, you want? Okay. I felt sorry for him, bleeding heart that I am. He was in shock and he sure had been pushed around that night. If he didn't always make plain sense, all I can say is that I wouldn't have made sense, either." Zeigler waited.

"I will admit," said the doctor between puffs, "that there have been some instances of sudden catharsis." He cocked a sandy eyebrow.

"Don't bother to translate," said Zeigler, crossing the trouser legs of his good suit, because the reporter got around these days and needed front. "I dig. How many instances?"

"A few.

"Quite a few? But no miracles. Didn't do a bit of good, eh?"

"Sometimes treatment was expedited." The doctor grinned at his own verbiage. "We *are* aware of a running undercurrent. One patient advises another, 'All right, you can go and talk to him.'"

"So if he doesn't preach, what does he do?"

"I don't know. They talk their hearts to him."

"Why don't you find out?" said Zeigler in astonishment.

"Tell me this, Saul. On that night, was he annoyed with *you* in any way?"

"Might have been." Zeigler frowned. "He sure brushed me off. But he had taken quite a beating. I didn't blame him."

"Why don't you go and see him?" the doctor said. "I'd be interested in the reaction. Afterward, come by and we'll make Milly feed us a bite of lunch."

"Where can I find him?" Zeigler was out of the chair.

"How should I know?" said the doctor. "Ask around."

Zeigler went to the door, turned back. "I don't want to hurt him, Doc. How shall I—"

"Just be yourself," the doctor said.

Zeigler came out into the sunshine of the lovely day. He had never been to this place before and it astonished him. He had expected a grim building with barred windows, and here he was on what looked like the sleepy campus of some charming little college, set between hills and sprawling fields, with the air freshened by the not-too-distant sea. There were green lawns and big trees and some mellow-looking buildings of Spanish design. There was even ivy.

It was very warm in the sun. He unlocked his car, tossed his jacket inside, and snatched the PRESS card away from the windshield. He locked the car again and began to walk. Ask around, eh? There were lots of people around, ambling on the broad walks, sitting on the grass, going in and out of buildings. Zeigler realized that he couldn't tell the patients from the staff. What a place!

The fourth person he asked was able to direct him.

The Reverend Hugh Macroy was sitting on a bench along the wide mall under one of the huge pepper trees. He was wearing wash trousers and a short-sleeved white shirt without a tie. He seemed at ease—just a handsome, well tanned, middle-aged gentleman growing quietly older in the shade.

Zeigler had begun to feel, although he couldn't tell who was who around here, that *they* could and were watching him. He approached the man with some nervousness.

"Mr. Macroy?"

"Yes?"

"Do you remember me, sir? Saul Zeigler."

"I don't believe I do, Mr. Zeigler. I'm sorry."

Zeigler remembered the voice well. But the face was not the old mask of agony and strain. The mouth was smiling, the dark eyes were friendly.

Zeigler said smoothly, "I'm not surprised you don't remember. I met you only once, a long time ago, and very briefly. Is it all right if I sit down?"

"Of course." The minister made a token shifting to give him more welcoming room on the bench and Zeigler sat down. "This place is sure a surprise to me," said Zeigler.

The minister began to chat amiably about the place. He seemed in every way perfectly rational. Zeigler felt as if he were involved in a gentle rambling conversation with a pleasant stranger. But it wasn't getting him anywhere.

He was pondering how to begin again when Macroy said, "But you are not a patient, Mr. Zeigler. Did you come especially to see me?"

"Yes, I did," said Zeigler, becoming bold. "I'm a writer. I was going to write a story about you but I'm not allowed to. Well, I wanted to see you, anyway."

"A story?"

"A story about all the good you do here."

"The good *I* do?" said the man.

"I've heard rumors about the good you've done some of these—er—patients."

"That isn't any story." Macroy seemed amused.

"So I'm told. And even if it is, I'm not going to be permitted to write it. I've given my word. Honestly, I won't write it."

The minister was looking at him with a pleasant smile. "I believe you," he said.

Zeigler found himself relaxing. "The truth is, I want in the worst way," he admitted, "to know what it is that you do here. Do you—well, preach to them? I know you're a minister."

"No, sir. I'm not. Not any more. And so, of course, I don't preach."

"Then what?"

"Oh, I listen to them. Some of them. Sometimes."

"But that's what the doctors do, isn't it? Do you listen *better*?"

Macroy said, as if to correct him gently, "The doctors here, and all the staff, are just as kind and understanding as they can be."

"Yes. But maybe you listen *differently*?"

Macroy looked thoughtful.

"The point is," pressed Zeigler, "if there's some kind of valuable insight that you have, shouldn't it be told to the world?"

"I'm not saving the world, Mr. Zeigler," said Macroy drily. "I'm not *that* crazy. Or that good, either." He was smiling.

Ziegler, who had momentarily forgotten that this man was supposed to be insane, said, "Just a mystery, eh? You don't know yourself?"

"It may be," said Macroy melodiously, "because I'm one of them. For I understand some of these sheep."

"In what way do you understand them, sir? I'm asking only for myself. Last time I saw you—Well, it's bothered me. I've wished I could understand." Zeigler really meant this.

Macroy was looking far away at the pleasant hills beyond the grounds. Then, as if he had reached into some pigeonhole and plucked this out, he murmured, "One hell of a newspaperman."

"Yes, sir," said Zeigler, suddenly feeling a little scared.

But Macroy didn't seem perturbed. In a moment he went on pleasantly, "Some of them don't speak, you know. Some, if they do, are not coherent. What man can really understand them? But there are others whom I recognize and I know that I love them."

"That's the secret?" Zeigler tried not to sound disappointed. "Love?"

Macroy went on trying to explain. "They've fallen out of mesh—out of pattern, you know. When they've lost too many of their connections and have split off from the world's ways too far, they can't function in the world at all."

Elementary, my dear Watson, thought Zeigler.

"But it seems to me," Macroy continued, "that quite a few of them didn't do what they were pressured to do, didn't depart from the patterns, because they could sense—oh, they couldn't say how, they couldn't express it. Yet they simply knew that somehow the mark was being missed, and what the world kept pressuring them to do and be just wasn't good enough. Some, poor seekers, not knowing where there was any clue, have made dreadful mistakes, have done dreadful things, wicked things. And yet—" He seemed to muse.

Zeigler was scarcely breathing. Wicked things? Like murdering your wife, for instance? "In what way," he asked quietly, "are you one of *them,* sir?"

"Oh." The minister was smiling. "*I* always wanted to be good, too. I was born yearning to be good. I can't remember not listening, beyond and through all the other voices, for the voice of God to speak to me, His child."

He smiled at Zeigler, who was feeling stunned. "I don't mean to preach. I only say that, because I have it—this yearning, this listening, this *hearing*—"

In a moment Zeigler said, rather vehemently, "I don't want to upset you. I don't want to trouble you in any way. But I just don't see—I can't understand why you're not back in the pulpit, sir. Of course, maybe you're expecting to leave here someday soon?"

"I really don't know," said Macroy. "I cannot return to the ministry, of course. Or certainly I don't expect to. I must wait—as I would put it—on the Lord. And it may be that I belong here."

He caught Zeigler's unsatisfied expression. "Excuse me. The obvious trouble is, Mr. Zeigler, that every time they take me into town, as on occasion they do, sooner or later I stop in my tracks and burst into tears. Which wouldn't make me very useful in the pulpit, I'm afraid."

"I guess," said Zeigler, "you've had a pretty rough deal. In fact, I know you've had, but—"

"No, no," said Macroy. "That's not the point. It isn't what anyone did to me. It's what I couldn't do. And still can't. Of course, here it is much easier. I can love these people, almost all of them."

"And you can't help trying to help them, can you?" Zeigler said, finding himself irresistibly involved. "Why do you say you don't expect to return to the ministry?"

"Oh, that's very simple." Macroy smiled a little ruefully. "I've explained, it seems to me, to a great many people." He sighed.

"I wish you'd explain it to me," said Zeigler earnestly.

"Then of course I'll try," said Macroy. "But I hope you'll understand that, while I must use certain terms, I don't mean to exhort you to become a Christian, for instance."

"I understand," said Zeigler.

"Christians were given two commandments," Macroy began slowly. "You, too, were given much the same ones, I believe, although in a different form."

"Go on," said Zeigler eagerly.

"The first is to love God, which God knows I do. But I was also committed to the second commandment and that one I could not obey. Oh, I longed to—I even thought that I was obeying. But it isn't, I discovered, a thing that you can force yourself to do. And when that Grace—I mean, when it didn't come to me and I simply was not able—"

"To do what, sir?"

"To love them all."

"All!" Zeigler's hair stirred.

"That's what He said." Macroy was calm and sure. The voice was beautiful. "Thy neighbor? Thy enemy?"

And suddenly Zeigler saw it. "You took it literally!" he burst out.

"Yes."

"But, listen," said Zeigler in agitation, "that's just too hard. I mean, that's just about impossible!"

"It was certainly too hard for me," said Macroy sadly, yet smiling.

"But—" Zeigler squirmed. "But that's asking too much of *any* human being. How *can* you love all the rotten people in the whole damn world—excuse me, sir. But surely you realize you were expecting too much of yourself."

"So they keep telling me," said Macroy, still smiling. "And since that's my point, too, I know it very well. What I don't feel they quite understand, and is so perfectly plain to me—" He turned to Zeigler, mind-to-mind. "Suppose you're committed to follow Him, to feed His sheep, to feed His lambs, to be His disciple—which is a discipline, isn't it?—and suppose you cannot make the grade? Then, when you see that you cannot, mustn't you leave the ministry? How could I be a hypocrite when He said not to be?

"Let me put it in analogy," Macroy continued, warming to argument. "Some young men who wish to become airplane pilots wash out. Isn't that the term? They just can't make the grade. So they may not be pilots. They would endanger people. They may, of course, work on the ground."

Zeigler was appalled. He couldn't speak.

"So if I have necessarily left the ministry," said Macroy, "that doesn't mean that I may not love as *many* as I can."

Zeigler saw the image of a ray of light that came straight down, vertical and one-to-one. Suddenly there was a cross-piece, horizontal, like loving arms spread out—but it had broken. Zeigler's heart seemed to have opened and out of it flooded a torrent of such pity, such affectionate pity, that he thought he was going to cry.

A thousand schemes began to whirl in his brain. Something should be done. This man should be understood. Zeigler would storm into the doctor's office. Or he *would* write a story, after all.

He said, his voice shaking, "Thanks, Mr. Macroy, for talking to me. And may the Lord lift up His countenance upon you and shine upon you and give you peace."

Macroy looked up. His look made Zeigler turn and almost run away.

Speeding along the walk, he was glad no one else had heard him sounding off in singing scripture, like some old rabbi, for God's sake! Okay, he'd felt like doing it and he'd done it and what was it with the human race that you'd better not sound as if you felt something like that?

Maybe that man *is* crazy! But I love him!

Just the same, Zeigler wasn't going back to Doctor Norman's office—not right now. There'd been a reaction, all right, but he didn't care to have it seen all over his face. He'd go see Milly Norman, who would give him some coffee and gossip. She always did. He'd take time to cool it. Or figure out how to translate it—

No, let the man alone, let him stay where he was. Why should Zeigler say one word to help get Hugh Macroy back into the stinking world, which would kill him. Sure as hell, it would.

Zeigler was blind and ran slambang into a man and murmured an apology.

"Hey," said the man, moving to impede him further, "hey, Press, you get any good news outta the nutty preacher?"

"Nothing I can use," said Zeigler bitterly. He started off, but he thought, Love them *all*?

So he stopped and looked experimentally at this stranger. Here was a patient. Zeigler didn't doubt it. A middle-aged, foxy-faced, shambling man with salted red hair, little beady eyes, and soft, repellent lips. A more unlovable sight Zeigler had seldom seen.

Just the same, he said aloud and heartily, "Hey, don't you worry about a thing, old-timer," and then—with his eyes stinging but telling himself to stop being so much the way he was, because he'd never make it, anyhow—suddenly it was too much for him and Zeigler sprinted to his car.

✝ ✝ ✝

In a little while a man shambled up to where Macroy still sat on the bench under the pepper tree.

"Hey, you the Reverend Macroy?"

"I'm Hugh Macroy. Not a Reverend."

"Well—er—my name's Leroy Chase."

"How do you do, Mr. Chase?"

"Glad to meetcha. Say, listen, there's something I guess I gotta tell you."

"Sit down," said Macroy cordially.

The man sat down. He put his unkempt hands through his greying red hair. "I'm kinda nervous."

"You needn't tell me anything."

"Yeah, but I wish—I mean, I want to."

"Well, I'm listening."

"It's a kinda long story."

"Go ahead."

"Well, see, I was up Salinas this time and I was hitching back down to L.A."

Macroy had turned his body slightly toward his companion.

"Well," the man said, "I guess you know that hitchers can't be choosers. Hah! So I get this ride and this stupe, he takes California One." Chase's little eyes shifted nervously.

Macroy said, "I see."

"So he dumps me in Big Sur, which is nowhere. So when I finally get another hitch south, I figure I'm lucky. Only trouble is, I find out this bird is juiced up pretty strong, and when the fog starts rolling in, believe me, I'm scared. So I want out. So I *get* out. So there I am."

The man was speaking in short bursts. "In that fog, what am I? A ghost or something? Who can see a thumb? Nobody's going to take his eye off the white line to look, even. And it gets dark. And what can I do?"

Macroy was listening intently, but he kept silent.

The red-headed man chewed on his mouth for a moment before he went on. "Well, I got my blanket-roll on me, so I figure I'll just bed down and wait out the fog. Why not? So I find this big rock and I nest myself down behind it, where no car is going to plow into me, see? And there I am, dozing and all that. Then there's this car pulls off the road and stops right ten, fifteen feet in front of me."

The man leaned suddenly away to blow his nose. Macroy looked away, flexed one ankle, then let it relax. He said nothing.

"So I wonder, should I jump up and beg a ride? But it's all so kinda weird, see—white air, you could say?" Chase was gesturing now, making slashes in the air for emphasis. "A man gets out with a flashlight. It's like a halo. And the other party gets out, see. Well, I dunno what's up. I can't see too good. I know they can't see me. I got a grey blanket. I'm practically another rock. And I'm lying low and thinking, why bother? What's the matter with where I am? It's kinda wild out there that night—the white air and all. And I can hear the sea. I always liked listening to the sea, especially by myself, you know?"

Macroy nodded. His eyes were fixed on the man's face.

"Listen, you know what I'm trying to—"

"I'm listening."

"So when this person starts coming along with the flash, I turn my face, so it won't show—"

"Yes" said Macroy, with a strange placidity.

"Then the light goes down on the ground. It don't fall, see? It's just pointing down. And I'm wondering what the hell—excuse me—when—" The voice was getting shrill. "My God, I know what she's gonna do! Listen, no man can take a thing like that, for God's sake!"

The man was crying now. "So I think, Oh, no, you don't—not on *me*, you don't!" So I just give a big heave and, holy God, it's too close and over she goes! Oh, I never meant—I never—but who could take a thing like that?"

Chase was now on the edge of the bench. "Before I know what I'm doing, I drag my roll and I'm running up the edgy side, north. My life is in my feet, brother, but I gotta get out of there. It's just instinct, see? I could hear you calling—"

"You heard me?" Macroy was looking at the sky.

"'Listen. Listen. So I'm about half, three-quarters of a mile away and now here comes this car going south. So I figure to look like I been going south the whole while. That way, I never *was* there. And damned if this guy don't stop in the fog and pick me up. Well, I soon find out *he* ain't exactly cold sober, but by this time I don't care. Then what does he have to do but stop for you? But you tell him to send help and we just—we just went on by."

Chase slumped.

"If you had told me then—" Macroy had shut his eyes.

"Oh, listen, maybe you're some kind of saint or something, but I didn't know, not then. Didn't even know you was a preacher."

"And you had two chances."

"Well, I had—well, three really. But look, nobody coulda said I'd done that on purpose. Maybe manslaughter. Who knows? What I couldn't take was the—was the *motive*. See, it's too damned hilarious. What I couldn't take was the big ha-ha. I mean, I knew she never saw me, I know that—she wouldn't have done a thing like that. But all I thought at the time was, Hey, this I don't have to take. If I would have stopped for one second—but here it comes, outta the night, you could say—who's going to understand? Because what a screaming howl, right?"

Chase was sobbing. He wasn't looking at Macroy. He sobbed into the crook of his own elbow.

Macroy said musingly, "Yes, it is supposed to be quite funny."

"Listen, what I did do." Chase gathered voice. "This happy-boy, he finally gets to that gas station, and he don't even know what day it is. The message is long gone from his mind. So *I* made the call to the Sheriff. That was the third chance. But I chickened out. I hung up. And I say 'so long' to this happy character and go in the cafe. When I see the cop car I figure I done all I could and maybe she's okay. I'm praying she's okay. It was the best that I could do."

They were silent then, in the sunshine that had crept around the tree.

Macroy said in a moment or two, "Why are you here?"

Chase mopped his face with his sleeve. "Oh, I fall apart, see?" he said rather cheerfully. "I practically never been what they'd call 'together.' You talk about chances. I had plenty chances. But not me, I wouldn't stay in school. I coulda even gone to college. But I wouldn't go. So I'm forty years old and I'm crying in my wine, when I can get any, like a baby whining after a shining star, too far—" The man controlled his wailing rhyme abruptly. "Well. So now they don't know what else to do with me. So I'm a nut. That's okay."

He relaxed against the back of the bench with a thump. "So now," he spoke quietly, "I'll do anything. I mean, clear your name if you want. What can they do to me?"

Macroy didn't speak.

"I wish—" said Chase. "Well, anyhow, now you know it wasn't your fault and it wasn't her fault, either. And it wasn't—" He stopped and seemed to listen, anxiously.

"Excuse me," said Macroy. "I was wondering what I would have done. I'm no saint." He turned his face. "And never was."

"But I didn't know you, Mr. Macroy." Chase began to be agitated again. "You got to remember, for all I knew you mighta killed me."

Macroy said, "I might have. I *think* not. But I wouldn't have laughed."

Chase drew in breath, an in-going sob. "Ah, you don't know me, either. All I *ever* been is a bum, all my life. I never did no good or been no good."

"But you wish you had? You wish you could?"

"God knows!" The cry came out of him, astonished.

"Yes. And I believe you." Macroy bent his head. "I'm sorry. I'm sorry. That woman was very dear to me. Very dear."

"Don't I believe it?" cried Chase as if his heart had split. "Oh God, don't I *know*! I heard you calling her. I knew it in your voice." Chase was sobbing. "I remember a thing—what they say in church—I remember.

Don't tell me it was good enough, the best I could do. Because it wasn't, and that's what I know."

Chase was on his knees, hanging onto the minister's knees and sobbing. "Oh, listen, listen. I'm sorry. I got a broken heart. Believe me? Please believe me!"

Holy Living and Holy Dying

Robert Barnard

WHEN THE ACT OF LOVE was over, or the act of intimacy, or whatever lying euphemism you cared to call it by, Gordon Chitterling rolled over on to his back, stared at the off-brown ceiling, and sighed. The girl, who had said her name was Jackie (didn't they all?) reached over for her cigarettes on the bedside table, took one as if this was an invariable habit, and lit it.

"Come a bit quick, didn't you?" she said, in her horrible Midlands accent. "You can have another go for an extra twenty. I've nothing fixed till half past eight."

"I'm not made of money," said Gordon irritably. "I'm a journalist."

"Shouldn't have thought journalists went short," said Jackie. "There's a gentleman on the *Sun* has me regular on expenses."

"That doesn't happen with the *Catholic Weekly.*"

"Is that religious?" Jackie asked, blowing out smoke. Gordon immediately regretted having told her.

"Not really. It means we are Catholic in our interests. Wide-ranging," Gordon lied.

Jackie frowned, trying to understand, but soon gave it up.

"Fifteen," she said. "I can't say fairer than that, can I? It'll save me the hassle of going out again."

Gordon raised his eyebrows to heaven. This was beginning to resemble a street bazaar in Cairo. At any moment she'd be throwing in Green Shield stamps. He jumped off the bed and began pulling on his clothes.

"Some other time," he said, buttoning his flies. Gordon was one of the few men in London who still had button-up flies. There was an all-or-nothing quality about zips that he distrusted. "Duty calls," he added, in his tight-lipped way.

He grabbed at his attaché case, but either because he was clumsy, or because he hadn't shut it properly before, it fell open and spilled its contents on to the linoleumed floor.

"Damn and blast."

"There, I told you you shouldn't rush away, all excited like that."

About as worked up as Calvin Coolidge on a wet Monday, thought Gordon, as he bent down to retrieve his papers. Jackie had idly rolled over on the bed to have a look.

"Coo, look at that. It's old Mossy. One of my regulars."

She was pointing to a large, glossy photograph of a distinguished gentleman in his fifties. Gordon snatched it up.

"You are quite mistaken."

"'Course I'm not. Comes regular. Real old sport. I think he's something in the world of finance."

"You certainly are mistaken. He was a Bishop."

"Go on! Well, he never lets on. Dirty old Bish!"

"I mean you are altogether mistaken in the man," said Gordon, shutting his briefcase with an irritable click. "You must have confused him with another . . . client. Bishop Bannerman was a highly respected figure in the Catholic Church. In addition to which he is dead."

"I didn't say he'd been recently."

"He was a very fine man. Highly respected. Unimpeachable character. Almost saintly."

He was shutting the door when Jackie shouted:

"And he had a strawberry birthmark the shape of Australia on his left shoulder."

Gordon gave the game away by his pause after he had shut the door. Jackie must have registered that it was a full ten seconds before he clattered down the bare floorboards on the stairs and out into Wardour

Street. In fact, he knew she had registered, because he heard her hideous shrill laugh as he descended.

Gordon Chitterling walked through Soho in the direction of Victoria Street, a frown on his rather insignificant face.

The first thing that concerned him was that Bishop Bannerman might become a subject for scandal and concern—or, rather, that *he* might be the cause of his so becoming. If he hadn't spilled that damned attaché case . . . If he hadn't gone to her straight from work. But somehow it was straight after work that he most felt like it.

His profile of Bishop Bannerman, who had died two months previously, was already fully researched and was only waiting to be written up. The outlines of his career were clear. Born in 1930 into a middle-class family in Warwick, where his father had been a chartered accountant, Anthony Bannerman had begun the process of conversion to Catholicism at the early age of seventeen. Many such early enthusiasms were to be put down to the powerful tug of religion working on the impressionable adolescent mind, but Bannerman's had held, and had stuck with him through university, so that by the time he had his BA, his aim of then studying for the priesthood had been accepted both by the church into which he had been received, and by his family.

After that it had been onwards and upwards: exemplary parish priest, much-loved broadcaster on *Lift Up Your Hearts* and *Thought for the Day,* eventually Bishop of West Ham, and strongly tipped for the Westminster job, when or if it became vacant. That was not to be: he had been struck down by a heart attack while attending a conference in Venice . . . Death in Venice . . . Well, at least he had not been *that* way inclined.

Gordon Chitterling let himself into the *Catholic Weekly* offices, and went along to his own neat little cubicle. There was nobody much about, and he switched on his desk light and sat there thinking. Imagine! that much-loved pastor, that fearless campaigner against apartheid, that helper among AIDS sufferers, that tireless worker for peace and reconciliation in Northern Ireland—to patronize a common prostitute. Regularly. But then, to patronize one regularly would be safer than picking up just anyone off the streets. Safer too to choose an ignorant little tart like Jackie.

Ah well, that was one aspect of the Bishop that would not get into the Profile.

Yet everything else, *everything,* had been so positive, so enthusiastic, so admiring. He opened his bottom drawer, and pulled out the thick sheaf of transcribed interviews. He leafed through them: "caring pastor"

. . . "concerned, committed crusader" . . . It had all seemed of a piece. Here was the interview with his brother, where he'd talked about the birthmark the shape of Australia: "He always said it meant he would end up Archbishop of Sydney, but actually he never even went there . . ."

A phrase caught his eye: "He was essentially a man of the people, among people, at home with people." He stopped and read on. It was an interview with Father O'Hara, a parish priest in the borough of Camden. It went on:

"I once saw him in a pub in my parish. I'd been visiting the wife of the publican. It was the Duck and Whistle—*not* an up-market pub, in fact rather a dubious place, with a lot of dubious characters among the regulars. Bishop Bannerman was in 'civvies,' talking and laughing with Snobby Noakes, a petty crook who'd been in and out of jail. They were completely man-to-man. I even saw money changing hands. I expect he was putting a bet on a horse—something he loved to do now and then. When he saw me he came over, and he talked to me just as naturally as he'd been talking to Snobby. You got the feeling that he'd chat with the Queen in exactly the same way he'd chat with a housewife in a block of council flats. That was the kind of man he was . . ."

It had seemed admirable at the time. The man of God who was at home in all worlds. Now it made Gordon wonder. There was no reason why it should: bishops went into pubs: bishops talked to criminals. The fact that, apparently, on occasion he used a prostitute did not mean there was anything less than innocent about his talking in a pub with a petty criminal.

And yet . . . and yet . . . That money changing hands. Gordon Chitterling did not like that at all.

The next day, when he sat down to write the Profile, his pen seemed to be weighted with lead. Not that his words were normally winged. Gordon was a reliable, competent journalist rather than an inspired one. Yet it was that very reliability that prevented the clichés of his pen-picture attaining any sort of conviction. Words and phrases like "saintly humility," "committed campaigner," "a man of God who was also a man among men" seemed to snicker back at him from the page. "You don't believe that, do you?" they seemed to say. It is not easy to work for a religious newspaper. You have to believe what you write. So much simpler to work for Murdoch.

To light upon a Bishop who broke his vows worried Gordon. His own sins worried him only a little, but then—he had taken no vows as a reporter on the *Catholic Weekly*. He knew he was going to have to go to the Duck and Whistle. What he was going to do when he got there he did not know, but he knew he was going to have to go.

In the event the Duck and Whistle, over the next two or three weeks, came to know him quite well. It was, as Father O'Hara had said, a decidedly down-market pub, with men doing dubious deals in nooks and corner. There was a juke-box, the blare from which was used to cover muttered conversations. The first evening Gordon spent there Snobby Noakes simply breezed in, downed a whisky and water, and breezed out again. Gordon did no more than identify him, from the landlord's greeting, and the talk of other customers. Snobby was a thin, perky character, rather better or more flashily dressed than the others in the bar. These mostly had a look that was decidedly seedy, and as his visits became regular Gordon—for his was the outlook and talents of the chameleon—came to merge with his surroundings and become seedier: he resurrected an old raincoat, made sure he wore a shirt with frayed cuffs.

His first talk with Snobby was innocuous—about horses and dogs, the kind you bet on, of course. Snobby was man-of-the-world, and rather condescending to Gordon's shabbiness. Snobby had once worked as a bookie's runner, and was adept at the smart disappearance when a big pay-out was due. What Snobby loved, it became apparent in later conversations, was a "wheeze"—a smart idea for a quick financial killing. Any other kind of killing was way outside his territory, for his heroes were shysters and con men. Where others might hero-worship Cromwell or Napoleon, Snobby saved his admiration for an Horatio Bottomley or a Maundy Gregory.

Gordon he accepted as a small-time con artist, rather on his own level, though less prosperous. "Though you've got a touch of class in the voice," he once said, flatteringly. "You could sell encyclopaedias, you could."

"The best cons," Snobby would say expansively over a drink, especially if Gordon bought it for him, "are the simple cons. Look at the South Sea Bubble. Learnt about that at school—always stayed with me. Simple, effective, beautiful!"

Gordon nodded wisely. He was never quite sure when Snobby was being humorous. Snobby had a sense of humour, where Gordon had very little.

"The other thing about your simple con is, it's them that clean up the biggest," Snobby went on. "Take the bloke that thought up the wheeze that Venice is sinking. Brilliant. He must have pulled in millions over the years."

"You're not suggesting Lord Norwich—"

"Whoever he was. Some smart little Mafia con I'd've thought. A real little beauty. Because bleedin' Venice isn't sinking, any more than Southend is. All high and dry and dandy. Mind you the bloke who thought of building it there in the first place was something of an artist too. Did you ever see a more obvious tourist trap? A man ahead of his time he must have been."

Snobby winked. Quite unprompted by Gordon, the conversation had begun to take a turn he liked.

"You seem taken with Venice," he said casually.

"Oh, I was. Lovely little place. Only drawback that I could see was you couldn't do a good snatch there, because the getaway presents problems."

"Been there often?"

"Just the once. A church conference."

Gordon's heart rose.

"Well!" he said. "I wouldn't have thought of you as a Christian."

Snobby laughed.

"That's why I was there, though. The Fourth Ecumenical Conference. You know: Catholic and C. of E. clergymen holding hands in gondolas. *That* was a right occasion. Tell you about it some day."

He didn't, though, not over the next two evenings spent chewing over the great cons, past and present. In the end Gordon had the brainwave of bringing the conversation round to clergymen.

"I don't know about you," he said, with the air of long and disreputable experience, "but I never found there was much to be got out of the clergy. They're supposed to be so bloody other-worldly, but somehow there's never anything much to be got there. Maybe they're too hard up."

Snobby's face assumed a relishing smile.

"True. Most of them are that. Church of England, anyhow." He leaned forward confidingly. "But I'll tell you this, me boy: there's money to be got not *from* the Church, but *by* the Church. That's for sure."

"What do you mean? Collection boxes, appeals, that kind of thing?" asked Gordon innocently.

"No, I do not mean that at all. Let me put it to you like this: if a man wants to lead a comfortable life, and enjoys tacking over to the windy side of the law, what better trade to enter than the Church? And here I'm talking about the Catholic Church, me boy. Very comfortable life, especially the higher you go. The celibacy rule doesn't bother you, because you've no intention of abiding by it. And as a way into the criminal life it has one great, glorious advantage."

"What's that?"

"Who hears most secrets? A bank manager? A politician? A social worker? No—it's a priest."

Gordon's heart almost stopped beating.

"My God—you don't mean—?"

"Right. The confessional. That's where the really interesting secrets are poured out." Snobby grinned. "I can see you're shocked, laddie. Supposed to be secret, isn't it? But think of it like this: there's this man— I have one in mind, but don't think you'll ever learn who—who goes into the Church purely and simply for what he can get out of it. Purely, simply and solely. Not an ounce of religious feeling in his whole make-up. He likes the good things of life, and this is his way of getting them—and a nice little bit of power to boot. From the beginning he knows that one of his ways will be using the confessional. I tell you, it's the most brilliant wheeze I ever knew."

"You mean—blackmail?" Gordon stuttered.

"'Course I mean blackmail. Used very, very discriminatingly. Which means it's a slow starter. When you're parish priest of Little Wittering-on-the-Wallop you don't try to blackmail Mary Sykes because she's sleeping with the local publican. Oh no—you take it slowly, get the notice of your superiors, emphasize that for you it's the *urban* parishes that present the real challenges to Christianity in the modern world, take up all the fashionable causes—famine, apartheid, battered wives. And little by little you get to the sort of parish, the sort of position, where you've got the real villains, and the people with things in their lives that are worth hiding."

"Say London," said Gordon.

"Say London," agreed Snobby, "though you needn't think you're going to get any more out of me than that."

"But what's the point? What's all the blackmail money going to be spent on?"

"High living, indulged in very discreetly, and in out-of-the-way places: the Azores, Curaçao, the Æolian islands."

Again there was that tiny click, as something fell into place. Somewhere in his notes there was a reference to a "tiny community" of religious brothers in the Azores, to which Bishop Bannerman had often gone in retreat. Also to periods of solitary prayer, on Lipari . . .

"What was your 'in' on all this?" Gordon asked, in his con-man-of-the-world manner. "How do you come to know so much about it?"

"Oh, I was the collector. I wasn't one of the faith—that wouldn't have done at all—but he'd got something on me, never mind what, from someone who was. I collected the dibs, handed it over intact, and collected my percentage. Miserable little percentage it was too, but it all added up. No, it was a beautiful scheme, and I was proud of my part in it—profitable and risk-free. Or so I thought."

"Not?"

"Well, my part was safe enough. You don't catch me taking any risks in a simple matter of picking up a parcel of ten-pound notes. Piece of cake, as I'm sure you know. On the other hand, the Bish—my religious friend—well, I'm afraid he overplayed his hand."

"Went for the really big villains?"

"Something like that, though not quite in the way you mean. Now, in this bloke's parish—we'll call it a parish—there were all sorts of villains, big, medium and small, from pimps to company directors, but naturally among the ones he knew best were the Mafia mob."

"Of course. But would they come to Confession?"

"Some of 'em. Very devout little shysters, some of 'em. So he'd hear all about the rackets involving the Iti restaurants, the fruit and veg markets, not to mention some of the fall-out from the Calvi affair, and the Banco Ambrosi-how's-yer-father. All very intriguing and profitable. And in among the rest, another little tit-bit. What that was precisely, I don't claim to know. Mostly I never *did* know. But the Mafia guy he got it from was a hard little pimp in Hackney, and I'd guess he'd been a hard little pimp in Palermo before that, so whatever it was, it was probably sexual. If it'd been something bigger he might have twigged . . ."

"So there was an Italian connection, was there? Hence Venice."

"Oh, there was an Italian connection all right. Though of course at Venice, at this 'ere conference I attended in an unofficial capacity, there were holy-rollers from all over, as well as C. of E., Methodists, Baptists, everything except the Reverend Ian Paisley, all making out they were matey as hell and brothers in Christ. It was all very affecting, if you didn't listen to what they was saying behind each other's backs. O' course, I was just there on a package tour—"

"To collect the loot."

"That's it. The trouble was, in Italy I was a bit of a fish out of water." Snobby shook his head. "Or so the B—so my reverend bloke thought. He made a plan for picking up the loot, made it himself, and I was too bleeding ignorant to argue against it. If I'd known about gondoliers . . ."

"Gondoliers?"

"I mean, all I knew about was honeymoon couples steered through the canals by a bloke with a pole who needed a shave and sang 'O Sole mio.' I didn't know they were the biggest pimps and petty crooks in the business, and had been going back centuries, ever since they built that place on stilts."

"I suppose it was asking for a double-cross."

"Too right it was. Added to the fact that Mario, the punter *my* bloke employed, had a mother from Messina, and contacts with all the underworld characters in Venice and on the mainland, all the way down to sunny Sicily."

"What went wrong?"

"Everything. Every-bloody-thing. Oh, the Iti Bishop came along—"

"Italian Bishop?"

"That's right. Him that my bloke had got the juicy little piece of information about, from the hard little crook in Hackney. He came along with his packet of ten-thousand-lira notes, and left it under the seat at the gondolier's end, just as he'd been told to in the note, and as I'd arranged with this Mario. Then I took my romantic little trip round the back canals, feeling a right berk, since I hadn't got anyone to hold 'ands with, not even a gay vicar. And then we went out into the lagoon and I transferred the package to my little briefcase—all as ordered, though somehow I didn't feel happy about it even then."

"I suppose you were followed when you got back to dry land?"

"Must've been. And very cleverly too, because I know all the wheezes an English follerer will get up to. Naturally I didn't go straight to my bloke and say 'Here's the loot.' I went up and down these dark little streets and alleyways, stopped for a cappucino, stopped for a plate of spaghetti, though I got most of it down my shirt-front. Must've been pretty conspicuous, looking back on it, because I'm not the type to carry a briefcase. Eventually, as per arrangement, I went into this scruffy bar, went to make a phone call, and dropped the parcel. My bloke, in civvies, went in immediately after, and hey presto it went into *his* brief-case. Trouble was, I wasn't followed any longer. He was. Then it was child's play to find out which hotel room he was in, and who he was. So from then on his fate was sealed."

"His . . . fate?"

"Well, it's obvious, isn't it? Mind you, he made it easier for them himself. He'd palled up with his victim, him who was Bishop of this big town in Sicily which shall be nameless. Oh, right palsy-walsy they were, swapping jokes in Latin and I don't know what. Gave my bloke a good laugh, and that nice little feeling of power to boot—for as long as it lasted. He was in this Iti Bishop's room when he died."

"When he had his heart attack?"

Snobby, well launched into his story, was oblivious to Gordon's mistake: so far he had not mentioned any such thing as a heart attack.

"Whatever you care to call it. Sharing a bottle of Corvo they was, a nice thick Sicilian red, in the Italian Bish's hotel room. And what does he do, this Bish, when my bloke falls down and starts eating the carpet? Does he ring the hotel Reception and say "Get me the hotel doctor"? Oh no he does not. He rings a buddy-pal, practising in Venice, brought up in the same little village on the slopes of Mount Etna. No problems about a certificate from *him*. What's the betting he was alerted in advance, eh?"

"You're not saying this bishop . . . *murdered* your man?" said Gordon, aghast. Snobby sat back in his chair and looked at him pityingly.

"You haven't understood a word I've been saying, have you? That's the whole point—they were two of a kind. They'd both gone into the Church for the same reason. That Bish was the Mafia's spiritual arm back in their home island. Confessions heard daily and passed straight on. Once he knew that his blackmailer was a priest, he knew exactly how he'd got on to him, and exactly what to do." Snobby pushed his beer-mug away and felt for his scarf. "Which leads me to my final words of advice to you tonight: there's no con so brilliant that two people can't think it up. And if two people running the same con bump into each other—wait for the explosion."

He pushed back his chair and got up, but as he did so he caught sight of Gordon's troubled expression, and seemed as if he was seeing the real man for the first time. He sat down again and looked at him seriously.

"It's fair bowled you over, hasn't it?" he said. "You're a serious chap at heart, aren't you? Sympathetic too. People must talk to you, I shouldn't mind betting. You ever thought of going in for the Church?"

✝

Mea Culpa

Jan Burke

It was going to be my turn next, and I should have been thinking about my sins, but I never could concentrate on my own sins—big as they were—once Harvey started his confession. I tried not to listen, but Harvey was a loud talker, and there was just no way that one wooden door was going to keep me from hearing him. There are lots of things I'm not good at anymore, but my hearing is pretty sharp. I wasn't trying to listen in on him, though. He was just talking loud. I tried praying, I tried humming "Ave Maria" to myself, but nothing worked. Maybe it was because Harvey was talking about wanting to divorce my mother.

It was only me and Father O'Brien and Harvey in the church then, anyway. Just like always. Harvey said he was embarrassed about me, on account of me being a cripple, and that's why he always waited until confessions were almost over. That way, none of his buddies on the parish council or in the Knights of Columbus would see him with me. But later, I figured it was because Harvey didn't want anybody to know he had sins.

Whatever the reason, on most Saturday nights, we'd get into his black Chrysler Imperial—a brand-spanking-new soft-seated car, with big fins on the back, push-button automatic transmission and purple dashlights.

We'd drive to church late and wait in the parking lot. When almost all the other cars were gone, he'd tell me to get out, to go on in and check on things.

I would get my crutches and go up the steps and struggle to get one of the big doors open and get myself inside the church. (That part was okay. Lots of other folks would try to do things for me, but Harvey let me do them on my own. I try to think of good things to say about Harvey. There aren't many, but that is one.)

I'd bless myself with holy water, then take a peek along the side aisle. Usually, only a few people were standing in line for confession by then. I'd go on up into the choir loft. I learned this way of going up the stairs real quietly. The stairs were old and wooden and creaked, but I figured out which ones groaned the loudest and where to step just right, so that I could do it without making much noise. I'd cross the choir loft and stand near one of the stained glass windows that faced the parking lot and wait to give Harvey the signal.

I always liked this time the best, the waiting time. It was dark up in the loft, and until the last people in line went into the confessional, I was in a secret world of my own. I could move closer to the railing and watch the faces of the people who waited in line. Sometimes, I'd time the people who had gone into the confessionals. If they were in there for a while, I would imagine what sins they were taking so long to tell. If they just went in and came out quick, I'd wonder if they were really good or just big liars.

Sometimes I would pray and do the kind of stuff you're supposed to do in a church. But I'm trying to tell the truth here, and the truth is that most often, my time up in that choir loft was spent thinking about Mary Theresa Mills. Her name was on the stained glass window I was supposed to signal from. It was a window of Jesus and the little children, and at the bottom it said it was "In memory of my beloved daughter, Mary Theresa Mills, 1902–1909." If the moon was bright, the light would come in through the window. It was so beautiful then, it always made me feel like I was in a holy place.

Sometimes I'd sit up there and think about her like a word problem in arithmetic: *Mary Theresa Mills died fifty years ago. She died when she was seven. If she had lived, how old would she be today, in 1959?* Answer: Fifty-seven; except if she hasn't had her birthday yet, so maybe fifty-six. (That kind of answer always gets me in trouble with my teacher, who would say it should just be fifty-seven. Period.)

I thought about her in other ways, too. I figured she must have been a good kid, not rotten like me. No one will ever make a window like that in my memory. It was kind of sad, thinking that someone good had died young like that, and for the past fifty years, there had been no Mary Theresa Mills.

There was a lamp near the Mary Theresa Mills window. The lamp was on top of the case where they kept the choir music, and that case was just below the window. When the last person went into the confessional, I'd turn the lamp on, and Harvey'd know he could come on in without seeing any of his friends. I'd wait until I saw him come in, then I'd turn out the lamp and head downstairs.

Once, I didn't wait, and I reached the bottom of the stairs when Harvey came into the church. A lady came down the aisle just then, and when she saw me she said, "Oh, you poor dear!" I really hate it when people act like that. She turned to Harvey, who was getting all red in the face and said, "Polio?"

I said, "No," just as Harvey said, "Yes." That just made him angrier. The lady looked confused, but Harvey was staring at me and not saying anything, so I just stared back. The lady said, "Oh dear!" and I guess that snapped Harvey out of it. He smiled real big and laughed this fake laugh of his and patted me on the head. Right then, I knew I was going to get it. Harvey only acts smiley like that when he has a certain kind of plan in mind. It fooled the lady, but it didn't fool me. Sure enough, as soon as she was out the door, I caught it from Harvey, right there in the church. He's no shrimp, and even openhanded, he packs a wallop.

Later, I listened, but he didn't confess the lie. He didn't confess smacking me, either, but Harvey told me a long time ago that nowhere in the Ten Commandments does it say, "Thou shalt not smack thy kid or thy wife." I wish it did, but then he'd probably just say that it didn't say anything about smacking thy stepkid. That's why, after that, I waited until Harvey had walked in and was on his way down the aisle before I came down the stairs.

So Harvey had been in the confessional for a little while before I made my way to stand outside of it. I could have gone into the other confessional, and I would, just as soon as I heard Harvey start the Act of Contrition—the last prayer a person says in confession. You can tell when someone's in a confessional because the kneeler has a gizmo on it that turns a light on over the door. When the person is finished, and gets up off the kneeler, the light goes out. But I knew Harvey's timing and I waited for that prayer instead, because, since the accident, I can't kneel so good. And once I get down on my knees. I have a hard time getting up again. Father O'Brien once told me I didn't have to kneel, but it doesn't seem right to me, so now he waits for me to get situated.

Like I said, I was trying not to eavesdrop, but Harvey was going on and on about my mom, saying she was the reason he drank and swore and committed sins, and how he would be a better Catholic if there was just some way he could have the marriage annulled. I was getting angrier and angrier, and I knew that was a sin, too. I couldn't hear Father O'Brien's side of it, but it was obvious that Harvey wasn't getting the answer he wanted. Harvey started complaining about me, and that wasn't so bad, but then he got going about Mom again.

I was so mad, I almost forgot to hurry up and get into the confessional when he started the Act of Contrition. Once inside, I made myself calm down, and started my confession. It wasn't hard for me to feel truly sorry, for the first sin I confessed weighed down on me more than anything I have ever done.

"Bless me, Father, for I have sinned. I killed my father."

I heard a sigh from the other side of the screen.

"My son," Father O'Brien began, "have you ever confessed this sin before?"

"Yes, Father."

"And received absolution?"

"Yes, Father."

"And have you done the penance asked of you?"

"Yes, Father."

"You don't believe in the power of the Sacrament of Penance, of the forgiveness of sins?"

I didn't want to make him mad, but I had to tell him the truth. "If God has forgiven me, Father, why do I still feel so bad about it?"

"I don't think God ever blamed you in the first place," he said, but now he didn't sound frustrated, just kind of sad. "I think you've blamed yourself. The reason you feel bad isn't because God hasn't forgiven you. It's because you haven't forgiven yourself."

"But if I hadn't asked—"

"—for the Davy Crockett hat for your seventh birthday, he wouldn't have driven in the rain," Father O'Brien finished for me. "Yes, I know. He loved you, and he wanted to give you something that would bring you joy. You didn't kill your father by asking for a hat."

"It's not just that," I said.

"I know. You made him laugh."

I didn't say anything for a long time. I was seeing my dad, sitting next to me in the car three years ago, the day gray and wet, but me hardly noticing, because I was so excited about that stupid cap. We were going somewhere together, just me and my dad, and that was exciting, too. The radio was on, and there was something about Dwight D. Eisenhower on the news. I asked my dad why we didn't like Ike.

"We like him fine," my father said.

"Then why are we voting for Yodelai Stevenson?" I asked him.

See how dumb I was? I didn't even know that the man's name was Adlai. Called him Yodelai, like he was some guy singing in the Alps.

My dad started laughing. Hard. I started laughing, too, just because he's laughing so hard. So stupid, I don't even know what's so funny. But then suddenly, he's trying to stop the car and it's skidding, skidding, skidding and he's reaching over, he's putting his arm across my chest, trying to keep me from getting hurt. There was a loud, low noise—a bang—and a high, jingling sound—glass flying. I've tried, but I can't remember anything else that happened that day.

My father died. I ended up crippled. The car was totaled. Adlai Stevenson lost the election. My mom married Harvey. And just in case you're wondering, no, I never got that dumb cap, and I don't want one. Ever.

Father O'Brien was giving me my penance, so I stopped thinking about the accident. I made a good Act of Contrition and went to work on standing up again. I knew Harvey watched for the light to go off over the confessional door, used it as a signal that I would be coming out soon. I could hear his footsteps. He'd always go back to the car before I could manage to get myself out of the confessional.

On the drive home, Harvey was quiet. He didn't lecture to me or brag on himself. When I was slow getting out of the car, he didn't yell at me or cuff my ear. That's not like him, and it worried me. He was thinking hard about something, and I had a creepy feeling that it couldn't be good.

The next day was a Sunday. Harvey and my mom went over to the parish hall after Mass. There was a meeting about the money the parish needed to raise to make some repairs. I asked my mom if I could stay in the church for a while. Harvey was always happy to get rid of me, so he said okay, even though he wasn't the one I was asking. My mom just nodded.

The reason I wanted to stay behind was because in the announce-ments that Sunday, Father O'Brien had said something about the choir loft being closed the next week, so that the stairs could be fixed. I wanted to see the window before they closed the loft. I had never gone up there in the daylight, but this might be my only chance to visit it for a while. As I made my way up the stairs, out of habit I was quiet. I avoided the stairs that creaked and groaned the most. I guess that's why I scared the old lady who was sitting up there in the choir loft. At first, she scared me, too.

She was wearing a long, old-fashioned black dress and a big black hat with a black veil, which made her look spooky. She was thin and really, really old. She had lifted the veil away from her face, and I could see it was all wrinkled. She probably had bony hands, but she was wearing gloves, so that's just a guess.

I almost left, but then I saw the window. It made me stop breathing for a minute. Colors filled the choir loft, like a rainbow had decided to come inside for a while. The window itself was bright, and I could see details in the picture that I had never seen before. I started moving closer to it, kind of hypnotized. Before I knew it, I was standing near the old lady, and now I could see she had been crying. Even though she still looked ancient, she didn't seem so scary. I was going to ask her if she was okay, but before I could say anything, she said, "What are you doing here?"

Her voice was kind of snooty, so I almost said, "It's a free country," but being in church on a Sunday, I decided against it. "I like this window," I said.

"Do you?" She seemed surprised.

"Yes. It's the Mary Theresa Mills window. She died when she was lit-tle, a long time ago," I said. For some reason, I felt like I had to prove to this lady that I had a real reason to be up there, that I wasn't just some kid who had climbed up to the choir loft to hide or to throw spitballs down on the pews. I told her everything I had figured out about Mary Theresa Mills's age, including the birthday part. "So if she had lived, she'd be old now, like you."

The lady frowned a little.

"She was really good," I went on. "She was practically perfect. Her mother and father loved her so much, they paid a lot of money and put this window up here, so that no one would ever forget her."

The old lady started crying again. "She wasn't perfect," she said. "She was a little mischievous. But I did love her."

"You knew her?"

"I'm her mother," the lady said.

I sat down. I couldn't think of anything to say, even though I had a lot of questions about Mary Theresa. It just didn't seem right to ask them.

The lady reached into her purse and got a fancy handkerchief out. "She was killed in an automobile accident," she said. "It was my fault."

I guess I looked a little sick or something when she said that, because she asked me if I was all right.

"My dad died in a car accident."

She just tilted her head a little, and something seemed different about her eyes, the way she looked at me. She didn't say, "I'm so sorry," or any of the other things people say just to be saying something. And the look wasn't a pity look; she just studied me.

I rubbed my bad knee a little. I was pretty sure there was rain on the way, but I decided I wouldn't give her a weather report.

"Is there much pain?" she asked, watching me.

I shrugged. "I'm okay."

We sat there in silence for a time. I started doing some figuring in my head, and realized that I had been in my car accident at the same age her daughter died in one.

"Were you driving?" I asked.

"Pardon?"

"You said it was your fault she died. Were you driving?"

"No," she said. "Her father was driving." She hesitated, then added, "We were separated at the time. He asked if he could take her for a ride in the car. Cars were just coming into their own then, you know."

"You mean you rode horses?" I asked.

"Sometimes. Mostly I rode in a carriage or a buggy. My parents were well-to-do, and I was living with them at the time. I don't think they trusted automobiles much. Cars were becoming more and more popular, though. My husband bought one."

"I thought you were divorced."

"No, not divorced, separated. We were both Catholics. We weren't even legally separated. In fact, the day they died, I thought we might be reconciling."

"What's that?"

"Getting back together. I thought he had changed, you see. He stopped drinking, got a job, spoke to me sweetly. He pulled up in a shiny new motor car, and offered to take Mary Theresa for a ride. They never came back. He abducted her—kidnapped her, you might say. She was his daughter, there was no divorce, and nothing legally barring him from doing exactly what he did."

"How did the accident happen?"

"My husband tried to put a great distance between us by driving all night. He fell asleep at the wheel. The car went off the road and down an embankment. They were both killed instantly, I was told. I've always prayed that was true."

I didn't say anything. She was crying again. I pulled out a couple of tissues I had in my pocket and held them out to her, figuring that lace hankie was probably soaked already.

She thanked me and took one of them from me. After a minute, she said, "I should have known! I should have known that a leopard doesn't change his spots! I entrusted the safety of my child to a man whom I knew to be unworthy of that trust."

I started to tell her that it wasn't her fault, that she shouldn't blame herself, but before the words were out of my mouth, I knew I had no business saying anything like that to her. I knew how she was feeling. It bothered me to see her so upset. Without really thinking much about what I was doing, I started telling her about the day my father died.

Since I'm being completely honest here, I've got to tell you that I had to use that other tissue. She waited for me to blow my nose, then said, "Have you ever talked to your mother about how you feel?"

I shook my head. "She wanted me to, but since the accident—we aren't as close as we used to be, I guess. I think that's why she got together with Harvey. I think she got lonely."

About then, my mother came into the church, and called up to me. I told her I'd be right down. She said they'd be waiting in the car.

As I got up, the old lady put a hand on me. "Promise me that you will talk to your mother tonight."

"About what?"

"Anything. A boy should be able to talk to his mother about anything. Tell her what we talked about, if you like. I won't mind."

"Okay, I will," I said, "but who will you talk to when you start feeling bad about Mary Theresa?"

She didn't answer. She just looked sad again. Just before I left, I told her which steps to watch out for. I also told her to carry an umbrella if she went out that evening, because it was going to rain. I don't know if she took any of my good advice.

In the car, I got worried again. I was expecting Harvey to be mad because I kept them waiting. But he didn't say anything to me, and when he talked to my mom, he was sweet as pie. I don't talk when I'm in a car anymore, or I might have said something about that.

Harvey went out not long after we got home. My mother said we'd be eating Sunday dinner by ourselves, that Harvey had a business meeting he had to go to. I don't think she really believed he had a business meeting on a Sunday afternoon. I sure didn't believe it. My mom and I don't get to be by ourselves too much, though, so I was too happy about that to complain about Harvey.

My promise to Mary Theresa's mother was on my mind, so when my mother asked me what I was doing up there in the choir loft, I took it as a sign. I told her the whole story, about the window and Mary Theresa and even about the accident. It was the second time I had told it in one day, so it wasn't so rough on me, but I think it was hard on her. She didn't seem to mind, and I even let her hug me.

It rained that night, just like my knee said it would. My mom came in to check on me, saying she knew that the rain sometimes bothered me. I was feeling all right, though, and I told her I thought I would sleep fine. We smiled at each other, like we had a secret, a good secret. It was the first time in a few years that we had been happy at the same time.

I woke up when Harvey came home. When I heard him put the Imperial in the garage, I got out of bed and peeked from behind my bedroom door. I knew he had lied to my mom, and if he was drunk or started to get mean with her, I decided I was gonna bash him with one of my crutches.

He came in the front door. He was wet. I had to clamp my hand over my mouth to keep from laughing, because I realized that he had gone out without his umbrella. He looked silly. The rain and wind had messed up his hair, so that his long side—the side he tries to comb over his bald spot—was hanging straight down. He closed the front door, really carefully, then he went into the bathroom near my bedroom, instead of the one off of his room. At first I thought he was just sneaking in and trying not to wake up my mom, but he was in there a long time. When he came out, he was in his underwear. I almost busted a gut trying not to laugh. He tiptoed past me and went to bed. The clock was striking three.

I waited until I thought he might be asleep, then I went into the bathroom. There was water all over the place. He hadn't mopped up after himself, so I took a towel and dried the floor and counter. It was while I was drying the floor that I saw the book of matches. It had a red cover on it, and it came from a place called Topper's, an all-night restaurant down on South Street. I picked up the matchbook. A few of the matches had been used. The name "Mackie" was written on the inside, and just below that, "1417 A-3." I closed the cover and looked at the address for Topper's. 1400 South Street. I knew Harvey's handwriting well enough to know that he had written that name and address.

What was he doing with matches? Harvey didn't smoke. He hated smoke. I knew, because he had made a big speech about it on the day he threw away my dad's pipes. I had gone into the trash and taken them back out. I put them in a little wooden box, the same one where I kept a photo of my dad. I never looked at the photo or the pipes, but I kept them anyway. I thought my mom might have found the place I hid them, but so far, she hadn't ratted on me.

I opened the laundry hamper. Harvey's wet clothes were in there. I reached in and pulled out his shirt. No lipstick stains, and even without lifting it close to my nose, I could tell it didn't have perfume on it. It could have used some. It smelled like smoke, a real strong kind of smoke. Not like a fire or anything, but stronger than a cigarette. A cigar, maybe. I had just put the shirt back in the hamper when the door flew open.

"What are you doing?" Harvey asked.

I should have said something like, "Ever heard of knocking?" or made some wisecrack, but I was too scared. I could feel the matchbook in my hand, hot, as if I had lit all the matches in it at once.

Luckily, my mom woke up. "Harvey?" I heard her call. It sounded like she was standing in the hall.

"Oh, did I wake you up, sweetheart?" he said.

My jaw dropped open. Harvey never talked to her like that after they got married.

"What's wrong?" she asked.

"I was just checking on the boy," he said, He looked at me and asked, "Are you okay, son?"

Son. That made me sick to my stomach. I swallowed and said, "Just came in to get some aspirin."

"Your leg bothering you because of this rain?" he asked, like he cared.

"I'll be all right. Sorry I woke you up."

My mom was at the door then, so I said, "Okay if I close the door? Now that I'm up . . . well, you know . . ."

Harvey laughed his fake laugh and put an arm around my mom. He closed the door.

I pulled a paper cup out of the dispenser in the bathroom. I turned the cup over and scratched the street numbers for Mackie and Topper's, then put the matchbook back where I found it. By now, I was so scared I really did have to go, so I didn't have to fake that. I flushed the toilet, then washed my hands. Finally, I put a little water in the cup. I opened the door. I turned to pick up the cup, and once again thought to myself that one of the things that stinks about crutches is that they take up your hands. I was going to try to carry the cup in my teeth, since it wasn't very full, but my mom is great about seeing when I'm having trouble, so she said, "Would you like to have that cup of water on your nightstand?"

I nodded.

Harvey watched us go into my bedroom. He went into the bathroom again. My mom started fussing over me, talking about maybe taking me to a new doctor. I tried to pay attention to what she was saying, but the whole time, I was worrying about what Harvey was thinking. Could he tell that I saw the matchbook? After a few minutes he came back out, and he had this smile on his face. I knew the matches wouldn't be on the floor now, that he had figured out where he had dropped them and that he had picked them up. He felt safe. I didn't. I drank the water and saved the bottom of the cup.

✝   ✝   ✝

The next morning I got up early and went into the laundry room. Harvey's clothes were still in the bathroom, but I wasn't interested in them anyway. I put a load of his wash in the washing machine, checking his trouser pockets before I put them in. I made sixty cents just by collecting his change. I put it in my own pocket, right next to the waxy paper from the cup.

I had just started the washer when my mom and Harvey came into the kitchen. My mom got the percolator and the toaster going. Harvey glared at me while I straightened up the laundry room and put the soap away.

"You're gonna turn him into a pansy, lettin' him do little girl's work like that," he said to my mom when she brought him his coffee and toast.

"I like being able to help." I said, before she could answer.

We both waited for him to come over and cuff me one for arguing with him first thing in the morning, but he just grunted and stirred a bunch of sugar into his coffee. He always put about half the sugar bowl into his coffee. You'd think it would have made him sweeter.

That morning, it seemed like it did. Once he woke up a little more, he started talking to her like a guy in a movie talks to a girl just before he kisses her. I left the house as soon as I could.

Before I left, I told my mom that I might be home late from school. I told her that I might catch a matinee with some of the other kids. I never do anything with other kids, and she seemed excited when I told her that lie. I felt bad about lying, even if it made her happy.

All day, I was a terrible student. I just kept thinking about the matchbook and about Mary Theresa's father and Harvey and leopards that don't change their spots.

After school, I took the city bus downtown. I got off at South Street, right in front of Topper's.

The buildings are tall in that part of town. There wasn't much sunlight, but up above the street, there were clotheslines between the buildings. The day was cloudy, so nobody had any clothes out, although I could have told them it wasn't going to rain that afternoon. Not that there was anything to rain on—nothing was growing there. The sidewalks and street were still damp, though, and not many people were around. I was a little nervous.

I thought about going into Topper's and asking if anybody knew a guy named Mackie, but decided that wouldn't be too smart. I started down the street. 1405 was the next address. Linden's Tobacco Shop. I had already noticed that sometimes they skip numbers downtown. I stopped, thinking maybe that was where Harvey got the smoke on his clothes. Just then a man came out of the door and didn't close it behind him as he left the shop. As I stood in the doorway, a sweet, familiar smell came to me, and I felt an ache in my chest. It was pipe tobacco. It made me think of my father, and how he always smelled like tobacco and Old Spice After-Shave. A sourpussed man came to the door, said, "No minors," and shut it in my face. The shop's hours were painted on the door. It was closed on Sundays.

I moved down the sidewalk, reading signs, looking in windows. "Buzzy's Newsstand—Out-of-Town Papers," "South Street Sweets—Handmade Chocolates," "Moore's Hardware—Everything for Home and Garden," "Suds-O-Mat—Coin-Operated Laundry." Finally, I came to "The

Coronet—Apartments to Let." The address was 1417 South Street. The building looked older than Mary Theresa's mother.

Inside, the Coronet was dark and smelled like a mixture of old b.o. and cooked cabbage. There was a thin, worn carpet in the hallway. A-3 was the second apartment on the left-hand side. I put my ear to the door. It was quiet. I moved back from the door and was trying to decide what to do when a man came into the building. I turned and pretended to be waiting for someone to answer the door of A-4.

The man was carrying a paper sack and smoking a cigar. The cigar not only smelled better than the hallway, it smelled exactly like the smoke on Harvey's clothes. It had to be Mackie.

Mackie's face was an okay face, except that his nose looked like he had run into a wall and stayed there for a while. He was big, but he didn't look clumsy or dumb. I saw that the paper sack was from the hardware store. When he unlocked his door, I caught a glimpse of a shoulder holster. As he pulled the door open, he saw me watching him and gave me a mean look.

"Whaddaya want?" he said.

I swallowed hard and said, "I'm collecting donations for the Crippled Children's Society."

His eyes narrowed. "Oh yeah? Where's your little collection can?"

"I can't carry it and move around on the crutches," I said.

"Hmpf. You won't get anything there," he said, nodding toward the other apartment. "The place is empty."

"Oh. I guess I'll be going then."

I tried to move past him, but he pushed me hard against the wall, making me drop one of my crutches. "No hurry, is there?" he said. "Let's see if you're really a cripple."

That was easy. I dropped the other crutch, then reached down and pulled my right pant leg up. He did what anybody does when they see my bad leg. They stare at it, and not because it's beautiful.

I used this chance to look past him into his apartment. From what I could see of it, it was small and neat. There was a table with two things on it: a flat, rectangular box and the part of a shot they call a syringe. It didn't have a needle on it yet. You might think I'm showing off, but I knew it was called a syringe because I've spent a lot of time getting stuck by the full works, and sooner or later some nurse tells you more than you want to know about anything they do to you.

Mackie picked up my crutches. I was trying to see into the paper sack, but all I could make out was that it was some kind of can. When Mackie straightened up again, his neck and ears were turning red. Maybe that's what made me bold enough to say, "I lied."

His eyes narrowed again.

"I'm not collecting for Crippled Children. I was just trying to raise some movie money."

He started laughing. He reached in his pocket and pulled out a silver dollar. He dropped it into my shirt pocket. "Kid, you earned it," he said and went into his apartment.

I leaned against the wall for another minute, my heart thumping hard against that silver dollar. Then I left and made my way to the hardware store.

No other customers were in there. The old man behind the counter was reading a newspaper. I cleared my throat. "Excuse me, sir, but Mackie sent me over to pick up another can."

"Another one? You can tell Mackie he's got to come here himself." He looked up at me and then looked away really fast. I'm used to it. "Look," he said, talking into the newspaper, "I'm not selling weed killer to any kid, crippled or no. The stuff's poisonous." That's the way he said it: "crippled or no." Like I had come in there asking for special treatment.

I had too much on my mind to worry about it. I was thinking about why a guy who lived in a place like the Coronet would need weed killer. "What's weed killer got in it, anyway?" I asked.

He folded his newspaper down and looked at me like my brain was as lame as my leg. "Arsenic. Eat a little of that and you're a goner."

† † †

At home that night, I kept an eye on Harvey. I noticed that even though he was still laying it on thick with my mom, he was nervous. He kept watching the clock on the mantle. My mom was in the kitchen, making lunches, and he kept looking between the kitchen and the clock. When the phone rang at eight, he jumped up to answer it, yelling. "I got it." To the person on the phone, he said, "Just a sec." He turned to me and said, "Get ready for bed."

I thought of arguing, but changed my mind. I went into the hallway, and waited just out of sight. I hoped he'd talk as loud as he usually did.

He tried to speak softly, but I could still hear him.

"No, no, that's too soon. I have some arrangements to make." He paused, then said, "Saturday, then. Good."

✝ ✝ ✝

That night, when my mom came in to say good night, I told her not to let Harvey fix her anything to eat, or take anything from him that came in a rectangular box. "He wants to poison you, Mom," I whispered.

She laughed and said, "That matinee must have been a detective movie. I was waiting for you to tell me about your afternoon. Did you have a good time?"

It wasn't easy, but I told her the truth. "I didn't go to a movie," I said.

"But I thought . . ."

"I went downtown. To South Street."

She looked more scared than when I told her that her husband wanted to poison her.

"Please don't tell Harvey!" I said.

"Don't tell Harvey what?" I heard a voice say. He was standing in my bedroom door.

"Oh, that he got a bad grade on a spelling test," my mom said. "But you wouldn't get angry with him over a little thing like that, would you, dear?"

"No, of course not, sweetheart," he said to her. He faked another laugh and walked off.

Although I don't think Harvey knew it, she hadn't meant it when she called him "dear." And she had lied to him for my sake. Just when I had decided that meant she believed me about the poison, she said, "You and I will have a serious talk very soon, young man. Good night." She kissed me, but I could tell she was mad.

✝ ✝ ✝

That was a terrible week. Harvey was nervous, I was nervous, and my mom put me on restriction. I had to come straight home after school every day. I never got far enough in the story to tell her what happened when I went downtown; she just said that where Harvey went at night was his business, not mine, and that I should never lie to her again about where I was going.

We didn't say much to one another. On Friday night, when she came in to say good night, I couldn't even make myself say good night back. She stayed there at my bedside and said, "We were off to such a good start this week. I had hoped . . . well, that doesn't matter now." I know you're angry with me for putting you on restriction, but you gave me a scare. You're all I have now, and I couldn't bear to lose you."

"You're all I have, too." I said, "I don't mind the restriction. It's just that you don't believe anything I say."

No, that's not it. It's just that I think Harvey is trying to be a better husband. Maybe Father O'Brien has talked to him, I don't know."

"A leopard doesn't change his spots," I said.

"Harvey's not a leopard."

"He's a snake."

She sighed again. She kept sitting there.

All of a sudden, I remembered that Harvey had mentioned Saturday, which was the next day, and I sat up. I hugged her hard. "Please believe me," I said. "Just this once."

She was startled at first, probably because that was two hugs in one week, which was two more than I'd given her since she married Harvey. She hugged back, and said, "You really are scared, aren't, you?"

I nodded against her shoulder.

"Okay. I won't let Harvey fix any meals for me or give me anything in a rectangular box. At least not until you get over this." She sounded like she thought it was kind of funny. "I hope it will be soon, though."

"Maybe as early as tomorrow," I whispered, but I don't think she heard me.

I hardly slept at all that night.

The next morning, Harvey left the house and didn't come back until just before dinner. He wasn't carrying anything with him when he came in the house, just went in and washed up. I watched every move he made, and he never went near any food.

"C'mon," he said to me after dinner, "let's go on down to the church."

A new thought hit me. What if the weed killer was for someone else? What if Harvey had hired Mackie to shoot my mom? "I don't want to go," I said.

"No more back talk out of you, buster. Let's go. Confessions will be over if we don't get down there."

I looked at my mom.

"Go on," she said. "I'll be fine."

As Harvey walked with me to the car, I kept trying to think up some way to stay home. I knew what Mackie looked like. I knew he carried his gun in a shoulder holster. I knew he liked silver dollars, because I had one of his in my pocket. I knew—

I looked up, because Harvey was saying something to me. He had opened the car door for me, which was more than he usually did. "Pardon?"

"I said, get yourself situated. I've got a surprise for your mother."

Before I could think of anything to say, he was opening the back door and picking up a package. A rectangular package. As he walked past me, I saw there was a label on it. South Street Sweets.

My mother took it from him, smiling and thanking him. "You know I can't resist chocolates," she said.

"Have one now," he said.

I was about to yell out "No!", thinking she'd forgotten everything I said, but she looked at me over his shoulder, and something in her eyes made me keep my mouth shut.

Harvey followed her glance, but before he could yell at me, she said, "Oh Harvey, his knee must be bothering him. Be a dear and help him. I'm going to go right in and put my feet up and eat about a dozen of these." To me, she said, "Remember what we talked about last night. You be careful."

All the way to the church, Harvey was quiet. When we got there, he sent me in first, as usual.

"But the choir loft is closed," I said.

"It hasn't fallen apart in a week. They haven't even started work on it. Go on."

I went inside. He was right. Even though there was a velvet rope and a sign that said, "Closed," it didn't look like any work had started. I wanted to be near Mary Theresa's window anyway. But as I got near the top of the stairs, I noticed they sounded different beneath my crutches. Some of the ones that were usually quiet were groaning now.

I waited until almost everyone was gone. By that time I had done more thinking. I figured Harvey wouldn't give up trying to kill my mom, even if I had wrecked his chocolate plan. He wanted the house and the money that came with my mom, but not her or her kid. I couldn't keep watching him all the time.

I turned the lamp on and waited for him to come into the church. As usual, he didn't even look toward me. He went into the confessional. I took one last look at the window and started to turn the lamp off, when I got an idea. I left the lamp on.

I knew the fourth step from the top was especially creaky. I went down to the sixth step from the top, then turned around. I held on to the rail, and then pressed one of my crutches down on the fourth step. It creaked. I leaned most of my weight on it. I felt it give. I stopped before it broke.

I went on down the stairs. I could hear Harvey, not talking about my mom this time, but not admitting he was hoping she was already dead. I went into the other confessional, but I didn't kneel down.

I heard Harvey finish up and step outside his confessional. Then I heard him take a couple of steps and stand outside my confessional door.

For a minute, I was afraid he'd open the door and look 'nside. He didn't. He took a couple of steps away, and then stopped again. I waited. He walked toward the back of the church, and I could tell by the sound of his steps that he was mad. I knocked on the wall between me and Father O'Brien, "All right if I don't kneel this time, Father?" I asked.

"Certainly, my son," he said.

"Bless me, Father, for I have sinned. I lied three times, I stole sixty cents, and . . ."

I waited a moment.

"And?" the priest said.

There was a loud groaning sound, a yell, and a crash.

"And I just killed my stepfather."

✝   ✝   ✝

He didn't die, he just broke both of his legs and knocked himself out. A policeman showed up, but not because Father O'Brien had told anyone my confession. Turned out my mother had called the police, showed them the candy, and finally convinced them they had to hurry to the church and arrest her husband before he harmed her son.

The police talked to me and then went down to South Street and arrested Mackie. At the hospital, a detective went in with me to see Harvey when Harvey woke up. I got to offer Harvey some of the chocolates he had given my mom. Instead of taking any candy, he made another confession that night. Before we left, the detective asked him why he had gone up into the choir loft. He said I had left a light on up there. The detective asked me if that was true, and of course I said, "Yes."

The next time I was in church, I put Mackie's silver dollar in the donation box near the candles and lit three candles: one for my father, one for Mary Theresa Mills, and one for the guy who made up the rule that says priests can't rat on you.

After I lit the candles, I went home and took out my wooden box. I put my father's pipes on the mantle, next to his photo. My mom saw me staring at the photo and came over and stood next to me. Instead of thinking of him being off in heaven, a long way away, I imagined him being right there with us, looking back at us from that picture. I imagined him knowing that I had tried to save her from Harvey. I thought he would have liked that.

My mom reached out and touched one of the pipes very carefully. "It wasn't your fault," she said.

You know what? I believed her.

THE WRONG SHAPE

G. K. CHESTERTON

CERTAIN OF THE GREAT ROADS going north out of London continue far into the country a sort of attenuated and interrupted spectre of a street, with great gaps in the building, but preserving the line. Here will be a group of shops, followed by a fenced field or paddock, and then a famous public-house, and then perhaps a market garden or a nursery garden, and then one large private house, and then another field and another inn, and so on. If anyone walks along one of these roads he will pass a house which will probably catch his eye, though he may not be able to explain its attraction. It is a long, low house, running parallel with the road, painted mostly white and pale green, with a veranda and sunblinds, and porches capped with those quaint sort of cupolas like wooden umbrellas that one sees in some old-fashioned houses. In fact, it is an old-fashioned house, very English and very suburban in the good old wealthy Clapham sense. And yet the house has a look of having been built chiefly for the hot weather. Looking at its white paint and sun blinds one thinks vaguely of pugarees and even of palm trees. I cannot trace the feeling to its root; perhaps the place was built by an Anglo-Indian.

Anyone passing this house, I say, would be namelessly fascinated by it; would feel that it was a place about which some story was to be told.

And he would have been right, as you shall shortly hear. For this is the story—the story of the strange things that did really happen in it in the Whitsuntide of the year 18—:

Anyone passing the house on the Thursday before Whit-Sunday at about half-past four P.M. would have seen the front door open, and Father Brown, of the small church of St. Mungo, come out smoking a large pipe in company with a very tall French friend of his called Flambeau, who was smoking a very small cigarette. These persons may or may not be of interest to the reader, but the truth is that they were not the only interesting things that were displayed when the front door of the white-and-green house was opened. There are further peculiarities about this house, which must be described to start with, not only that the reader may understand this tragic tale, but also that he may realize what it was that the opening of the door revealed.

The whole house was built upon the plan of a T, but a T with a very long cross piece and a very short tail piece The long cross piece was the frontage that ran along in face of the street with the front door in the middle; it was two stories high, and contained nearly all the important rooms. The short tail piece, which ran out at the back immediately opposite the front door, was one story high, and consisted only of two long rooms, the one leading into the other. The first of these two rooms was the study in which the celebrated Mr. Quinton wrote his wild Oriental poems and romances. The farther room was a glass conservatory full of tropical blossoms of quite unique and almost monstrous beauty, and on such afternoons as these was glowing with gorgeous sunlight. Thus when the hall door was open, many a passerby literally stopped to stare and gasp; for he looked down a perspective of rich apartments to something really like a transformation scene in a fairy play: purple clouds and golden suns and crimson stars that were at once scorchingly vivid and yet transparent and far away.

Leonard Quinton, the poet, had himself most carefully arranged this effect; and it is doubtful whether he so perfectly expressed his personality in any of his poems. For he was a man who drank and bathed in colours, who indulged his lust for colour somewhat to the neglect of form—even of good form. Thus it was that he had turned his genius so wholly to eastern art and imagery; to those bewildering carpets or blinding embroideries in which all the colours seem fallen into a fortunate chaos, having nothing to typify or to teach. He had attempted, not perhaps with complete artistic success, but with acknowledged imagination

and invention, to compose epics and love stories reflecting the riot of violent and even cruel colour; tales of tropical heavens of burning gold or
blood-red copper; of eastern heroes who rode with twelve-turbaned
mitres upon elephants painted purple or peacock green; of gigantic jewels that a hundred negroes could not carry, but which burned with
ancient and strange-hued fires.

In short (to put the matter from the more common point of view), he
dealt much in eastern heavens, rather worse than most western hells; in
eastern monarchs, whom we might possibly call maniacs; and in eastern
jewels which a Bond Street jeweller (if the hundred staggering negroes
brought them into his shop) might possibly not regard as genuine.
Quinton was a genius, if a morbid one; and even his morbidity appeared
more in his life than in his work. In temperament he was weak and
waspish, and his health had suffered heavily from oriental experiments
with opium. His wife—a handsome, hard-working, and, indeed, over-
worked woman—objected to the opium, but objected much more to a
live Indian hermit in white and yellow robes, whom her husband had
insisted on entertaining for months together, a Virgil to guide his spirit
through the heavens and the hells of the east.

It was out of this artistic household that Father Brown and his friend
stepped on to the door-step; and to judge from their faces, they stepped
out of it with much relief. Flambeau had known Quinton in wild student
days in Paris, and they had renewed the acquaintance for a week-end; but
apart from Flambeau's more responsible developments of late, he did not
get on well with the poet now. Choking oneself with opium and writing
little erotic verses on vellum was not his notion of how a gentleman
should go to the devil. As the two paused on the doorstep, before taking
a turn in the garden, the front garden gate was thrown open with vio-
lence, and a young man with a billycock hat on the back of his head tumbled up the steps in his eagerness. He was a dissipated-looking youth
with a gorgeous red necktie all awry, as if he had slept in it, and he kept
fidgeting and lashing about with one of those little jointed canes.

"I say," he said breathlessly, "I want to see old Quinton. I must see
him. Has he gone?"

"Mr. Quinton is in, I believe," said Father Brown, cleaning his pipe,
"but I do not know if you can see him. The doctor is with him at present."

The young man, who seemed not to be perfectly sober, stumbled into
the hall; and at the same moment the doctor came out of Quinton's study,
shutting the door and beginning to put on his gloves.

"See Mr. Quinton?" said the doctor coolly. "No, I'm afraid you can't. In fact, you mustn't on any account. Nobody must see him; I've just given him his sleeping draught."

"No, but look here, old chap," said the youth in the red tie, trying affectionately to capture the doctor by the lapels of his coat. "Look here. I'm simply sewn up, I tell you. I—"

"It's no good, Mr. Atkinson," said the doctor, forcing him to fall back; "when you can alter the effects of a drug I'll alter my decision," and, settling on his hat, he stepped out into the sunlight with the other two. He was a bull-necked, good-tempered little man with a small moustache, inexpressibly ordinary, yet giving an impression of capability.

The young man in the billycock, who did not seem to be gifted with any tact in dealing with people beyond the general idea of clutching hold of their coats, stood outside the door, as dazed as if he had been thrown out bodily, and silently watched the other three walk away together through the garden.

"That was a sound, spanking lie I told just now," remarked the medical man, laughing. "In point of fact, poor Quinton doesn't have his sleeping draught for nearly half an hour. But I'm not going to have him bothered with that little beast, who only wants to borrow money that he wouldn't pay back if he could. He's a dirty little scamp, though he is Mrs. Quinton's brother, and she's as fine a woman as ever walked."

"Yes," said Father Brown. "She's a good woman."

"So I propose to hang about the garden till the creature has cleared off," went on the doctor, "and then I'll go in to Quinton with the medicine. Atkinson can't get in, because I locked the door."

"In that case, Dr. Harris," said Flambeau, "we might as well walk round at the back by the end of the conservatory. There's no entrance to it that way but it's worth seeing, even from the outside."

"Yes, and I might get a squint at my patient," laughed the doctor, "for he prefers to lie on an ottoman right at the end of the conservatory amid all those blood-red poinsettias; it would give me the creeps. But what are you doing?"

Father Brown had stopped for a moment, and picked up out of the long grass, where it had almost been wholly hidden, a queer, crooked Oriental knife, inlaid exquisitely in coloured stones and metals.

"What is this?" asked Father Brown, regarding it with some disfavour.

"Oh, Quinton's, I suppose," said Dr. Harris carelessly; "he has all sorts of Chinese knick-knacks about the place. Or perhaps it belongs to the mild Hindoo of his whom he keeps on a string."

"What Hindoo?" asked Father Brown, still staring at the dagger in his hand.

"Oh, some Indian conjurer," said the doctor lightly; "a fraud, of course.

"You don't believe in magic?" asked Father Brown without looking up.

"Oh crikey! magic!" said the doctor.

"It's very beautiful," said the priest in a low, dreaming voice; "the colours are very beautiful. But it's the wrong shape."

"What for?" asked Flambeau, staring.

"For anything. It's the wrong shape in the abstract. Don't you ever feel that about Eastern art? The colours are intoxicatingly lovely; but the shapes are mean and bad—deliberately mean and bad. I have seen wicked things in a Turkey carpet."

"*Mon Dieu!*" cried Flambeau, laughing.

"They are letters and symbols in a language I don't know; but I know they stand for evil words," went on the priest, his voice growing lower and lower. "The lines go wrong on purpose—like serpents doubling to escape."

"What the devil are you talking about?" said the doctor with a loud laugh.

Flambeau spoke quietly to him in answer. "The Father sometimes gets this mystic's cloud on him, " he said; "but I give you fair warning that I have never known him have it except when there was some evil quite near."

"Oh, rats!" said the scientist.

"Why, look at it," cried Father Brown, holding out the crooked knife at arm's length, as if it were some glittering snake. "Don't you see it is the wrong shape? Don't you see that it has no hearty and plain purpose? It does not point like a spear. It does not sweep like a scythe. It does not *look* like a weapon. It looks like an instrument of torture."

"Well, as you don't seem to like it," said the jolly Harris, "it had better be taken back to its owner. Haven't we come to the end of this confounded conservatory yet? This house is the wrong shape, if you like."

"You don't understand," said Father Brown, shaking his head. "The shape of this house is quaint—it is even laughable. But there is nothing *wrong* about it."

As they spoke they came round the curve of glass that ended the conservatory, an uninterrupted curve, for there was neither door nor window by which to enter at that end. The glass, however, was clear, and the sun still bright, though beginning to set; and they could see not only the flamboyant blossoms inside, but the frail figure of the poet in a brown velvet coat lying languidly on the sofa, having, apparently, fallen half asleep over a book. He was a pale, slight man, with loose, chestnut hair and a fringe of beard that was the paradox of his face, for the beard made him look less manly. These traits were well known to all three of them; but even had it not been so, it may be doubted whether they would have looked at Quinton just then. Their eyes were riveted on another object.

Exactly in their path, immediately outside the round end of the glass building, was standing a tall man, whose drapery fell to his feet in faultless white, and whose bare, brown skull, face, and neck gleamed in the setting sun like splendid bronze. He was looking through the glass at the sleeper, and he was more motionless than a mountain.

"Who is that?" cried Father Brown, stepping back with a hissing intake of his breath.

"Oh, it is only that Hindoo humbug," growled Harris; "but I don't know what the deuce he's doing here."

"It looks like hypnotism," said Flambeau, biting his black moustache.

"Why are you unmedical fellows always talking bosh about hypnotism?" cried the doctor. "It looks a deal more like burglary."

"Well, we will speak to it, at any rate," said Flambeau, who was always for action. One long stride took him to the place where the Indian stood. Bowing from his great height, which overtopped even the Oriental's, he said with placid impudence:

"Good evening, sir. Do you want anything?"

Quite slowly, like a great ship turning into a harbour, the great yellow face turned, and looked at last over its white shoulder. They were startled to see that its yellow eyelids were quite sealed, as in sleep. "Thank you," said the face in excellent English. "I want nothing." Then, half opening the lids, so as to show a slit of opalescent eyeball, he repeated, "I want nothing." Then he opened his eyes wide with a startling stare, said, "I want nothing," and went rustling away into the rapidly darkening garden.

"The Christian is more modest," muttered Father Brown; "he wants something."

"What on earth was he doing?" asked Flambeau, knitting his black brows and lowering his voice.

"I should like to talk to you later," said Father Brown.

The sunlight was still a reality, but it was the red light of evening, and the bulk of the garden trees and bushes grew blacker and blacker against it. They turned round the end of the conservatory, and walked in silence down the other side to get round to the front door. As they went they seemed to wake something, as one startles a bird, in the deeper corner between the study and the main building; and again they saw the white-robed fakir slide out of the shadow, and slip round towards the front door. To their surprise, however, he had not been alone. They found themselves abruptly pulled up and forced to banish their bewilderment by the appearance of Mrs. Quinton, with her heavy golden hair and square pale face, advancing on them out of the twilight. She looked a little stern, but was entirely courteous.

"Good evening, Dr. Harris," was all she said.

"Good evening, Mrs. Quinton," said the little doctor heartily. "I am just going to give your husband his sleeping draught."

"Yes," she said in a clear voice. "I think it is quite time." And she smiled at them, and went sweeping into the house.

"That woman's over-driven," said Father Brown; "that's the kind of woman that does her duty for twenty years, and then does something dreadful."

The little doctor looked at him for the first time with an eye of interest. "Did you ever study medicine?" he asked.

"You have to know something of the mind as well as the body," answered the priest; "we have to know something of the body as well as the mind."

"Well," said the doctor, "I think I'll go and give Quinton his stuff."

They had turned the corner of the front façade, and were approaching the front doorway. As they turned into it they saw the man in the white robe for the third time. He came so straight towards the front door that it seemed quite incredible that he had not just come out of the study opposite to it. Yet they knew that the study door was locked.

Father Brown and Flambeau, however, kept this weird contradiction to themselves, and Dr. Harris was not a man to waste his thoughts on the impossible. He permitted the omnipresent Asiatic to make his exit, and then stepped briskly into the hall. There he found a figure which he had already forgotten. The inane Atkinson was still hanging about, humming and poking things with his knobby cane. The doctor's face had a spasm of disgust and decision, and he whispered rapidly to his companion: "I must lock the door again, or this rat will get in. But I shall be out again in two minutes."

He rapidly unlocked the door and locked it again behind him, just balking a blundering charge from the young man in the billycock. The young man threw himself impatiently on a hall chair. Flambeau looked at a Persian illumination on the wall; Father Brown, who seemed in a sort of daze, dully eyed the door. In about four minutes the door was opened again. Atkinson was quicker this time. He sprang forward, held the door open for an instant, and called out: "Oh, I say, Quinton, I want—"

From the other end of the study came the clear voice of Quinton, in something between a yawn and a yell of weary laughter.

"Oh, I know what you want. Take it, and leave me in peace. I'm writing a song about peacocks."

Before the door closed half a sovereign came flying through the aperture and Atkinson, stumbling forward, caught it with singular dexterity.

"So that's settled," said the doctor, and, locking the door savagely, he led the way out into the garden.

"Poor Leonard can get a little peace now," he added to Father Brown; "he's locked in all by himself for an hour or two."

"Yes," answered the priest; "and his voice sounded jolly enough when we left him." Then he looked gravely round the garden, and saw the loose figure of Atkinson standing and jingling the half-sovereign in his pocket, and beyond, in the purple twilight, the figure of the Indian sitting bolt upright upon a bank of grass with his face turned towards the setting sun. Then he said abruptly: "Where is Mrs. Quinton?"

"She has gone up to her room," said the doctor. "That is her shadow on the blind."

Father Brown looked up, and frowningly scrutinized a dark outline at the gas-lit window.

"Yes," he said, "that is her shadow," and he walked a yard or two and threw himself upon a garden seat.

Flambeau sat down beside him; but the doctor was one of those energetic people who live naturally on their legs. He walked away, smoking, into the twilight, and the two friends were left together.

"My father," said Flambeau in French, "what is the matter with you?"

Father Brown was silent and motionless for half a minute then he said: "Superstition is irreligious, but there is something in the air of this place. I think it's that Indian—at least, partly."

He sank into silence, and watched the distant outline of the Indian, who still sat rigid as if in prayer. At first sight he seemed motionless, but as Father Brown watched him he saw that the man swayed ever so slightly with a rhythmic movement, just as the dark tree-tops swayed ever so slightly in the little wind that was creeping up the dim garden paths and shuffling the fallen leaves a little.

The landscape was growing rapidly dark, as if for a storm, but they could still see all the figures in their various places. Atkinson was leaning against a tree, with a listless face; Quinton's wife was still at her window; the doctor had gone strolling round the end of the conservatory; they could see his cigar like a will-o'-the-wisp; and the fakir still sat rigid and yet rocking, while the trees above him began to rock and almost to roar. Storm was certainly coming.

"When that Indian spoke to us," went on Brown in a conversational undertone, "I had a sort of vision, a vision of him and all his universe. Yet he only said the same thing three times. When first he said, 'I want nothing,' it meant only that he was impenetrable, that Asia does not give itself away. Then he said again, 'I want nothing,' and I knew that be meant that he was sufficient to himself, like a cosmos, that he needed no God, neither admitted any sins. And when he said the third time, 'I want nothing,' he said it with blazing eyes. And I knew that he meant literally what he said; that nothing was his desire and his home; that he was weary for nothing as for wine; that annihilation, the mere destruction of everything or anything—"

Two drops of rain fell; and for some reason Flambeau started and looked up, as if they had stung him. And the same instant the doctor down by the end of the conservatory began running towards them, calling out something as he ran.

As he came among them like a bombshell the restless Atkinson happened to be taking a turn nearer to the house front; and the doctor clutched him by the collar in a convulsive grip. "Foul play!" he cried; "what have you been doing to him, you dog?"

The priest had sprung erect, and had the voice of steel of a soldier in command.

"No fighting," he cried coolly; "we are enough to hold anyone we want to. What is the matter, doctor?"

"Things are not right with Quinton," said the doctor, quite white. "I could just see him through the glass, and I don't like the way he's lying. It's not as I left him, anyhow."

"Let us go in to him," said Father Brown shortly. "You can leave Mr.

Atkinson alone. I have had him in sight since we heard Quinton's voice."

"I will stop here and watch him," said Flambeau hurriedly. "You go in and see."

The doctor and the priest flew to the study door, unlocked it, and fell into the room. In doing so they nearly fell over the large mahogany table in the centre at which the poet usually wrote; for the place was lit only by a small fire kept for the invalid. In the middle of this table lay a single sheet of paper, evidently left there on purpose. The doctor snatched it up, glanced at it, handed it to Father Brown, and crying, "Good God, look at that!" plunged towards the glass room beyond, where the terrible tropic flowers still seemed to keep a crimson memory of the sunset.

Father Brown read the words three times before he put down the paper. The words were: "I die by my own hand; yet I die murdered!" They were in the quite inimitable, not to say illegible, handwriting of Leonard Quinton.

Then Father Brown, still keeping the paper in his hand, strode towards the conservatory, only to meet his medical friend coming back with a face of assurance and collapse. "He's done it," said Harris.

They went together through the gorgeous unnatural beauty of cactus and azalea and found Leonard Quinton, poet and romancer, with his head hanging downward off his ottoman and his red curls sweeping the ground. Inside his left side was thrust the queer dagger that they had picked up in the garden, and his limp hand still rested on the hilt.

Outside, the storm had come at one stride, like the night in Coleridge, and garden and glass roof were darkening with driving rain. Father Brown seemed to be studying the paper more than the corpse; he held it close to his eyes; and seemed trying to read it in the twilight. Then he held it up against the faint light, and, as he did so, lightning stared at them for an instant so white that the paper looked black against it.

Darkness full of thunder followed, and after the thunder Father Brown's voice said out of the dark: "Doctor, this paper is the wrong shape."

"What do you mean?" asked Doctor Harris, with a frowning stare.

"It isn't square," answered Brown. "It has a sort of edge snipped off at the corner. What does it mean?"

"How the deuce should I know?" growled the doctor. "Shall we move this poor chap, do you think? He's quite dead."

"No," answered the priest; "we must leave him as he lies and send for the police." But he was still scrutinizing the paper.

As they went back through the study he stopped by the table and picked up a small pair of nail scissors. "Ah," he said with a sort of relief; "this is what he did it with. But yet—" And he knitted his brows.

"Oh, stop fooling with that scrap of paper," said the doctor emphatically. "It was a fad of his. He had hundreds of them. He cut all his paper like that," as he pointed to a stack of sermon paper still unused on another and smaller table. Father Brown went up to it and held up a sheet. It was the same irregular shape.

"Quite so," he said. "And here I see the corners that were snipped off." And to the indignation of his colleague he began to count them.

"That's all right," he said, with an apologetic smile. "Twenty-three sheets cut and twenty-two corners cut off them. And as I see you are impatient we will rejoin the others."

"Who is to tell his wife?" asked Dr. Harris. "Will you go and tell her now, while I send a servant for the police?"

"As you will," said Father Brown indifferently. And he went out to the hall door.

Here also he found a drama, though of a more grotesque sort. It showed nothing less than his big friend Flambeau in an attitude to which he had long been unaccustomed, while upon the pathway at the bottom of the steps was sprawling with his boots in the air the amiable Atkinson, his billycock hat and walking-cane sent flying in opposite directions along the path. Atkinson had at length wearied of Flambeau's almost paternal custody, and had endeavoured to knock him down, which was by no means a smooth game to play with the Roi des Apaches, even after that monarch's abdication.

Flambeau was about to leap upon his enemy and secure him once more, when the priest patted him easily on the shoulder.

"Make it up with Mr. Atkinson, my friend," he said. "Beg a mutual pardon and say 'Good night.' We need not detain him any longer." Then, as Atkinson rose somewhat doubtfully and gathered his hat and stick and went towards the garden gate, Father Brown said in a more serious voice: "Where is that Indian?"

They all three (for the doctor had joined them) turned involuntarily towards the dim grassy bank amid the tossing trees, purple with twilight, where they had last seen the brown man swaying in his strange prayers. The Indian was gone.

"Confound him," said the doctor, stamping furiously. "Now I know that it was that nigger that did it."

"I thought you didn't believe in magic," said Father Brown quietly.

"No more I did," said the doctor, rolling his eyes. "I only know that I loathed that yellow devil when I thought he was a sham wizard. And I shall loathe him more if I come to think he was a real one."

"Well, his having escaped is nothing," said Flambeau. "For we could have proved nothing and done nothing against him. One hardly goes to the parish constable with a story of suicide imposed by witchcraft or auto-suggestion."

Meanwhile Father Brown had made his way into the house, and now went to break the news to the wife of the dead man.

When he came out again he looked a little pale and tragic; but what passed between them in that interview was never known, even when all was known.

Flambeau, who was talking quietly with the doctor, was surprised to see his friend reappear so soon at his elbow; but Brown took no notice, and merely drew the doctor apart. "You have sent for the police, haven't you?" he asked.

"Yes," answered Harris. "They ought to be here in ten minutes."

"Will you do me a favour?" said the priest quietly. "The truth is, I make a collection of these curious stories, which often contain, as in the case of our Hindoo friend, elements which can hardly be put into a police report. Now, I want you to write out a report of this case for my private use. Yours is a clever trade," he said, looking at the doctor gravely and steadily in the face. "I sometimes think that you know some details of this matter which you have not thought fit to mention. Mine is a confidential trade like yours, and I will treat anything you write for me in strict confidence. But write the whole."

The doctor, who had been listening thoughtfully with his head a little on one side, looked the priest in the face for an instant, and said: "All right," and went into the study, closing the door behind him.

"Flambeau," said Father Brown, "there is a long seat there under the veranda, where we can smoke, out of the rain. You are my only friend in the world, and I want to talk to you. Or, perhaps, be silent with you."

They established themselves comfortably in the veranda seat; Father Brown, against his common habit, accepted a good cigar and smoked it steadily in silence, while the rain shrieked and rattled on the roof of the veranda.

"My friend," he said at length, "this is a very queer case. A very queer case."

"I should think it was," said Flambeau, with something like a shudder.

"You call it queer, and I call it queer," said the other, "and yet we mean quite opposite things. The modern mind always mixes up two different ideas: mystery in the sense of what is marvellous, and mystery in the sense of what is complicated. That is half its difficulty about miracles. A miracle is startling; but it is simple. It is simple because it *is* a miracle. It is power coming directly from God (or the devil) instead of indirectly through nature or human wills. Now you mean that this business is marvellous because it is miraculous, because it is witchcraft worked by a wicked Indian. Understand, I do not say that it was not spiritual or diabolic. Heaven and hell only know by what surrounding influences strange sins come into the lives of men. But for the present my point is this: If it was pure magic, as you think, then it is marvellous; but it is not mysterious—that is, it is not complicated. The quality of a miracle is mysterious, but its manner is simple. Now, the manner of this business has been the reverse of simple."

The storm that had slackened for a little seemed to be swelling again, and there came heavy movements as of faint thunder. Father Brown let fall the ash of his cigar and went on:

"There has been in this incident," he said, "a twisted, ugly, complex quality that does not belong to the straight bolts either of heaven or hell. As one knows the crooked track of a snail, I know the crooked track of a man."

The white lightning opened its enormous eye in one wink, the sky shut up again, and the priest went on:

"Of all these crooked things, the crookedest was the shape of that piece of paper. It was crookeder than the dagger that killed him."

"You mean the paper on which Quinton confessed his suicide," said Flambeau.

"I mean the paper on which Quinton wrote, 'I die by my own hand,'" answered Father Brown. "The shape of that paper, my friend, was the wrong shape; the wrong shape, if ever I have seen it in this wicked world."

"It only had a corner snipped off," said Flambeau, "and I understand that all Quinton's paper was cut that way."

"It was a very odd way," said the other, "and a very bad way, to my taste and fancy. Look here, Flambeau, this Quinton—God receive his soul!—was perhaps a bit of a cur in some ways, but he really was an artist, with the pencil as well as the pen. His handwriting, though hard to read, was bold and beautiful. I can't prove what I say; I can't prove anything. But I tell you with the full force of conviction that he could never have cut that mean little piece off a sheet of paper. If he had wanted to cut down paper for some purpose of fitting in, or binding up, or what not, he would have made quite a different slash with the scissors. Do you remember the shape? It was a mean shape. It was a wrong shape. Like this. Don't you remember?"

And he waved his burning cigar before him in the darkness, making irregular squares so rapidly that Flambeau really seemed to see them as fiery hieroglyphics upon the darkness—hieroglyphics such as his friend had spoken of, which are undecipherable, yet can have no good meaning.

"But," said Flambeau, as the priest put his cigar in his mouth again and leaned back, staring at the roof. "Suppose somebody else did use the scissors. Why should somebody else, cutting pieces off his sermon paper, make Quinton commit suicide?"

Father Brown was still leaning back and staring at the room, but he took his cigar out of his mouth and said: "Quinton never did commit suicide."

Flambeau stared at him. "Why, confound it all," he cried; "then why did he confess to suicide?"

The priest leaned forward again, settled his elbows on his knees, looked at the ground, and said in a low distinct voice: "He never did confess to suicide."

Flambeau laid his cigar down. "You mean," he said, "that the writing was forged?"

"No," said Father Brown; "Quinton wrote it all right."

"Well, there you are," said the aggravated Flambeau; "Quinton wrote: 'I die by my own hand,' with his own hand on a plain piece of paper."

"Of the wrong shape," said the priest calmly.

"Oh, the shape be damned!" cried Flambeau. "What has the shape to do with it?"

"There were twenty-three snipped papers," resumed Brown unmoved, "and only twenty-two pieces snipped off. Therefore one of the pieces had been destroyed, probably that from the written paper. Does that suggest anything to you?"

A light dawned on Flambeau's face, and he said: "There was something else written by Quinton, some other words. 'They will tell you I die by my own hand,' or 'Do not believe that—'"

"Hotter, as the children say," said his friend. "But the piece was hardly half an inch across; there was no room for one word, let alone five. Can you think of anything hardly bigger than a comma which the man with hell in his heart had to tear away as a testimony against him?"

"I can think of nothing," said Flambeau at last.

"What about quotation marks?" said the priest, and flung his cigar far into the darkness like a shooting star.

All words had left the other man's mouth, and Father Brown said, like one going back to fundamentals:

"Leonard Quinton was a romancer, and was writing an Oriental romance about wizardry and hypnotism. He—"

At this moment the door opened briskly behind them and the doctor came out with his hat on. He put a long envelope into the priest's hands.

"That's the document you wanted," he said, "and I must be getting home. Good night."

"Good night," said Father Brown, as the doctor walked briskly to the gate. He had left the front door open, so that a shaft of gaslight fell upon them. In the light of this Brown opened the envelope and read the following words:

"DEAR FATHER BROWN—*Vicisti, Galilœe!* Otherwise, damn your eyes, which are very penetrating ones. Can it be possible that there is something in all that stuff of yours after all?

"I am a man who has ever since boyhood believed in Nature and in all natural functions and instincts, whether men called them moral or immoral. Long before I became a doctor, when I was a schoolboy keeping mice and spiders, I believed that to be a good animal is the best thing in the world. But just now I am shaken; I have believed in Nature; but it seems as if Nature could betray a man. Can there be anything in your bosh? I am really getting morbid.

"I loved Quinton's wife. What was there wrong in that? Nature told me to, and it's love that makes the world go round. I also thought, quite sincerely, that she would be happier with a clean animal like me than with that tormenting little lunatic. What was there wrong in that? I was only facing facts, like a man of science. She would have been happier.

"According to my own creed I was quite free to kill Quinton, which was the best thing for everybody, even himself.

But as a healthy animal I had no notion of killing myself. I resolved, therefore, that I would never do it until I saw a chance that would leave me scot free. I saw that chance this morning.

"I have been three times, all told, into Quinton's study to-day. The first time I went in he would talk about nothing but the weird tale, called 'The Curse of a Saint,' which he was writing, which was all about how some Indian hermit made an English colonel kill himself by thinking about him. He showed me the last sheets, and even read me the last paragraph, which was something like this: 'The conqueror of the Punjab, a mere yellow skeleton, but still gigantic, managed to lift himself on his elbow and gasp in his nephew's ear: "I die by my own hand, yet I die murdered!"' It so happened, by one chance out of a hundred, that those last words were written at the top of a new sheet of paper. I left the room, and went out into the garden intoxicated with a frightful opportunity.

"We walked round the house, and two more things happened in my favour. You suspected an Indian, and you found a dagger which the Indian might most probably use. Taking the opportunity to stuff it in my pocket I went back to Quinton's study, locked the door, and gave him his sleeping draught. He was against answering Atkinson at all, but I urged him to call out and quiet the fellow, because I wanted a clear proof that Quinton was alive when I left the room for the second time. Quinton lay down in the conservatory, and I came through the study. I am a quick man with my hands, and in a minute and a half I had done what I wanted to do. I had emptied all the first part of Quinton's romance into the fireplace, where it burnt to ashes. Then I saw that the quotation marks wouldn't do, so I snipped them off, and to make it seem likelier, snipped the whole quire to match. Then I came out with the knowledge that Quinton's confession of suicide lay on the front table, while Quinton lay alive, but asleep, in the conservatory beyond.

"The last act was a desperate one; you can guess it: I pretended to have seen Quinton dead and rushed to his room. I delayed you with the paper; and, being a quick man with my hands, killed Quinton while you were looking at his confession of suicide. He was half-asleep, being drugged, and I put his own hand on the knife and drove it into his body. The knife was of so queer a shape that no one but an operator could have calculated the angle that would reach his heart. I wonder if you noticed this.

"When I had done it the extraordinary thing happened. Nature deserted me. I felt ill. I felt just as if I had done something wrong. I think my brain is breaking up; I feel some sort of desperate pleasure in thinking I have told the thing to somebody; that I shall not have to be alone with it if I marry and have children. What is the matter with me? . . . Madness . . . or can one have remorse, just as if one were in Byron's poems! I cannot write any more.

—JAMES ERSKINE HARRIS."

Father Brown carefully folded up the letter and put it in his breast pocket just as there came a loud peal at the gate bell, and the wet waterproofs of several policeman gleamed in the road outside.

Brother Orchid

Richard Connell

"Be smart," the warden said. "Go straight."

A grin creased the leather face of Little John Sarto.

"I *am* goin' straight," he said. "Straight to Chi."

"I wouldn't if I were you, Sarto."

"Why not? I owned that burg once. I'll own it again."

"Things have changed in ten years."

"But not me," said Little John. "I still got what it takes to be on top."

"You didn't stay there," the warden observed.

"I got framed," Sarto said. "Imagine shovin' me on the rock on a sissy income tax rap!"

"It was the only charge they could make stick," the warden said. "You were always pretty slick, Sarto."

"I was, and I am," said Little John.

The warden frowned. "Now look here, Sarto. When a man has done his time and I'm turning him loose, I'm supposed to give him some friendly advice. I do it, though I know that in most cases it's a farce. You'd think men who'd done a stretch here in Alcatraz ought to have a sneaking notion that crime does not pay, but while I'm preaching my lit-

tle sermon I see a faraway look in their eyes and I know they're figuring out their next bank job or snatch."

"Don't class me with them small-time heisters and petty-larceny
yeggs," said Little John. "I'm a born big shot."

"You're apt to die the same way," said the warden dryly.

"That's okay, net, by me," said Little John. "When I peg out I want
to go with fireworks, flowers and bands; but you'll have a beard to your
knees before they get out the last extra on Little John Sarto. I got a lot
of livin' to do first: I got to wash out the taste of slum with a lakeful of
champagne, and it'll take half the blondes in the Loop to make me forget them nights in solitary. But most of all I got to be myself again, not
just a number. For every order I've took here on the rock, I'm goin' to
give two. I'm goin' to see guys shiver and jump when I speak. I've
played mouse long enough. Watch me be a lion again."

The warden sighed. "Sarto," he said, "why don't you play it safe?
Stay away from Chicago. Settle in some new part of the country. Go into
business. You've got brains and a real gift for organization. You ran a big
business once—"

"Million a month, net," put in Sarto.

"And you're only forty-six and full of health," the warden went on.
"You can still make a fresh start."

"Using what for wampum?" asked Little John.

"You've got plenty salted away."

Sarto laughed a wry laugh.

"I got the ten bucks, and the ticket back to Chi, and this frowsy suit
the prison gimme, and that's all I got," he said.

"Don't tell me you're broke!"

"Flat as a mat," said Little John. "I spent it like I made it—fast. A
king's got to live like a king, ain't he? When I give a dame flowers, it was
always orchids. My free-chow bill ran to a grand a week. They called me
a public enemy but they treated me like a year-round Sandy Claws. . . .
But I ain't worryin'. I was born broke. I got over it."

† † †

A prison guard came in to say that the launch was ready to take Sarto
to the mainland.

"Well, goodbye, Warden," said Sarto jauntily. "If you ever get to Chi
gimme a buzz. I'll throw a party for you."

"Wait a minute," said the warden. "I can't let you go till I make one last attempt to start you on the right track. I know a man who'll give you a job. He runs a big truck farm and—"

He stopped, for Sarto was shaking with hoarse laughter.

"Me a rube?" Little John got out. "Me a bodyguard to squashes? Warden, the stir-bugs has got you."

"It's a chance to make an honest living."

"Save it for some cluck that would feel right at home livin' with turnips," Sarto said. "I got other plans."

The siren on the launch gave an impatient belch.

"So long, Warden," said Little John. "I won't be seein' you."

"You're right there," the warden said.

Sarto's face darkened at the words.

"Meanin' Chi might be bad for my health?"

"I've heard rumors to that effect," replied the warden.

"I've heard 'em for years," said Little John. "They're a lotta rat spit. Plenty guys has talked about what they was goin' to do to me. I always sent flowers to their funerals—you heard about that."

He chuckled.

"A big heart of forget-me-nots with 'Sorry, Pal' in white orchids on it."

"All right, wise guy," the warden said. "Go to Chicago. The sooner you get rubbed out, the better for everybody. You're no good and you never will be."

"Atta clown," said Little John Sarto. "Always leave 'em laughin' when you say goodbye."

Laughing, he started out toward the big gray gate.

Deep in the woods in an out-of-the-world corner of Michigan, squat, unkempt Twin Pine Inn hides itself. It was silent that summer night, and dark save for a single window in the taproom. Behind the customerless bar, Fat Dutchy was drinking his fourth rock-and-rye.

"Stick 'em up. This is a heist."

The voice, low and with a snarl in it, came from the doorway behind him. Up went Fat Dutchy's hands.

"Easy with the rod," he whimpered. "There ain't a sawbuck in the joint."

"Not like the good old days," the voice said.

Dutchy turned his head. Little John Sarto was standing there with nothing more lethal in his hand than a big cigar. Dutchy blinked and goggled.

"Well, greaseball, do I look funny?" Sarto demanded.

"No—no—boss, you ain't changed a bit."

"I don't change," Sarto said. "Gimme a slug of bourbon."

Fat Dutchy sloshed four fingers of whisky into a glass. His hand trembled. Liquor splashed on the bar.

"What you got the jits about?" asked Sarto.

"You gimme a turn comin' in like you was a ghost or sumpin'," said Fat Dutchy. He wiped sweat from his mottled jowls with the bar rag. Sarto gulped his drink.

"Business bad, eh?"

"It ain't even bad, boss. It just ain't."

"Cheer up, big puss. You'll soon be scoffin' filly miggnons smothered with century notes," Sarto said. "I'm back."

† † †

Fat Dutchy rubbed his paunch and looked unhappily at the floor. "Things is different," he said.

Sarto banged his glass down on the bar.

"If one more lug tells me that, I'll kick his gizzard out," he said. "Now, listen. I'm holin' up here till I get my bearin's. Soon as I get things set, I'm goin' to town. But first I gotta contact some of the boys."

Fat Dutchy played nervously with the bar rag.

"Gimme another slug," Sarto ordered. "I got a ten-year thirst."

Fat Dutchy poured out the drink. Again his shaking hands made him spill some of it.

"Here's to me," said Sarto, and drank. "Now, listen: I want you to pass the office along to certain parties that I'm here and want to see 'em, pronto. For a starter, get in touch with Philly Powell, Ike Gelbert, Ouch O'Day, Willie the Knife, Benny Maletta, French Frank, Hop Latzo, Al Muller and that fresh kid that was so handy with a tommy gun—"

"Jack Buck?"

"Yeah. I may need a torpedo. When I fell out, he had the makin's of a good dropper. So get that phone workin', lard head—you know where they hang out."

"Sure," said Fat Dutchy. He held up his hand and ticked off names on his thick fingers.

"Ike Gelbert and Al Muller is in the jug doin' life jolts," he said. "Philly Powell and French Frank was crossed out right at this bar. Ouch O'Day throwed an ing-bing and was took to the fit house; the G-boys filled Benny Maletta with slugs and sent Willie the Knife to the hot squat; I dunno just where Hop Latzo is but I've heard talk he's at the bottom of Lake Mich in a barrel of concrete. So outa that lot there's only Jack Buck left and I don't guess you wanna see him—"

"Why not?"

"He's growed up," said Fat Dutchy. "He's the loud noise now. What rackets there is, Jack Buck's got 'em in his pocket."

"I'll whittle him down to his right size," said Sarto.

"Jack's in strong. He's waitin' for you, boss, and he ain't foolin'. The boys tell me it's worth three G's to the guy that settles you."

Sarto snorted. "Only three grand!" he said indignantly.

"That's serious sugar nowadays," said Fat Dutchy. "I'm tellin' you times is sour. Jack Buck has cornered the few grafts that still pay. He's got a mob of muzzlers that was in reform school when you was head man. You ain't nothin' fo'em but a name and a chance to earn three thousand fish."

Sarto sipped his drink. Lines of thought furrowed his face.

"I'll stay here till I figure out an angle," he announced.

"Boss," said Fat Dutchy, "I don't wanna speak outa turn, but wouldn't it be a smart play to take it on the lam for a while?"

"Where to?"

Fat Dutchy shrugged his stout shoulders.

"I wouldn't know, boss," he said. "When the heat's on—"

"Yeah, I know," cut in Sarto. "You're smoked wherever you go."

"What are you goin' to do, boss?"

"I'm goin' to hit the sheets and dream I'm out," said Little John.

Dog-tired though he was, he could not get to sleep. His mind yanked him away from dreams, back to prison, to the death-house, where men were lying in the dark, as he was, trying to sleep.

"They got the bulge on me, at that," he thought. "They *know* when they're goin' to get it."

He felt like a man reading his own obituary, complete but for two facts: where and when.

He knew he was safe where he was, but not for long. They'd comb all the known hideouts. He tried to think of some friend he could trust to hide him. Name after name he considered and rejected. He had come to the ninety-sixth name and found no one he could count on when he fell asleep.

✝   ✝   ✝

A light in his eyes and a voice in his ear jerked him awake.

A man was bending over him, smiling and saying:

"Wake up, dear. You'll be late for school."

He was a huge, soft-looking young man with a jovial freckled face. His suit was bottle-green and expensive. Sarto had never seen him before.

"Up, up, pet," he said, and waved at Sarto a big blue-black automatic.

A second man watched from the other side of the bed. He was younger and smaller than the first man, and his flour-white face was perfectly blank. Sarto did not know him either.

Sarto sat up in bed.

"Listen, fellas," he said, "if I get a break you get five grand."

"Got it on you, darling?" asked the freckled man.

"Nope. But I can dig it up inside a week."

"Sorry. We do a strictly cash business," the freckled man said.

"I'll make it ten grand," said Little John. He addressed the pallid man. "Wadda you say, bud? Ten G's."

The freckled man chuckled.

"He'd say 'no' if he could say anything," he said. "He doesn't hear, either. His eyes are good, though. His name is Harold, but we call him Dummy."

Sarto held his naked, flabby body very stiff and straight.

"Do your stuff," he said.

Dummy took his hand from his pocket. There was a pistol in it. The freckled man brushed the gun aside.

"We don't want to give this charming place a bad name," he explained to Sarto. "For Dutchy's sake."

"So that fat rat tipped you," said Sarto.

"Yes," said the freckled man. "For a modest fee. Come along, baby."

They were speeding through open farm country. The speedometer hit seventy-five. Sarto closed his mouth and his eyes.

"Praying?" asked the freckled man.

"Naw!"

"Better start, toots."

"I know nuttin' can help me."

"That's right," said the freckled man cheerfully. "Nothing but a miracle. But you might pray for your soul."

"Aw, go to hell."

They turned into a rutty, weed-grown road. As they bumped along through a tunnel of trees, suddenly, silently Little John Sarto began to pray.

"Listen! This is Little John Sarto of Chicago, Illinois, U.S.A. I know I got no right to ask any favors. I guess I got a bad rep up there. Well, I ain't goin' to try to lie away my record. Everything on the blotter is true. I don't claim I rate a break. All I say is I need one bad and I'll pay for it. I don't know how; but look me up in the big book. It ought to say that when I make a deal I never run out on it. If I'm talkin' out of turn, forget it. But I won't forget if—"

"Last stop. All out," sang out the freckled man. He halted the car by a thicket of thigh-high brush.

Sarto got out of the car. Dummy got out, too. He kept his gun against Little John's backbone.

"Goodbye, now," said the freckled man, and lit a cigarette.

Dummy marched Sarto off the road and into the thicket. Abruptly, like a spotlight, the moon came out. Dummy spun Sarto around. Sarto could see his face. It held neither hate nor pity. Dummy raised his pistol. As he brought it up on a level with Sarto's forehead, the breeze whipped a straggling branch of a wild rosebush across the back of his hand, and the thorns cut a wet, red line. For part of a second Dummy dropped his eyes to his bleeding hand. Sarto wheeled and dove into the underbrush. Dummy fired three quick shots. One missed. One raked across Sarto's skull. One seared his shoulder. He staggered, but kept plunging on. Dummy darted after him. Then the moon went out.

As Sarto floundered on he could hear Dummy crashing through the brush behind him. But Dummy could not hear his quarry. Dizzy and weak, the wounded man fought his frantic way through tar-black brush. Thorns stabbed him, briers clawed. A low branch smashed him on the nose, and he reeled and nearly went down. Bending double, he churned on. Then his head hit something hard, and he dropped, stunned for a moment. He reached out an unsteady hand and felt an ivy-covered wall. No sound of pursuit came to his ears.

Painfully he dragged himself up to the top of the wall. Not a sob of breath was left in him. He straddled the wall and clung to it. Then he fainted.

† † †

In the monastery of the Floratines, today was like yesterday and yesterday was like a day in the ninth century when the order was founded. Neither time nor war nor the hate of kings had changed their humble habits or their simple creed. Over the door this creed was carved: "Be poor in purse, pure in heart, kind in word and deed and beautify the lives of men with flowers."

These were the words of the Blessed Edric, their founder, and, ever since his day, Floratines in every land had lived by them, harming no one, helping man, raising flowers.

When King Henry VIII set his face against other monks, he let no hostile hand be laid on the few Floratines.

"They do much good," the monarch said, "and, in sooth, they have nothing worth the taking, these Little Brothers of the Flowers."

They kept the name, and it gave rise to a custom. When a man left the world behind to enter their ranks, he left his name, too, and took the name of a flower.

In the first light of a new day they sat in their refectory, forty-four men in snuff-hued robes, most of them growing old. Their tonsured polls were brown from the sun, their faces serene from inner peace.

"Brother Geranium is late with the milk," observed Brother Tulip, eyeing his dry porridge.

"Perhaps the cow kicked him," suggested Brother Hollyhock.

"She wouldn't. She's fond of him," said Brother Nasturtium. "I'll go down to the dairy and see if anything has happened to him," volunteered Brother Nasturtium. But as he rose from his bench, Brother Geranium, popeyed and panting, burst into the room.

"There's a naked man lying in the petunia bed," he gasped out. "I think he's dead."

† † †

Little John Sarto thought he was dead, too, when he opened his eyes in the infirmary and saw Abbot Jonquil and Brother Nasturtium at his bedside.

"I made it," he exclaimed huskily. "I beat the rap."

"Take it easy, son," said the abbot. "You've been badly hurt."

"But I ain't in hell," said Little John. Then he added, "Or if I am what are you guys doing here?"

"You're alive and in a safe place."

Sarto stared at him.

"Say, do you know who I am?" he asked.

"No."

"You musta seen my mug in the papers."

"We don't see newspapers here," the abbot said. "And we don't ask who a man is if he needs help."

Sarto touched his bandaged head.

"How long am I in for?" he inquired.

"Until you are well and strong again."

"I got no money."

"Neither have we," said the abbot. "So that makes you one of us, doesn't it?"

"That's one for the book, mister," said Little John.

"I'm Abbot Jonquil. This is Brother Nasturtium, your nurse. If you wish us to notify your friends—"

"I got no friends," grunted Little John.

"You have now," said the abbot.

"I tell you I'm broke."

"You poor fellow," said the abbot gently "What a life you must have led!"

"I been round long enough to know you never get sumpin' for nuttin'."

"I think you have talked enough for the present," the abbot said. "Try to rest and try not to worry—about anything. You may stay here as long as you wish, as our guest."

He went to the door.

"I'll look in again this evening," the abbot said. "Meantime, if you need anything, tell Brother Nasturtium."

His sandals shuffled softly away down the stone corridor.

Sarto squinted at the bulky monk.

"Get me a slug of bourbon, Nasty," he said.

"If you don't mind, I'd rather be called Brother Nasturtium," said the other mildly.

"Whatever you say, only gimme a snort."

Brother Nasturtium brought him a glass of water.

"Try it," he said. "'Twill give you strength."

"Water?" said Sarto disdainfully.

"Look at lions and tigers," said Brother Nasturtium.

As he drank the water, Little John studied the man. He noted the dented nose, gnarled ears, lumpy knuckles and the jaw like an anvil.

"You was a fighter, wasn't you?" said Sarto.

"We don't ask questions like that," said Brother Nasturtium. "What we were, rich or poor, big or small, good or bad, does not matter here."

"That's double jake by me, " said Little John. "I think I'm going to like it here."

"I hope so."

"Say, tell me sumpin', big boy. What's your graft?"

Brother Nasturtium's eyes twinkled.

"'Tis twenty years and more since I've heard such talk," he said. "We raise flowers and sell them in the city."

"There's a good gelt in that," said Sarto. "You boys must be cuttin' up a nice profit."

"What we clear, and it isn't much, goes to the poor."

"That's a nutsy way to run a business," observed Little John.

✝　✝　✝

He closed his eyes. Presently he said:

"How does a guy join up with this outfit?"

"It's fairly easy," Brother Nasturtium told him, "if a man wants to be a lay brother—"

"A which?"

"Lay brother. I'm one. They don't take holy orders. They have few religious duties, chiefly saying their prayers. They are not permitted to go outside the walls, and they must obey their superiors. The discipline is rather severe. Some men say it's like being in prison—"

"They do, do they?" said Little John.

"Except that there are no bars."

"That might make a slight difference," conceded Little John. "What are the other catches?"

"Before a man can take his first vow as a lay brother, he must be on probation for a year. That means—"

"I know about probation," said Little John. "Where do I sign?"

"You'll have to talk to the abbot."

"Shoo him in."

"Lay brothers do not shoo abbots."

"Then tell him I wanta proposition him."

"If you're in earnest about this," Brother Nasturtium said, "you might be choosing the name we are to call you."

"Just call me 'Lucky.'"

"It must be the name of a flower."

Little John thought a moment.

"I've picked my new tag," he announced.

"What is it?"

"Brother Orchid."

At dusk Brother Nasturtium left the sickroom to get his patient's supper.

When he had gone, Little John began to laugh. It hurt him to laugh, but he couldn't help it.

"Boy, oh, boy!" he said. "What a hideout!"

As he weeded the rose garden Brother Orchid sang softly:

> *Johnny saw Frankie a-coming,*
> *Out the back door he did scoot.*
> *Frankie took aim with her pistol,*
> *And the gun went rooty-toot-toot.*
> *He was her man—*

He turned the tune deftly into "Abide with Me" as he saw Brother Nasturtium come out of the greenhouse and head toward him.

Three nights before he had taken the vows that made him a full-fledged lay brother. As he flicked a ladybug from a leaf, he reflected that it hadn't been such a tough year. The routine didn't bother him; he was used to one far more rigid; but he was not used to men like Abbot Jonquil, Brother Nasturtium and the rest. At first he felt sure that some sly, dark purpose lay behind their kindness to him. He watched, warily, for the trap. No trap was sprung. Always they were thoughtful, patient, pleasant with him and with one another.

"Maybe I've got into a high-class whacky house," he thought.

Whatever it was, he decided, it was perfect for his plans. There he could bide his time, snug and safe, ready to strike. He was old enough to know the wonders time can work. And he was wise enough to know that while Jack Buck reigned as czar he must remain in exile. If he ventured back to his old kingdom now, he might just as well go straight to the morgue and book a slab. But czars slip, and czars fall, sometimes suddenly in this violent world. He'd wait and be ready.

"Well, Brother Orchid, your roses are doing well," said Brother Nasturtium as he came up.

"Lay you three to one they bring more than your lilies," said Brother Orchid.

"It's a hundred to one they won't bring anything," said Brother Nasturtium, somberly. Brother Orchid looked up and saw that the face, usually so benign, was grave.

"What's the gag?" he asked.

"Our market is gone."

"How come?"

"They won't handle our flowers."

"Who won't?"

"The wholesalers. We don't belong to the association."

"Why don't we join it?"

"They won't let us. Not a flower can be sold in the city that isn't grown in their own nurseries."

"I get it," said Brother Orchid. "The old chisel. Who's the wheels in this shakedown?"

"A man named Buck is behind it, I believe. So Abbot Jonquil learned when he was in town. He tried to see this Mr. Buck to plead with him not to take away our only means of livelihood. One of Buck's ruffians kicked him downstairs."

"I suppose the abbot was sucker enough to go to the coppers," said Brother Orchid.

"He did go to the police."

"What did *they* do—slug him?"

"No. They were polite enough. But they said that so far as they knew the Floral Protective Association was a legitimate business concern."

"The bulls still know the answers," said Brother Orchid. "And the D.A. said he'd like to do sumpin', but his hands is tied, because you gotta have evidence, and all the witnesses is scared to talk."

"You seem to know all about it."

"I seen movies," said Brother Orchid.

He weeded away, deep in thought.

"Have we got any jack in the old sack?" he asked suddenly.

"About four hundred dollars, the abbot told me."

"Peanuts," said Brother Orchid. "But enough for a couple of secondhand choppers. You and me could handle 'em. We'd need roscoes for the rest of the boys. But I know an armory that's a soft touch. You and me and Geranium and Lilac could charge out tonight, hustle a hot short, and knock it off. Once we was heeled we could move in on Buck and his gorillas and—"

"Man alive, what sort of talk is that?" demanded the scandalized Brother Nasturtium.

"Forget it, pal," said Brother Orchid. "I guess this sun has made me slap-happy. What are we goin' to do?"

"Be patient and pray."

"And eat what?"

"Heaven knows."

"Yeah, and they claim it helps guys that help themselves."

"Maybe Mr. Buck will see the light."

Brother Orchid plucked up a clump of sour grass.

"Maybe this weed'll turn into an American Beauty," he said. He wrung the weed's neck and hurled it into his basket.

"That's the only way to treat weed," he said.

"But is it?" said Brother Nasturtium. "Wasn't everything put into the world for some good use, if man had the sense to find out what that use is?"

"That's a lot of words," said Brother Orchid. "Weeds is weeds."

"No," said Brother Nasturtium, as he turned away, "weeds are flowers out of place."

† † †

Hungry after their day of work, the Little Brothers of the Flowers waited in the refectory for their abbot to come in and say grace. They tried to make light talk of events in their small world. But there was a shadow over them.

Abbot Jonquil entered, walking slowly. It came to them for the first time that he was a very old man.

"I'm afraid I have more bad news," he said. "Our funds have been taken from my safe. Of course none of us took them—"

He stopped and looked down the long table.

"Where is Brother Orchid?" he asked.

"Maybe he's in his cell, praying," said Brother Nasturtium. "Shall I fetch him?"

"Yes, please."

Brother Nasturtium came back alone. His big ruddy face was twisted with trouble.

"Maybe I was wrong about weeds," he said.

In his office, Thomas Jefferson Brownlow, special prosecutor of rackets, was talking to the press. The reporters liked him. He was so earnest and so green.

"Same old story, boys," he said. "All I can tell you is that men are selfish animals, and that's not news. I know Buck is back of all these new rackets. So do you. But I can't prove it in a court of law. The men who can simply will not go before the grand jury and tell their stories. They put their skins before their civic duty. I'm not blaming them. But the fact remains I can't force them to testify. They're not afraid of *me*. I wish they were. That's all today, gentlemen."

The reporters filed out. Brownlow bent morosely over the indictment of a jobless man who had stolen a peck of potatoes.

Swerling, his assistant, bustled in. He was excited.

"Chief," he said, "they're back."

"Who?"

"Those florists and laundrymen and fruit peddlers. And they're ready to talk."

"The devil you say!"

"Better grab 'em while they're hot, Chief," urged Swerling.

"But what's got into 'em?"

"You have me there."

"It doesn't matter," said Brownlow, "if they'll talk. Send 'em in and lock all the doors."

Once they started to talk Thomas Jefferson Brownlow had a hard job to stop them. The Grand Jury was back before its seats in the box had cooled off, and shortly thereafter Jack Buck and three of his top aides were passengers on a special train that would not stop till it had

carried them to a station near a big, gray gate. Most of his lesser lieu-
tenants also took trips, accompanied by large, official-looking men,
who returned alone. A few escaped, some by taking to their heels, others by wriggling through loopholes in the law.

Mr. Brownlow was walking toward his office, debating whether he
should run for governor or the Senate, when he bumped into Mr. Chris
Poppadoppalous, emerging from the room where witnesses are paid
their fees. Mr. Poppadoppalous beamed, bowed, and handed Mr.
Brownlow a large box.

"Gardenias," he said. "I brink dem for you."

"Thanks," said Brownlow. "And there's one more thing you can do
for me."

"Anythink," said Mr. Poppadoppalous with another bow.

"One day you boys were afraid to talk. The next day you talked. Why?"

"We were afraid not to," said Mr. Poppadoppalous.

"Afraid of me?" asked Brownlow, rather pleased.

Mr. Poppadoppalous tittered apologetically.

"Oh, no, sir," he said. "You're a nice man. You don't say, 'Talk, you
Greek so-and-so, or I'll tear out your heart and eat it before your eyes.'"

"Did somebody say that to you?"

"Yes, sir. To all us boys."

"Who?"

"The little fellow," said Mr. Poppadoppalous, and bowed, and scurried away.

✝   ✝   ✝

From his hotel window Little John Sarto looked out over the lighted city
spread at his feet. Somebody knocked on his door.

"Come in," said Sarto.

The freckled young man came in. He had on a new suit, mossgreen
this time, and he was still jovial.

"Hello, sweetheart," he said.

"Hello, Eddie," said Sarto.

"You know why I'm here."

"Sure," said Sarto. "Have a drink?"

"Why not?" said Eddie, and poured out a drink from a bottle of
bourbon on the table. Sarto took one, too.

"Nice going, boss," said Eddie, raising his glass. "We'll run this town right."

"We?"

"You will, I mean," said Eddie. "I'll be glad to work under a man with your brains. Poor Jack didn't have many. Nerve, yes. But he never looked ahead. You do. Well, what do you say, boss? Dummy and some of the boys are waiting downstairs for the answer. They're solid for you, boss. Anything you say goes."

Sarto didn't say anything. He went to the window and looked out over the city.

"Of course, things are rather ragged right now," said Eddie. "We'll have to take it slow and easy for a while. But the boys are counting on you to work out some nice, new, juicy angles. The town's yours."

"I don't want it," said Little John.

"What do you mean?" Eddie was not jovial now.

"I got other plans."

"You can't run out on us."

"I'm walking out," said Sarto. "Right now."

"The boys won't like that."

"I'm doing what *I* like."

"That's always expensive," said Eddie.

"I know all about that."

Eddie shrugged his shoulders.

"Okay," he said, and sauntered out of the room.

Hurriedly, Little John Sarto began to strip off his loud, plaid suit.

"I'm right," said the warden to the chaplain, laying down the morning paper. "You say all men have some good in them. I say some men are all bad and nothing can change them. Take this fellow, Sarto. Last night in Chicago, as he was getting on a bus, he was filled full of lead."

"That hardly proves your point." The chaplain smiled. "Bullets are very democratic. They'll kill good men as well as bad, you know."

"There was nothing good about Sarto. Just listen to this: 'The police say Sarto plotted to return to power in the underworld. They are at a loss to explain why, at the time of his death, he was disguised as a monk.' Why, the scheming wolf! Whether there's any good whatsoever in such a man, I leave it to you to judge."

"He does sound pretty bad, I grant you," the chaplain said. "But. even so, I hate to condemn him or any man. I might be reversed by a higher Judge."

THE MONK'S TALE

P. C. DOHERTY

THE FEAST OF THE ASSUMPTION 1376
(15th August)

I have begun this journal because my Prior has asked me. I received his letter and, I say this in the spirit of obedience, his remarks about my past cut like barbs. I know I have sinned before God and man but here in the parish of St. Erkonwald in Southwark I daily atone for my sins. I observe most strictly the rule of St. Dominic and spend both day and night in the care of souls. God knows, the harvest here is great; the filthy alleyways, piss-strewn runnels and poor hovels shelter broken people whose minds and souls have been bruised and poisoned by grinding poverty. The great fat ones of the land do not care but hide behind empty words, false promises and a lack of compassion which even Dives would have blushed at.

My house is no more than a white-washed shed with two rooms and a wooden door and casement which do not fit. My horse, an aged destrier, whom I call Philomel, eats as if there is no tomorrow but can go no faster than a shuffling cat. He drains my purse of money. I simply mention these matters to remind myself of my present state and to advise my Prior that his strictures are not necessary. As I have said, my purse is empty, shrivelled up and tight as a usurer's soul. My collection boxes have been stolen, the chancel screen is in disrepair, the altar is marked and stained and the nave of the church is often covered with huge pools of water, for our roof serves as more of a colander than a covering.

God knows I atone for my sins. I seem to be steeped in murder, bloody and awful, it taxes my mind and reminds me of my own great crime. I have served the people here six months now. I have also taken on those duties assigned by my Prior as clerk and scrivener to Sir John Cranston, coroner of the city. Time and again he takes me with him to sit over the body of some man, woman or child pitifully slain. "Is it murder, suicide or an accident?" he asks. And so the dreadful stories begin. Of stupidity, a woman who forgets how dangerous it is for a child to play out on the cobbled streets, dancing between the hooves of iron-shod horses or the creaking wheels of huge carts as they bring their produce up from the river. Still, a child is slain, the little body flung bruised and marked while the young soul goes out to meet its Christ. But there are more dreadful deaths. Men drunk in taverns, their bellies awash with cheap ale; their souls dead and black as the deepest night as they lurch at each other with sword, dagger or club. When the wound is made and the soul fled, Cranston and I arrive. I mean no offence for Sir John, despite his portly frame, plum red face, balding pate and watery eyes is, I think, in heart a good man. An honest official. A rare man indeed, who does not take bribes, searches for the truth, ever patient before declaring the true cause of death and I am always with him. I and my writing trays, my pens and inkpots, transcribing the lies, the deceits, the stories which flourish like weeds about any death.

I always keep a faithful record and every word I hear, every sentence I write, every time I visit the scene of the murder, I am back on that bloody field fighting for Edward, the Black Prince. I, a novice monk who has broken his vows and taken his younger brother off to war. Every night I dream of that battle: the press of steel men, the lowered pikes, the screams and shouts. Each time the nightmare goes like a mist clearing above the river, leaving only me kneeling beside the corpse of my dead brother, screaming into the darkness for his soul to return, I know it never will.

However, I beg Christ's pardon for I wander from the story. I was in my church long before dawn on the eve of the feast of St. John saying my office, quietly kneeling before the chancel screen, the only light being that of a taper lit before the statue of the Madonna. I confess I had not slept that night. Instead, I had climbed to the top of the church tower to observe the stars for I do admit that the movements of the heavens still have the same fascination for me as they did when I studied at Oxford in Friar Bacon's observatory on Folly Bridge. I was tired and slightly fearful for Godric, a well known murderer and assassin, had begged for sanctuary in the church and while I prayed he lay, curled up like a dog, in the corner. He had eaten my supper, pronounced himself well satisfied and settled down to a good night's sleep. How is it, I ask, that such men can sleep so well? Godric had slain a man, struck him down in the market place, taken his purse and fled. He hoped to escape but had the misfortune to encounter a group of city officials and their retainers, who raised the hue and cry and pursued him here. I was attempting to repair the chancel screen and let him in after he hammered on the door. Godric brushed by me, gasping, waving the dagger, still bloody from his crime, and ran up the nave breathlessly shouting,

"Sanctuary! Sanctuary!"

The officials did not come into church though they expected me, as clerk to Sir John Cranston, to have handed him over but I could not.

"This is God's house!" I shouted, "Protected by Holy Mother Church and the King's decree!"

So they left him alone though they placed a guard on the door and swore they would kill him if he attempted to escape. Godric will either have to give himself up or abjure the realm.

Anyway, I digress, my prayers were again disturbed by a commotion outside the church and I thought the city authorities had sent armed retainers to take Godric, for we live in turbulent times. Our present King, Edward III, God bless him, is past his prime and the mighty men of war have their own way in most matters. I took the taper and hurried down the church, splashing through the puddles as there had been a violent thunderstorm, you may remember it, two days previously. Outside, the city guards had been disturbed from their sleep and were locked in fierce argument with Sir John Cranston, who bellowed as soon as he saw me,

"For God's sake, Father, tell these oafs who I am!" He patted the neck of his horse and glared around. "We have work to do, priest, another death murder at Bermondsey, one of the great ones of the land. Come! Ignore these dolts!"

"They did not know who you are, Sir John." I replied, "Because you are muffled in robe and hood worse than any monk."

I then explained to the men that Sir John Cranston was coroner of the

City of London and had business with me. They backed off like beaten mastiffs, their dark faces glowering with a mixture of anger and fear.

"Leave Godric be!" I warned. "You are not to enter the church!"

They nodded, I locked the church door and went over to my own house. I stuffed my panniers with parchment, quills and ink, saddled Philomel and rejoined Sir John. The coroner was in good spirits, thoroughly enjoying his altercation with the city guard for Sir John hates officialdom, damns them loudly along with goldsmiths, priests and even, he looked slyly at me and grinned, Dominican monks who study the stars!

"Ever heavenwards," I quipped in reply, "We must look up at the sky and study the stars."

"Why?" Cranston replied brusquely. "Surely you do not believe in that nonsense about planets and heavenly bodies governing our lives? Even the church fathers condemn it."

"In which case," I answered. "They condemn the Star of Bethlehem."

Sir John belched, grabbed the wineskin slung over his saddle horn, took one deep gulp and, raising his bottom, farted as loudly as he could. I decided to ignore Sir John's sentiments, verbal or otherwise. He means well and his wine is always the best that Gascony can grow.

"What business takes us to Bermondsey?" I asked.

"Abbot Hugo," he replied. "Or rather Hugo who was once Abbot. Now he is as dead as that cat over there." He pointed to a pile of refuse, a mixture of animal and human excrement, broken pots and, lying on top, a mangy cat, its white and russet body now swollen with corruption.

"So, an Abbot has died?"

"No, murdered! Apparently Abbot Hugo was not beloved by his brethren. After Prime this morning he had his customary daily meeting with the leading officials of the Abbey and, as usual, infringed the rule of St. Benedict by breaking his fast in his own private chamber, a jug of Malmesy wine and the best bread the abbey ovens can bake. His door was locked. Some time later, when he did not attend Divine Service, the brothers came and found his door still barred. When they forced it open, Hugo was lying dead at his table. At first they thought it was apoplexy, a stroke or the falling sickness but the Infirmarian, a Brother Stephen, smelt the wine cup and said it contained Belladonna. So," Sir John looked sideways at me, "We hunt murder in a monastery. Priests who kill. Tut! Tut! What is the world coming to?"

"God only knows!" I replied. "When coroners drink and fart, and make cutting remarks about men who are still men with all their failings, be they priest or prelate!" Sir John laughed, pushing his horse near mine, slapping me affectionately on the shoulder.

"I like you, Brother Athelstan!" he bellowed. "But God knows," he mimicked my words, "Though God knows why your order sent you to Southwark and your Prior ordered you to be a coroner's clerk."

We have had this conversation before. Sir John probing whilst I defended. Some day I will tell him the full truth though I think he surmises it already.

"Is it reparation?" he queried.

"Curiosity," I replied, "Can be a grave sin, Sir John." But the coroner laughed and deftly turned the conversation to other matters.

We rode along the river bank arriving at Bermondsey shortly before noon. I was glad to be free of the city, the stinking streets, the shoving and pushing in the market place, the houses which rear up and block the sun. The great swaggering lords who ride through on their fierce, iron-shod destriers in a blaze of silks and furs, their heads held high, proud, arrogant and as ruthless as the hawks they carry. The women are no better with their plucked eyebrows and white pasted faces: their soft, sensuous bodies are clothed in lawn and samite, their heads covered by a profusion of lacy veils; while only a coin's throw away a woman, pale and skeletal, sits crooning over her dying baby, begging for a crust to eat. God should send fire on the city or a leader to raise up the poor, but there again I preach sedition and remember my vow to keep silent.

At Bermondsey the great door to the abbey was kept fast. Sir John had to clang the bell as if raising the "Hue and Cry," before the gates squeaked open and we were led into the abbey forecourt by a most anxious-looking lay brother. The abbey was a great facade of stone, carved and sculptured, soaring up into the heavens, man's ladder to God. The place was subdued and quiet. The cloisters were empty, the hollowed stone passageways ghostly, even menacing. I felt I was entering a house of shadows. The lay brother took us to the Prior's office, a large comfortable room, the floor, so polished it could serve as a mirror, was covered here and there by thick woollen rugs. The black granite walls were draped and decorated with cloths of gold. The Prior was waiting for us; like all his kind, a tall, severe man, completely bald, with features as sharp as any knife and grey eyes as hard as flint. He greeted Sir John Cranston with forced warmth but, when I introduced myself and described my office, he smiled chillingly, dismissing me with a flicker of his eyes.

"Most uncommon," he murmured, "For a friar to be free of his order and serving in such a lowly office." Sir John snorted rudely and would have intervened if I had not.

"Prior Wakefield," I replied. "My business is my own. Like you, I am a priest, a man as learned as yourself, who now wonders why murder should be committed in a Benedictine monastery."

"Who said it was murder?"

"The Infirmarian who sent the message," Sir John interrupted. "He told us the Abbot had been poisoned, even naming the substance found in the cup." The Prior shrugged.

"You are correct," he murmured. "Evil news seems to have wings of its own."

"We are here to see the body!" Cranston bluntly reminded him.

The Prior led us out into the cloisters which lay to the south side of the abbey church. Its centre or garth had been carefully cultivated, laid out with raised vegetable beds, herb gardens and the sweet-smelling roses now in full bloom under a hot mid-day sun. As the rule of Benedict laid down, there was silence, except for the scratching of pens from carrels where monks studied or pored over painted manuscripts. The doors of their cells were wide open because of the oppressive heat.

The Prior led us down more passageways and out to the Abbot's personal residence, a large, spacious, two-storied building. The ground floor was the Abbot's own refectory. We passed through it, up some wooden stairs into what the Prior termed the Abbot's private chambers: a large study sumptuously decorated, the walls painted red with golden stars, thick rugs on the floor and a huge oaken desk and table. There were cupboards full of books, the rich, leather coverings exuding their own special perfume so my fingers itched to open them. Behind this lay the Abbot's bedroom and I was struck by its austerity, no glazed or coloured windows here and the walls were just white, freshly painted with lime. The only furniture were a stool, a small table and a huge four-poster bed now stripped of any coverings, it bore the Abbot's corpse, rigid, silent, accusing under its linen sheet.

Cranston did not wait for the Prior but pulled back the linen cloth to expose a skull-like head and skeletal features made even uglier by the rictus of death. Abbot Hugo had been an old man, well past his sixtieth summer. Cranston pulled the sheet down further, revealing how the Abbot had been laid out for burial in the thick, brown smock of his order with coarse sandals strapped round the bare feet. The Abbot's face, like the features of any murdered victim, fascinated me; the slight purplish

tinge in his face and sunken cheeks. The monks had attempted to close
his eyes in death and, unable to, had placed a coin over each of his eyes,
one of these had slipped off and the Abbot glared sightlessly at the ceiling. Cranston indicated I should examine the body more closely, not that
he is squeamish, I just think he enjoys making me pore over some corpse,
the more revolting the better.

"I must open the robe." I said turning to the Prior. The fellow nodded
angrily.

"Get on with it!"

Taking the hem of the Abbot's robe, I lifted it and pushed it right up
to his neck to expose a thin, emaciated body, a dirty white, like the underbelly of a rat. There were no contusions or bruises and the same was true
of the neck and chest; the only marks were the ink stains on two fingers
of his left hand.

"Nothing unusual about that," the Prior remarked, "Abbot Hugo was
a great writer." I nodded and looked closer. The ink seemed to be stained
permanently but there was no cut on the fingers and, when I raised the
cold hand, I detected nothing untoward. I re-arranged the Abbot's robe
and, muttering the Requiem, pulled the linen sheet back up to his chin
before examining the half-open mouth. The Infirmarian was right, even
the most stupid of physicians would have detected poison. I gently prised
open the lips, still not yet fully rigid in death, revealing yellow stumps of
teeth. The gums, tongue and palate, however, were now stained black
and, when I leant down and smelt, I detected the sour sweet tang of a
powerful poison.

"How do we know," I asked, "that the Abbot died alone?"

Wakefield shrugged.

"Quite easily. Two lay brothers always stayed at the foot of the stairs
leading to his chambers. They would sit there, pray, meditate or be on call
when the Abbot rang a small bell on his desk."

"That could be heard at the foot of the stairs?"

"Yes."

"And these two lay brothers maintain no one went up?" The Prior
smiled thinly.

"I didn't say that. They did allow the servant through with a tray bearing wine and bread, as well as the Abbot's Secretarius, Brother
Christopher."

"Ah, yes, Brother Christopher." I replied. "And how long was he in
there?"

"A very short while."

Cranston slumped on the foot of the bed.

"Abbot Hugo, you liked him?" he barked.

The Prior nodded.

"I respected him deeply."

"And your brethren?"

"Abbot Hugo was a hard man but a holy one. He was a zealot who upheld the rule but could be capable of great compassion."

"When was the meal served?" I asked him.

"I asked the servant. He said the cellarer had laid the bread and wine out during the fourth hour after midnight. That was customary. Abbot Hugo's instructions were always to bring it when the hour candle had burnt mid-way between five and six."

The Prior looked down at the floor. He was embarrassed, uneasy.

"There is something else?" I asked.

"What do you mean?"

"Oh, you know full well what I mean." I said curtly.

The Prior coughed nervously.

"You are right," he answered after a while. "The Infirmarian, he has kept the Abbot's wine and bread locked away but he went down to the kitchen to inspect the jug of wine which the Cellarer had used. He found a large stain on the table. It smelt of Belladonna."

"Ah!" Cranston let out a long sigh.

I watched the Prior closely.

"Did anything happen in the days leading up to Abbot Hugo's death?" The Prior was silent.

"Answer the question!" Cranston snapped.

The Prior rubbed his eyes with the back of his hand and glanced up. He looked grey and exhausted.

"Yes, today is. . . ."

"Wednesday!" Cranston interjected.

"On Sunday evening after Compline, the Abbot met us here in his own quarters. He announced he was going to resign, retire."

"Why?"

"He claimed he was too old to continue as Abbot and wished to go into retreat. Go to another house, revert to being a simple monk and so prepare for his death."

"What was the reaction to this?"

"We were all horror-struck. We had our differences with the Abbot.

That is only natural in an enclosed community but we did revere him."

There was a pause as Cranston and I eyed each other. We both knew what question we would like to ask next.

"If the Abbot had retired," I began slowly. "Who would have been elected as his successor?"

The Prior's face softened as if he was preparing me for what came next.

"I think I would have been." His face flushed as he looked at both of us. "I know what you're thinking, what you're hinting at." He got up. "To slay someone is an abominable act, a mortal sin. To be guilty of the murder of a man like Abbot Hugo would be nothing more than blasphemous sacrilege."

"Tush, Prior Wakefield," Cranston said softly. "We did not say that."

The Prior flung a look of hate at me.

"He did!" he said.

"My Lord Prior," I replied. "I did not. Before God I did not!" I looked at Cranston. "Sir John, we must interview the lay brothers. My Lord Prior, Sir John will use the Abbot's study. First, we would like to question the lay brothers; the servant who brought the bread and wine as well as the two who stood guard at the foot of the stairs."

The Prior nodded and, giving a hasty bow to Sir John Cranston, stalked out of the room. Once he was gone I closed the door, opened one of my panniers and, bringing out a sharp needle which I use to sew parchment together, went over to the corpse and pulled back the shroud. Abbot Hugo's face, still stared, transfixed by death. I pressed the lower jaw down and, using the needle, scraped between the yellow teeth.

"What is it?" Cranston asked.

I went over to the casement window and opened the wooden shutter to look more carefully at what the needle had dug out for me. A soft, greyish, pulpy mass. Cranston came over to stand by me, a look of disgust on his face.

"What do you think it is?" he asked.

I grimaced.

"The remains of a meal the night before or even the bread. God knows!"

Cranston, apparently bored by my mysterious attitude, pulled the shroud back over Abbot Hugo and told me to join him in the Abbot's study where he slumped unceremoniously into the great chair behind the table. He waved me to a small stool which stood alongside, gripping the side of the desk as he studied it carefully. A book of hours in one corner, the clasp broken, allowing us a glimpse of the golds and blues of the illuminated writing. Rolls of parchment, a writing tray similar to the one I used, bearing an ink pot, a long quill pen and a small battered, wooden cross which the Abbot must have used when meditating. Nothing remarkable but Cranston told me to list it. After all, it is quite common after such inquisitions for the coroner to be accused of filching the dead man's goods.

After this, the Prior returned with the lay brothers whom Cranston wished to question. They were all old, rather venerable men, who had been taken into the abbey for good services performed in the King's wars or in some nobleman's household. Cranston questioned them carefully, tolerating their garrulous replies but dismissed them, for what they said corroborated the Prior's story.

During the afternoon Cranston and I pieced together the events leading up to the Abbot's sudden death, only the distant booming of the abbey bell or the soft patter of sandalled feet in the corridor outside interrupted our deliberations. For once in his long, hard-drinking life, Sir John refrained from downing goblet after goblet of rich red wine. Perhaps it was his concentration and sober attitude which made me guess that Sir John had been directed here by some powerful personage at court.

"Look, Athelstan," he said, using his fat, stubby fingers to list events. "Abbot Hugo was a holy but strict man; he rises and sings the morning office with his brethren. He then returns to his room. In the kitchen the cellarer pours a goblet of wine and lays out a dish of freshly baked bread. These are brought up by a lay brother who leaves it outside the room on a bench: the staircase is guarded by two lay brothers: the Abbot's Secretarius brings the bread and wine in and leaves. No one else comes up but later Abbot Hugo cannot be roused. The next thing is that the Abbot's door has been broken down and the Prior, who had been talking to the Sub-Prior, Brother Paul, at the time, comes into the room. The Sub-Prior is with him." Cranston paused and looked at me. "What then?"

I sighed and shrugged.

"According to Prior Wakefield and the lay brothers," I replied, "Wakefield and Brother Paul found the Abbot slouched back in his chair. The Prior removes the body himself and lays it on the ground. A few minutes later the Infirmarian arrives. It is he who smells the wine and detects the poison."

"Had the Abbot eaten or drunk anything?" Cranston queried.

"According to Prior Wakefield," I replied, "He had, a little. They found this when they removed the cup of wine and bread. They have kept it under lock and key as evidence." Cranston shook his head and sighed in exasperation.

"I see," he said despondently, "no solution in this."

"Who wants a solution?" I asked Sir John abruptly. The coroner looked at me slyly.

"News was sent immediately to the court and, within an hour, the order to come here had arrived at my house." He chewed his lip thoughtfully. "But what answer can I give? Was the bread and wine poisoned in the kitchen and, if so, by whom? Or did Brother Christopher or one of the lay servants perpetrate the crime?"

I shook my head, unable to offer Cranston any solution.

The day drew on. Cranston asked for food and this was brought; a jug of ale, some small white loaves and two bowls of rich broth stew, garnished with onions and leeks and heavily seasoned. Cranston, eating noisily, slurped from his bowl, using the special pewter spoon he always carried with him. As he ate he summarised what we knew.

"We have an old Abbot who intends to resign. He attends the first part of the Divine Office just after midnight and retires here to his chamber, though he is expected back in the abbey church about six to sing Prime. He locks himself in his room, the only visitor is his Secretarius, Brother Christopher, who brings in the bread and wine brought up by one of the servants. Brother Christopher," he continued, "is only there for a few minutes. But the cup he has brought in is poisoned." Cranston rose and, after stretching himself, walked round the room. "The solution is quite simple. The murderer either must be one of the following: the Cellarer, for there was a poison stain found in the kitchen, the old servant who brought it up or, more likely, Brother Christopher. No one else could have done it for the stairs were guarded."

I agreed and was about to make my own suggestion when the great bell of the abbey began to toll for Vespers.

"Sir John," I asked, "What shall we do now?"

"What do you mean?"

"Are we to return to the city or to stay here?"

"We have come so far we might as well see the matter through," he replied.

"Then, if you don't mind," I retorted. "I would like to join my brothers in Christ in church," Cranston shrugged.

"Do what you like."

I left Cranston in the Abbot's study and went quickly down to the church. The great west door was open. I went inside. Torches had been lit which only increased the sense of watchful silence, making the shadows dance and slither across the great pillars. The sunlight still streamed through the coloured glass windows but I thought the church must always be dark. I went up through the heavily ornamented rood screen, past the pulpit and into the sanctuary, a small chapel in itself with choir stalls of carved wood on either side. Each stall had a richly decorated canopy at the back with a desk in front. The monks were now filing in from another door; ghostly figures with their hoods pulled up. They looked indistinguishable, despite the fire of the torches and the light of the huge beeswax candles placed on the altar. A dark figure loomed over me, pulling his cowl back. I recognised Prior Wakefield.

"You wish to join us?" he whispered.

"Yes, Father."

He waved me to an empty stool.

"Brother Anselm is sick, we would be only too pleased for you to help us with our singing."

I could not decide if he was being helpful or sarcastic but I murmured my thanks and took my place, waiting for the other monks to join us. I caught the faint, fragrant smell of incense but my soul sensed something else. The figures lining up in their stalls were quiet, calm, possessed of one intent, to use all their energy in the praise of God. Nevertheless, I caught the awful smell of fear and knew that each man must be wondering which of their brethren had committed the horrible crime of murder. The Abbot's empty seat, which stood at the west end of the choir, dominated the gathering, its very emptiness turning it into an accusatory finger as if the Abbot was stretching his hand out beyond death, seeking his killer here, at the very foot of God's throne.

I leaned against the stall seat and waited until the leading cantor moved up to the lectern, a huge brass stand in the shape of an eagle with outstretched wings. In a clear angelic voice he began the chant.

"Oh, Lord, arise in haste to help me!"

The monks thundered their reply, answering ea⌐¹
response. I joined in, forgetful of sin, blasphemy and
pleased to be back amongst my fellow priests, singing ⌐
chant of the church.

After the service I joined the monks as they filed ⌐

darkening cloister into the refectory or frater, a long, well lit room roofed in timber and generously served by huge windows; some filled with horn, others with beautiful decorated glass. The high table on the dais at the end was empty except for the Prior who stood there intoning the "Benedicite." The monks sat down, pulling back their cowls, sitting patiently while the lay brothers served them and a young monk, standing at a pulpit built in the refectory wall, read from the writings of Jerome. Apart from the reading, the meal was eaten in complete silence. No one seemed concerned by my presence, though I sensed an atmosphere of menace and I knew their very detachment masked close scrutiny, indeed resentment at my presence. So intense was this feeling that I gulped my food and, forgetting all etiquette, hastily rose, bowed to the great crucifix which hung above the dais and gratefully fled back to the cloisters.

Cranston was waiting for me in the Abbot's chamber, noisily eating a better meal than I had been served in the refectory and taking great gulps of wine from a shallow bowl.

"Did you enjoy yourself, Brother?" he asked his mouth full.

"An interesting experience," I replied. "Though one I would not like to repeat."

Whilst Cranston gobbled his meal I went over and picked up the book of hours, trying to calm myself by studying the beautiful paintings, a feast of colour and light. Cranston announced he had finished eating by noisily smacking his lips, slouching back in the Abbot's great chair and belching as loudly as a trumpet blast.

"And what has my Lord Coroner decided to do now?" I said sarcastically.

Cranston shrugged.

"I have told that whey-faced Prior I wish to see the following: himself, the Sub-Prior, the Infirmarian, the Cellarer and, of course, dear Brother Christopher. We shall question these to throw some light on our dark mystery."

He had hardly finished speaking when there was a knock at the door and Prior Wakefield entered, a file of monks behind him. Cranston, now full of his own importance as well as good wine, made no attempt at welcome. He imperiously waved them in front of the desk and, after instructing me to light candles, ordered me to take careful note of what was said. The young man who had been the leading cantor in the church helped me find a tinder and light the branched candlestick bringing the room to life.

"Good," murmured Sir John, revelling in his authority. "Those things that were done in the dark," he added, misquoting scripture, "shall be examined on the mountain top."

"There is no need to treat us like errant scholars, Sir John." Prior Wakefield insisted.

"I am not," Cranston replied brusquely. "But I am the King's Coroner."

"You have no jurisdiction in this abbey," Wakefield interrupted.

"I have every jurisdiction. The King's writ rules here as it does anywhere else. So, my Lord Prior, please introduce me to your brethren."

Wakefield, swallowing his pride, gestured towards his fellow monks. The Sub-Prior Brother Paul, small, chubby-faced and great bellied, he could have taken the part in any mummer's play as Robin Hood's Friar Tuck. The Infirmarian, Brother Stephen, tall, scholarly looking, a man full of his own importance with a great nose and arrogant eyes. If I had not known better I would have sworn he was the Prior. Brother Ambrose, the Cellarer, surprisingly lean, sallow-faced, a look of constant worry souring his mouth. Finally, Brother Christopher the Secretarius, the young man with the voice of an angel.

Once the introductions were over, Cranston went through what we had learnt so far and no one demurred.

"Right!" Sir John barked, using his stubby fingers to score points. "We know you, the Cellarer, poured the drink and prepared the bread during the fourth hour after midnight. It stood in the monastery kitchens until taken up by the lay brother, who placed it outside the Abbot's lodging on the same bench later used to break the door down. The only visitor was you, Brother Christopher." The young man nodded, a look of intense fear in his eyes as he nervously ran his fingers through his close cropped, blond hair. "You did take the wine in?" Again Brother Christopher nodded. "Speak up, man." Prior Wakefield was about to intervene but Cranston stopped him with a warning glance. "You have a tongue, Brother Christopher?"

"Yes, I have a tongue," he answered softly. "I took the tray in, as usual Abbot Hugo was kneeling on his *prie dieu.*" He nodded towards the far corner before pointing to the book of hours on the table. "I placed the tray on the table."

"Did the Abbot say anything?"

"He whispered '*Gratias.*'"

"What then?" I interrupted. "After you left, what would Abbot Hugo do?"

The young man spread his hands.

"As customary, he would sit where you are and write letters whilst breaking his fast. A few minutes before Prime he would leave his chamber and join us in the abbey church."

"Did the Abbot write anything the night he died?" I asked.

"No," the Cellarer, interrupted, "He simply checked my accounts. The roll was found on his desk."

"Who has it now?"

"Brother Christopher later gave it over to me," the Prior answered. "I have looked at it. There's nothing untoward."

Sir John grimaced.

"Are you hinting that Brother Christopher did anything wrong?" Wakefield asked peevishly.

"Oh, no, Brother Christopher would not do anything untoward!"

Cranston and I looked in surprise at Brother Paul's clever mimicry of the Prior's words. Wakefield, his face flushed with anger, turned on the Sub-Prior.

"Brother Paul, I suggest you keep your mouth shut!" Wakefield smiled at the Secretarius. "Do not worry, Christopher, we know you did nothing wrong."

"How do you know?" the Sub-Prior interrupted, "He was the last man to see the Abbot alive. He did carry the wine in."

Brother Christopher fell to his knees, sobbing into his upraised hands. Cranston and I were both transfixed by this tableau. The calm composure of these monks now broken by the child-like weeping of Brother Christopher and the look of hatred exchanged between the Prior and Brother Paul. I was about to intervene but Cranston waved me to silence.

"We both know how you looked after your darling Christopher!" the Sub-Prior spat spitefully.

"What are you hinting at, Brother?"

Wakefield drew himself up to his full height and I was surprised at the way that the small Sub-Prior, his smiling face now hard and impassive, stood his ground.

"Oh, we know how you interceded with the Abbot," he commented, throwing a knowing look at Cranston, "To beg for mercy when this young man was found stealing from the monastery at night, dressed in multi-coloured hose, red shoes and velvet jacket, to enjoy the pleasures of the city."

"That was years ago," Brother Christopher sobbed.

"We are forgetting one thing," Brother Stephen, the Infirmarian interrupted. "Traces of the Belladonna poison were found in the kitchen."

"What are you implying?" the Cellarer shouted. "You are the Infirmarian, you had access to poisons!"

The Infirmarian was about to yell back when Cranston clapped his hands.

"Enough is enough is enough!" he bellowed. "Prior Wakefield," he continued evenly as the brothers regained some composure. "I suggest we interview each of you separately and I will begin with you. The rest should wait outside."

He was about to continue when he was interrupted by a knock on the door and the lay brother who had earlier admitted to bringing the wine and bread from the kitchen shuffled in, head down, hands hanging dejectedly on either side of him. He went over to Prior Wakefield and knelt at his feet.

"Peccavi," the old man whispered, "I have sinned."

"What is it, Brother Wulfstan?"

"It is true," the old man whispered in a now still room. "I brought up the wine as usual and, as usual, I drank from it." There was a few moments silence, shattered by the uproar the lay brother's words caused.

"See!" the Cellarer shouted. "I am innocent!"

"It must have been poisoned later," the Infirmarian added gleefully, "And the only person who touched it was our darling Brother Christopher."

The young monk, unable to accept this, howled in protest and, before anyone could stop him, fled from the room.

Cranston rose to his feet.

"Prior Wakefield, you will wait on me now. Brother Ambrose," he indicated to where the lay brother still lay sobbing at the Prior's feet. "Take this man away and, Brother Stephen," he turned to the Infirmarian, "Bring back the Secretarius. Now! Go, all of you!"

Once the room was cleared, Cranston sat down and turned to me, a look of complete surprise on his face.

"So, my dear Athelstan, Chaucer's words are true, the cowl doesn't make the monk."

"No more than the robe makes the judge or armour the knight." I replied, "Though I agree, we have uncovered a filthy plot of passions here."

Cranston grimaced.

"The murderer must be Christopher. We must find out why."

I shook my head.

"Too easy," I replied.

But Cranston just shrugged, shouting for Prior Wakefield to come back into the room.

The Prior had regained his composure and, not waiting for Cranston's invitation, pushed across a small stool to sit opposite him. He did not even bother to stare at me but sat fingering the tassel of his cord, waiting for Cranston to begin. The coroner smiled.

"Prior Wakefield, your relations with Brother Paul, the Sub-Prior, are not what they should be?"

"What do you mean?"

"There is very little charity between two brother priests."

"I do not like Brother Paul." Wakefield replied evenly. "Read your Aquinas, Sir John, one can draw distinctions between loving and liking. I do not like Brother Paul because he is arrogant, with great ambition but not the talent to match."

"Nor," continued Cranston drily, "does he like your protégé, Brother Christopher."

"Brother Christopher is a weak vessel, he fell from grace some years ago. I recommended him to the post of Secretarius so both I and Father Abbot could keep an eye on him."

"Your Sub-Prior is hinting at something else."

Wakefield's sallow face flushed.

"Brother Paul will have to atone for his sin," he answered. "He hints at an unnatural love between Brother Christopher and myself. That is not true."

"Who sent the messenger to me?" Cranston interrupted.

"I believe it was the Infirmarian, Brother Stephen." Cranston nodded.

"Then we will see him next."

"He has brought the Abbot's wine and bread with him."

"Good." Cranston replied.

Brother Stephen entered the room as soon as Wakefield left, placing the bread and wine triumphantly on the table before Cranston as if laying an altar for Mass. Cranston sniffed at both before handing them to me. There was a tinge of mould on the bread so I snapped it in two and held it close against my nose but I could detect nothing. The wine cup was a different matter. A silver chased goblet, it was still half-full of wine but reeked of that sour-sweet stench I detected from Abbot Hugo's lips. Cranston watched me pull a face.

"What made you think of poison?" he asked Brother Stephen abruptly.

"What do you mean?" the Infirmarian snapped back.

"Well," Cranston smiled. "Abbot Hugo was an old man. You found him dead over his desk?"

"I did not find him."

"Agreed, your Prior did, but you came into the room and immediately checked the cup. Was it spilled?"

"Of course not."

"So why examine it?"

"I do not know," Brother Stephen replied crossly. "Perhaps I am naturally suspicious. I looked around, everything was in order."

"Everything?" I interjected. A slow doubt began to form in my mind, "You are sure about that, Brother Stephen?"

"Yes. I simply picked up the cup out of curiosity. But the smell of Belladonna was so strong I knew immediately it was drugged."

"Are you so proficient in poisons?" Cranston asked, "That you can detect it even when it's laced with wine?" Brother Stephen looked at him arrogantly.

"Of course. I am a specialist in poisons: Nightshade, Belladonna, the juice of the foxglove. Not that," he looked at us both in one sweeping glance, "Not that I am the only person with access to them. We use poison in keeping our beehives, to get rid of rats and mice and in the garden. Indeed, any of the brothers could mix poisons from the herbs we grow."

"So, why did you send for Sir John?" I asked. "Why the King's coroner?"

"Sir John knows that himself," Brother Stephen replied artfully and, before I could intervene, Cranston smoothly dismissed the Infirmarian, telling him to send Brother Christopher in.

After a short while the young monk entered, escorted by Prior Wakefield. He was white-faced, red-eyed, his cheeks stained by tears.

"Sit down," Cranston said kindly. "We have no need for you, Prior Wakefield."

The Prior seemed reluctant to move.

"I repeat myself, my Lord Prior, there is no need for you to stay."

Once Wakefield was gone, Cranston leaned across the table.

"Brother Christopher, let us be brief. We know when the wine left the kitchen it was not poisoned or the lay brother who drank from it would have died. We have also learnt that no one approached the wine whilst it was outside Abbot Hugo's study. The only conclusion we can draw is that you must have poisoned the cup before bringing it in and stained the kitchen table to spread confusion. Well, what do you have to say?"

The young monk, looking totally crestfallen, shook his head.

"I am innocent!" he stuttered, "Completely in this matter!"

"Oh, no, you're not!" Cranston snapped. "My Lord Prior!" he bellowed.

Wakefield, waiting outside, re-entered immediately.

"I would be grateful," Cranston declared and broke off yawning, "If Brother Christopher could be taken and locked in some cell. I believe you have armed retainers?"

The Prior nodded and, before he could object, Cranston rose.

"By the King's authority, I order this and I do not wish my orders questioned."

Wakefield took the young Secretarius by the arm as if he was some small boy and led him out of the room. Cranston stretched and turned.

"I would like to be civil, Brother Athelstan but, with all due respect to yourself, I have had enough of monks for one day. So I bid you good-night."

Cranston nodded his head and scurried off whilst I stayed in the Abbot's study and sent for the Infirmarian.

After some time, Brother Stephen arrived, cross-faced and sleep laden.

"What is it, Friar?" he brusquely asked.

"One question, monk!" I snapped back. "And one question only. If you gave me Belladonna in wine, how long would it take for me to die?"

The fellow seemed to find that a pleasant thought.

"No more than a few seconds," he replied.

I gave out a great sigh and grinned.

"Then Brother Stephen, I demand this on the King's authority; you are to rouse Prior Wakefield and tell him to take Brother Christopher from custody and bring him here. Now!" I shouted, seeing the arrogant obstinacy in his face. The monk shrugged, dismissed me with a supercilious glance and padded out of the room. Well over half an hour passed before I heard footfalls in the corridor outside.

"Come in!" I shouted. "Do not let us wait on idle ceremony!" Wakefield entered, holding up a now distraught Christopher, white-faced, wild eyed. I momentarily wondered if he had lost his wits. "Brother

Christopher," I began kindly, "Sit on the stool. Prior Wakefield, please stay outside." I leaned across the table. "Brother Christopher, I do not think you are the murderer." I was pleased to see the look of relief in the young man's eyes. "But you must gather your wits. You put the tray bearing the wine down on the table?"

The young monk nodded.

"Then come!" I rose. "Come here, Brother Christopher, and sit in the Abbot's chair."

The young man did so, slowly like a dream walker, his eyes staring fixedly at the table top.

"Now, Brother, you are the Abbot. You have drunk your wine. What would you do next?"

The young man picked up the quill, dipped it in the inkhorn and, taking a piece of paper, began scratching words upon it. I went round and noted ruefully that the young monk had written the words of the Chief Priest from Christ's trial in the Gospel—"What need we of proof?"

"I need proof," I said quietly. "Now please pretend you are the Abbot, imitate his every mannerism."

I sat on the stool and watched Brother Christopher play-act. As I urged him on, my suspicions firmed into certainty. I asked him a few questions about what had happened on the day before. He answered that he had worked in his office, he told me who had visited him. When he mentioned one name, I remembered something said earlier in the day.

"Thank you, Brother," I said. "Just one final question. You brought the wine and bread into Father Abbot? When did you see him previously? I mean, by yourself?"

"Oh," the young monk answered. "I brought him a letter, sealed by the Prior." He stopped and gazed into the air. "That was the previous evening. Then, just before retiring, I came back with the writing tray."

"The one that is on the desk now?" I asked.

Brother Christopher nodded.

"Yes, it is. Why?"

I shrugged.

"It's of little matter. I thank you, Brother. You may join Prior Wakefield and inform him, on my authority, as well as that of Sir John Cranston, that you may return to your cell on one condition, you are to stay there until we leave."

Early next morning, woken from my sleep in the Abbot's chair by the booming of the bells for Prime, I stretched my aching body and went

down to rouse Sir John Cranston. The old coroner was snoring like a pig
and I confess I took great joy in waking him. I told him of my conclusions. At first he argued vehemently against me, angry that I had ordered
Brother Christopher's release, so I went through my arguments again. Sir
John, sitting up in bed, still dressed in the clothes he wore the previous
day, reluctantly agreed to what I asked. Cranston rose, washed himself at
the Lavararium and followed me round the cloisters back to the Abbot's
lodgings. An old lay brother sat dozing on the low cloister wall, half listening to the dawn chant of the monks in the abbey choir. I gently roused
him and told him to bring Prior Wakefield and the Sub-Prior to us as
soon as the service was over. This time Cranston did not sit in the Abbot's
chair but dramatically waved me into it, as if his own presence was no
longer necessary. Playing the role he had assigned me, I placed two stools
before the table and we waited quietly until Prior Wakefield and Brother
Paul entered. I gestured at them to sit.

"Prior Wakefield," I said. "Tell me what you were doing when the
news of Abbot Hugo's death was brought to you?"

The Prior, his eyes still red from lack of sleep, yawned as he rubbed
his brow, trying to remember.

"Yes, I have told you," he snapped peevishly. "I was in my office talking to Brother Paul. He had asked to see me on some matter. I forget now."
Brother Paul nodded in agreement.

"Then what?" I asked.

"The lay brother came down, saying something was wrong, Brother
Paul and I ran up here and, once the door was forced, we both entered
the room."

"What then?" I asked.

"Abbot Hugo was lying back in his chair. Brother Paul pulled the
chair back, I picked the Abbot up. He was no weight and I laid him gently on the floor. I checked his breath and felt for the blood beat in his neck
but there was nothing."

"Is that when you changed the pens, Brother Paul?" I asked abruptly,
Never have I seen a monk's face go so ashen.

"What do you mean?" he asked hoarsely.

"You know what I mean," I replied. "Like Brother Christopher, you
know how the Abbot often sucked the end of a quill whilst writing or
preparing to write. So you coated it with poison and, the previous
evening, went into Brother Christopher's office and placed the poisoned
quill on the Abbot's writing tray. You knew when Abbot Hugo would pick

it up and I suggest you kept very close to the Prior, hence your request for a meeting just before Prime on that fatal day. You had no reason to doubt anything would go wrong. Abbot Hugo's routine was established. He was a creature of habit."

"This is. . . ."

"I would be grateful if you did not interrupt me!" I snapped, "and let me finish. You had to be with the Prior so when the body was discovered you gained immediate access to the room. After that it was simple. While Prior Wakefield moved Abbot Hugo's body you poured the poison into the cup and replaced the poisoned quill with an untainted one. A few seconds, the phial of poison and the quill already hidden in the voluminous sleeves of your robe. No one would dream of examining where the writing tray was placed. I am sure if we check the Cellarer's account, we would find places where the Abbot used the quill to tally amounts. He would have then leaned back in the chair, unwittingly drinking the poison as he licked the quill. He would feel ill, place it down and fall back into death." I paused. "Later on, a little poison was dropped on the table down in the kitchen and you successfully spread the seeds of suspicion. Any one of your brothers could have poisoned the Abbot's wine, even when the old lay brother admitted to sipping from the cup, you thought you were safe. For the only possible culprit could be Brother Christopher."

"That is ridiculous!" the Sub-Prior muttered. "You have no proof!"

"Oh, yes I do," I replied. "First, you did visit Brother Christopher's office the night beforehand on some petty errand which engaged the young Secretarius' attention. Secondly, the fresh pen you used to replace the poisoned one. You made sure that it had been dipped in ink and certainly used by yourself. Now you are a right-handed man, when you use a quill the tip is worn away on the right side but Abbot Hugo was left-handed, his quill should have been worn down on the left." I picked up the quill from the writing tray. "This is the untainted quill you brought in." I pointed to the tip. "Look, it is worn down on the right side. When I checked Abbot Hugo's corpse I noticed the ink stain on his left hand. This quill could never have been used by him. Finally, Belladonna is a quick-acting, powerful poison. If the Abbot had raised the cup to his lips he would never have had time to place it back on the table. It would either have fallen on the table or the floor.

"Why?" Prior Wakefield asked, glaring at the Sub-Prior.

"Oh, I think I can answer that," Cranston interrupted. "There is no love lost between you two. If Abbot Hugo had retired; you, Prior Wakefield, could well have replaced him. That's the last thing Brother Paul wanted. So Abbot Hugo dies in mysterious circumstances. A feeling of suspicion is created and your superiors may well have been tempted to place someone else, an outsider, in charge."

"A mummer's tale!" Brother Paul sneered. "A fable, nothing else."

"In which case," I remarked, digging into the pocket of my own robe, "You will not object to placing the tip of this quill in your mouth?" I drew out a battered quill and held it up. "Look, Brother Paul, it's worn on the left side and is still stained with ink. I ask you to put it into your mouth."

"That's not the quill that Abbot Hugo used," Brother Paul snapped back and immediately raised his hand to his lips to bite back his words.

"You are correct! How do you know that, Brother Paul?"

"I don't! I don't!" the Sub-Prior murmured. "I will say no more."

"What are you going to do?" Prior Wakefield asked, for the first time ever looking at me squarely in the face. "I ask you, Brother Athelstan, not Sir John Cranston, for you too are a disgraced monk aren't you?" he smiled thinly. "Oh, I made a few enquiries, a little digging amongst the gossip, Brother Athelstan, who fled his novitiate to join the King's army and took his own younger brother, only to get him killed. A man who not only broke his monastic vows but the hearts of his parents."

God forgive me, I could not stop the tears welling up in my eyes. Wakefield's words stirred my memory and I recalled the tragic, tear-stained faces of my mother and father.

"I have sinned," I replied. "And my sin is always before me and let that be Brother Paul's sentence. You, Prior Wakefield, will be elected Abbot. Brother Paul will resign as Sub-Prior and stay in this monastery for the rest of his life being ruled by a man he hates. I could not think of a worse form of hell. That is," I added crisply, "if Sir John agrees."

Cranston, who had been watching me closely, nodded and rose, not bothering to give the still seated Brother Paul a glance.

"I would be grateful, Lord Prior, if you would ensure that this malignant was locked away until we leave. Of course, he may object to Brother Athelstan's sentence, in which case he can take his chances before the King's Justices in the Guildhall. I suggest he does not do that."

Prior Wakefield nodded and patted Brother Paul on the shoulder, who followed him as meekly as a lamb out of the room.

Once they had left, Cranston came up and nudged me gently on the chest.

"They are bailiffs in cowls," he said, quoting a current proverb about monks. "I don't like monks" he continued evenly. "I am not too sure whether I like you but I do respect you, Athelstan. Now let's be gone from this hell pit!"

Our journey back into London was uneventful but, before we parted, Cranston pulled back his hood and leaned closer to me.

"I agree with your sentence, Athelstan" he said, "But the Infirmarian sent for me because Abbot Hugo had once been spiritual confessor to our dread King, Edward III. I will let the court know what happened. I am sure Brother Paul will meet with an accident before Michaelmas Day."

I left Cranston to go back to my own church. The pools of water were still on the floor and the church door hung loose. Someone had stolen the small statue of the Virgin from its niche. Godric the murderer had been taken, snatched by officials of the Mayor, or so Ranulf the rat-catcher told me when I found him sleeping on the steps of the sanctuary. I gave him a coin and dismissed him. I knelt before the crucifix and said the "De Profundis" for Godric's soul and for that of Abbot Hugo and for my own brother, Francis. Souls sent before their time to stand before the throne of God. So now I have related this story, perhaps I will look once more at the stars, say my Office and go merrily to bed. Pray God Cranston gives me peace.

WHEN YOUR BREATH FREEZES

KATHLEEN DOUGHERTY

THERE ARE SEVEN OF US.

I am Sister Ellen: the youngest, the ugliest, the least devout, the most fragile. I need the vast silences of northern Alaska and the imposed silence of this cloister. The souls of these women are quiet, their musings as distant as the Chukchi Sea. The nuns have taken me in for the winter, an act of charity, a, charity they might well regret. But they don't know about my special ability, my accursed gift. If they did, they'd shun me as others have. Their unspoken thoughts, though, are safe from me. Nothing could compel me again to peruse the mind of another. What you see there are the ugly shapes of nightmares.

Under my white robes, the color for a novice, are a pair of expeditionweight long johns, the fabric a heat-retaining, sweat-wicking synthetic; then a pair of wind-blocking pile pants. We have no television, no radio, yet we have the latest in underwear.

Off come the sturdy black shoes and on go the insulated knee-high boots. I unpin the white novice's veil from my hair and hang the veil on a wall peg. I slide a black ski mask over my head, position the mouth and eye holes. I like wearing the mask; its blank anonymity hides my facial scars. There is only one mirror here, in the infirmary. I have little use for mirrors.

I wrap my neck with the wool scarf knitted by Sister Gabrielle. I think tenderly of her gnarled hands, twisted by arthritis, the black yarn, and the slow clack of the needles. She had embroidered "Ellen" on a cloth tag. My fingers worked a stretch cap on top of the ski mask, then I shrug on the anorak with its thick pile of yellow fleece lining, its rich fringe of fox fur around the hood. The drawstring snugs the hood low on my forehead and up over my mouth. The fur tickles and has that dusty aroma of animal skin.

Last are the glove liners and the padded mittens with Velcro wrist bands. Even before I open the heavy wooden door, I imagine I hear the cows lowing, though that's not possible. The wind's voice whips away sound and, deceptively, mimics the wail of a cat, a distant locomotive, an unhappy ghost.

I flick on the outdoor lights and step beyond the door, pulling it closed behind me. The frigid air steals my breath. Outside all is the white of an unusually bitter February. Though midmorning, there are hours before dawn bleaches the sky. My teeth chatter. It is colder than death out here.

The north wind pauses in its cold rush. I spit. The saliva crackles, freezing in midair, and shatters like glass on the walkway. Cold, very cold, even by the standards of northern Alaska. More than seventy below. Gusts sweep snow pellets, hard as gravel, across the covered walkway to the barn. That wooden structure, like the convent, appears to sprout from the mountainside.

During the Yukon gold rush, miners hewed these caverns, clawing from granite the shelters that shielded them from brutal winters. The southfacing walls are wood; north-facing walls and much of the ceiling are the smoothed underbelly of the mountain. Snaking into the earth from those north walls are tunnels; a few lead to steaming pools of hot springs, potable—though slightly sulfurous—water. After the Second World War, the exhausted claim was purchased by the Immaculata order, and this remote land, once brimming with the harsh voices and greed of prospectors, became the refuge of silent nuns.

The gale blasts against my long skirts and I cover the walkway in a graceless stagger. The barn door sticks, its hinges cranky with cold. I wrench open the door and step inside to rich aromas: cow hide, dung, hay, bird droppings, wood smoke. The miners had used the large room as a barracks. Humid air fogs a tunnel entrance, one which leads to the hot springs, where the nuns take paying guests during the brief summers.

The barn houses two cows, a mangy good-for-nothing goat, and a chicken-wire enclosure with a dozen hens and an irritable cock. The hens set up a comical squawking and fluttering, shocked to their very cores every few hours when I come to tend the wood stove. The cows regard me with their calm brown eyes, aware that it's morning and hoping for fresh fodder. These are, as far as I've seen, the only cows in Alaska, a gift from a rancher in the lower forty-eight. He'd stayed here last summer, Leonidist said, soaking in the convent's hot sulfur springs, and was convinced he'd been miraculously healed of gout.

Pine logs dropped into the wood stove make the coals flare. The stove stands in an isolated hollow scooped from the mountain. The flue disappears into the rocky ceiling.

I milk the cows and the sullen goat, gather eggs from the hens. I slap the cow's haunches, urging them up and down the center aisle. They don't like the enforced exercise, but their shanks tend to develop abscesses. Sister Fiske, a paramedic and our only source of medical expertise during these frozen months, prescribed aerobics. The cows want only to stare into their food bins and meditate golden hay into existence. Their resistance makes the stroll hard work and I wonder about the medical benefits for any of us. After half an hour, I stop, panting. Their bony heads study me quietly, a pitying look which makes me smile.

I muck out the stalls and coop, spread down fresh straw, and rake the soiled material to the far entrance. I switch on the outdoor lights. This part gets tricky. If drifts have built up in the past hours, a path will have to be cleared. That means shoveling for two minutes, dashing into the warmth of the barn and scaring the heck out of the chickens, shoveling another two minutes, and so on.

To my delight, the door swings open easily and the path to the garden appears clear. I rake the straw outside and drag the mound a few yards when a snow-dusted rock catches my eye. A mound of black, a large stone that hadn't been there before . . . and with awful clarity the form resolves into that of a huddled person. My chest tenses with shock. I am kneeling next to the shape without memory of moving closer.

She is curled into the fetal position. The ebony veil, hard and shiny, has frozen into place, covering most of the profile, but there's enough exposed to see the broad jaw, the deep etch of lines from nose to mouth, the dark brown mole with its two stiff hairs stark against ashen flesh. Frost has made a mask of the features, smoothed out the web of wrinkles on her full cheeks, lessened the downward draw of persimmon lips. It is

Sister Praxades, our cook, who refuses—refused—to bake white bread. In the kitchen with her black sleeves rolled up over dimpled forearms, she taught me to knead whole-grain dough. She smelled of flour and yeast and discontent.

With my right glove and liner off, I touch her throat where, in life, the carotid artery throbs. Her neck is frozen solid, hard and unyielding.

Her pudgy hands and feet are bare, pale as alabaster. How can this be? No one would willingly tromp barefoot in Alaska's winter.

My thoughts are slow lizards, too long in the cold.

My right hand signs the cross over the body. I mentally begin an Act of Contrition, but retreat to the barn when the air hurts my lungs. Chickens cackle and the goat bleats while I finish the prayer for Sister Praxades, an inadequate charity for a woman who had been more than tolerant of a newcomer.

Tears burn my cheeks. I, who have so little opportunity for love, loved her.

There had been seven of us.

Now there are six.

✝ ✝ ✝

Reverend Mother thinks in German, a language I don't comprehend. Snatches of words, swirling in her mind-winds, fly out: *schnee, tot, unschuld, verlassen.* She is in her late forties, the youngest except for me, yet authority is a mantle she wears with ease. Her bearing is military, her oval face composed, her gray eyes sharp. Only now her gaze reveals disquiet upon my panicked report of Sister Praxades's death. Reverend Mother's face shutters down; her thoughts whirl. Rosary beads rattle within the folds of her black robes. Her pale lips shape the English words, "Jesus, Mary, Joseph," a favored indulgence of this order. Each nun says this prayer so often that the rhythm becomes one with each inhale and exhale. When the rare words seep from their minds, that is what I sense: JesusMaryJoseph.

Reverend Mother orients on me. Her lapse of control is over. Her fingers sign, *You—lead me—Praxades.* Even now Reverend Mother does not break the quiet meditation.

Her hand halts me as I turn. She shapes sentences fast, too fast, and I shake my head in confusion. She places a long index finger to her lips, then signs, *No tell—others.*

Why not tell the others? They'll know Sister Praxades is missing. I gesture for permission to speak, my sign language inept. Reverend Mother slices her hand in the negative, a command that reminds me of my position here. The shock of finding Sister Praxades has made me exceed my bounds. Flushing, I bow my head in apology, nod compliance, and we exit her office. It is up to Reverend Mother, not the distraught pseudo-novice "Sister" Ellen, to decide when to tell the nuns. If she waits until after the Angelus, before the noon meal when contemplation officially ends, Sister Praxades will not be any less dead for the delay.

In the hall Sister Leonidist, standing on a foot stool, scrapes tallow from a wall sconce. Candle glow highlights the postmenopausal down of her cheeks and chin. Thick red eyebrows shadow her sockets, making her pale blue eyes seem large and black. Leon the Lion, my pet name for her in my head, is the one I'd have gone to first to share the terrible discovery. She performs a modified curtsy from her perch in respect of Reverend Mother as we pass. I look longingly over my shoulder at Leon. She grins and winks, pretends to stick a finger up one wide nostril.

At the side door, before Reverend Mother dons her anorak, she removes her black headdress. Her hair is a flattened, short gray-brown, and its thinness somehow diminishes her authority. I focus on the splintered wood planks, embarrassed. It is disrespectful to see her so. After a moment, she nudges me, not unkindly. It is time to go out into the cold.

† † †

One voice: "*Dominus vobiscum.*" The Lord be with you.

Five voices: "*Et cum spiritu tuo.*" And with your spirit.

It is noon and the hours of silence end. Reverend Mother observes us from the lectern. Her hands clutch the frame on either side of the Bible. Her knuckles whiten. She is, I know, gathering strength to talk about Sister Praxades. The nuns do not speak. Their minds are suspended in a sea of expectation; no gleanings travel from their consciousness to mine, not even the Jesus, Mary, Joseph prayer. Leon catches my attention with a raised bushy eyebrow and looks pointedly at her lap. She signs: *Cook sick?*

The others may think that. We are not allowed in our cells except to sleep or to rest if we're ill. How I wish Sister Praxades were on her pallet, tucked under quilts, resting away a fever instead of curled miserably outside, the door of her mind forever frozen closed. I hope that whatever malady caused her to wander in the snow also prevented the cook from suffering.

My vision blurs and I drop my gaze to the pine table. In front of me and the four seated nuns are blue ceramic bowls of potato soup, our lunch. In the kitchen I simmered the potatoes in chicken stock—no wonder those fowl squawk with such alarm—and added cream, butter, salt, pepper, and a dash of crisp Chardonnay. As Sister Praxades taught, I tasted and added more butter, cream, tasted and added more spices, tasted and added more wine . . . and still the broth seemed bland.

Rich yellow butter dots the soup's surface, my poor attempt to duplicate the dead woman's craft. Only the bread, a thick, sweet rye, can be trusted. The large, round, crusty loaves were baked by the cook yesterday.

Reverend Mother's sharp inhale pulls my attention to the lectern. Her lips pressed together. "Sister Ellen found Sister Praxades outside this morning. Sister Praxades is dead." The bald statements straighten every spine, including my own.

"No," cries Sister Gabrielle, an old friend of the cook, eldest nun, knitter of woolens for the likes of me. Her misshapen hand fists, hits the table, and spoons jump. Her anguish bolts to my heart. She cries again: "No!"

"Sister Gabrielle," comes the cautioning, authoritative voice of Reverend Mother.

The old nun's mouth gapes, showing too-even dentures. Tears diffuse down cheeks as creased as parchment. She hunches over the table, gasping with hushed sobs, and a thread of saliva descends from her lips. Sister Fiske, the medic, sits next to the stricken woman. Her chin lifts, her eyes narrow behind magnified glasses. A sharp, disapproving line creases between her brows and her mouth thins, a compassionless look from a woman who frets about the abscesses of cows.

At a nod from Reverend Mother, Fiske rises, accompanies the crying Gabrielle into the stone corridor. The old woman's voice muffles in decrescendo. After a moment, the thin creak of the chapel door reveals their location. And in this room . . . silence. Leon stares at her lap. Sister Xavier, our housekeeper, an angular woman with a jaw as square as a box, fingers a soup spoon. She rarely speaks even when conversation is allowed.

Reverend Mother sighs deeply and bows her head. She says, "Why did you doubt?" Stress has made her German accent noticeable. Their shared emotion builds critical mass and penetrates my carefully erected barriers.

Each is deeply, piercingly ashamed.

Reverend Mother restricts me to the kitchen with my bowl of cooling soup while she conducts a private meeting with the others in the dining room. At the pine counter where Praxades taught me to shape loaves of whole wheat, I force myself to finish my lunch. Food is never wasted. Each tight swallow emphasizes my hurt: grief for the cook and, to my chagrin, the wound of being excluded from the nuns' discussion. I don't belong here, I chide myself. Why should Reverend Mother behave as though I'll stay beyond the spring thaw?

After I eat and feed more coal to the stove, the temptation to eavesdrop wins. I press my ear against the swinging door to the dining room. Not even hushed conversation seeps through the wood. Pushing the door open a crack—my toes still on the kitchen floor so there isn't technical disobedience—I see the five blue bowls on the table, still full. The nuns are gone.

Determined to be a help and to demonstrate a charity I'm not exactly feeling, I busy myself in the pantry, planning dinner. Surveying the shelves, my gaze touches opaque brown vials, medicines that Sister Praxades took on a complicated schedule. The names on the labels don't mean anything to me; once she showed me the collection on her chubby palm, pointing out one for blood pressure, another for cholesterol, and so on.

I pop the cap of one bottle and spill out beautiful azure capsules into my hands. Whatever her medications were supposed to do, they hadn't done their job last night. Sighing, I return the pills to their container and scoop the half-dozen prescriptions into my pocket. Fiske will want these returned to the infirmary.

I decide on tuna casserole, a dish I'm unlikely to ruin. I gather the canned fish, mushroom soup, noodles, and a stale bag of potato chips. The planks squeak under my tread and I see Praxades of last night, after dinner, sashaying and spinning her robes in exaggerated mockery of Sister Fiske, floorboards complaining under her weight. Mimicry was her gift and no one, myself included, was exempt, but Fiske was the cook's specialty.

At the sink I twist the crank of the opener around the tuna can and indulge the sweet sorrow of memories. Oddly enough, Praxades was liberal while the much younger Fiske was conservative. Praxades wanted a satellite dish and television so she could learn recipes from Julia Child; she wanted a subscription to *Gourmet* magazine, deliverable by bush pilot when weather allowed. In the common room, the arguments between Praxades and Fiske were high entertainment. Fiske struggled to control her indignation, I'll give her that. However, Praxades was a master of provocation. The cook's suggestions would become more and more extreme: the nuns should forgo habits and wear fleece slacks and shirts, the L. L. Bean catalogue had them in black.

Last night the cook's trump card, so to speak, enraged Fiske to unusual heights. Praxades suggested that evenings be passed by rousing games of stud poker, using holy cards as chips. The silent Sister Xavier grinned. Leon always looked happy, as though her features were incapable of any other expression. Fiske sprang to her feet, hands clenched by her sides, her complexion red; she'd flung her book to the floor. She sputtered, "You . . . you . . . you sacrilegious old fool, you disgusting—"

"Enough," interrupted Reverend Mother, a regal lift to her chin. "Sister Praxades, hold your tongue. Sister Fiske, you allow the cook to bait you every evening. Both of you must learn control and tolerance." However, Reverend Mother's eyes held a glitter of amusement; not, I'm sure, because of Fiske's fury but because of the cook's inane ideas.

Smug satisfaction brightened Praxades's plump face. Fiske retrieved *The Lives of the Saints,* touched the cover to her lips in apology—to the book, which must have been blessed—and returned to her chair, hands trembling. I felt the heat of her hate for the cook, an emotion as searing as any that had touched me in the cities. It is Lent, weeks of sacrifice in preparation for Easter, but she definitely wasn't offering up her aggravation to the Lord, Fiske even lacked the control to school her expression. She darted a withering, mean look at Reverend Mother, then dropped her gaze to her book. Her face was murderous.

The fork in my hand stops scooping out the tuna. An uneasy resonance jingles in my mind. Had Fiske looked surprised at Reverend Mother's dire announcement? I recall only Fiske's disapproving expression over Gabrielle's outburst.

Perhaps Fiske had nothing to be surprised about.

Fiske, while not a physician, plays the part of one by doling out medications. In my habit's pocket, my fingers clutch the containers of pills.

No one would know if they had been tampered with. No one, that is, except for Fiske.

No, I think, please. Not here.

Not again.

Reverend Mother imposes an afternoon of silence in memory of the cook. When I enter her office and request permission to speak, she signs, "later." Minutes afterward, swaddled in my anorak, I tromp through the barn, chickens squawking in terror, and exit by the rear door. If Praxades was disoriented by medication, probably Fiske had to lead her outside. Snow squeaks like plastic pellets under my boots. Wind whips up millions of grains as fine as baby powder, shoving me nearly off my feet. My polarized lenses fog. I push the goggles above my eyes with awkward mittens and squint. The body is gone. While I was sequestered in the kitchen, the nuns moved the cook.

The day's dilute glow is muted by dark-bellied clouds, and though I search, crouching near the ground, crabwalking the path, there's no evidence that anyone has been here: not the dead cook, not the nuns, and—as I look at ground near my boots—not even Sister Ellen. The harsh land of winter has wiped away the traces. A spasm of shivering makes my jaw muscles tremble. I straighten. Abruptly a gale whites out the world and my name floats through the whirl: "*Ellen.*"

I pivot, pulse galloping, half-expecting to see Praxades levitating from the ground. That movement is a dangerous mistake. The wind increases, howling and spinning drifts, shoving so hard that I stagger. The mad swirl of snow is blinding. Panic shoots through my very core, more invasive than the cold. Which way is the barn? How long have I been out here? Two minutes? Three? Already my fingers are deadened, ice freezing together my eyelashes, narrowing my view to thin, blurry slits.

I must move. My feet stumble, forcing my body against the wind, and again I hear my name, swallowed by the squall, but definitely from my left. If I'm hallucinating, if hypothermia is creating a false call, then I'm dead. I fight, moving to my left for an eternity of seconds; finally arms grab and pull me into the thick smell and chicken cackles of the barn. Violent shivers drop me to my knees on the straw. The door latch clunks closed. My rescuer drags me to the heat of the wood stove.

My gloves are pulled off, then the liners, and my frozen fingers are clasped in hands so warm they burn my flesh. When the ice melts from my lashes, I'm staring into the kind, silent face of Sister Xavier. I know her the least, yet I know this: She will perform extra penance for the sin of breaking silence when she called my name.

† † †

In the infirmary, I proffer Sister Praxades's medicines. Fiske's cold fingers remove the bottles from my palm.

I speak, violating the imposed quiet. "Why would Sister Praxades go outside?"

The woman is still a moment, studying me, and the intensity of her stare and the knowledge of my scars make my cheeks warm. Then she shrugs, a who-knows gesture. That motion is a lie. I feel her dissembling, controlling body language. She walks across the rough brick floor, twirling her robes in the way that Praxades mocked. For a moment the mirrored cabinet bounces her image at me, then her double swings away as she opens the cabinet. I follow. "The cook was fine last night. What would make her do such a thing?"

Fiske ignores me, reads the label on one vial, and places it on a shelf cabinet. In my cell, under my pallet, is a list of the prescriptions and one pill from each container. Feeble evidence. The thought strikes me that if Fiske decides to remove any other thorn in her side, by persisting like this, I'm making Sister Ellen the next likely target. Fiske's pinched face last night rises to mind, her seething fury at the cook . . . and, now I recall, toward Reverend Mother.

Anger, however, isn't an omen of murder. "What do you think caused her odd behavior?" I ask, observing her profile as she shelves the remaining vials. "The mix of drugs she'd been taking?"

Her lips curl slightly in contempt. This impugning of her medical care prompts her to talk. "Not at all."

During the next pause, I expect her to announce that Praxades was befuddled by a stroke or low blood sugar. Instead, she closes the wall cabinet. I'm careful not to look into the mirror. Fiske says, "Separation from God."

"What?"

"That's what killed your precious Sister Praxades."

She turns in a flair of robes and for a moment a silly picture forms, a ballet of nuns in long black habits. I catch her by the arm. With slow disdain, she rotates her head to fix a dark gaze on my hand. I don't let go. "She . . . you're saying she died from, what, weak faith? That's your clinical diagnosis?"

She raises her eyes to meet mine. Behind thick lenses her irises glint as though forged of hard, shiny metal. "No, Sister Ellen. That's my spiritual diagnosis."

Our gazes lock. I almost do the thing that I vowed never to do again under any circumstances: invade the mind of another.

If I forcibly examine her thoughts, she will know. They always knew. The last time I used this accursed ability, I destroyed everyone around me.

Fiske stares, a smirking, superior look. It strikes me that she knows all about me, but that's impossible. Her hands shape the words *Look, Files, Top, Ellen.* With a nod she indicates the tall file cabinet.

I release Fiske. She strides away, footfalls slapping the brick floor, and exits the infirmary. As I look at the file cabinet, my stomach clenches in sudden, inexplicable fear. *I,* of all people, understand that some things are better left alone. Yet minutes later I have scanned the thick files bearing my name. Everything is there: the *Journal of the American Medical Association* study about a woman with provable telepathy; the Duke University professor's interview in *People* magazine and a photo of me hooked to an EEG machine; the *Newsweek* and *Time* articles about my assisting with various murder investigations nationwide; the *New York Times* report about how Gardini the Magician, a debunker of so-called psychics, finally paid a quarter of a million dollars to a bona fide mindreader.

Dozens of newspaper and magazine articles cover the famous psychic's last murder case: Psychic's Husband and Brother Guilty of Business Partner's Murder. Then the same grainy photograph shows up in report after report: my disfigured features after the men my brother hired attacked me with acid. Long before that, though, everyone I came into contact with was leery of me. And weeks before acid ate away my features, I decided never again to snare thoughts from another's mind. After plastic surgeons had done the best they could with flesh that scarred so badly, I sought anonymity, a location where my history and notoriety might be unknown, where I might find, if not peace, at least isolation.

I thought that the nuns hadn't questioned me about my past or my scars due to their otherworldliness. Now I see that they had no need to interview me.

I stand in front of the infirmary mirror, holding the heavy file and gazing at my wretched reflection.

During dinner, while heads bend over a surprisingly tasty tuna casserole, first Leon, then Reverend Mother read passages from the Bible. Dinners are a time to fortify our bodies and our spirits. Reverend Mother, now at the podium, chooses the verses describing Jesus walking on the sea. The expressions of Leon, Xavier, Reverend Mother, and Gabrielle—especially Gabrielle—are serious and downcast. Fiske, to my eye, appears artificially solemn. I swallow a second helping of casserole, eager for the meal to end so that I can interrogate Leon over the dishes. After a minute, the only sound of fork against plate is my own. I look up. Fiske, Xavier, Gabrielle, and Leon are rapt with attention on Reverend Mother. She reads:

> "But when he saw that the wind was boisterous, he was afraid;
> and beginning to sink he cried out, saying, 'Lord, save me!'
> And immediately Jesus stretched out His hand and caught him,
> and said to him, 'O you of little faith, why did you doubt?'"

Reverend Mother closes the Bible, kisses the gold-embossed cover, and returns to her place at the table. Everyone resumes eating, but something has happened which I've missed. The heavy cloud of their mood has lifted. On a psychological level, the dim dining room is bright.

In the cavern, Leon and I wear headlamps to light our way to the spring. The earth-generated heat keeps the temperatures from dropping below fifty, yet the high humidity is chilling. The damp mist blurs her shape and when our buckets accidentally clang together as we walk, my pulse jumps. She appears comfortable with how the cook died. She explains that Sister Praxades was moved to a mining shaft north of the barn. After leaving the corpse, they barricaded the entrance. When the ground thaws and, with the approval of the medical examiner—from two-hundred-mile-away Lygon—and Praxades's relatives, a burial plot will be prepared. Until then, her body will remain frozen and will be safe from the occasional arctic fox.

Her chipper tone nonpluses me. She might be discussing the disposal of the goat. We reach the pool and kneel down to draw water. I ask, "Why can't we have a memorial service now?"

"To mourn her would be to question God's will."

I set my full bucket down impatiently; water sloshes over the lip. "Leon, *talk* to me."

The desperation in my voice must have moved her. She sets her pail next to mine and says, "Of course I miss Sister Praxades. She brought this place alive. She made us laugh." Through the steam I see her grin. "Well, everyone except Sister Fiske," Leon amends. "Ellen, look at it this way. If you died, would you want those you love to feel grief, to suffer over losing you?"

I wouldn't. Still, I'm troubled by the acceptance of the cook's death. Even the elderly Gabrielle appears adjusted to her friend's absence, though perhaps that's not true. She might be numb with grief.

Leon places her hand on my shoulder. In the steam, her headlamp creates a bright halo. "Perhaps it's easier for us. Our beliefs treat death as a natural part of the soul's journey. It wouldn't make sense for us to behave as though Sister Praxades is gone forever."

I wish I believed in the immortality of the soul. "What if Fiske messed with Praxades's medication?"

Leon is quiet a moment. I know I've surprised her. "I guarantee that Sister Fiske is innocent of everything except anger. She's devoted to safeguarding our health, not endangering it."

Leon could probably find good in Judas. We trudge back through the tunnel toward the living quarters. An aura radiates from her, and in that aura three words ring over and over: JesusMaryJoseph.

I assume the duties of the cook, though joy has evaporated for me. The others appear inexplicably cheered, except for Reverend Mother, who wears a preoccupied expression as though straining to hear a faint voice just beyond the audible range. A snowstorm blankets the grounds with one foot, then two feet of powder. I watch Fiske, who ignores me. The weather rages and we turn inward; the times of silence are natural for them. This spiritual hibernation makes me edgy, though my bread-baking improves. Two days pass.

On the third morning, Gabrielle vanishes.

✝ ✝ ✝

I sleep. I wake with a start, furious with my failed vigil. Today Leon, Xavier, and I search outside for Gabrielle, but our efforts were thwarted by the storm's bluster. She disappeared in the night, like Praxades. The spirits of the nuns are visibly leadened, even Fiske's. My mind is groggy; confused speculations stick in my skull. Why is everyone so resigned— about Praxades, now Gabrielle? Why does Reverend Mother appear fatigued? She walks hesitantly, as if movement is an effort. Is Fiske poisoning Reverend Mother? Has Fiske killed Gabrielle?

A distant sound travels from the corridor. I sit up. Was that the timbers creaking? I toss off the comforter; chill seeps through my habit, cold slipping like spiders under the thermal underwear. In a few seconds I light the hurricane lamp, pull on my insulated boots, and tiptoe into the dark hall. All but one of the cell doors are closed. I peer into that room and my candlelight glows to an empty pallet. Seeing the tidy vacant room is a blow. I run to the kitchen, the dining room, the infirmary, the sitting room, the chapel, my search as fruitless as I feared. At the entryway door, I yank on anorak, gloves, cap and let myself out into the clear, breezy night, the cold so sharp my lungs inhale reflexively with the shock. It is always like this after a storm, as though fierce weather hones winter to better express its nature. The northerly has swept the entryway clear of all but a half-foot of powder, though drifts smooth the side wall clear up to the eaves. I round the building and find wind and deep snow . . . and heartache.

A figure glows in the frosty moonlight, skin gleaming whitely, a wide sweep of black and jiggling buttocks. "Leon!" I cry. She turns, a statue of salt, merging into the colorless world except for dark thatches of hair at crotch and head. My boots sink deep into the fresh powder as I struggle to her side.

"Please don't worry," Leon said. "I have faith." Syllables slur from frozen lips. "I'm getting warmer. My feet—"

"Leon, for the love of God, *please*." Unshed tears chill my eyes. "You're not getting warmer. You're freezing."

My own face is ice. My stiff fingers won't grip. I loop my arm under hers and guide her toward the building. She resists; her red-lashed eyes blink sleepily under the narcotic of hypothermia.

"Damn you, Leon, *walk*."

Her pale mouth opens in a semblance of a smile, the muscles of her jaw stiff with cold. "I'm walking, Ellen," she mumbles. "I'll come back. Reverend Mother did." Her arm slips like mist from mine and she stumbles away, wading through fresh snow, moving with speed I wouldn't have thought possible. But she is numb. My legs drag through thigh-deep drifts and, trailing her, I fall, flounder deep in powdery whiteness. My freezing arms thrash for purchase in a substance as unstable as flour. Snow blankets my vision. I regain my footing, breathing hard, brushing ice from my face. Every muscle trembles so violently, my body straining to produce heat, that I can barely stand. I am alone in a landscape as pale and barren as the moon, and I suddenly understand who the murderer is.

I race through the corridor to Reverend Mother's room and enter without knocking, throat parched from cold and panic. A single candle flickers from the floor. Reverend Mother lies on her bed in full habit, fingers laced at her waist, thick black socks on her feet. The down comforter and blankets have been kicked to the floor. I lean over her. "I don't know what rot you've been telling these women, but Leon's out there and you're going to help me get her inside. If she hears you calling, she'll come in." Part of me says it's already too late for Leon, but I can't listen to that.

Reverend Mother stares at me, eyes glittering as though a fire blazes inside her skull. "It's Lent. The Lord calls her. She's being tested."

I pull her to a sitting position and her heat radiates like a furnace. Fever has glossed her skin with perspiration. "This is not Christ asking the apostles to walk on water, damn it. This is Alaska and she'll die out there. No one can survive that cold."

Her hands clutch my shoulders with a frenzied strength. "I did."

An odor pierces my hysteria, a fetid smell. It isn't a chamberpot stink, but a scent of putrefaction and decay. With horror, I look at her feet, which she suddenly tucks under her skirts, a childlike gesture. I pull back the material. She isn't wearing thick, dark socks; frost-bitten toes and heels have swelled, rotted, and blackened. I slide up the polypro of her long underwear. Dark streaks on the calves disappear under the fabric, infection spreading toward her groin. Sickened, I cover her legs. Reverend Mother lies back against her pallet, and whispers a few words in German, the gist of which I understand. "Yes," I nod sadly, "you have faith."

The pilot and I haven't spoken. I'm his only passenger and wear heavy, insulated ear muffs to dull the engine noise; conversation is impossible. I'm also wearing a thin gauze mask that Sister Xavier fashioned at my request before I left the cloister. The pilot didn't ask about it. He probably thinks the mask is a religious garment. Below us is Anchorage, refreshingly green in its springtime mantle.

Xavier and I hunted but never found Leon's body. We speculated that she must have entered an abandoned mine shaft. After the start of the thaw, I found Gabrielle not far from the tunnel where the others had barricaded Praxades, and where we had entombed the corpse of Reverend Mother. I spent the last four months meditating on my own considerable responsibility in these terrible deaths. At first I raged at the twisted beliefs that corralled this small, insular society into suicidal behaviors. After talking awhile with Fiske and Xavier, though, I saw that I could have played a part in bringing a sort of heathen reasoning to their lives. However, my goal was self-protection and isolation, not involvement. Perversely, I managed to neither protect myself nor remain uninvolved. Guilt will always reside within me, a hard, frozen shard of northern Alaska.

After the pilot lands, I step down from the plane, pull the mask below my chin, and walk toward the terminal.

Travelers at the airport stare, but I've taken a gift—and a lesson— from my months in the cloister. In my soul spreads a vast emptiness, images and ideas bright stars with light-years of distance in between.

STATE OF GRACE

LOREN D. ESTLEMAN

"RALPH? THIS IS LYLA."

"Who the hell is Lyla?"

"Lyla Dane. I live in the apartment above you, for chrissake. We see each other every day."

"The hooker."

"You live over a dirty bookstore. What do you want for a neighbor, a freaking rocket scientist?"

Ralph Poteet sat up in bed and rumpled his mouse-colored hair. He fumbled the alarm clock off the night table and held it very close to his good eye. He laid it face down and scowled at the receiver in his hand. "It's two-thirty ayem."

"Thanks. My watch stopped and I knew if I called you you'd tell me what time it is. Listen, you're like a cop, right?"

"Not at two-thirty ayem."

"I'll give you a hundred dollars to come up here now."

He blew his nose on the sheet. "Ain't that supposed to be the other way around?"

"You coming up or not? You're not the only dick in town. I just called you because you're handy."

"What's the squeal?"

"I got a dead priest in my bed."

He said he was on his way and hung up. A square gin bottle slid off the blanket. He caught it before it hit the floor, but it was empty and he dropped it. He put on his Tyrolean hat with a feather in the band, found his suit pants on the floor half under the bed, and pulled them on over his pajamas. He stuck bare feet into his loafers and because it was October he pulled on his suitcoat, grunting with the effort. He was forty-three years old and forty pounds overweight. He looked for his gun just because it was 2:30 A.M., couldn't find it, and went out.

Lyla Dane was just five feet and ninety pounds in a pink kimono and slippers with carnations on the toes. She wore her black hair in a page-boy like Anna May Wong, but the Oriental effect fell short of her round Occidental face. "You look like crap," she told Ralph at the door.

"That's what two hours' sleep will do for you. Where's the hundred?"

"Don't you want to see the stiff first?"

"What do I look like, a pervert?"

"Yes." She opened a drawer in the telephone stand and counted a hundred in twenties and tens into his palm.

He stuck the money in a pocket and followed her through a small living room decorated by K-Mart into a smaller bedroom containing a Queen Anne bed that had cost twice as much as all the other furniture combined and took up most of the space in the room. The rest of the space was taken up by Monsignor John Breame, pastor of St. Boniface, a cathedral Ralph sometimes used to exchange pictures for money, although not so much lately because the divorce business was on the slide. He recognized the monsignor's pontifical belly under the flesh-colored satin sheet that barely covered it. The Monsignor's face was purple.

"He a regular?" Ralph found a Diamond matchstick in his suitcoat pocket and stuck the end between his teeth.

"Couple of times a month. Tonight I thought he was breathing a little hard after. Then he wasn't."

"What do you want me to do?"

"Get rid of him, what else? Cops find him here the Christers'll run me out on a cross. I got a business to run."

"Cost you another hundred."

"I just gave you a hundred."

"You're lucky I don't charge by the pound. Look at that gut."

"*You* look at it. He liked the missionary position."

"What else would he?"

She got the hundred and gave it to him. He told her to leave. "Where'll I go?"

"There's beds all over town. You probably been in half of them. Or go find an all-night movie if you don't feel like working. Don't come back before dawn."

She dressed and went out after emptying the money drawer into a shoulder bag she took with her. When she was gone Ralph helped himself to a Budweiser from her refrigerator and looked up a number in the city directory and called it from the telephone in the living room. A voice like ground glass answered.

"Bishop Stoneman?" Ralph asked.

"It's three ayem," said the voice.

"Thank you. My name is Ralph Poteet. I'm a private detective. I'm sorry to have to inform you Monsignor Breame is dead."

"Mary Mother of God! What happened?"

"I'm no expert. It looks like a heart attack."

"Mary Mother of God. In bed?"

"Yeah."

"Was he—do you know if he was in a state of grace?"

"That's what I wanted to talk to you about," Ralph said.

✝   ✝   ✝

The man Bishop Stoneman sent was tall and gaunt, with a complexion like wet pulp and colorless hair cropped down to stubble. He had on a black coat buttoned to the neck and looked like an early martyr. He said his name was Morgan. Together they wrapped the monsignor in the soiled bedding and carried him down three flights of stairs, stopping a dozen times to rest, and laid him on the backseat of a big Buick Electra parked between streetlamps. Ralph stood guard at the car while Morgan went back up for the monsignor's clothes. It was nearly 4:00 A.M. and their only witness was a skinny cat who lost interest after a few minutes and stuck one leg up in the air to lick itself.

After a long time Morgan came down and threw the bundle onto the front seat and gave Ralph an envelope containing a hundred dollars. He said he'd handle it from there. Ralph watched him drive off and went back up to bed. He was very tired and didn't wake up until the fire sirens were grinding down in front of the building. He hadn't even heard the explosion when Lyla Dane returned to her apartment at dawn.

"Go away."

"That's no way to talk to your partner," Ralph said.

"Ex-partner. You got the boot and I did, too. Now I'm giving it to you. Go away."

Dale English was a special investigator with the sheriff's department who kept his office in the City-County Building. He had a monolithic face and fierce black eyebrows like Lincoln's, creating an effect he tried to soften with pink shirts and knobby knitted ties. He and Ralph had shared a city prowl car for two years, until some evidence turned up missing from the property room. Both had been dismissed, English without prejudice because unlike the case with Ralph, none of the incriminating items had been found in English's possession.

"The boot didn't hurt you none," Ralph said.

"No, it just cost me my wife and my kid and seven years' seniority. I'd be a lieutenant now."

Ralph lowered his bulk onto the vinyl-and-aluminum chair in front of English's desk. "I wouldn't hang this on you if I could go to the city cops. Somebody's out to kill me."

"Tell whoever it is I said good luck."

"I ain't kidding."

"Me neither."

"You know that hooker got blown up this morning?"

"The gas explosion? I read about it."

"Yeah, well, it wasn't no accident. I'm betting the arson boys find a circuit breaker in the wall switch. You know what that means."

"Sure. Somebody lets himself in and turns on the gas and puts a breaker in the switch so when the guy comes home the spark blows him to hell. What was the hooker into and what was your angle?"

"It's more like who was into the hooker." Ralph told him the rest.

"This the same Monsignor Breame was found by an altar boy counting angels in his bed at the St. Boniface rectory this morning?" English asked.

"Thanks to me and this bug Morgan."

"So what do you want?"

"Hell, protection. The blowup was meant for me. Morgan thought I'd be going back to that same apartment and set it up while I was waiting for him to come down with Breame's clothes."

"Bishops don't kill people over priests that can't keep their vows in their pants."

Ralph screwed up his good eye. Its mate looked like a sour ball someone had spat out. "What world you living in? Shape the Church is in, he'd do just that to keep it quiet."

"Go away, Ralph."

"Well, pick up Morgan at least. He can't be hard to find. He looks like one of those devout creeps you see skulking around in paintings of the Crucifixion.

"I don't have jurisdiction in the city."

"That ain't why you won't do it. Hey, I told IAD you didn't have nothing to do with what went down in Property."

"It would've carried more weight if you'd submitted to a lie detector test. Mine was inconclusive." He paged through a report on his desk without looking at it. "I'll run the name Morgan and the description you gave me through the computer and see what it coughs up. There won't be anything."

"Thanks, buddy."

"You sure you didn't take pictures? It'd be your style to try and put the squeeze on a bishop."

"I thought about it, but my camera's in hock." Ralph got up. "You can get me at my place. They got the fire out before it reached my floor."

"That was lucky. Gin flames are the hardest to put out."

✝   ✝   ✝

He was driving a brand-new red Riviera he had promised to sell for a lawyer friend who was serving two years for suborning to commit perjury, only he hadn't gotten around to it yet. He parked in a handicapped zone near his building and climbed stairs smelling of smoke and firemen's rubber boots. Inside his apartment, which was also his office, he rewound the tape on his answering machine and played back a threatening call from a loan shark named Zwingman, a reminder from a dentist's receptionist with a Nutra-Sweet voice that last month's root canal was still unpaid for, and a message from a heavy breather that he had to play back three times before deciding it was a man. He was staring toward the door, his attention on the tape, when a square of white paper slithered over the threshold.

That day he was wearing his legal gun, a short-nosed .38 Colt, in a clip on his belt, and an orphan High Standard .22 magnum derringer in an ankle holster. Drawing the Colt, he lunged and tore open the door just in time to hear the street door closing below. He swung around and crossed to the street window. Through it he saw a narrow figure in a long black coat and the back of a closecropped head crossing against traffic to the other side. The man rounded the corner and vanished.

Ralph holstered the revolver and picked up the note. It was addressed to him in a round, shaped hand.

> Mr. Poteet:
> If it is not inconvenient, your presence at my home could prove to your advantage and mine.
>
> Cordially,
Philip Stoneman,
Bishop-in-Ordinary

Clipped to it was a hundred-dollar bill.

Bishop Stoneman lived in a refurbished brownstone in a neighborhood that the city had reclaimed from slum by evicting its residents and sandblasting graffiti off the buildings. The bell was answered by a youngish bald man in a dark suit and clerical collar who introduced himself as Brother Edwards and directed Ralph to a curving staircase, then retired to be seen no more. Ralph didn't hear Morgan climbing behind him until something hard probed his right kidney. A hand patted him down and removed the Colt from its clip. "End of the hall."

The bishop was a tall old man, nearly as thin as Morgan, with iron-gray hair and a face that fell away to the white shackle of his collar. He rose from behind a redwood desk to greet his visitor in an old-fashioned black frock that made him look like a crow. The room was large and square and smelled of leather from the books on the built-in shelves and pipe tobacco. Morgan entered behind Ralph and closed the door.

"Thank you for coming, Mr. Poteet. Please sit down."

"Thank Ben Franklin." But he settled into a deep leather chair that gripped his buttocks like a big hand in a soft glove.

"I'm grateful for this chance to thank you in person," Stoneman said, sitting in his big swivel. "I'm very disappointed in Monsignor Breame. I'd hoped that he would take my place at the head of the diocese."

"You bucking for cardinal?"

He smiled. "I suppose you've shown yourself worthy of confidence. Yes, His Holiness has offered me the red hat. The appointment will be announced next month."

"That why you tried to croak me? I guess your right bower cashing in in a hooker's bed would look bad in Rome."

One corner of the desk supported a silver tray containing two long-stemmed glasses and a cut-crystal decanter half full of ruby liquid. Stoneman removed the stopper and filled both glasses. "This is an excellent Madeira. I confess that the austere life allows me two mild vices. The other is tobacco."

"What are we celebrating?" Ralph didn't pick up his glass.

"Your new appointment as chief of diocesan security. The position pays well and the hours are regular."

"In return for which I forget about Monsignor Breame?"

"And entrust all related material to me. You took pictures, of, course." Stoneman sipped from his glass.

Ralph lifted his. "I'd be pretty stupid not to, considering what happened to Lyla Dane."

"I heard about the tragedy. That child's soul could have been saved."

"You should've thought about that before your boy Morgan croaked her," Ralph gulped off half his wine. It tasted bitter.

The bishop laid a bony hand atop an ancient ornate Bible on the desk. His guest thought he was about to swear his innocence. "This belonged to St. Thomas. More, not Aquinas. I have a weakness for religious antiques."

"Thought you only had two vices." The air in the room stirred slightly. Ralph turned to see who had entered, but his vision was thickening. Morgan was a shimmering shadow. The glass dropped from Ralph's hand. He bent to retrieve it and came up with the derringer. Stoneman's shout echoed. Ralph fired twice at the shadow and pitched headfirst into its depths.

✝ ✝ ✝

He awoke feeling pretty much the way he did most mornings, with his head throbbing and his stomach turning over. He wanted to turn over with it, but he was stretched out on a hard, flat surface with his ankles strapped down and his arms tied above his head. He was looking up at water-stained tile. His joints ached.

"The sedative was in the stem of your glass," Stoneman was saying. He was out of Ralph's sight and Ralph had the impression he'd been talking for a while. "You've been out for two hours. The unpleasant effect is temporary, rather like a hangover."

"Did I get him'?" Ralph's tongue moved sluggishly.

"No, you missed rather badly. It required persuasion to get Morgan to carry you down here to the basement instead of killing you on the spot. He was quite upset."

Ralph squirmed. There was something familiar about the position he was tied in. For some reason he thought of Mrs. Thornton, his ninth-grade American Lit. teacher. *What is the significance of Poe's "Pit and the Pendulum" to the transcendentalist movement?* His organs shriveled.

"Another antique," said the bishop. "The Inquisition did not end when General Lasalle entered Madrid, but went on for several years in the provinces. This Particular rack was still in use after Torquemada's death. The gears are original. The wheel is new, and of course I had to replace the ropes. Morgan?"

A shoe scraped the floor and a spoked shadow fluttered across Ralph's vision. His arms tightened. He gasped.

"That's enough. We don't want to put Mr. Poteet back under." To Ralph: "Morgan just returned from your apartment. He found neither pictures nor film nor even a camera. Where are they?"

"I was lying. I didn't take no pictures."

"Morgan."

Ralph shrieked.

"Enough! His Holiness is sensitive about scandal, Mr. Poteet. I won't have Monsignor Breame's indiscretions bar me from the Vatican. Who is keeping the pictures for you?"

"There ain't no pictures, honest."

"Morgan!"

A socket started to slip. Ralph screamed and blubbered.

"Enough!" Stoneman's fallen-away face moved into Ralph's vision. His eyes were fanatic. "A few more turns will sever your spine. You could be spoon-fed for the rest of your life. Do you think that after failing to kill you in that apartment I would hesitate to cripple you? Where are the pictures?"

"I didn't take none!"

"Morgan!"

"*No!*" It ended in a howl. His armpits were on fire. The ropes creaked.

"Police! Don't move!"

The bishop's face jerked away. The spoked shadow fluttered. The tension went out of Ralph's arms suddenly, and relief poured into his joints. A shot flattened the air. Two more answered it. Something struck the bench Ralph was lying on and drove a splinter into his back. He thought at first he was shot, but the pain was nothing; he'd just been through worse. He squirmed onto his hip and saw Morgan, one black-clad arm stained and glistening, leveling a heavy automatic at a target behind Ralph's back. Scrambling out of the line of fire, Ralph jerked his bound hands and the rack's wheel, six feet in diameter with handles bristling from it like a ship's helm, spun around. One of the handles slapped the gun from Morgan's hand. Something cracked past Ralph's left ear and Morgan fell back against the tile wall and slid down it. The shooting stopped.

Ralph wriggled onto his other hip. A man he didn't know in a houndstooth coat with a revolver in his hand had Bishop Stoneman spread-eagled against a wall and was groping in his robes for weapons. Dale English came off the stairs with the Luger he had been carrying since Ralph was his partner. He bent over Morgan on the floor, then straightened and holstered the gun. He looked at Ralph. "I guess you're okay."

"I am if you got a pocketknife."

"Arson boys found the circuit breaker in the wall switch just like you said." He cut Ralph's arms free and sawed through the straps on his ankles. "When you didn't answer your telephone I went to your place and found Stoneman's note."

"He confessed to the hooker's murder."

"I know. I heard him."

"How the hell long were you listening?"

"We had to have enough to pin him to it, didn't we?"

"You son of a bitch. You just wanted to hear me holler."

"Couldn't help it. You sure got lungs."

"I got to go to the toilet."

"Stick around after," English said. "I need a statement to hand to the city boys. They won't like County sticking its face in this."

Ralph hobbled upstairs. When he was through in the bathroom he found his hat and coat and headed out. At the front door he turned around and went back into the bishop's study, where he hoisted Thomas More's Bible under one arm. He knew a bookseller who would probably give him at least a hundred for it.

Jemima Shore's First Case

Antonia Fraser

AT THE SOUND OF THE first scream, the girl in
bed merely stirred and turned over. The second scream was much louder
and the girl sat up abruptly, pushing back the meagre bedclothes. She
was wearing a high-necked white cotton nightdress with long sleeves
which was too big for her. The girl was thin, almost skinny, with long
straight pale-red hair and oddly shaped slanting eyes in a narrow face.

Her name was Jemima Shore and she was fifteen years old.

The screams came again: by now they sounded quite blood-curdling
to the girl alone in the small room—or was it that they were getting
nearer? It was quite dark. Jemima Shore clambered out of bed and went
to the window. She was tall, with long legs sticking out from below the
billowing white cotton of the nightie, legs which like the rest of her body
were too thin for beauty. Jemima pulled back the curtain which was
made of some unlined flowered stuff. Between the curtain and the glass
was an iron grille. She could not get out. Or, to put it another way, whatever was outside in the thick darkness, could not get in.

It was the sight of the iron grille which brought Jemima properly to
her senses. She remembered at last exactly where she was: sleeping in a
ground-floor room at a boarding-school in Sussex called the Convent of

the Blessed Eleanor. Normally Jemima was a day-girl at the Catholic boarding-school, an unusual situation which had developed when her mother came to live next door to Blessed Eleanor's in her father's absence abroad. The situation was unusual not only because Jemima was the only day-girl at Blessed Eleanor's but also because Jemima was theoretically at least a Protestant: not that Mrs. Shore's vague ideas of religious upbringing really justified such a positive description.

Now Mrs. Shore had been called abroad to nurse her husband who was recovering from a bad attack of jaundice, and Reverend Mother Ancilla, headmistress of the convent, had agreed to take Jemima as a temporary boarder. Hence the little ground-floor room—all that was free to house her—and hence for that matter the voluminous nightdress, Mrs. Shore's ideas of nightclothes for her teenage daughter hardly according with the regulations at Blessed Eleanor's. To Jemima, still staring uncomprehendingly out into the darkness which lay beyond the grille and the glass, as though she might perceive the answer, none of this explained why she should now suddenly be awakened in the middle of the night by sounds which suggested someone was being murdered or at least badly beaten up: the last sounds you would expect to hear coming out of the tranquil silence which generally fell upon the Blessed Eleanor's after nine o'clock at night.

What *was* the time? It occurred to Jemima that her mother had left behind her own smart little travelling-clock as a solace in the long conventual nights. Squinting at its luminous hands—somehow she did not like to turn on the light and make herself visible through the flimsy curtains to whatever was outside in the night world—Jemima saw it was three o'clock. Jemima was not generally fearful either of solitude or the dark (perhaps because she was an only child) but the total indifference with which the whole convent appeared to be greeting the screams struck her as even more alarming than the noise itself. The big red-brick building, built in the twenties, housed not only a girls' boarding-school but the community of nuns who looked after them; the two areas were divided by the chapel.

The chapel! All of a sudden Jemima realized not only that the screams were coming from that direction but also—another sinister thought—she might conceivably be the only person within earshot. The so-called "girls' guest-room" (generally old girls) was at the very edge of the lay part of the building. Although Jemima had naturally never visited the nuns' quarters on the other side, she had had the tiny windows of their cells pointed out by her best friend Rosabelle Powerstock, an authority on the whole fascinating subject of nuns. The windows were high up, far away from the chapel.

Was it from a sense of duty, or was it simply due to that ineradicable curiosity in her nature to which the nuns periodically drew grim attention suggesting it might be part of her unfortunate Protestant heritage . . . at all events, Jemima felt impelled to open her door a crack. She did so gingerly. There was a small night-light burning in the long corridor before the tall statue of the Foundress of the Order of the Tower of Ivory—Blessed Eleanor, dressed in the black habit the nuns still wore. The statue's arms were outstretched.

Jemima moved warily in the direction of the chapel. The screams had ceased but she did hear some other sound, much fainter, possibly the noise of crying. The night-light cast a dim illumination and once Jemima passed the statue with its long welcoming arms—welcoming, that is, in daylight; they now seemed to be trying to entrap her—Jemima found herself in virtual darkness.

As Jemima cautiously made her way in to the chapel, the lingering smell of incense began to fill her nostrils, lingering from that night's service of benediction, that morning's mass, and fifty other years of masses said to incense in the same place. She entered the chapel itself—the door was open—and perceived a few candles burning in front of a statue to her left. The incense smell was stronger. The little red sanctuary lamp seemed far away. Then Jemima stumbled over something soft and shapeless on the floor of the central aisle.

Jemima gave a sharp cry and at the same time the bundle moved, gave its own anguished shriek and said something which sounded like: "Zeeazmoof, Zeeazmoof." Then the bundle sat up and revealed itself to be not so much a bundle as an Italian girl in Jemima's own form called Sybilla.

At this point Jemima understood that what Sybilla was actually saying between sobs was: "She 'as moved, she 'as moved," in her characteristic strong Italian accent. There was a total contrast between this sobbing creature and the daytime Sybilla, a plump and rather jolly dark-haired girl, who jangled in illicit gold chains and bracelets, and wore more than a hint of equally illicit make-up. Jemima did not know Sybilla particularly well despite sharing classes with her. She pretended to herself that this was because Sybilla (unlike Jemima and her friends) had no interest in art, literature, history or indeed anything very much except Sybilla herself; pleasure, parties and the sort of people you met at parties, principally male. Sybilla was also old for her form—seventeen already—whereas Jemima was young for it, so that there was a considerable age gap between them. But the truth was that Jemima avoided Sybilla because she was a princess (albeit an Italian one, not a genuine British Royal) and Jemima, being middle class and proud of it, had no wish to be accused of snobbery.

The discovery of Sybilla—Princess Maria Sybilla Magdalena Graffo di Santo Stefano to give her her full title—in the chapel only deepened the whole mystery. Knowing Sybilla, religious mania, a sudden insane desire to pray alone in the chapel at night, to make a novena for example, simply could not be the answer to her presence. Sybilla was unashamedly lazy where religion was concerned, having to be dragged out of bed to go to mass even when it was obligatory on Sundays and feast days, protesting plaintively, like a big black cat ejected from the fireside. She regarded the religious fervour of certain other girls, such as Jemima's friend Rosabelle Powerstock, with goodnatured amazement.

"So boring" she was once overheard to say about the Feast of the Immaculate Conception (a holiday of obligation). "Why do we have this thing? I think we don't have this thing in Italy." It was fortunate that Sybilla's theological reflections on this occasion had never come to the ears of Reverend Mother Ancilla who would have quickly set to rights this unworthy descendant of a great Roman family (and even, delicious rumour said, of a Pope or two).

Yes, all in all, religious mania in Princess Sybilla could definitely be ruled out.

"Sybilla," said Jemima, touching her shoulder, "don't cry—"

At that moment came at last the sound for which Jemima had been subconsciously waiting since she first awoke: the characteristic swoosh of a nun in full habit advancing at high speed, rosary at her belt clicking, rubber heels twinkling down the marble corridor.

"Sybilla, *Jemima?*" The rising note of surprise on the last name was evident in the sharp but controlled voice of Sister Veronica, the Infirmarian. Then authority took over and within minutes nun-like phrases such as "To bed at once both of you" and "No more talking till you see Reverend Mother in the morning" had calmed Sybilla's convulsive sobs. The instinctive reaction of nuns in a crisis, Jemima had noted, was to treat teenage girls as children; or perhaps they always mentally treated them as children, it just came to the surface in a crisis. Sybilla after all was nearly grown-up, certainly if her physical appearance was any guide. Jemima sighed; was she to be hustled to bed with her curiosity, now quite rampant, unsatisfied?

It was fortunate for Jemima that before dispatching her charges, Sister Veronica did at least make a quick inspection of the chapel—as though to see what other delinquent pupils might be lurking there in the middle of the night.

"What happened, Sybilla?" Jemima took the opportunity to whisper. "What frightened you? I thought you were being murdered—"

Sybilla extended one smooth brown arm (unlike most of the girls at Blessed Eleanor's, she was perpetually sun-tanned, and unlike Jemima, she had somehow avoided wearing the regulation white nightdress).

"Oh, my God, Jemima!" It came out as "Omigod, Geemima! I am telling you. She 'as moved!"

"Who moved, Sybilla?"

"The statue. You know, the one they call the Holy Nelly. She moved her arms towards me. She 'as touched me, Jemima. It was *miraculo*. How do you say? A mir-a-cul."

Then sister Veronica returned and imposed silence, silence on the whole subject.

But of course it was not to be like that. The next morning at assembly the whole upper school, Jemima realized, was buzzing with excitement in which words like "miracle," "Sybilla's miracle" and "there was a miracle, did you hear" could be easily made out. Compared to the news of Sybilla's miracle—or the Blessed Eleanor's miracle depending on your point of view—the explanation of Sybilla's presence near the chapel in the middle of the night passed almost unnoticed: except by Jemima Shore that is, who definitely did not believe in miracles and was therefore still more avid to hear about Sybilla's experiences than she had been the night before. Jemima decided to tackle her just after Sister Hilary's maths lesson, an experience calculated to leave Sybilla unusually demoralized.

Sybilla smiled at Jemima, showing those dimples in her pinkish-olive cheeks which were her most attractive feature. (Come to think of it, was that pinkish glow due to a discreet application of blush-on? But Jemima, no nun, had other things on her mind.)

"Eet's ridiculous," murmured Sybilla with a heavy sigh; there was a clank as her gold charm bracelet hit the desk; it struck Jemima that the nuns' rosaries and Sybilla's jewellery made roughly the same sound and

served the same purpose, to advertise their presence. "But you know
these nuns, they won't let me write to my father. So boring. Oh yes, they
will let me *write*, but it seems they must read the letter. Mamma made
them do that, or maybe they did it, I don't know which. Mamma is so
holy, Omigod, she's like a nun . . . Papa"—Sybilla showed her dimples
again—"Papa, he is—how do you say—a bit of a bad dog."

"A gay dog," suggested Jemima helpfully. Sybilla ignored the inter-
ruption. She was busy speaking affectionately, even yearningly, of Prince
Graffo di Santo Stefano's bad (or gay) dog-like tendencies which seemed
to include pleasure in many forms. (The Princess being apparently in
contrast a model of austere piety, Jemima realized that Sybilla was very
much her father's daughter.) The Prince's activities included racing in
famous motor cars and escorting famously beautiful women and skiing
down famous slopes and holidaying on famous yachts, and other
things, amusing things. "Papa he 'ates to be bored, he 'ates it!" These
innocuous pursuits had according to Sybilla led the killjoy Princess to
forbid her husband access to his daughter: this being Italy there could
of course be no divorce either by the laws of the country or for that matter by the laws of Mother Church to which the Princess at least strictly
adhered.

"But it's true, Papa, he doesn't want a divorce either," admitted
Sybilla. "Then he might have to marry—I don't know who but he might
have to marry this woman or that woman. That would be terrible for
Papa. So boring. No, he just want some money, poor papa, he has no
money, Mama has all the money, I think it's not fair that, she should *give*
him the money, *si*, he is her *marito*, her 'usband, she should give it to
him. What do you think, Jemima?"

Jemima, feeling the first stirrings of primitive feminism in her breast
at this description of the Santo Stefano family circumstances, remained
politely silent on that subject.

Instead: "And the statue, Sybilla?" she probed gently.

"Ah." Sybilla paused. "Well, you see how it is, Jemima. I write to
him. I write anything, amusing things. And I put them in a letter but I
don't like the nuns to read these things so—" she paused again. "So I am
making an arrangement with Gregory," ended Sybilla with a slight but
noticeable air of defiance.

"Yes, Gregory," she repeated. "That man. The gardener, the chauffeur,
the odd-things man, whatever he is, the taxi-man."

Jemima stared at her. She knew Gregory, the convent's new odd-job

man, a surprisingly young fellow to be trusted in this all-female estab-
lishment, but all the same—

"And I am placing these letters under the statue of the Holy Nelly in
the night," continued Sybilla with more confidence. "To wake up?
Omigod, no problem. To go to sleep early, *that* is the problem. They
make us go to bed like children here. And he, Gregory, is collecting them
when he brings the post in the morning. Later he will leave me an
answer which he takes from the post office. That day there will be one
red flower in that big vase under the statue. And so we come to the night
when I am having my *miraculo*," she announced triumphantly.

But Jemima, who did not believe in miracles, fell silent once more at
what followed: Sybilla's vivid description of the statue's waving arms,
warm touch just as she was about to hide the letter (which she then
retrieved) and so forth and so on—an account which Jemima had a feeling was rapidly growing even as she told it.

"So you see I am flinging myself into the chapel," concluded Sybilla.
"And sc-r-r-reaming and sc-r-r-reaming. Till you, Jemima *cara*, have
found me. Because you only are near me!"

Well, that at least was true, thought Jemima: because she had formed
the strong impression that Sybilla, for all her warmth and confiding
charm was not telling her the truth; or not the whole truth. Just as
Jemima's reason would not let her believe in miracles, her instinct would
not let her believe in Sybilla's story, at any rate not all of it.

Then both Jemima and Sybilla were swirled up in the sheer drama
of Sister Elizabeth's lesson on her favourite Wordsworth ("Oh, the lovely
man!").

"Once did she hold the gorgeous East in fee," intoned Sister Liz in a
sonorous voice before adding rather plaintively: "Sybilla, do wake up;
this is *your* Venice after all, as well as dear Wordsworth's." Sybilla raised
her head reluctantly from her desk where it had sunk as though under
the weight of the thick dark hair, unconfined by any of the bands prescribed by convent rules. It was clear that her thoughts were very far
from Venice, "hers" or anyone else's, and even further from Wordsworth.

Another person who did not believe in miracles or at any rate did
not believe in this particular miracle was Reverend Mother Ancilla.
Whether or not she was convinced by Sybilla's explanation of sleepwalking—"since a child I am doing it"—Mother Ancilla dismissed the
mere idea of a moving statue.

"Nonsense child, you were asleep at the time. You've just said so. You dreamt the whole thing. No more talk of miracles please, Sybilla; the ways of Our Lord and indeed of the Blessed Eleanor may be mysterious but they are not as mysterious as *that*," announced Mother Ancilla firmly with the air of one to whom they were not in fact at all that mysterious in the first place. "Early nights for the next fourteen days—no, Sybilla, that is what I said, you need proper rest for your mind which is clearly, contrary to the impression given by your report, over-active . . ."

Even Sybilla dared do no more than look sulky-faced with Mother Ancilla in such a mood. The school as a whole was compelled to take its cue from Sybilla: with no further grist to add to the mill of gossip, gradually talk of Sybilla's miracle died away to be replaced by scandals such as the non-election of the Clitheroe twins Annie and Pettie (short for Annunziata and Perpetua) as Children of Mary. This was on the highly unfair grounds that they had appeared in a glossy magazine in a series called "Cloistered Moppets" wearing some Mary Quantish version of a nun's habit.

Jemima Shore did sometimes wonder whether Sybilla's illicit correspondence still continued. She also gazed from time to time at Gregory as he went about his tasks, all those tasks which could not be performed by the nuns themselves (surprisingly few of them as a matter of fact, picking up and delivering the post being one of them). Gregory was a solid-looking individual in his thirties with nice thick curly hair cut quite short, but otherwise in no way striking; were he not the only man around the convent grounds (with the exception of visiting priests in the morning and evening and parents at weekends) Jemima doubted whether she would have remembered his face. But he was a perfectly pleasant person, if not disposed to chat, not to Jemima Shore at least. The real wonder was, thought Jemima, that Sybilla had managed to corrupt him in the first place.

It was Jemima's turn to sigh. She had better face facts. Sybilla was rich—that much was obvious from her appearance—and she was also voluptuous. Another sigh from Jemima at the thought of Sybilla's figure, so much more like that of an Italian film star—if one fed on dollops of spaghetti—than anything Jemima could achieve. No doubt both factors, money and figure, had played their part in enabling Sybilla to capture Gregory. It was time to concentrate on other things—winning the English Prize for example (which meant beating Rosabelle) or securing the part of Hamlet in the school play (which meant beating everybody).

When Sybilla appeared at benediction on Saturday escorted by a middle-aged woman, and a couple of men in camel-haired coats, one very tall and dark, the other merely dark, Jemima did spare some further thought for the Santo Stefano family. Were these relations? The convent rules were strict enough for it to be unlikely they were mere friends, especially when Mamma Principessa was keeping such a strict eye on access to her daughter. Besides, the woman did bear a certain resemblance to Sybilla, her heavily busted figure suggesting how Sybilla's voluptuous curves might develop in middle age.

Jemima's curiosity was satisfied with unexpected speed: immediately after benediction Sybilla waved in her direction, and with wreathed smiles and much display of dimple, introduced her cousin Tancredi, her Aunt Cristiana and her Uncle Umberto.

"Ah now, Jemima, you come with us, you come with us for dinner? Yes, I insist. You have saved me. *Si, si,* it was her"—to her relations. To Jemima she confided: "I am not expecting them. They come to spy on the naughty Sybilla," dimples again. "But listen, Tancredi, he is very much like my Papa, now you know what Papa looks like, 'andsome, yes? And Papa, he like Tancredi very much, so you come?"

"I don't have a Permission—" began Jemima rather desperately. One look at Tancredi had already told her that he approximated only too wonderfully to her latest ideal of masculine attraction, derived partly from the portrait of Lord Byron at the front of her O-level text, and partly from a character in a Georgette Heyer novel called *Devil's Cub.* (Like many would-be intellectuals, Jemima had a secret passion for Georgette Heyer. Jemima, with Rosabelle, Annie, Pettie and the rest of her coterie, were relieved when from time to time some older indisputably intellectual female would announce publicly in print, tribute perhaps to her own youth, that Georgette Heyer was an important if neglected literary phenomenon.)

Alas, Jemima felt in no way ready to encounter Tancredi, the man of her dreams, at this precise juncture: she was aware that her hair, her best feature, hung lankly, there having been no particular reason in recent days to wash it. Her "home clothes" in which she would be allowed to emerge from the convent, belonged to a much shorter girl (the girl Mrs. Shore had in fact bought the clothes for, twelve months previously), nor could they be passed off as mini-skirted because they were too unfashionable.

One way and another, Jemima was torn between excitement and apprehension when Sybilla, in her most wayward mood, somehow overrode these very real difficulties ("But it's charming, the long English legs; Tancredi has seen you, *ma che bella!* Yes, yes, I am telling you . . .") and also, even more surprisingly, convinced Mother Ancilla to grant permission.

"An unusual friendship, dear Jemima," commented the Reverend Mother drily, before adding: "But perhaps you and Sybilla have both something to learn from each other." Her bright shrewd little eyes beneath the white wimple moved down Jemima's blouse and that short distance covered by her skirt.

"Is that a mini-skirt?" asked Mother Ancilla sharply. "No, no, I see it is not. And your dear mother away . . ." Mother Ancilla's thoughts were clearly clicking rapidly like the beads of her rosary. "What will the Marchesa think? Now, child, go immediately to Sister Baptist in the sewing-room, I have a feeling that Cecilia Clitheroe"—she mentioned the name of a recent postulant, some relation to Annie and Pettie—"is about your size." Marvelling, not for the first time, at the sheer practical world-liness of so-called unworldly nuns, Jemima found herself wearing not so much a drooping blouse and outmoded skirt as a black suit trimmed in beige braid which looked as if it had come from Chanel or thereabouts.

Without the suit, would Jemima really have captured Tancredi in quite the way she did at the dinner which followed? For undoubtedly, as Jemima related it to Rosabelle afterwards, Tancredi *was* captured and Rosabelle, summing up all the evidence, agreed that it must have been so. Otherwise why the slow burning looks from those dark eyes, the wine glass held in her direction, even on one occasion a gentle pressure of a knee elegantly clad in a silk suit of a particular shade of blue just a little too bright to be English? As for Tancredi himself, was he not well worth capturing, the muscular figure beneath the dandyish suit, nothing effeminate about Tancredi, the atmosphere he carried with him of inter-national sophistication—or was it just the delicious smell of *Eau Sauvage?* (Jemima knew it was *Eau Sauvage* because on Rosabelle's rec-ommendation she had given some to her father for Christmas; not that she had smelt it on him subsequently beyond one glorious whiff at Christmas dinner itself.)

As for Sybilla's uncle and aunt, the Marchesa spoke very little but when she did so it was in careful English, delivered, whether intention-ally or not, in a reproachful tone as though Jemima's presence at dinner demanded constant explanation if not apology. Jemima's answers to the Marchesa's enquiries about her background and previous education seemed to disgust her particularly; at one point, hearing that Jemima's father was serving in the British army, the Marchesa simply stared at her. Jemima hoped that the stare was due to national prejudice based on wartime memories, but feared it was due to simple snobbery.

Uncle Umberto was even quieter, a short pock-marked Italian who would have been plausible as a waiter, had he not been an Italian nobleman. Both uncle and aunt, after the first unfortunate interrogation, spoke mainly in Italian to their niece: family business, Jemima assumed, leaving Tancredi free for his pursuit of Jemima while their attention was distracted.

The next day: "You 'ave made a conquest, Jemima" related Sybilla proudly. "Tancredi finds you so int-ell-igent"—she drawled out the word—"and he asks if all English girls are so int-ell-igent, but I say that you are famous for being clever, so clever that you must find him so stu-pid!"

"I'm not all *that* clever, Sybilla." Jemima despite herself was nettled; for once she had hoped her attraction lay elsewhere than in her famous intelligence. That might win her the English Prize (she had just defeated Rosabelle) but intelligent was not quite how she wished to be regarded in those sophisticated international circles in which in her secret daydreams she was now dwelling.

Tancredi's letter, when it came, did not however dwell upon Jemima's intelligence but more of her particular brand of English beauty, her strawberries-and-cream complexion (Sybilla's blush-on had been liberally applied), her hair the colour of Italian sunshine and so forth and so on in a way that Jemima had to admit could scarcely be bettered even in daydream. The method by which the letter arrived was less satisfactory: the hand of Sybilla, who said that it had been enclosed in a letter from Tancredi's sister Maria Gloria (letters from accredited female relations were not generally opened). Had Sybilla read the letter which arrived sealed with sellotape? If she had, Jemima was torn between embarrassment and pride at the nature of the contents.

Several more letters followed until one day—"He wants to see you again. Of course he wants to see you again!" exclaimed Sybilla. "He loves you. Doesn't he say so always?" Jemima shot her a look: so Sybilla did know the letters' contents. To her surprise Jemima found that she was not exactly eager to see Tancredi again, despite the fact that his smuggled letters had become the centre of her emotional existence. Tancredi's passion for Jemima had something of the miraculous about it—Jemima smiled to herself wryly, she who did not believe in miracles—and she couldn't help being worried that the miracle might not happen a second time. . . . It was in the end more sheer curiosity than sheer romance which made Jemima continue to discuss Sybilla's daring idea for a rendezvous. This was to be in Jemima's own ground-floor room no less—Tancredi to be admitted through the grille left open for the occasion.

"The key!" cried Jemima "No, it's impossible. How would we ever get the key?"

"Oh Jemima, you who are so clever," purred Sybilla, looking more than ever like a fat black cat denied its bowl of cream. "Lovely Jemima . . . I know you will be thinking of something. Otherwise I am thinking that Tancredi goes to Italy and you are not seeing him. So boring. He has so many girls there."

"Like Papa?" Jemima could not resist asking. But Sybilla merely pouted.

"I could give such a long, long letter to Papa if you say yes," she sighed. "I'm frightened to speak to Gregory now, you know. Papa thinks—" She paused. "He's a bit frightened too. That moving statue." Sybilla shuddered.

"No, Sybilla," said Jemima.

Nevertheless in her languorously persistent way, Sybilla refused to let the subject of Tancredi's projected daring expedition to Blessed Eleanor's drop. Jemima for her part was torn between a conviction that it was quite impossible to secure the key to the grille in front of her ground-floor window and a pride which made her reluctant to admit defeat, defeat at the hands of the nuns. In the end pride won, as perhaps Jemima had known all along that it would. She found by observing Sister Dympna, who swept her room and was responsible for locking the grille at darkness, that the grille was opened by a key, but snapped shut of its own accord. From there it was a small step to trying an experiment: a piece of blackened cardboard between grille and jamb, and the attention of Sister Dympna distracted at the exact moment the busy little nun was slamming the grille shut.

It worked. Jemima herself had to close the grille properly after Sister Dympna left. That night Jemima lay awake, conscious of the outer darkness and the window through which Tancredi would come if she wanted him to come. She began to review the whole thrilling affair, beginning so unpropitiously as it had seemed at the time, with Sybilla's screams in the night. She remembered that night in the chapel with the terrified girl, the smell of incense in her nostrils, and then switched her thoughts to her first and so far her only encounter with Tancredi . . . Her own personal miracle. She heard Sybilla's voice: "*Miraculo.*"

But I don't believe in miracles, said the coldly reasonable voice of Jemima enclosed in the darkness, away from the seductive Mediterranean charm of Sybilla. And there's something else too: my instinct. I thought she was lying that first night, didn't I? Why did the statue move? A further disquieting thought struck Jemima. She got out of bed, switched on the light, and gazed steadily at her reflection in the small mirror over the basin.

"Saturday," said Jemima the next morning; she sounded quite cold. "Maria Gloria had better pass the message." But Sybilla, in her pleasure at having her own way, did not seem to notice the coldness. "And Sybilla—" added Jemima.

"Cara?"

"Give me the letter for your father in good time because I've got permission to go over to my own house to borrow some decent dresses of my mother's, she's coming back, you know. As I may not see you later, give me the letter before I go." Sybilla enfolded Jemima in a soft, warm, highly scented embrace.

By Saturday, Jemima found herself torn between two exactly contradictory feelings. Half of her longed for the night, for the rendezvous—whatever it might bring—and the other half wished that darkness would never come, that she could remain for the rest of her life, suspended, just waiting for Tancredi . . . Was this what being in love meant? For Jemima, apart from one or two holiday passions, for her father's young subalterns, considered that she had never been properly in love; although it was a matter much discussed between herself and Rosabelle (of her other friends the Clitheroe twins, Annie and Pettie being too merrily wanton and Bridget too strictly pious to join in these talks). Then there was another quite different side to her character, the cool and rational side, which simply said: I want to investigate, I want to find out what's going on, however painful the answer.

Jemima made her visit to her parents' home driven by the silent Gregory and chaperoned by Sister Veronica who was cross enough at the waste of time to agree with Jemima that the garden was in an awful state, and rush angrily at the neglected branches—"Come along, Jemima, we'll do it together." Jemima took a fork to the equally neglected beds and dug diligently out of range of Sister Veronica's conversation. (Gregory made no move to help but sat in the car.) Jemima herself was also extremely quiet on the way back, which with Gregory's enigmatic silence, meant that Sister Veronica could chatter on regarding the unkempt state of the Shore home ("Your poor dear mother . . . no gardener") to her heart's content. For the rest of the day and evening, Jemima had to keep the investigative side of her nature firmly to the fore. She found her emotional longings too painful.

Darkness fell on the convent. From the corner of her window— unbarred or rather with a crack left in the grille, so that only someone who knew it would open would be able to detect it—Jemima could watch as the yellow lights in the high dormitories were gradually extinguished. Sybilla was sleeping somewhere up there in the room which she shared with a monkey-like French girl called Elaine, who even in the summer at Blessed Eleanor's was huddled against the cold: "She is too cold to wake up. She is like your little mouse who sleeps," Sybilla had told Jemima. But Sybilla now was certainly watched at night and could not move about freely as she had once done.

On the other side of the building were the nuns, except for those on duty in the dormitories or Sister Veronica in the infirmary. Jemima had no idea where Mother Ancilla slept—alone perhaps in the brief night allowed to nuns before the early morning mass? But Mother Ancilla was another subject about which Jemima preferred not to think; the nun was so famously percipient that it had required some mental daring for Jemima even to say goodnight to her. She feared that the dark shrewd eyes might see right through to her intentions.

In her room, Jemima decided not to change into her convent night gown; she snuggled under the covers in jeans (collected that afternoon from home—strictly not allowed at Blessed Eleanor's)—and a skimpy black polo-necked jersey. In spite of herself, convent habits inspired in her a surprising desire to pray.

Reflecting that to do so even by rationalist standards, could not exactly do any *harm*, Jemima said three Hail Marys.

Oddly enough it was not until Jemima heard the faint—very faint— sound of someone rapping on the window, which was her clue to wind back the grille, that it occurred to Jemima that what she was doing might not only be foolhardy but actively dangerous. By then of course it was too late. She had no course now but to pull back the grille as silently as possible—since Sybilla's escapade the nuns had taken to patrolling the outside corridor from time to time. She raised the window cautiously.

Over the sill, dressed as far as she could make out entirely in black, at any rate in black jersey (remarkably similar to her own) and black trousers, with black rubber-soled shoes, came Tancredi. The smell of *Eau Sauvage* filled the room: for one wild moment the sweetness of it made Jemima regret . . . then she allowed herself to be caught into Tancredi's arms. He kissed her, his rather thin lips forcing apart her own.

Then Tancredi stood back a little and patted her lightly on her denim-clad thigh, "What protection! You are certainly not anxious to seduce me, *cara*," he said softly. Jemima could sense him smiling in the darkness. "This is a little bit like a nun, yes?" He touched her breast in the tight black jersey. "This not so much."

"Tancredi, you mustn't, I mean—" What did she mean? She knew what she meant. She had it all planned, didn't she?

"Tancredi, listen, you've simply got to take Sybilla's packet, her letter that is, it's quite thick, the letter, you must take it and then go. You see, the nuns are very suspicious. I couldn't let you know, but I have a feeling someone suspects . . . Mother Ancilla, she's the headmistress, she's awfully beady." Jemima was conscious she was babbling on. "So you must take the letter and go."

"Yes, I will take the letter. In good time. Or now, *tesoro*, if you like. I don't want to make tr-r-rouble for you." Tancredi sounded puzzled. "But first, oh I'm so tired, all that walking through this park, it's enor-mous, let's sit down a moment on this ridiculous little bed. Now this is really for a nun, this bed."

"I think you should just collect the letter and go," replied Jemima, hoping that her voice did not quaver.

"Collect, you mean you don't have it?" Tancredi was now a little brisker, more formal.

"I—I hid it. By the statue outside. You see we have inspection on Saturdays, drawer inspection, cupboard inspection, everything. I didn't dare keep it. So I used her place, Sybilla's place. Look, I'll explain where you go—"

To Jemima's relief, yes, it really was to her relief, she found Tancredi seemed to accept the necessity for speed, and even for a speedy depar-ture. The embrace he gave her as he vanished into the ill-lit corridor was quite perfunctory, only the lingering smell of *Eau Sauvage* in her room reminded her of what a romantic tryst this might under other circum-stances have turned out to be. Jemima sat down on the bed suddenly and waited for Tancredi's return. Then there would be one last embrace, perhaps perfunctory, perhaps a little longer, and he would vanish into the darkness from which he had come, out of her life.

She waited.

But things did not turn out quite as Jemima had planned. One moment Tancredi was standing at the door again, with a clear view of the big statue behind him; he had a pencil torch in his hand and a packet opened at one end. The next moment he had leapt towards her and caught her throat in the fingers of one strongly muscled hand.

"Where is it?" he was saying in a fierce whisper, "Where is it? Have you taken it? Who has taken it?" And then, with more indignation— "What is *this?*" He was looking at some white Kleenex which protruded from the packet, clearly addressed to the Principe Graffo di Santo Stefano in Sybilla's flowing hand. The fingers tightened on Jemima's throat so that she could hardly speak, even if she had some answer to the fierce questioning.

"Tancredi, I don't know what—" she began. Then beyond Tancredi, at the end of the corridor, to Jemima's horror she saw something which looked to her very much like the statue of the Blessed Eleanor moving. Jemima gave a scream, cut off by the pressure of Tancredi's fingers. After that a lot of things happened at once, so that later, sorting them out for Rosabelle (under very strict oath of secrecy—the Clitheroe twins and Bridget definitely not to be informed) Jemima found it difficult to get the exact order straight. At one moment the statue appeared to be moving in their direction, the next moment a big flashlight, of quite a different calibre from Tancredi's pencil torch, was shining directly on both of them. It must have been then that Jemima heard the voice of Gregory, except that Gregory was saying something like: Detective Inspector Michael Vann, Drugs Squad, and Michael Vann of Drugs Squad was, it seemed, in the process of arresting Tancredi.

Or rather he might have intended to be in the process, but an instant after Tancredi heard his voice and was bathed in the flashlight, he abandoned his hold on Jemima, dived in the direction of the window, pulled back the grille and vanished.

Then there were more voices, an extraordinary amount of voices for a tranquil convent at night, and phrases were heard like "Never mind, we'll get him," and words like "Ports, airports," all of which reverberated in the mind of Jemima without making a particularly intelligible pattern. Nothing seemed to be making much sense, not since the statue had begun to move, until she heard someone—Gregory—say:

"And after all that, he's managed to take the stuff with him."

"He hasn't," said Jemima Shore in a small but firm voice. "It's buried in the garden at home."

✝ ✝ ✝

It was so typical of Mother Ancilla, observed Jemima to Rosabelle when the reverberations of that night had at long last begun to die away, so typical of her that the very first thing she should say was: "You're wearing jeans, Jemima."

"I suppose she had to start somewhere," commented Rosabelle. "Personally, I think it's a bit much having the Drugs Squad moseying round the convent even if it is the biggest haul etc. etc. and even if the Principe is a wicked drug pusher etc. etc. Thank goodness it's all over in time for the school play." Rosabelle had recently been cast as Hamlet (Jemima was cast as Laertes—"that dear misguided *reckless* young man, as Sister Elizabeth put it, with a meaning look in Jemima's direction). Rosabelle at least had the school play much on her mind. "Did Mother Ancilla give any proper explanation?" Rosabelle went on.

"You know Mother Ancilla," Jemima said ruefully, "She was really amazingly lofty about the whole thing. That is, until I remarked in a most innocent voice that the nuns obviously agreed with the Jesuits that the ends justify the means."

"Daring! Then what?"

"Then I was told to write an essay on the history of the Society of Jesus by Friday—you can't win with Mother Ancilla."

"Sybilla and Co. certainly didn't. Still, all things considered, you were quite lucky, Jem. You did save the cocaine. You didn't get struck down by Tancredi, and you didn't get ravished by him."

"Yes, I was lucky; wasn't I?" replied Jemima in a tone in which Rosabelle thought she detected just a hint of wistfulness.

The reverberations of that night had by this time included the precipitate departure of Sybilla from the convent, vast amounts of expensive green velvety luggage surrounding her weeping figure in the convent hall the next day. She refused to speak to Jemima beyond spitting at her briefly: "I '*ate* you, Jemima, and Tancredi, he '*ates* you too, he thinks you are *ugly*." Then Sybilla shook her black head furiously so that the long glittering earrings, which she now openly flaunted, jangled and glinted.

What would happen to Sybilla? The Drugs Squad were inclined to be lenient towards someone who was so evidently under the influence of a father who was both pleasure-loving and poverty-stricken (a bad combination). Besides, thanks to a tip-off, they had had her watched since her arrival in England, and the Prince's foolproof method of bringing drugs into the country via his daughter's school luggage—clearly labelled "Blessed Eleanor's Convent, Churne, Sussex"—had never in fact been as foolproof as he imagined. For that matter, Gregory, the enigmatic gardener, had not been as subornable as Sybilla in her confident way and Jemima in her envious one, had imagined.

Gregory however, as an undercover operative, had not been absolutely perfect; it had been a mistake for example to let Sybilla glimpse him that night by the statue, provoking that fit of hysterics which had the effect of involving Jemima in the whole affair. Although it could be argued—and was by Jemima and Rosabelle—that it was Jemima's involvement which had flushed out Tancredi, the Prince's deputy, after Sybilla had become too frightened to contact Gregory. Then there was Jemima's valiant entrapment of Tancredi and her resourceful preservation of the cocaine.

All the same, Jemima Shore herself had not been absolutely perfect in the handling of the whole matter, as Mother Ancilla pointed out very firmly, once the matter of the jeans had been dealt with. It was only after some very frank things had been said about girls who kept things to themselves, things best confided to authority, girls who contemplated late-night trysts with males (albeit with the highest motives as Mother Ancilla accepted) that Mother Ancilla put her bird's head on one side: "But, Jemima dear child, what made you—how did you guess?"

"I just never believed in the second miracle, Mother," confessed Jemima.

"The second miracle, dear child?"

"I didn't believe in the first miracle either, the miracle of Sybilla's waving statue. The second miracle was Tancredi, the cousin, falling in love with me. I looked in the mirror, and well . . ." Her voice trailed away. Mother Ancilla had the effect of making her confess things she would rather, with hindsight, have kept to herself.

Mother Ancilla regarded Jemima for a moment. Her gaze was quizzical but not unkind.

"Now Jemima, I am sure that when we have finished with you, you will make a wonderful Ca— . . . a wonderful wife and mother"—she had clearly intended to say "Catholic wife and mother" before realizing who sat before her.

Jemima Shore saw her first and doubtless her last chance to score over Mother Ancilla.

"Oh, no, Reverend Mother," she answered boldly, "I'm not going to be a wife and mother. I'm going into television," and having already mentioned one of Mother Ancilla's pet banes, she was inspired to add another: "I'm going to be an investigative reporter."

The Witch's Tale

Margaret Frazer

*The gretteste clerkes been noght
wisest men, As whilom to the wolf
thus spak the mare.*
—Geoffrey Chaucer,
The Reeve's Tale

The night's rain had given way to a softened sky streaked with thin clouds. The air was bright with spring, and the wind had a kindness that was not there yesterday. In the fields the early corn was a haze of green across the dark soil, and along the sheltered southward side of a hedgerow Margery found a dandelion's first yellow among the early grass. The young nettles and wild parsley were up, and in a few days would be far enough along to gather for salad, something fresh after the long winter's stint of dried peas and beans and not enough porridge.

Margery paused under a tree to smile over a cuckoo-pint, bold and blithe before the cuckoo itself was heard this spring. Farther along the hedge a chaffinch was challenging the world, sparrows were squabbling with more vigor than they had had for months, and a muted flash of red among the bare branches showed where a robin was about his business. As she should be about hers, she reminded herself.

She had set out early to glean sticks along the hedgerows but there was not much deadwood left so near the village by this end of winter; her sling of sacking was barely a quarter full, and all of it was wet and would need drying before it was any use. But she must go home. Jack would be

coming for his dinner and then Dame Claire at the priory was expecting
her.

Though she and Jack were among the village's several free souls and
not villeins, Margery's one pride was that she worked with Dame Claire,
St. Frideswide's infirmarian. They had met not long after Margery had
married Jack and come to live in Priors Byfield. In the untended garden
behind the cottage she had found a plant she could not identify despite
the herb lore she had had from her mother and grandmother. With her
curiosity stronger than her fear, she had gone hesitantly to ask at the nunnery gates if there were a nun who knew herbs. In a while a small woman
neatly dressed and veiled in Benedictine black and white had come out to
her and kindly looked at the cutting she had brought.

"Why, that's bastard agrimony," she had said. "In your garden? It must
have seeded itself from ours. It's hardly common in this part of England
and I've been nursing ours along. It's excellent for strengthening the lungs
and to ease the spleen and against dropsy, you see."

"Oh, like marjoram. Wild marjoram, not sweet. Only better, I suppose?" Margery had said; and then had added regretfully, "I suppose you
want it back?"

Dame Claire had regarded her with surprise. "I don't think so. We still
have our own." She looked at the cutting more closely. "And yours seems
to be doing very well. Tell me about your garden."

Margery had told her and then, drawn on by Dame Claire's questions,
had told what she knew of herbs and finally, to her astonishment, had
been asked if she would like to see the priory's infirmary garden. One
thing had led on to another, that day and others; and with nothing in
common between them except their love of herbs and using them to help
and heal, she and Dame Claire had come to work together, Margery gathering wild-growing herbs for Dame Claire's use as well as her own and
growing plants in her garden to share with the infirmarian, as Dame
Claire shared her own herbs and the book-knowledge Margery had no
way of having. And for both of them there was the pleasure of talking
about work they both enjoyed, each with someone as knowledgeable as
herself.

Now, this third spring of their friendship, the soil would soon be dry
enough, God willing, for this year's planting. Margery and Dame Claire
had appointed today to plan their gardens together, so that Dame Claire
could ask the priory steward to bring back such cuttings as they needed
when he went to Lady Day fair in Oxford.

But Margery had to hurry. Her husband Jack wanted both her and his dinner waiting for him when he came into the house at the end of the morning's work, and his displeasure was ugly when she failed him. She had left herself time enough this morning, she was sure, even allowing for her dawdling along the hedgerow; but as she let herself into her garden by the back gate from the field path she saw with a familiar sick feeling that Jack was standing in the cottage's back doorway, fists on his hips and a mean grin on his fleshy mouth. He was back early from hedging—Margery would have sworn he was early—and neither she nor his food was waiting and no excuse would make any difference to what he would do now.

Wearily, Margery set down her bundle on the bench beside the door and looked up at him. It was better to see it coming.

"Y'know better than to be late," he accused. "Y'know I've told you that."

"I can have your dinner on in hardly a moment." She said it without hope. Nothing would help now; nothing ever did.

"I don't want to wait!" Jack put his hand flat between her breasts and shoved her backward. He always began with shoving. "I shouldn't *have* to wait!"

Margery stumbled back. Jack came after her and she turned sideways, to make a smaller target, for all the good it would do her. He shoved her again, staggering her along the path, then caught her a heavy slap to the back of her head so that she pitched forward, her knees banging into the wooden edging of a garden bed, her hands sinking into the muddy soil. She scrambled to be clear of him long enough to regain her feet. So long as she was on her feet he only hit. Once she was down, he kicked. His fists left bruises, sometimes cuts. His feet were worse. There were places in her that still hurt from last time, three weeks ago. From experience she knew that if she kept on her feet until he tired, he did not kick her so long.

But her fear made her clumsy. He was yelling at her now, calling her things she had never been, never thought of being. A blow alongside of her head sent her stumbling to one side, into her herb bed among the straw and burlap meant to protect her best plants through the winter. She scrambled to be out of it but Jack came in after her, crushing his feet down on anything in his way.

Margery cried out as she had not for her own pain. "Stop it! Leave my plants be!" Jack laughed and stomped one deliberately.

"Them and you both," he said, enjoying himself "You'll learn to do what you're told."

Margery fumbled in the pouch under her apron and, still scrambling to keep beyond his reach and get out from among her herbs, snatched out a small packet of folded cloth not so big as the palm of her hand. She brandished it at him and screamed, "You stop! You stop or I'll use this!"

For a wonder Jack did stop, staring at her in plain surprise. Then he scoffed, "You've nothing there, y'daft woman!" and grabbed for her.

Margery ducked from his reach, still holding out the packet. "It's bits of you, Jack Wilkins!" she cried. "From when I cut your hair last month and then when you trimmed your nails. Remember that? It's bits of you in here and I've made a spell, Jack Wilkins, and you're going to die for it if you don't leave me alone and get out of my garden!' "

"It's not me that's going to die!" he roared, and lurched for her.

After two days of sun the weather had turned back to low-trailing clouds and rain. But it was a gentle, misting rain that promised spring after winter's raw cold, and Dame Frevisse, leaving the guest hall where everything was readied should the day bring guests to St. Frideswide's, paused at the top of the stairs down into the courtyard to look up and let the rain stroke across her face. Very soon the cloister bell would call her into the church with the other nuns for the afternoon's service of Vespers, and she would be able to let go the necessities of her duties as the priory's hosteler to rise into the pleasure of prayer.

But as she crossed the yard toward the cloister door, Master Naylor overtook her. He was the priory's steward, a long-faced man who kept to his duties and did them well but managed to talk with the nuns he served, as little as possible. Bracing herself for something she probably did not want to hear, Frevisse turned to him. "Master Naylor?"

"I thought you'd best know before you went in to Vespers," he said, with a respectful bow of his head. Master Naylor was ever particular in his manners. "There's a man come in to say Master Montfort and six of his men will be here by supper time."

Frevisse felt her mouth open in protest, then snapped it closed. Among her least favorite people in the realm was Master Morys Montfort, crowner for northern Oxfordshire. It was his duty to find out what lay behind unexpected deaths within his jurisdiction, then to bring the malefactor—if any—to the sheriff's attention, and to see to it that whatever fines or confiscations were due King Henry VI were duly collected.

Frevisse had no quarrel with any of that, but Master Montfort had the regrettable tendency to prefer the least complicated solution to any problem and find his facts accordingly. He and Frevisse had long since struck a level of mutual hostility neither was inclined to abate. She was not happy to hear of his coming, and she said, "I trust he's just passing on his way to somewhere else? There's no one dead hereabouts that I've heard of."

Master Naylor shrugged. "It's Jack Wilkins in the village, the day before yesterday. They tolled the village bell for him but you were likely in church for Sext then."

"But why is Montfort coming? Is there doubt about the way this Wilkins died?"

"No doubt. His wife shook a charm at him and cast a spell, and he fell down dead. At least three of their neighbors saw it. I'd not have thought it of Margery," he added. "She's never been known to put her herbs to aught but good, that I've heard."

"*Margery?* Dame *Claire's* Margery?"

"That's her, the herbwife who visits here sometimes."

"Does Dame Claire know?"

"No more than you, I doubt. It was witchcraft and murder certain enough. Montfort will have it done a half hour after he's seen her and talked to her neighbors. He'll probably be on the road to Banbury with her before noon tomorrow and she'll be in the bishop's hands not long after that. I'd have reported it all to Domina Edith come week's end with the other village business." He seemed to think that was all the dealing there needed to be with the matter; Jack and Margery were not among the priory's villeins, and so not his responsibility. The lethal use of witchcraft wasn't usual; on the other hand, all herbwives used spells in their medicines, and it was but a small step to misuse them. He would not have mentioned it except he knew of Margery's link with Dame Claire.

The bell for Vespers began to ring. Frevisse said impatiently, "Where is she being kept?"

Master Naylor pointed through the gateway toward the outer yard. "She's in one of the sheds there. I've two of our men guarding her. She's gagged so it's all right; they're safe. There's nothing to be done."

"Dame Claire will want to see her after Vespers," Frevisse said. "Please you, tell the guesthall servants for me that Montfort is coming. I have to go."

The Vespers she had expected to enjoy was instead a prolonged discomfort of impatience; and afterwards she had to wait until supper was finished and the nuns went out into the garden for recreation time—the one hour of the day their Benedictine rule allowed for idle talk—before she could tell Dame Claire what was to hand.

"*Margery?*" Dame Claire exclaimed in her deep voice. Disbelief arched her eyebrows high toward her veil. "Killed her husband with witchcraft? I very much doubt it. In fact I don't believe it at all! I want to see her."

That was easily done. Frevisse waited at the foot of the stairs to the prioress' parlor while Dame Claire went up to ask permission. Then they went together, out of the cloister and across the inner yard—Frevisse noting there were lights in the guesthall window so Montfort and his entourage must have arrived—through the gateway to the outer yard where a stable hand, surprised to see them outside the cloister, pointed to the shed at the end of the stables where the prisoner was being kept.

"I should have thought to bring a cloak for her, and something warm to eat," Dame Claire regretted as they went. "These spring nights are cold, and she must be desperate, poor thing."

As Master Naylor had said, two stolid stable men were keeping guard inside the shed door, and Margery was gagged and her hands bound at her waist. But a clay lamp set in the corner on the bare earth floor gave a comforting yellow glow to the rough boards of her prison, and by its light as they stood in the doorway—Dame Claire explaining to the guards that they were come with permission to talk with Margery—Frevisse saw that Margery had several blankets, a cloak, and a straw-stuffed pillow to make her a bed along the farther wall, and that beside it were a pot of ale and various plates with three different kinds of bread and parts of two cheeses. Frevisse knew that in such cases as Margery the nunnery provided a blanket and an occasional piece of bread. So who had done this much for Margery?

Margery herself had risen to her feet as the nuns entered. Despite her crime, she was much as Frevisse had remembered her, a middling sort of woman—of middling build, middling young, middling tall, with nothing particular about her, except—to judge by her eyes above the gag—that she was frightened. As well she should be.

Dame Claire finished with the men, and crossed the shed to her, Frevisse following. As Margery curtseyed, Dame Claire said, "Let me loose your hands so you can take off the gag. I've told them you won't do anything. We want to talk to you."

Dame Claire freed Margery's hands, and gratefully she unknotted the cloth behind her head. "Thank you, my lady," she said hoarsely.

"Have something to drink." Dame Claire indicated the ale kindly. "Have they let you eat?"

Margery nodded over the rim of the clay pot as she drank thirstily. When she had finished, she said, "They've been as kind as might be. And village folk have brought me things." She gestured at her bed and food and lamp. She was clearly tired as well as frightened, worn out by too many strange things happening to her. "But I hoped you'd come, so I could tell you why I didn't come t'other day when I said I would."

"I wondered what happened to you," Dame Claire answered. "But I never thought this."

Margery hung her head. "Nor did I."

"They say you killed your husband."

Margery nodded. "I did that."

"Margery, no!" Dame Claire protested.

"Jack came at me, the way he's done ever since we married whenever I've not done right. But this time we were in my garden and he was trampling my plants." It plainly mattered very much to her that Dame Claire understand. "I told him to stop but he didn't care, and I—lost my temper."

"You truly did kill him?" Dame Claire asked, still disbelieving it.

"Oh, yes. Sure as sure. I didn't know the spell would work that way but it did. Took him off afore he could hit me again, just like that."

"What—exactly—did you do?" Frevisse asked carefully. Murder, serious enough in itself, was worse for the murderer when done by witchcraft. Charms and spells were simply part of healing; every herbwife knew some. But if they were turned to evil, they became part of the Devil's work and a matter for the Church as well as lay law.

Margery looked at Frevisse with mingled shyness and guilt, and did not answer.

"Tell us, please," Dame Claire urged. "Dame Frevisse and I want to help you."

"There's no help for me!" Margery said in surprise. "I killed him."

"How?" Frevisse persisted.

Margery hung her head. She twisted her hands in her apron and, low-voiced with embarrassment, said, "I'd been saving bits of him this while. Hair, you know, and his nail cuttings."

"Margery! That's wicked!" Dame Claire exclaimed.

"I know it!" Margery said piteously. "But I was only going to make a small charm. When I'd money for the wax to make the figure. Not kill him, like, but weaken his arm so he couldn't hit me so hard. That's all I wanted to do. Just weaken him."

"But you hadn't made the figure yet?" Frevisse asked. Margery shook her head dumbly. Frevisse pressed, "What did you do then, that you think you killed him?"

"I had the—things in a little packet. I held it up and told him what it was and that he'd better stop what he was doing. That I'd made a charm and I'd kill him if he didn't stop."

"But you hadn't made a charm yet. You said so," said Dame Claire.

"That I hadn't. But I meant to. I really did." She looked anxiously from one nun to the other. "If I make confession and do penance before they hang me, I won't have to burn in hell, will I? Not if I'm truly penitent?"

"Surely not," Dame Claire reassured her.

"But if you didn't have the charm, what happened?" Frevisse asked.

Margery shuddered. "Jack kept hitting and shoving. I knew he'd near to kill me, once he had his hands on me, and I'd never have another chance to make a charm against him, not now he knew. I was that frighted, I grabbed the first words that came to me, thinking to scare him off with them. I didn't even think what they were. I just said them at him and shook the packet like I was ill-wishing him. I just wanted to keep him back from me, I swear that's all. Just hold him off as long as might be."

She broke off, closing her eyes at the memory.

"And then?" Dame Claire prompted.

Faintly, tears on her cheeks, Margery said, "He stopped. All rigid like I'd hit him with a board. He stared at me with his mouth open and then grabbed his chest, right in the center, and bent over double. He was gasping like he hurt, or couldn't catch his breath. Then he fell over. In the path, away from my herbs. He curled up and went on gasping and then— he stopped. He just stopped and was dead."

A little silence held them all. Frevisse was aware of the two men at her back, and knew that everything they were hearing would be told later all around the nunnery and village.

"Margery," Dame Claire said, "you can't wish a man dead. Or rather, you can wish it, but it won't happen, not that simply."

"But it did," Margery said.

And there would probably be no convincing anyone otherwise. But for Dame Claire's sake, Frevisse asked, "What was it you said to him? A spell?"

Margery nodded. "The one for—"

Master Naylor interrupted her with a firm rap on the door frame. He inclined his head respectfully to Frevisse and Dame Claire, and said, "The crowner wants to see her now."

"So late?" Dame Claire protested.

"He hopes to finish the matter tonight so he can be on his way at earliest tomorrow. He has other matters to see to," Master Naylor explained.

Matters more important than a village woman who was surely guilty, Frevisse thought. A woman who was the more inconvenient because she would have to be sent for examination before a bishop before she could be duly hanged.

"We'll come with her," said Dame Claire.

Master Montfort had been given the guesthall's best chamber, with its large bed and plain but sufficient furnishings. The shutters had been closed against the rainy dusk, the lamps lighted, and at a table against the farther wall his clerk was hunched over a parchment, quill in hand and inkwell ready.

The crowner himself stood by the brazier in the corner, his hands over its low warmth. He was short in the leg for the length of his body, and had begun to go fat in his middle, but to his own mind any shortcomings he might have—and he was not convinced that he had any—were amply compensated for by the dignity of his office; he no more than glanced over his shoulder as Master Naylor brought Margery in, then sharpened his look on Frevisse and Dame Claire following her. A flush spread up his florid face and over the curve of his balding head.

"You can stay, Naylor," he said. "But the rest of you may go." Belatedly, ungraciously, he added, "My ladies."

With eyes modestly downcast and her hands tucked up either sleeve of her habit, Frevisse said, "Thank you, but we'll stay. It would not be seemly that Margery be here unattended."

She had used that excuse in another matter with Master Montfort. He had lost the argument then, and apparently chose not to renew it now. His flush merely darkened to a deeper red as he said tersely, "Then stand to one side and don't interfere while I question her."

They did so. Master Montfort squared up in front of Margery and announced in his never subtle way, "I've questioned some several of your neighbors already and mean to see more of them before I'm to bed tonight so you may as well tell what you have to tell straight out and no avoiding it. Can you understand that?"

Margery did not lift her humbly bowed head. "Yes, m'lord."

"You killed your husband? Now, mind you, you were heard and seen so there's no avoiding it."

Margery clearly had no thought of avoiding anything. While the clerk's pen scratched busily at his parchment, recording her words, she repeated what she had already told Frevisse and Dame Claire. When she had finished, Master Montfort rocked back on his heels, smiling grimly with great satisfaction. "Very well said, and all agreeing with your neighbors' tales. I think there's no need for more."

"Except," Dame Claire said briskly, knowing Master Montfort would order her to silence if she gave him a chance, "I doubt her husband died of anything more than apoplexy."

The crowner turned on her. In a tone intended to quell, he said, "I beg your pardon, my lady?"

Dame Claire hesitated. Frevisse, more used to the crowner's bullying, said helpfully, "Apoplexy. It's a congestion of the blood—"

Master Montfort's tongue caught up with his indignation. "I know what it is!"

Frevisse turned to Master Naylor. As steward of the priory's properties he had far better knowledge of the villeins than she did. "What sort of humor was this Jack Wilkins? Hot-tempered or not?"

"Hot enough it's a wonder he was in so little trouble as he was," Master Naylor said. "He knocked a tooth out of one of his neighbors last week because he thought the man was laughing at him. The man wasn't, being no fool, but Jack Wilkins in a temper didn't care about particulars. It wasn't the first time he's made trouble with his temper. And he was known to beat his wife."

"Choleric," said Dame Claire. "Easily given to temper. People of that sort are very likely to be struck as Jack Wilkins was, especially in the midst of one of their furies. He was beating his wife—

"As he had every right to do!" Master Montfort declared.

As if musing on his own, Master Naylor said, "There's a feeling in the village that he did it more often and worse than need be."

But Dame Claire, refusing to leave her point, went on over his words,

"—and that's heavy work, no matter how you go about it. Then she defied him, maybe even frightened him when she said her spell—"

"And down he fell dead!" the crowner said, triumphant. "That's what I'm saying. It was her doing and that's the end of it."

"What was the spell she said?" Frevisse interjected. "Has anyone asked her that?"

Master Montfort shot her an angry look; determined to assert himself, he swung back on Margery. "That was my next question, woman. What did you actually say to him? No, don't look at anyone while you say it! And say it slow so my clerk can write it down."

Eyes turned to the floor, voice trembling a little, Margery began to recite, "Come you forth and get you gone . . ."

If Master Montfort was expecting a roaring spell that named devils and summoned demons, he was disappointed. The clerk scratched away busily as Margery went through a short verse that was nevertheless quite apparently meant to call the spirit out of the body and cast it away. Part way through, Dame Claire looked startled.

In the pause after Margery finished speaking, the clerk's pen scritched on. Master Montfort, ever impatient, went to hover at his shoulder and, as soon as he had done, snatched the parchment away. While he read it over, Frevisse leaned toward Dame Claire, who whispered briefly but urgently in her ear. Before Frevisse could respond, Master Montfort demanded at Margery, "That's it? just that?" Margery nodded. Master Montfort glared at his clerk and recited loudly, "Come you forth . . ."

The man's head jerked up to stare with near-sighted alarm at his master. The crowner went on through the spell unheeding either his clerk's dismay or Master Naylor's movement of protest. Margery opened her mouth to say something, but Frevisse silenced her with a shake of her head, while Dame Claire pressed a hand over her own mouth to keep quiet.

When Master Montfort had finished, a tense waiting held them all still, most especially the clerk. When nothing happened after an impatient minute, Master Montfort rounded on Margery. "How long is this supposed to take?"

Margery fumbled under his glare. "My husband—he—almost on the instant, sir. But—"

"Spare me your excuses. If it worked for you, why didn't it work for me? Because I didn't have clippings of his hair or what?"

Keeping her voice very neutral, Frevisse suggested, "According to

Robert Mannying in his *Handling Sin*, a spell has no power if said by someone who doesn't believe in it. Margery uses herbs and spells to help the villagers. She believes in what she does. You don't. Do you believe in your charm, Margery? This one that you said at your husband?"

"Yes, but—"

"She's a witch," Master Montfort interrupted. "And whatever good you claim she's done, she's used a spell to kill a man this time, and her husband at that. Who knows what else she's tried." He rounded on Margery again and said in her face, "There's a question for you, woman. Have you ever used this spell before?"

Margery shrank away from him but answered, "Surely. Often and often. But—"

"God's blood!" Master Montfort exclaimed. "You *admit* you've murdered other men?"

"Margery!" Frevisse interposed, "*What* is the spell *for*?"

Driven by both of them, Margery cried out, "It's for opening the bowels!"

A great quiet deepened in the room. Margery looked anxiously from face to face. Frevisse and Dame Claire looked carefully at the floor. Red darkened and mounted over Master Montfort's countenance again. Master Naylor seemed to struggle against choking. The clerk ducked his head low over his parchment. Nervously Margery tried to explain. "I make a decoction with gill-go-on-the-ground, and say the spell over it while it's brewing, to make it stronger. It provokes urine, too, and ... and ..." She stopped, not understanding their reactions, then finished apologetically, "They were the first words that came into my head, that's all. I just wanted to fright Jack off me, and those were the first words that came. I didn't mean for them to kill him."

Master Montfort, trying to recover lost ground, strangled out, "But they did kill him, didn't they? That's the long and short of it, isn't it?"

Margery started to nod, but Frevisse put a stilling hand on her arm; and Dame Claire said, "It's a better judgement that her husband died not from her words but from his own choler, like many another man before him. It wasn't Margery but his temper that did for him at the last."

Master Montfort glared at her. "That's women's logic!" he snapped. "His wife warns him she has bits of him to use against him, and cries a spell in his face, and he drops down dead, and it's *his* fault? Where's the sense of that? No! She's admitted her guilt. She was seen doing it. There's no more questioning needed. Naylor, keep her until morning. Then I'll take her in charge."

† † †

The twilight had darkened to deep dusk but the rain had stopped as they came out of the guest hall. Master Naylor steadied Margery by her elbow as they went down the steps to the yard. No matter how much she had expected her fate, she seemed dazed by the crowner's pronouncement, and walked numbly where she was taken. Frevisse and Dame Claire followed with nothing to say, though Frevisse at least seethed with frustration at their helplessness and Montfort's stupidity. Even the acknowledgement of the *possibility* of doubt from him would have been something.

Margery's two guards were waiting at the foot of the steps in the spread of light from the lantern hung by the guest hall door. They stood aside, then followed as the silent group made their way around the rain-puddles among the cobbles to the gateway to the outer yard. Beyond it was the mud and deeper darkness of the outer yard where the lamplight showing around the ill-fitted door of Margery's prison shed was the only brightness. Busy with her feet and anger, Frevisse did not see the knot of people there until one of them swung the shed door open to give them more light, and Master Naylor said in surprise, "Tom, what brings you out? And the rest of you?"

Frevisse could see now that there were seven of them, four women and three men, all from the village. The women curtseyed quickly to her, Dame Claire, and Master Naylor as they came forward to Margery. Crooning to her like mothers over a hurt child, they enveloped her with their kindness; and one of them, with an arm around her waist, soothed, "There now, Margery-girl, we can see it didn't go well. You come in-by. We've something warm for you to eat." Together they drew her into the shed, leaving the men to front the priory-folk.

Tom, the village reeve and apparently their leader in this, ducked his head to her and Dame Claire, and again to Master Naylor before he said, "She's to go then? No help for it?"

"No help for it," Master Naylor agreed. "The crowner means to take her with him when he goes in the morning."

The men nodded as if they had expected no less. But Tom said, "It makes no difference that there's not a body in the village but's glad to have

Jack gone? He was a terror and no mistake and she didn't do more than many of us have wanted to."

"I can't argue that, but it changes nothing," Master Naylor said. "Margery goes with the crowner in the morning, and be taken before the bishop for what she's done."

"She didn't do anything!" Dame Claire said with the impatience she had had to curb in Master Montfort's presence.

Frevisse agreed. "This Jack died from his own temper, not from Margery's silly words!"

"It was apoplexy," said Dame Claire. "People who indulge in ill temper the way Jack Wilkins did are like to die the way Jack Wilkins did."

"If you say so, m'lady," Tom said in a respectful voice. "But Margery cried something out at him, and Jack went down better than a poled ox. God keep his soul," he added as an after-thought, and everyone crossed themselves . Jack Wilkins was unburied yet; best to say the right things for he would make a wicked ghost.

"It wasn't even a spell to kill a man. Margery says so herself."

"Well, that's all right then," Tom said agreeably. "And a comfort to Margery to know it wasn't her doing that killed Jack, no matter what the crowner says. But what we've come for is to ask if some of us can stand Margery's guard tonight, for friendship's sake, like, before she goes."

Dim with distance and the mist-heavy dusk, the bell began to call to Compline, the nuns' last prayers before bed. Frevisse laid a hand on Dame Claire's arm, drawing her away. Master Naylor could handle this matter. There was nothing more for the two of them to do here. Better they go to pray for Margery's soul. And Jack Wilkins', she thought belatedly.

✝   ✝   ✝

Watery sunshine was laying thin shadows across the cloister walk next morning as Frevisse went from chapter meeting toward her duties. She expected Master Montfort and his men and Margery would be gone by now, ridden away at first light; and she regretted there had been nothing that could be done to convince anyone but herself and Dame Claire that Margery had not killed her lout of a husband with her poor little spell and desperation. But even Margery had believed it, and would do penance for it as if her guilt were real, and go to her death for it.

Frevisse was distracted from her anger as she neared the door into the courtyard by the noise of Master Montfort's raised voice, the words unclear but his passion plain. She glanced again at the morning shadows. He was supposed to be miles on his way by this time. She opened the door from the cloister to the courtyard.

Usually empty except for a passing servant and the doves around the well, the yard was half full of villagers crowded to the foot of the guest hall steps. Master Montfort stood above them there, dressed for riding and in a rage.

"You're still saying there's no trace of her?" he ranted. Frevisse stopped where she was with a sudden hopeful lift of her spirits. "You've been searching the wretched place since dawn! My men have scoured the fields for miles! *Someone* has to know where she is! Or if she's truly bolted, we have to set the hounds to her trail!"

Even from where she was, Frevisse could see the sullen set of every villein's shoulders. But it was clear that the main thrust of his words was at Master Naylor, standing straight-backed at the head of the villeins, deliberately between them and the crowner's rage. With a hard-edged patience that told Frevisse he had been over this already more than once, he answered in his strong, carrying voice, "We have no hounds to set to her trail. This is a priory of nuns. They're not monks; they don't ride to hunt here."

Standing close behind the steward, Tom the reeve growled so everyone could hear, "And where she went, you wouldn't care to follow!"

Master Montfort pointed at him, furious. "You! You're one of the fools who slept when you were supposed to be guarding her! Dreaming your way to perdition while she walks off free as you please! What do you mean, 'where she went'? Hai, man, what do you mean?"

"I mean it wasn't a natural sleep we had last night!" Tom answered loudly enough to send his words to the outer yard, to Master Montfort's entourage and a number of priory servants clustered just beyond the gateway. Frevisse saw them stir as he spoke. "Aye, it wasn't a natural sleep and there's not one of us will say it was. We fell to sleep all at once and together, between one word and another. That's not natural! No more than Jack Wilkins falling down dead was natural. We're lucky it was only sleep she did to us! That's what I say! And anybody who tried to follow her is asking for what happens to him!"

Behind and around him the other villeins glanced at each other and nodded. One of the bolder men even spoke up, "Tom has the right of it!"

A woman—Frevisse thought she was one of four who had come to Margery last night—said shrilly, "You can't ask any decent man to follow where she's gone!"

Master Montfort pointed at her. "You know where she's gone? You admit you know?"

"I can make a fair guess!" the woman flung back. "Flown off to her master the devil, very like, and you'll find no hound to go that trail!"

"Flown off?" Master Montfort raged. "*Flown* off? I'm supposed to believe that? Naylor, most of these folk are the priory's villeins! Warn them there's penalties for lying to the king's crowner and hiding murderers. She's around here somewhere!"

"If she is, we haven't found her yet for all our searching," Master Naylor said back. "Twice through the village is enough for one day, and there's no sign where she might have gone across country. As you say, these are our villeins and I can say I've never known them given to such lying as this. Maybe they've the right of it. You said yourself last night she was a witch, and now she seems to have proved it!"

Master Montfort stared at him, speechless with rage.

"What we say," shouted another of the men, "is you're welcome to come search us house to house yourself, you being so much smarter than the rest of us. But if you find her, you'd better hope she doesn't treat you like she did her husband!"

There was general angry laughter among all the villeins at that; and some from beyond the gateway. For just a moment Master Montfort lost the stride of his anger, paused by the man's words. Then he gathered himself together and rounded on Master Naylor. With a scorn that he meant to be withering, he said, "I've greater matters to see to than hunting down some petty village witch. She was in your charge, Naylor, and the loss is to you, not to me. There'll be an amercement to pay for losing the king's prisoner, and be assured I'll see the priory is charged it to the full!"

"I'm assured you will," Master Naylor returned tersely, his scorn stronger than Master Montfort's.

For a balanced moment he and the crowner held each other's eyes. Then Master Naylor gestured sharply for the villeins to move back from the foot of the steps. Crowding among themselves, they gave ground. Master Montfort's mouth opened, then closed, and with great, stiff dignity he descended, passed in front of them to his horse being held for him beyond the gateway, and mounted. He glared around at them one final time and, for good measure, across the courtyard at Frevisse still standing in the doorway, then jerked his horse around and went.

No one moved or spoke until the splash and clatter of his going, and his entourage after him, were well away. And even then the response

among them all seemed no more than a long in-drawn breath and a slow
release of tension. Heads turned to one another, and Frevisse saw smiles,
but no one spoke. There were a few chuckles but no more as they all
drifted out of the gateway, some of them nodding to Master Naylor as they
passed him. He nodded back, and did not speak either; and when they
were gone, he stayed where he was, waiting for Frevisse to come to him.

She did, because there in the open courtyard they could most easily
talk without chance of being overheard so long as they kept their voices
low. "Master Naylor," she said as she approached him.

He inclined his head to her. "Dame Frevisse."

"I take it from what I heard that Margery Wilkins escaped in the
night?"

"It seems her guards and the friends who came to keep her company
slept. When they awoke this dawn, she was gone."

"And cannot be found?"

"We've searched the village twice this morning, and Master Montfort's
men have hunted the near countryside."

"They think she used her witch-powers to escape?"

"So it would seem. What other explanation is there?"

"I can think of several," Frevisse said dryly.

Master Naylor's expression did not change. "Just as you and Dame
Claire could think of some other reason for Jack Wilkins' death besides
his wife's words striking him down."

"And the fine to the priory for your carelessness in losing your
witch?"

"It was villeins who had the watch of her and lost her. I mean to make
an amercement on the village to help meet the fine our crowner will
surely bring against the priory."

"Won't there be protest over that?"

"Villeins always protest over paying anything. But in this I think
there'll be less arguing than in most. She's their witch. Let them pay for
her. Dear-bought is held more dear."

"They still truly believe she killed her husband?" Frevisse asked.
"Despite what we told them last night, they still believe she's a witch with
that much power?"

"What else can they believe?" the steward asked quietly in return.
"They saw her do it."

"What do you believe?" Frevisse asked, unable to tell from his neutral
expression and voice.

Instead of an answer to that, Master Naylor said, "I think a straw-filled loft is not an uncomfortable place to be for a week and more this time of year. And that by the time summer comes there'll be a new herb-wife in the village, maybe even with the same first name but someone's widowed sister from somewhere else, freeborn like Margery was and no questions asked."

"And after all, witchcraft in itself is no crime or sin," Frevisse said. "The wrong lies in the use it's put to."

"And all the village knows Margery has ever used her skills for good, except this one time, if you judge what she did was ill. All her neighbors judge it wasn't," Master Naylor said solemnly.

"They mean to keep her even if it costs them?" Frevisse asked.

"They know she's a good woman. And now that they're certain she has power, she's not someone they want to lose."

"Or to cross," Frevisse said.

Master Naylor came as near to a smile as he ever came, but only said, "There'll likely be no trouble with anyone beating her ever again."

Ⴇ urder Ⴇ ysteries

Ⴖ eil Gaima ⴖ

The Fourth Angel says:
Of this order I am made one,
From Mankind to guard this place
That through their Guilt they have foregone,
For they have forfeited His Grace;
Therefore all this must they shun
Or else my Sword they shall embrace
And myself will be their Foe
To flame them in the Face.
—Chester Ⴇ ystery Cycle:
The Creatio ⴖ , a ⴖ d Ada Ⴇ a ⴖ d Eve, 1461.

THIS IS TRUE.

Ten years ago, give or take a year, I found myself on an enforced stopover in Los Angeles, a long way from home. It was December, and the California weather was warm and pleasant. England, however, was in the grip of fogs and snowstorms, and no planes were landing there. Each day I'd phone the airport, and each day I'd be told to wait another day.

This had gone on for almost a week.

I was barely out of my teens. Looking around today at the parts of my life left over from those days, I feel uncomfortable, as if I've received a gift, unasked, from another person: a house, a wife, children, a vocation. Nothing to do with me, I could say, innocently. If it's true that every seven years each cell in your body dies and is replaced, then I have truly inherited my life from a dead man; and the misdeeds of those times have been forgiven, and are buried with his bones.

I was in Los Angeles. Yes.

On the sixth day I received a message from an old sort-of-girlfriend from Seattle: she was in LA too, and she had heard I was around on the friends-of-friends network. Would I come over?

I left a message on her machine. Sure.

That evening: a small, blonde woman approached me, as I came out of the place I was staying. It was already dark.

She stared at me, as if she were trying to match me to a description, and then, hesitantly, she said my name.

"That's me. Are you Tink's friend?"

"Yeah. Car's out back. C'mon; she's really looking forward to seeing you."

The woman's car was one of the huge old boat-like jobs you only ever seem to see in California. It smelled of cracked and flaking leather upholstery. We drove out from wherever we were to wherever we were going.

Los Angeles was at that time a complete mystery to me; and I cannot say I understand it much better now. I understand London, and New York, and Paris: you can walk around them, get a sense of what's where in just a morning of wandering. Maybe catch the subway. But Los Angeles is about cars. Back then I didn't drive at all; even today I will not drive in America. Memories of LA for me are linked by rides in other people's cars, with no sense there of the shape of the city, of the relationships between the people and the place. The regularity of the roads, the repetition of structure and form, mean that when I try to remember it as an entity all I have is the boundless profusion of tiny lights I saw one night on my first trip to the city, from the hill of Griffith Park. It was one of the most beautiful things I had ever seen, from that distance.

"See that building?" said my blonde driver, Tink's friend. It was a red-brick art deco house, charming and quite ugly.

"Yes."

"Built in the 1930s," she said, with respect and pride.

I said something polite, trying to comprehend a city inside which fifty years could be considered a long time.

"Tink's real excited. When she heard you were in town. She was so excited."

"I'm looking forward to seeing her again."

Tink's real name was Tinkerbell Richmond. No lie.

She was staying with friends in small apartment clump, somewhere an hour's drive from downtown LA.

What you need to know about Tink: she was ten years older than me, in her early thirties; she had glossy black hair and red, puzzled lips, and very white skin, like Snow White in the fairy stories; the first time I met her I thought she was the most beautiful woman in the world.

Tink had been married for a while at some point in her life, and had a five-year-old daughter called Susan. I had never met Susan—when Tink had been in England, Susan had been staying on in Seattle, with her father.

People named Tinkerbell name their daughters Susan.

Memory is the great deceiver. Perhaps there are some individuals whose memories act like tape recordings, daily records of their lives complete in every detail, but I am not one of them. My memory is a patchwork of occurrences, of discontinuous events roughly sewn together: the parts I remember, I remember precisely, whilst other sections seem to have vanished completely.

I do not remember arriving at Tink's house, nor where her flatmate went.

What I remember next is sitting in Tink's lounge, with the lights low; the two of us next to each other, on the sofa.

We made small talk. It had been perhaps a year since we had seen one another. But a twenty-one-year-old boy has little to say to a thirty-two-year-old woman, and soon, having nothing in common, I pulled her to me.

She snuggled close with a kind of sigh, and presented her lips to be kissed. In the half-light her lips were black. We kissed for a little, and I stroked her breasts through her blouse, on the couch; and then she said:

"We can't fuck. I'm on my period."

"Fine."

"I can give you a blow job, if you'd like."

I nodded assent, and she unzipped my jeans, and lowered her head to my lap.

After I had come, she got up and ran into the kitchen. I heard her spitting into the sink, and the sound of running water: I remember wondering why she did it, if she hated the taste that much.

Then she returned and we sat next to each other on the couch.

"Susan's upstairs, asleep," said Tink. "She's all I live for. Would you like to see her?"

"I don't mind."

We went upstairs. Tink led me into a darkened bedroom. There were child-scrawl pictures all over the walls—wax-crayoned drawings of winged fairies and little palaces—and a small, fair-haired girl was asleep in the bed.

"She's very beautiful," said Tink, and kissed me. Her lips were still slightly sticky "She takes after her father."

We went downstairs. We had nothing else to say, nothing else to do. Tink turned on the main light. For the first time I noticed tiny crows' feet at the corners of her eyes, incongruous on her perfect, Barbie-doll face.

"I love you," she said.

"Thank you."

"Would you like a ride back?"

"If you don't mind leaving Susan alone . . . ?"

She shrugged, and I pulled her to me for the last time.

At night, Los Angeles is all lights. And shadows.

A blank, here, in my mind. I simply don't remember what happened next. She must have driven me back to the place where I was staying—how else would I have gotten there? I do not even remember kissing her goodbye. Perhaps I simply waited on the sidewalk and watched her drive away.

Perhaps.

I do know, however, that once I reached the place I was staying I just stood there, unable to go inside, to wash and then to sleep, unwilling to do anything else.

I was not hungry. I did not want alcohol. I did not want to read, or talk. I was scared of walking too far, in case I became lost, bedeviled by the repeating motifs of Los Angeles, spun around and sucked in so I could never find my way home again. Central Los Angeles sometimes seems to me to be nothing more than a pattern, like a set of repeating blocks: a gas station, a few homes, a mini-mall (donuts, photo developers, laundromats, fast-foods), and repeat until hypnotised; and the tiny changes in the mini-malls and the houses only serve to reinforce the structure.

I thought of Tink's lips. Then I fumbled in a pocket of my jacket, and pulled out a packet of cigarettes.

I lit one, inhaled, blew blue smoke into the warm night air.

There was a stunted palm tree growing outside the place I was staying, and I resolved to walk for a way, keeping the tree in sight, to smoke my cigarette, perhaps even to think; but I felt too drained to think. I felt very sexless, and very alone.

A block or so down the road there was a bench, and when I reached it I sat down. I threw the stub of the cigarette onto the pavement, hard, and watched it shower orange sparks.

Someone said, "I'll buy a cigarette off you, pal. Here."

A hand, in front of my face, holding a quarter. I looked up.

He did not look old, although I would not have been prepared to say how old he was. Late thirties, perhaps. Mid-forties. He wore a long, shabby coat, colorless under the yellow street lamps, and his eyes were dark.

"Here. A quarter. That's a good price."

I shook my head, pulled out the packet of Marlboros, offered him one. "Keep your money. It's free. Have it."

He took the cigarette. I passed him a book of matches (it advertised a telephone sex line; I remember that), and he lit the cigarette. He offered me the matches back, and I shook my head. "Keep them. I always wind up accumulating books of matches in America."

"Uh-huh." He sat next to me, and smoked his cigarette. When he had smoked it halfway down, he tapped the lighted end off on the concrete, stubbed out the glow, and placed the butt of the cigarette behind his ear.

"I don't smoke much," he said. "Seems a pity to waste it, though."

A car careened down the road, veering from one side to the other. There were four young men in the car: the two in the front were both pulling at the wheel, and laughing. The windows were wound down, and I could hear their laughter, and the two in the back seat ("*Gaary, you asshole! What the fuck are you onnn mannnn?*") and the pulsing beat of a rock song. Not a song I recognised. The car looped around a corner, out of sight.

Soon the sounds were gone, too.

"I owe you," said the man on the bench.

"Sorry?"

"I owe you something. For the cigarette. And the matches. You wouldn't take the money. I owe you."

I shrugged, embarrassed. "Really, it's just a cigarette. I figure, if I give people cigarettes, then if ever I'm out, maybe people will give me cigarettes."

I laughed, to show I didn't really mean it, although I did. "Don't worry about it."

"Mm. You want to hear a story? True story? Stories always used to be good payment. These days . . ." He shrugged. ". . . Not so much."

I sat back on the bench, and the night was warm, and I looked at my watch: it was almost one in the morning. In England a freezing new day would already have begun: a workday would be starting for those who could beat the snow and get into work; another handful of old people, and those without homes, would have died, in the night, from the cold.

"Sure," I said to the man. "Sure. Tell me a story."

He coughed, grinned white teeth—a flash in the darkness—and he began.

"First thing I remember was the Word. And the Word was God. Sometimes, when I get *really* down, I remember the sound of the Word in my head, shaping me, forming me, giving me life.

"The Word gave me a body, gave me eyes. And I opened my eyes, and I saw the light of the Silver City.

"I was in a room—a silver room—and there wasn't anything in it except me. In front of me was a window, that went from floor to ceiling, open to the sky, and through the window I could see the spires of the City, and at the edge of the City, the Dark.

"I don't know how long I waited there. I wasn't impatient or anything, though. I remember that. It was like I was waiting until I was called; and I knew that some time I would be called. And if I had to wait until the end of everything, and never be called, why, that was fine too. But I'd be called, I was certain of that. And then I'd know my name, and my function.

"Through the window I could see silver spires, and in many of the other spires were windows; and in the windows I could see others like me. That was how I knew what I looked like.

"You wouldn't think it of me, seeing me now, but I was beautiful. I've come down in the world a way since then.

"I was taller then, and I had wings.

"They were huge and powerful wings, with feathers the colour of mother-of-pearl. They came out from just between my shoulderblades. They were so good. My wings.

"Sometimes I'd see others like me, the ones who'd left their rooms, who were already fulfilling their duties, I'd watch them soar through the sky from spire to spire, performing errands I could barely imagine.

"The sky above the City was a wonderful thing. It was always light, although lit by no sun—lit, perhaps by the City itself: but the quality of light was forever changing. Now pewter-coloured light, then brass, then a gentle gold, or a soft and quiet amethyst..."

The man stopped talking. He looked at me, his head on one side. There was a glitter in his eyes that scared me. "You know what amethyst is? A kind of purple stone?"

I nodded.

My crotch felt uncomfortable.

It occurred to me then that the man might not be mad; I found this far more disquieting than the alternative.

The man began talking once more. "I don't know how long it was that I waited, in my room. But time didn't mean anything. Not back then. We had all the time in the world.

"The next thing that happened to me, was when the Angel Lucifer came to my cell. He was taller than me, and his wings were imposing, his plumage perfect. He had skin the colour of sea-mist, and curly silver hair, and these wonderful grey eyes . . .

"I say *he,* but you should understand that none of us had any sex, to speak of." He gestured towards his lap. "Smooth and empty. Nothing there. You know.

"Lucifer shone. I mean it—he glowed from inside. All angels do. They're lit up from within, and in my cell the angel Lucifer burned like a lightning storm.

"He looked at me. And he named me.

"'You are Raguel,' he said. 'The Vengeance of the Lord.'

"I bowed my head, because I knew it was true. That was my name. That was my function.

"'There has been a . . . a wrong thing,' he said. 'The first of its kind. You are needed.'

"He turned and pushed himself into space, and I followed him, flew behind him across the Silver City, to the outskirts, where the City stops and the Darkness begins; and it was there, under a vast silver spire, that we descended to the street, and I saw the dead angel.

"The body lay, crumpled and broken, on the silver sidewalk. Its wings were crushed underneath it and a few loose feathers had already blown into the silver gutter.

"The body was almost dark. Now and again a light would flash inside it, an occasional flicker of cold fire in the chest, or in the eyes, or in the sexless groin, as the last of the glow of life left it for ever.

"Blood pooled in rubies on its chest and stained its white wing-feathers crimson. It was very beautiful, even in death.

"It would have broken your heart.

"Lucifer spoke to me, then. 'You must find who was responsible for this, and how; and take the Vengeance of the Name on whomever caused this thing to happen.'

"He really didn't have to say anything. I knew that already. The hunt, and the retribution: it was what I was created for, in the Beginning; it was what I *was.*

"'I have work to attend to,' said the angel Lucifer.

"He flapped his wings, once, hard, and rose upwards; the gust of wind sent the dead angel's loose feathers blowing across the street.

"I leaned down to examine the body. All luminescence had by now left it. It was a dark thing; a parody of an angel. It had a perfect, sexless face, framed by silver hair. One of the eyelids was open, revealing a placid grey eye; the other was closed. There were no nipples on the chest and only smoothness between the legs.

"I lifted the body up.

"The back of the angel was a mess. The wings were broken and twisted; the back of the head staved in; there was a floppiness to the corpse that made me think its spine had been broken as well. The back of the angel was all blood.

"The only blood on its front was in the chest area. I probed it with my forefinger, and it entered the body without difficulty.

"*He fell,* I thought. *And he was dead before he fell.*

"And I looked up at the windows that ranked the street. I stared across the Silver City. *You did this,* I thought. *I will find you, whoever you are. And I will take the Lord's vengeance upon you.*"

The man took the cigarette stub from behind his ear, lit it with a match. Briefly I smelled the ashtray smell of a dead cigarette, acrid and harsh; then he pulled down to the unburnt tobacco, exhaled blue smoke into the night air.

"The angel who had first discovered the body was called Phanuel.

"I spoke to him in the Hall of Being. That was the spire beside which the dead angel lay. In the Hall hung the . . . the blueprints, maybe, for what was going to be . . . all this." He gestured with the hand that held the stubby cigarette, pointing to the night sky and the parked cars and the world. "You know. The universe."

"Phanuel was the senior designer; working under him were a multitude of angels labouring on the details of the Creation. I watched him from the floor of the hall. He hung in the air below the Plan, and angels flew down to him, waiting politely in turn as they asked him questions, checked things with him, invited comment on their work. Eventually he left them, and descended to the floor.

"'You are Raguel,' he said. His voice was high, and fussy. 'What need have you of me?'

"'You found the body?'

"'Poor Carasel? Indeed I did. I was leaving the hall—there are a number of concepts we are currently constructing, and I wished to ponder one of them,—*Regret* by name. I was planning to get a little distance from the City—to fly above it, I mean, not to go into the Dark outside, I wouldn't do that, although there has been a some loose talk amongst . . . but, yes. I was going to rise, and contemplate.

"'I left the Hall, and . . . ,' he broke off. He was small, for an angel. His light was muted, but his eyes were vivid and bright. I mean really bright. 'Poor Carasel. How could he do that to himself? How?'

"'You think his destruction was self-inflicted?'

"He seemed puzzled—surprised that there could be any other explanation. 'But of course. Carasel was working under me, developing a number of concepts that shall be intrinsic to the Universe, when its Name shall be spoken. His group did a remarkable job on some of the real basics—*Dimension* was one, and *Sleep* another. There were others.

"'Wonderful work. Some of his suggestions regarding the use of individual viewpoints to define dimensions were truly ingenious.

"'Anyway He had begun work on a new project. It's one of the really major ones—the ones that I would usually handle, or possibly even Zephkiel' He glanced upward. 'But Carasel had done such sterling work. And his last project was so remarkable. Something apparently quite trivial, that he and Saraquael elevated into . . .' He shrugged. 'But that is unimportant. It was this project that forced him into non-being. But none of us could ever have foreseen . . .'

"'What was his current project?'

"Phanuel stared at me. 'I'm not sure I ought to tell you. All the new concepts are considered sensitive, until we get them into the final form in which they will be Spoken.'

"I felt myself transforming. I am not sure how I can explain it to you, but suddenly I wasn't me—I was something larger. I was transfigured: I was my function.

"Phanuel was unable to meet my gaze.

"'I am Raguel, who is the Vengeance of the Lord,' I told him. 'I serve the Name directly. It is my mission to discover the nature of this deed, and to take the Name's vengeance on those responsible. My questions are to be answered.'

"The little angel trembled, and he spoke fast.

"'Carasel and his partner were researching *Death*. Cessation of life. An end to physical, animated existence. They were putting it all together. But

Carasel always went too far into his work—we had a terrible time with him when he was designing *Agitation*. That was when he was working on *Emotions* . . .'

"'You think Carasel died to—to research the phenomenon?'

"'Or because it intrigued him. Or because he followed his research just too far. Yes.' Phanuel flexed his fingers, stared at me with those brightly shining eyes. 'I trust that you will repeat none of this to any unauthorised persons, Raguel.'

"'What did you do when you found the body?'

"'I came out of the Hall, as I said, and there was Carasel on the side-walk, staring up. I asked him what he was doing and he did not reply. Then I noticed the inner fluid, and that Carasel seemed unable, rather than unwilling, to talk to me.

"'I was scared. I did not know what to do.

"The Angel Lucifer came up behind me. He asked me if there was some kind of problem. I told him. I showed him the body And then . . . then his Aspect came upon him, and he communed with the Name. He burned so bright.

"'Then he said he had to fetch the one whose function embraced events like this, and he left—to seek you, I imagine.

"'As Carasel's death was now being dealt with, and his fate was no real concern of mine, I returned to work, having gained a new—and I sus-pect, quite valuable—perspective on the mechanics of *Regret*.

"'I am considering taking *Death* away from the Carasel and Saraquael partnership. I may reassign it to Zephkiel, my senior partner, if he is will-ing to take it on. He excels on contemplative projects!'

"By now there was a line of angels waiting to talk to Phanuel. I felt I had almost all I was going to get from him.

"'Who did Carasel work with? Who would have been the last to see him alive?'

"'You could talk to Saraquael, I suppose—he was his partner, after all. Now, if you'll excuse me . . .'

"He returned to his swarm of aides: advising, correcting, suggesting, forbidding."

The man paused.

The street was quiet, now; I remember the low whisper of his voice, the buzz of a cricket somewhere. A small animal—a cat perhaps, or some-thing more exotic, a raccoon, or even a jackal—darted from shadow to shadow among the parked cars on the opposite side of the street.

"Saraquael was in the highest of the mezzanine galleries that ringed the Hall of Being. As I said, the Universe was in the middle of the Hall, and it glinted and sparkled and shone. Went up quite a way, too . . ."

"The Universe you mention, it was, what, a diagram?" I asked, interrupting for the first time.

"Not really. Kind of. Sorta. It was a blueprint; but it was full-sized, and it hung in the Hall, and all these angels went around and fiddled with it all the time. Doing stuff with *Gravity*, and *Music* and *Klar* and whatever. It wasn't really the universe, not yet. It would be, when it was finished, and it was time for it to be properly Named."

"But . . ." I grasped for words to express my confusion. The man interrupted me.

"Don't worry about it. Think of it as a model, if that makes it easier for you. Or a map. Or a—what's the word? Prototype. Yeah. A Model-T Ford universe." He grinned. "You got to understand, a lot of the stuff I'm telling you, I'm translating already; putting it in a form you can understand. Otherwise I couldn't tell the story at all. You want to hear it?"

"Yes." I didn't care if it was true or not; it was a story I needed to hear all the way through to the end.

"Good. So shut up and listen.

"So I met Saraquael, in the topmost gallery. There was no one else about—just him, and some papers, and some small, glowing models.

"'I've come about Carasel,' I told him.

"He looked at me. 'Carasel isn't here at this time,' he said. 'I expect him to return shortly.'

"I shook my head.

"'Carasel won't be coming back. He's stopped existing as a spiritual entity,' I said.

"His light paled, and his eyes opened very wide. 'He's dead?'

"'That's what I said. Do you have any ideas about how it happened?'

"'I . . . this is so sudden. I mean, he'd been talking about . . . but I had no idea that he would . . .'

"'Take it slowly.'

"Saraquael nodded.

"He stood up and walked to the window. There was no view of the Silver City from his window—just a reflected glow from the City and the sky behind us, hanging in the air, and beyond that, the Dark. The wind from the Dark gently caressed Saraquael's hair as he spoke. I stared at his back.

"'Carasel is . . . no, was. That's right, isn't it? *Was.* He was always so involved. And so creative. But it was never enough for him. He always wanted to understand everything—to experience what he was working on. He was never content to just create it—to understand it intellectually. He wanted *all* of it.

"'That wasn't a problem before, when we were working on properties of matter. But when we began to design some of the Named emotions . . . he got too involved with his work.

"'And our latest project was *Death.* It's one of the hard ones—one of the big ones, too, I suspect. Possibly it may even become the attribute that's going to define the Creation for the Created: if not for *Death,* they'd be content to simply exist, but with *Death,* well, their lives will have meaning—a boundary beyond which the living cannot cross . . .'

"'So you think he killed himself?'

"'I know he did,' said Saraquael. I walked to the window, and looked out. Far below, a *long* way, I could see a tiny white dot. That was Carasel's body I'd have to arrange for someone to take care of it. I wondered what we would do with it; but there would be someone who would know, whose function was the removal of unwanted things. It was not my function. I knew that.

"'How?'

"He shrugged. 'I know. Recently he'd begun asking questions—questions about *Death.* How we could know whether or not it was right to make this thing, to set the rules, if we were not going to experience it ourselves. He kept talking about it!

"'Didn't you wonder about this?'

"Saraquael turned, for the first time, to look at me. 'No. That *is* our function—to discuss, to improvise, to aid the Creation and the Created. We sort it out now, so that when it all Begins, it'll run like clockwork. Right now we're working on *Death.* So obviously that's what we look at. The physical aspect; the emotional aspect; the philosophical aspect . . .

"'And the *patterns.* Carasel had the notion that what we do here in the Hall of Being creates patterns. That there are structures and shapes appropriate to beings and events that, once begun, must continue until they reach their end. For us, perhaps, as well as for them. Conceivably he felt this was one of his patterns.'

"'Did you know Carasel well?'

"'As well as any of us know each other. We saw each other here; we

worked side by side. At certain times I would retire to my cell, across the
city. Sometimes he would do the same.'

"'Tell me about Phanuel.'

"His mouth crooked into a smile. 'He's officious. Doesn't do much—
farms everything out, and takes all the credit.' He lowered his voice,
although there was no other soul in the gallery. 'To hear him talk, you'd
think that Love was all his own work. But to his credit, he does make sure
the work gets done. Zephkiel's the real thinker of the two senior design-
ers, but he doesn't come here. He stays back in his cell in the City, and
contemplates; resolves problems from a distance. If you need to speak to
Zephkiel, you go to Phanuel, and Phanuel relays your questions to
Zephkiel . . .'

"I cut him short. 'How about Lucifer? Tell me about him.'

"'Lucifer? The Captain of the Host? He doesn't work here . . . He has
visited the Hall a couple of times, though—inspecting the Creation. They
say he reports directly to the Name. I have never spoken to him.'

"'Did he know Carasel?'

"'I doubt it. As I said, he has only been here twice. I have seen him
on other occasions, though. Through here.' He flicked a wingtip, indicat-
ing the world outside the window. 'In flight.'

"'Where to?'

"Saraquael seemed to be about to say something; then he changed his
mind. 'I don't know.'

"I looked out of the window, at the Darkness outside the Silver City.

"'I may want to talk with you some more, later,' I told Saraquael.

"'Very good.' I turned to go.

"'Sir? Do you know if they will be assigning me another partner? For
Death?'

"'No,' I told him. 'I'm afraid I don't.'

"In the centre of the Silver City was a park—a place of recreation and
rest. I found the Angel Lucifer there, beside a river. He was just standing,
watching the water flow.

"'Lucifer?'

"He inclined his head. 'Raguel. Are you making progress?'

"'I don't know. Maybe. I need to ask you a few questions. Do you
mind?"

"'Not at all.'

"'How did you come upon the body?'

"'I didn't. Not exactly. I saw Phanuel, standing in the street. He looked distressed. I enquired whether there was something wrong, and he showed me the dead angel. And I fetched you.'

"'I see.'

"He leaned down, let one hand enter the cold water of the river. The water splashed and rilled around it. 'Is that all?'

"'Not quite. What were you doing in that part of the City?'

"'I don't see what business that is of yours.'

"'It is my business, Lucifer. What were you doing there?'

"'I was . . . walking. I do that sometimes. Just walk, and think. And try to understand.' He shrugged.

"'You walk on the edge of the City?'

"A beat, then, 'Yes.'

"'That's all I want to know. For now.'

"'Who else have you talked to?'

"'Carasel's boss, and his partner. They both feel that he killed himself—ended his own life.'

"'Who else are you going to talk to?'

"I looked up. The spires of the City of the Angels towered above us. 'Maybe everyone.'

"'All of them?'

"'If I need to. It's my function. I cannot rest until I understand what happened, and until the vengeance of the Name has been taken on whomever was responsible. But I'll tell you something I do know.'

"'What would that be?' Drops of water fell like diamonds from the angel Lucifer's perfect fingers.

"'Carasel did not kill himself!

"'How do you know that?'

"'I am Vengeance. If Carasel had died by his own hand,' I explained to the Captain of the Heavenly Host, 'there would have been no call for me. Would there?'

"He did not reply.

"I flew upwards, into the light of the eternal morning.

"You got another cigarette on you?"

I fumbled out the red and white packet, handed him a cigarette.

"Obliged.

"Zephkiel's cell was larger than mine.

"It wasn't a place for waiting. It was a place to live, and work, and be. It was lined with books, and scrolls, and papers, and there were images and representations on the walls: pictures. I'd never seen a picture before.

"In the centre of the room was a large chair, and Zephkiel sat there, his eyes closed, his head back.

"As I approached him he opened his eyes.

"They burned no brighter than the eyes of any of the other angels I had seen, but somehow, they seemed to have seen more. It was something about the way he looked. I'm not sure I can explain it. And he had no wings.

"'Welcome, Raguel,' he said. He sounded tired.

"'You are Zephkiel?' I don't know why I asked him that. I mean, I knew who people were. It's part of my function, I guess. Recognition. I know who *you* are.

"'Indeed. You are staring, Raguel. I have no wings, it is true, but then, my function does not call for me to leave this cell. I remain here, and I ponder. Phanuel reports back to me, brings me the new things, for my opinion. He brings me the problems, and I think about them, and occasionally I make myself useful by making some small suggestions. That is my function. As yours is vengeance.'

"'Yes.'

"'You are here about the death of the angel Carasel?'

"'Yes.'

"'I did not kill him.'

"When he said it, I knew it was true.

"'Do you know who did?'

"'That is *your* function, is it not? To discover who killed the poor thing, and to take the Vengeance of the Name upon him.'

"'Yes.'

"He nodded.

"'What do you want to know?'

"I paused, reflecting on what I had heard that day. 'Do you know what Lucifer was doing in that part of the City, before the body was found?'

"The old angel stared at me. 'I can hazard a guess.'

"'Yes?'

"'He was walking in the Dark.'

"I nodded. I had a shape in my mind, now. Something I could almost grasp. I asked the last question:

"'What can you tell me about *Love*?'

"And he told me. And I thought I had it all.

"I returned to the place where Carasel's body had been. The remains had been removed, the blood had been cleaned away, the stray feathers collected and disposed of. There was nothing on the silver sidewalk to indicate it had ever been there. But I knew where it had been.

"I ascended on my wings, flew upward until I neared the top of the spire of the Hall of Being. There was a window there, and I entered.

"Saraquael was working there, putting a wingless mannikin into a small box. On one side of the box was a representation of a small brown creature, with eight legs. On the other was a representation of a white blossom.

"'Saraquael?'

"'Hm? Oh, it's you. Hello. Look at this: if you were to die, and to be, let us say, put into the earth in a box, which would you want laid on top of you—a spider, here, or a lily, here?'

"'The lily, I suppose.'

"'Yes, that's what I think, too. But why? I wish . . .' He raised a hand to his chin, stared down at the two models, put first one on top of the box then the other, experimentally. 'There's so much to do, Raguel. So much to get right. And we only get one chance at it, you know. There'll just be one universe—we can't keep trying until we get it right. I wish I understood why all this was so important to Him . . .'

"'Do you know where Zephkiel's cell is?' I asked him.

"'Yes. I mean, I've never been there. But I know where it is.'

"'Good. Go there. He'll be expecting you. I will meet you there.'

"He shook his head. 'I have work to do. I can't just . . .'

"I felt my function come upon me. I looked down at him, and I said, 'You will be there. Go now.'

"He said nothing. He backed away from me, toward the window, staring at me; then he turned, and flapped his wings, and I was alone.

"I walked to the central well of the Hall, and let myself fall, tumbling down through the model of the universe: it glittered around me, unfamiliar colours and shapes seething and writhing without meaning.

"As I approached the bottom, I beat my wings, slowing my descent, and stepped lightly onto the silver floor. Phanuel stood between two angels, who were both trying to claim his attention.

"'I don't care how aesthetically pleasing it would be,' he was explaining to one of them. 'We simply cannot put it in the centre. Background radiation would prevent any possible life-forms from even getting a foothold; and anyway, it's too unstable.'

"He turned to the other. 'Okay, let's see it. Hmm. So that's *Green*, is it?

It's not exactly how I'd imagined it, but. Mm. Leave it with me. I'll get back to you.' He took a paper from the angel, folded it over decisively.

"He turned to me. His manner was brusque, and dismissive. 'Yes?'

"'I need to talk to you.'

"'Mm? Well, make it quick. I have much to do. If this is about Carasel's death, I have told you all I know!

"'It is about Carasel's death. But I will not speak to you now. Not here. Go to Zephkiel's cell: he is expecting you. I will meet you there.'

"He seemed about to say something, but he only nodded, walked toward the door.

"I turned to go, when something occurred to me. I stopped the angel who had the *Green*. 'Tell me something.'

"'If I can, sir.'

"'That thing.' I pointed to the Universe. 'What's it going to be *for*?'

"'For? Why, it is the Universe.'

"'I know what it's called. But what purpose will it serve?'

"He frowned. 'It is part of the plan. The Name wishes it; He requires *such and such*, to these dimensions, and having *such and such* properties and ingredients. It is our function to bring it into existence, according to His wishes. I am sure He knows its function, but He has not revealed it to me.' His tone was one of gentle rebuke.

"I nodded, and left that place.

"High above the City a phalanx of angels wheeled and circled and dove. Each held a flaming sword which trailed a streak of burning brightness behind it, dazzling the eye. They moved in unison through the salmon-pink sky They were very beautiful. It was—you know on summer evenings, when you get whole flocks of birds performing their dances in the sky? Weaving and circling and clustering and breaking apart again, so just as you think you understand the pattern, you realise you don't, and you never will? It was like that, only better.

"Above me was the sky. Below me, the shining City. My home. And outside the City, the Dark.

"Lucifer hovered a little below the Host, watching their maneuvers.

"'Lucifer?'

"'Yes, Raguel? Have you discovered your malefactor?'

"'I think so. Will you accompany me to Zephkiel's cell? There are others waiting for us there, and I will explain everything.'

"He paused. Then, 'Certainly.'

"He raised his perfect face to the angels, now performing a slow revolution in the sky, each moving through the air keeping perfect pace with the next, none of them ever touching. 'Azazel!'

"An angel broke from the circle; the others adjusted almost imperceptibly to his disappearance, filling the space, so you could no longer see where he had been.

"'I have to leave. You are in command, Azazel. Keep them drilling. They still have much to perfect.'

"'Yes, sir.'

"Azazel hovered where Lucifer had been, staring up at the flock of angels, and Lucifer and I descended toward the city.

"'He's my second-in-command,' said Lucifer. 'Bright. Enthusiastic. Azazel would follow you anywhere.'

"'What are you training them for?'

"'War.'

"'With whom?'

"'How do you mean?'

"'Who are they going to fight? Who else is there?'

"He looked at me; his eyes were clear, and honest. 'I do not know. But He has Named us to be His army. So we will be perfect. For Him. The Name is infallible and all-just, and all-wise, Raguel. It cannot be other-wise, no matter what—' He broke off, and looked away.

"'You were going to say?'

"'It is of no importance.'

"'Ah.'

"We did not talk for the rest of the descent to Zephkiel's cell."

I looked at my watch: it was almost three. A chill breeze had begun to blow down the LA street, and I shivered. The man noticed, and he paused in his story. "You okay?" he asked.

"I'm fine. Please carry on. I'm fascinated."

He nodded.

"They were waiting for us in Zephkiel's cell: Phanuel, Saraquael, and Zephkiel. Zephkiel was sitting in his chair. Lucifer took up a position beside the window.

"I walked to centre of the room, and I began.

"'I thank you all for coming here. You know who I am; you know my function. I am the Vengeance of the Name: the arm of the Lord. I am Raguel.

"'The angel Carasel is dead. It was given to me to find out why he died, who killed him. This I have done. Now, the angel Carasel was a designer in the Hall of Being. He was very good, or so I am told . . .

"'Lucifer. Tell me what you were doing, before you came upon Phanuel, and the body.'

"'I have told you already I was walking.'

"'Where were you walking?'

"'I do not see what business that is of yours.'

"'*Tell me.*'

"He paused. He was taller than any of us; tall, and proud. 'Very well. I was walking in the Dark. I have been walking in the Darkness for some time now. It helps me to gain a perspective on the City—being outside it. I see how fair it is, how perfect. There is nothing more enchanting than our home. Nothing more complete. Nowhere else that anyone would want to be.'

"'And what do you do in the Dark, Lucifer?'

"He stared at me. 'I walk. And . . . there are voices, in the Dark. I listen to the voices. They promise me things, ask me questions, whisper and plead. And I ignore them. I steel myself and I gaze at the City. It is the only way I have of testing myself—putting myself to any kind of trial. I am the Captain of the Host; I am the first among the Angels, and I must prove myself.'

"I nodded. 'Why did you not tell me this before?'

"He looked down. 'Because I am the only angel who walks in the Dark. Because I do not want others to walk in the Dark: I am strong enough to challenge the voices, to test myself. Others are not so strong. Others might stumble, or fall.'

"'Thank you, Lucifer. That is all, for now.' I turned to the next angel. 'Phanuel. How long have you been taking credit for Carasel's work?'

"His mouth opened, but no sound came out.

"'Well?'

"'I . . . I would not take credit for another's work.'

"'But you did take credit for *Love*?'

"He blinked. 'Yes. I did.'

"'Would you care to explain to us all what *Love* is?' I asked.

"He glanced around uncomfortably. 'It's a feeling of deep affection and attraction for another being, often combined with passion or desire—a need to be with another.' He spoke dryly, didactically, as if he were reciting a mathematical formula. 'The feeling that we have for the Name, for our Creator—that is *Love* . . . amongst other things. *Love* will be an

impulse which will inspire and ruin in equal measure. We are . . .' He
paused, then began once more. 'We are very proud of it.'

"He was mouthing the words. He no longer seemed to hold any hope
that we would believe them.

"'Who did the majority of the work on *Love*? No, don't answer. Let me
ask the others first. Zephkiel? When Phanuel passed the details on *Love*
to you for approval, who did he tell you was responsible for it?'

"The wingless angel smiled gently. 'He told me it was his project.'

"'Thank you, sir. Now, Saraquael: whose was *Love*?'

"'Mine. Mine and Carasel's. Perhaps more his than mine, but we
worked on it together.'

"'You knew that Phanuel was claiming the credit for it?'

"'. . . Yes.'

"'And you permitted this?'

"'He—he promised us that he would give us a good project of our
own to follow. He promised that if we said nothing we would be given
more big projects—and he was true to his word. He gave us *Death*.'

"I turned back to Phanuel. 'Well?'

"'It is true that I claimed that *Love* was mine.'

"'But it was Carasel's. And Saraquael's.'

"'Yes.'

"'Their last project—before *Death*?'

"'Yes.'

"'That is all.'

"I walked over to the window, looked out at the silver spires, looked
at the Dark. And I began to speak.

"'Carasel was a remarkable designer. If he had one failing, it was that
he threw himself too deeply into his work.' I turned back to them. The
angel Saraquael was shivering, and lights were flickering beneath his skin.
'Saraquael? Who did Carasel love? Who was his lover?'

"He stared at the floor. Then he stared up, proudly, aggressively. And
he smiled.

"'I was.'

"'Do you want to tell me about it?"

"'No.' A shrug. 'But I suppose I must. Very well, then.

"'We worked together. And when we began to work on *Love* . . . we
became lovers. It was his idea. We would go back to his cell, whenever
we could snatch the time. There we touched each other, held each other,
whispered endearments and protestations of eternal devotion. His welfare

mattered more to me than my own. I existed for him. When I was alone I would repeat his name to myself, and think of nothing but him.

"'When I was with him . . .' He paused. He looked down. '. . . Nothing else mattered.'

"I walked to where Saraquael stood; lifted his chin with my hand, stared into his grey eyes. 'Then why did you kill him?'

"'Because he would no longer love me. When we started to work on *Death* he—he lost interest. He was no longer mine. He belonged to *Death*. And if I could not have him, then his new lover was welcome to him. I could not bear his presence—I could not endure to have him near me and to know that he felt nothing for me. That was what hurt the most. I thought . . . I hoped . . . that if he was gone then I would no longer care for him—that the pain would stop.

"'So I killed him; I stabbed him, and I threw his body from our window in the Hall of Being. But the pain has *not* stopped.' It was almost a wail.

"Saraquael reached up, removed my hand from his chin. 'Now what?'

"I felt my aspect begin to come upon me; felt my function possess me. I was no longer an individual—I was the Vengeance of the Lord.

"I moved close to Saraquael, and embraced him. I pressed my lips to his, forced my tongue into his mouth. We kissed. He closed his eyes.

"I felt it well up within me then: a burning, a brightness. From the corner of my eyes, I could see Lucifer and Phanuel averting their faces from my light; I could feel Zephkiel's stare. And my light became brighter and brighter, until it erupted—from my eyes, from my chest, from my fingers, from my lips: a white, searing fire.

"The white flames consumed Saraquael slowly, and he clung to me as he burned.

"Soon there was nothing left of him. Nothing at all.

"I felt the flame leave me. I returned to myself once more.

"Phanuel was sobbing. Lucifer was pale. Zephkiel sat in his chair, quietly watching me.

"I turned to Phanuel and Lucifer. 'You have seen the Vengeance of the Lord,' I told them. 'Let it act as a warning to you both.'

"Phanuel nodded. 'It has. Oh it has. I, I will be on my way, sir. I will return to my appointed post. If that is all right with you?'

"'Go.'

"He stumbled to the window, and plunged into the light, his wings beating furiously.

"Lucifer walked over to the place on the silver floor where Saraquael had once stood. He knelt, stared desperately at the floor as if he were trying to find some remnant of the angel I had destroyed: a fragment of ash, or bone, or charred feather; but there was nothing to find. Then he looked up at me.

"'That was not right,' he said. 'That was not just.' He was crying; wet tears ran down his face. Perhaps Saraquael was the first to love, but Lucifer was the first to shed tears. I will never forget that.

"I stared at him, impassively. 'It was justice. He killed another. He was killed in his turn. You called me to my function, and I performed it.'

"'But . . . he *loved*. He should have been forgiven. He should have been helped. He should not have been destroyed like that. That was *wrong*.'

"'It was His will.'

"Lucifer stood. 'Then perhaps His will is unjust. Perhaps the voices in the Darkness speak truly after all. How *can* this be right?'

"'It is right. It is His will. I merely performed my function.'

"He wiped away the tears, with the back of his hand. 'No,' he said, flatly. He shook his head, slowly, from side to side. Then he said, 'I must think on this. I will go now.'

"He walked to the window, stepped into the sky, and he was gone.

"Zephkiel and I were alone in his cell. I went over to his chair. He nodded at me. 'You have performed your function well, Raguel. Shouldn't you return to your cell, to wait until you are next needed?'"

The man on the bench turned towards me: his eyes sought mine. Until now it had seemed—for most of his narrative—that he was scarcely aware of me; he had stared ahead of himself, whispered his tale in little better than a monotone. Now it felt as if he had discovered me, and that he spoke to me alone, rather than to the air, or the City of Los Angeles. And he said:

"I knew that he was right. But I *couldn't* have left then—not even if I had wanted to. My aspect had not entirely left me; my function was not completely fulfilled. And then it fell into place; I saw the whole picture. And like Lucifer, I knelt. I touched my forehead to the silver floor. 'No, Lord,' I said. 'Not yet.'

"Zephkiel rose from his chair. 'Get up. It is not fitting for one angel to act in this way to another. It is not right. Get up!'

"I shook my head. 'Father, You are no angel,' I whispered.

"Zephkiel said nothing. For a moment my heart misgave within me.

I was afraid. 'Father, I was charged to discover who was responsible for Carasel's death. And I do know.'

"'You have taken your vengeance, Raguel.'

"'*Your* vengeance, Lord.'

"And then He sighed, and sat down once more. 'Ah, little Raguel. The problem with creating things is that they perform so much better than one had ever planned. Shall I ask how you recognised me?'

"'I . . . I am not certain, Lord. You have no wings. You wait at the centre of the City, supervising the Creation directly. When I destroyed Saraquael, You did not look away. You know too many things. You . . .' I paused, and thought. 'No, I do not know how I know. As You say, You have created me well. But I only understood who You were and the meaning of the drama we had enacted here for You, when I saw Lucifer leave.'

"'What did you understand, child?'

"'Who killed Carasel. Or at least, who was pulling the strings. For example, who arranged for Carasel and Saraquael to work together on *Love*, knowing Carasel's tendency to involve himself too deeply in his work?'

"He was speaking to me gently, almost teasingly, as an adult would pretend to make conversation with a tiny child. 'Why should anyone have "pulled the strings," Raguel?'

"'Because nothing occurs without reason; and all the reasons are Yours. You set Saraquael up: yes, he killed Carasel. But he killed Carasel so that *I* could destroy *him*.'

"'And were you wrong to destroy him?'

"I looked into His old, old eyes. 'It was my function. But I do not think it was just. I think perhaps it was needed that I destroy Saraquael, in order to demonstrate to Lucifer the Injustice of the Lord.'

"He smiled, then. 'And whatever reason would I have for doing that?'

"'I . . . I do not know. I do not understand—no more than I understand why You created the Dark, or the voices in the Darkness. But You did. You caused all this to occur.'

"He nodded. 'Yes. I did. Lucifer must brood on the unfairness of Saraquael's destruction. And that—amongst other things—will precipitate him into certain actions. Poor sweet Lucifer. His way will be the hardest of all my children; for there is a part he must play in the drama that is to come, and it is a grand role.'

"I remained kneeling in front of the Creator of All Things.

"'What will you do now, Raguel?' He asked me.

"'I must return to my cell. My function is now fulfilled. I have taken vengeance, and I have revealed the perpetrator. That is enough. But— Lord?'

"'Yes, child.'

"'I feel dirty. I feel tarnished. I feel befouled. Perhaps it is true that all that happens is in accordance with Your will, and thus it is good. But sometimes You leave blood on Your instruments.'

"He nodded, as if He agreed with me. 'If you wish, Raguel, you may forget all this. All that has happened this day.' And then He said, 'However, you will not be able to speak of this to any other angels, whether you choose to remember it or not.'

"'I will remember it.'

"'It is your choice. But sometimes you will find it is easier by far not to remember. Forgetfulness can sometimes bring freedom, of a sort. Now, if you do not mind,' He reached down, took a file from a stack on the floor, opened it, '— there is work I should be getting on with.'

"I stood up and walked to the window. I hoped He would call me back, explain every detail of His plan to me, somehow make it all better. But He said nothing, and I left His Presence without ever looking back."

The man was silent, then. And he remained silent—I couldn't even hear him breathing—for so long that I began to get nervous, thinking that perhaps he had fallen asleep, or died.

Then he stood up.

"There you go, pal. That's your story. Do you think it was worth a couple of cigarettes and a book of matches?" He asked the question as if it was important to him, without irony.

"Yes," I told him. "Yes. It was. But what happened next? How did you . . . I mean, if . . ." I trailed off.

It was dark on the street, now, at the edge of daybreak. One by one the streetlights had begun to flicker out, and he was silhouetted against the glow of the dawn sky. He thrust his hands into his pockets. "What happened? I left home, and I lost my way, and these days home's a long way back. Sometimes you do things you regret, but there's nothing you can do about them. Times change. Doors close behind you. You move on. You know?

"Eventually I wound up here. They used to say no one's ever originally from LA. True as Hell in my case."

And then, before I could understand what he was doing, he leaned down and kissed me, gently, on the cheek. His stubble was rough and prickly, but his breath was surprisingly sweet. He whispered into my ear: 'I never fell. I don't care what they say. I'm still doing my job, as I see it.'

My cheek burned where his lips had touched it.

He straightened up. "But I still want to go home."

The man walked away down the darkened street, and I sat on the bench and watched him go. I felt like he had taken something from me, although I could no longer remember what. And I felt like something had been left in its place—absolution, perhaps, or innocence, although of what, or from what, I could no longer say.

An image from somewhere: a scribbled drawing, of two angels in flight above a perfect city; and over the image a child's perfect handprint, which stains the white paper blood-red. It came into my head unbidden, and I no longer know what it meant.

I stood up.

It was too dark to see the face of my watch, but I knew I would get no sleep that day I walked back to the place I was staying, to the house by the stunted palm tree, to wash myself, and to wait. I thought about angels, and about Tink; and I wondered whether love and death went hand in hand.

The next day the planes to England were flying again.

I felt strange—lack of sleep had forced me into that miserable state in which everything seems flat and of equal importance; when nothing matters, and in which reality seems scraped thin and threadbare. The taxi journey to the airport was a nightmare. I was hot, and tired, and testy. I wore a T-shirt in the LA heat; my coat was packed at the bottom of my luggage, where it had been for the entire stay.

The airplane was crowded, but I didn't care.

The stewardess walked down the aisle with a rack of newspapers: the *Herald Tribune*, *USA Today*, and the *LA Times*. I took a copy of the *Times*, but the words left my head as my eyes scanned over them. Nothing that I read remained with me. No, I lie: somewhere in the back of the paper was a report of a triple murder: two women, and a small child. No names were given, and I do not know why the report should have registered as it did.

Soon I fell asleep. I dreamed about fucking Tink, while blood ran sluggishly from her closed eyes and lips. The blood was cold and viscous and clammy, and I awoke chilled by the plane's air-conditioning, with an unpleasant taste in my mouth. My tongue and lips were dry. I looked out of the scratched oval window, stared down at the clouds, and it occurred to me then (not for the first time) that the clouds were in actuality another land, where everyone knew just what they were looking for and how to get back where they started from.

Staring down at the clouds is one of the things I have always liked best about flying. That, and the proximity one feels to one's death.

I wrapped myself in the thin aircraft blanket, and slept some more, but if further dreams came then they made no impression upon me.

A blizzard blew up shortly after the plane landed in England, knocking out the airport's power supply. I was alone in an airport elevator at the time, and it went dark and jammed between floors. A dim emergency light flickered on. I pressed the crimson alarm button until the batteries ran down and it ceased to sound; then I shivered in my LA T-shirt, in the corner of my little silver room. I watched my breath steam in the air, and I hugged myself for warmth.

There wasn't anything in there except me; but even so, I felt safe, and secure. Soon someone would come and force open the doors. Eventually somebody would let me out; and I knew that I would soon be home.

The Bishop and the Hit Man
A Blackie Ryan Story

Andrew Greeley

"I've put down thirty-two men, Father," he told me. "I could give you all their names . . ."

"That won't be necessary," I assured him.

I have often argued that if the rule of celibacy is to be lifted partially for Catholic priests but only for a certain period each week, Sunday night would be the appropriate time. In a dark and lonely rectory, quiet for the only night of the week, the priest who mans the fort feels that he is isolated from the human condition. This is especially true if the rectory is a monumental monstrosity like that of Holy Name Cathedral, a place which at the best of times is filled with silent emanations from the past and an occasional spirit of a departed bishop—or even Cardinal—is said to walk the corridors.

I've never seen one such, however, being the most empirical and pragmatic of men.

It is perhaps an appropriate time and place to open the door at 720 North Wabash in the so-called Windy City (Richard M. Daley, mayor, and Michael Jordan, owner) and encounter a self-professed hit man.

"I don't know," he continued. "Some of them probably deserved it.

But I never asked about that. Like in any line of work, you do what you're told and don't ask questions. It's my line of work, Father."

"Indeed."

He talked like a character in one of the many films about the Outfit (as we call it in Chicago). However he did not look like Robert De Niro or any of the other stars who appear in such films. He was trim, of medium height, and dressed in a conservative three-piece charcoal gray suit (with a faint hint of a line in its weave). His thin brown hair receded only marginally from an utterly unremarkable face, and his skin was pale and bland. Only his hard blue eyes, innocent of emotion or mercy, suggested that he might be a psychopath.

"See this." He opened his expensive attaché case and revealed what looked like a toy weapon. "This is a twenty-five-millimeter automatic. Small, isn't it? Looks like a toy, huh? I don't carve any notches in, but I've put down ten men with it."

"Remarkable."

Who would put out a contract on an inoffensive little priest? I wondered.

"It's not loaded." He fitted an instrument which, from frequent attendance at the cinema, I identified as a silencer. "Some night soon I'm going to walk up behind Mr. Richard Powers as he's taking his walk down East Lake Shore Drive, confident that nothing can happen in that busy and affluent street, yell, 'Hey, Dick,' and put a bullet right between his eyes. No noise, no blood, no mess, and he's facing God."

"Astonishing."

He unfastened the silencer and put the gun away. My guardian angel and I began to breathe again.

"This is all under the seal of confession, isn't it?"

"As you wished."

When I had ushered him into the "counseling room" on the first floor of the Cathedral rectory and hung up his saturated raincoat he told me that he wanted to go to confession, a wish expressed less frequently now than it used to be because Catholics are freer from compulsions about minor matters ("I missed Mass on Sunday, but I was sick") than they used to be.

Multiple homicide was not, however, a minor matter.

"I'm the best there is in the country," my guest insisted. "No one is as neat or as professional as I am. Not a single arrest. The cops don't know who I am. Or where I live. Even my clients don't know who I am.

All the contact is indirect. My family and my neighbors think I have a small business, which I do as a cover. But this is my real line of work."

"Ah."

"I'm known only by my nickname—the Pro. Neat, isn't it?"

"Indeed."

"I don't do too many jobs anymore, Father. One, two a year, and that's all. I get two hundred big ones for each job, half on agreement, half on fulfillment. They don't want to pay that kind of money, they don't ask for the Pro, huh? A man needs that kind of money these days to put his kids through college, know what I mean?"

"A major expense."

"All my kids are in Catholic schools, Father. A boy in college, two high school kids, and one little doll that just made her First Communion. I'm raising them all to be good Catholics, Father."

"Admirable."

"I pray to God every night that they'll never find out what their daddy really does for a living."

Dickie Powers is not one of my favorite people. He is, not to put too fine an edge on things, to the right of Neil of the Nine Hostages, both politically and ecclesiastically. He presumes that because he's a highly successful developer (though he owns a lot of vacant land in our current recessionary times), he would more ably run the Archdiocese of Chicago than Sean Cardinal Cronin, presently, by the Grace of God and the impatient toleration of the Apostolic See, Archbishop of Chicago. Milord Cronin has a long record of more than holding his own against rich and conservative Catholics. However, Dick Powers also thinks that he knows more about how the Cathedral parish ought to be run—down to such tiny details as the Sunday Mass schedule—than the inoffensive and ineffectual little priest who actually does run it. And proposes to continue to run it. Democratically, of course.

His basic strategy for dealing with the problems the Church faces today is to purify it of all who may disagree with certain of its teachings.

"Throw out everyone who won't accept the birth control teaching! Get rid of them all! They're all going to hell anyway! We don't need them and don't want them!"

My problem with such a strategy is not merely that it would empty the Cathedral and that there would be no income to pay the heat and light bills and keep the schools (of which we have two) open. My problem is that even if we tried it, the laity would not leave. Despite Dickie

Powers, we no longer have an Inquisition available to turn the recalci-
trant over to the secular arm for suitable disposal.

I would not go so far as one of my young colleagues who, with lam-
entable lack of charity, remarked at the table the other night, "Dickie
Powers is one of the great assholes of the Western world."

I did not dispute the point, however.

"I don't know what this Powers guy did to offend my clients . . . you
can guess who they are, Father. Probably welched on a deal. My clients
don't like welchers. A deal is a deal, and if they let one guy get away
welching, then everyone would, isn't that so?"

"Arguably."

Recently Dickie had done something extraordinary which could
have increased the number of people who disliked him. He had taken
unto himself a new wife, twenty-five years younger than his fifty-five
years, his first wife having finally escaped him to her eternal reward—
helped by acute cirrhosis of the liver, in turn the result of, among other
things, chronic alcoholism.

"Being married to Dickie," Milord Cronin had remarked, again with
scandalous lack of charity, "would drive anyone to drink."

I may have added, "And a new wife would drive to the creature those
who have expectations of inheritance at the time of his departure for
whatever reward God may be planning for him."

To make matters worse for his allies on the Catholic right, Regina,
Dickie's intended young woman (as far as I can see quiet, presentable,
and intelligent and perhaps capable of taming Dickie), not only was not
of the household of the faith but had been married before—at twenty for
a brief period.

"I don't believe in those annulment things," Dickie had bellowed at
me. "So don't pull that stuff. Her first husband was a bastard. I want a
church wedding just like my first marriage."

Dickie was a big, strong, well-preserved man, handsome in a
rugged way with a square blunt face (usually red with anger) and thick
iron gray hair. His bride-to-be watched him intently, not with fear but
with admiration.

I explained that there would be certain difficulties since both his
bride-to-be and her first husband were baptized Christians. There were
some steps we might take—

"I don't want to take any steps," he had shouted. "I have been a good

Catholic all my life, and I demand to be married in this Church, by Father Martin, two weeks from today."

I don't make the current marriage rules for the Catholic Church, and I don't necessarily like them. But no way I was going to apply them to everyone else but Dickie Powers, a loudmouth shanty Irishman if I ever met one.

Nor, as far as I could see, would Father Martin, the head of a right-wing "secular institute," dare to violate publicly the Vatican's rules on such matters.

During the shouting match in my office (well, he was shouting anyway), I felt sorry for Regina, who knew nothing of our Church, was not seeing us at our best, and seemed astonished by the anger of her groom. I felt less sympathy with the Powers offspring, who had been brought along to the rectory for reasons that escaped me. Rick and Melissa—the sole issues of the marriage—smirked through the whole session, delighted at the spoke I had thrown into the wheel of their father's marriage bandwagon and triumphant over their prospective stepmother, to whom they blatantly refused to speak.

Both children were economically useless. Rick, an overweight, long-haired snob, who wanted passionately to produce "important" films, ran an "off-Loop" theater group which performed, with notable lack of critical or financial success, obscure modern plays, sometimes made more obscure because they were done in the original language—like Hungarian. Melissa, a brittle blonde, owned a boutique on Oak Street that sold, or rather did not sell, women's apparel that has been described to me by my nieces as "like totally *funky,* you know."

In that context the adjective was not spoken in admiration.

While he disapproved of the occupations of both his children and of their swinging-singles lifestyles, Dickie resolutely funded their efforts and kept them from not only starvation but the necessity of purchasing cheap liquor.

So Dickie and Regina were married in a civil ceremony by an elderly judge who was a friend of his. Most of the invited guests stayed away from the wedding, less for religious reasons than because they didn't like Dickie.

In addition to the union workers, who hated Dickie for hiring scabs, and the other developers, who resented his bidding tactics, and, according to my strange penitent, the Boys Out on the West Side, there were other actors who would benefit from his death before he changed his will to favor the new wife: Rick, Melissa, and Father Martin's happy little band of brothers, who were now, in alleged obedience to St. Paul and in imitation of the Amish, ostentatiously shunning their greatest benefactor.

"I've got cold feet for the first time in my life, Father," the hit man continued, his face narrowing into an anxious frown. "This is a tricky one. He'll probably have his own bodyguards, and there'll be cops, too. I've handled tough ones before, but this will be one of the toughest. What if they get me? What if I don't make it home?"

"Your children will know you are a criminal?"

"Nah. No one will link the hit man with me. I mean, they'll find out my real identity from my prints. But back home I'm someone else and no one has my prints." Tears appeared in his eyes. "As far as the wife and kids are concerned, I'll vanish from the face of the earth."

"Ah."

"No, what I'm scared about is God." He rubbed his hands together nervously. "God is pretty mad at me these days. He's not gonna like to see me when I show up. I don't figure I can cop a plea with him. It'll be curtains for me."

"You fear eternal damnation?"

"What else will I get? And no time off for good behavior either. I mean, I never really thought about dying before. I figured that I'd get a chance on my deathbed, and that way I'd make it. But what if I'm killed while I'm trying to hit someone else? Then it's the pit of hell for me, isn't it?"

I personally hold with the late Cardinal von Baltassar that salvation for everyone is not inconsistent with the Catholic tradition—and himself a favorite of the Pope at that. But I was not about to explain that position just at the moment.

"God's love is without limit," I said, "its fullness beyond our wildest imagination. One always gets second chances, opportunities to turn away from what separates us from God and to begin our life again."

"Yeah, Father"—he shook his head sadly—"but not professional killers."

"Yes, even mass murderers. Compared with some political leaders I might mention, you're small time."

"You mean, I might still make it?"

"Precisely."

"But what if I'm killed during the hit?"

"Cancel the hit, return the down payment, live off the income from your other business."

"My clients wouldn't like it, Father."

"I thought they couldn't find you."

"I'm a pro, Father. I do my work. I keep my promises. Besides, I need the money. I've got family expenses. I can't give it back. It costs a hell of a lot of money to put four kids through college."

"Nonetheless, you know you should get out of your line of work."

"I know that, Father. I know it. This will be the last one, I promise. Can you give me absolution now?"

"How can I invoke God's love to reconcile you with God's people when you tell me that you are going forth to kill someone?"

"Maybe he deserves to die."

"We all do, but in God's time."

"Yeah . . . but a job is a job. I'm a professional, Father. That's why they call me the Pro."

"You believe that God will accept that argument?"

Tears were pouring down his face. "Gee, how could He? I'm caught. Damned no matter what I do . . . You sure you can't give me absolution so I could receive Holy Communion tomorrow?"

I gave up on the new-fashioned theology of reconciliation and stated my position in old-Church terms: "I can't absolve you unless you have a firm purpose of amendment."

"Yeah, I have that, too."

"Not if you intend to kill someone."

"I don't want to kill him. I *have* to kill him. Damn it, Father, don't you understand that?"

"I'm afraid I don't. There is no excuse for murder, and you know that well."

"Yeah, Father, I guess I do."

He continued to weep. "Jeez, what would my ma say if she knew up in heaven?"

"Pretty much what I'm saying. Take this chance to change your life."

"It's too late." He stood up. "I'm damned already. Thanks for listening, Father. I gotta be going. Pray for me."

He extended his hand and shook mine firmly.

"Come back again if you want to," I said lamely.

What the hell do you say in such circumstances?

"You're sure this is under the seal of confession? You can't tell anyone?"

"Not a soul."

"Good-bye, Father," he said to me at the door. "You've been a big help. Remember to pray for me."

"I will certainly do that. Remember, it's never too late to begin again."

"Not for me," he said, and disappeared into the rain and the darkness.

I returned to my room, glanced briefly at the posters of the three Johns of my young adulthood—Pope, President, and quarterback of the Baltimore Colts—poured myself a generous amount of Jameson's twelve-year special reserve to calm my nerves, and sat back on my easy chair to think.

I thought for a long time.

The doorbell rang again. The hit man again.

"Nah, Father." He stood in the rain, water pouring off his anguished face. "Forget about that seal of confession thing. You can tell them that there's a contract out on Richard Powers and there's a professional hit man in town to do the job. Maybe that will help me with God."

Before I bad time to challenge his absurd reasoning, he had faded back into the watery darkness.

Upon return to my study, I found that the poltergeist that shares my quarters, had, as is his custom when I leave for a few minutes, finished my drink. I was constrained to fill my Waterford tumbler again.

Once more I thought for a long time.

Then I dialed Captain John Culhane of the Chicago Police Department, commander of Area Six Detectives, a smart and honest cop, at his private home phone.

"Culhane."

"Father Ryan, John."

"Yeah, what's up, Bishop?"

"Have there been any threats against the life of a certain Richard Patrick Powers lately?"

"How lately?"

"Recent weeks."

"Only four or five, the usual number. Lot of people hate tricky Dickie."

"So I've been led to believe. Any rumors of his being in trouble with the Boys Out on the West Side?"

"He's been in trouble with them for years. They're scared of him."

"Another threat was called to my attention tonight, purporting to be serious."

"Yeah, well, he's got his own bodyguards. Doesn't want us around because he says we're all crooks. I'll tell him about it and offer some police protection. I suspect he'll laugh in my face. Should I say the Outfit is involved?"

"You might mention that."

My obligations fulfilled, I retired for the night and slept peacefully.

After the morning Eucharist (what we now call the mass when we remember to do so) and breakfast, I made a phone call to an acquaintance who is what is known as a "friend of friends." I wanted some information on two questions. He was able to answer them both, as I thought he would, without consulting those friends.

John Culhane called me later in the morning, just as I returned from the grammar school and the eighth graders whom I enjoy greatly. But then I'm not their parent.

"Like I said, Bishop, Dickie Powers laughed in my face. Then, get this, he called back to apologize because his new wife made him. So it ends up with him saying thanks but no, thanks. She may be his salvation."

"Arguably. God usually knows what She is doing."

Two weeks passed, and there was no hit on Dickie Powers.

Then one evening, after I had listened to a husband and wife who once had been deeply in love spew hate at each other, John Culhane was on the phone.

"It went down tonight, Bishop. Dickie Powers. Classic mob hit. Dickie's walking down East Lake Shore Drive with his wife at night, his bodyguards a few yards behind him. A man with a turned-up coat collar comes out from beneath one of those canopies in front of the buildings on the street, calls, 'Dick,' softly, and puts him down with a twenty-two with a silencer. He jumps into a car that pulls up and is gone before the bodyguards see Dickie slump to the ground."

"Dead?"

"No, the hit man blows it. A bullet in the lung, but he's going to make it, I think. He's on his way to Northwestern."

"Lung?"

"Yeah, I know. They usually go for the head. Maybe this guy was going for the heart."

"Or can't shoot straight. I'm on my way to the hospital."

The Hit Man Who Couldn't Shoot Straight, not bad as a title for a film.

In the emergency room Dickie Powers was conscious when I administered the Sacrament of the Sick to him. His wife, her face stained with tears, clung to his hand and answered "amen" with him to the prayers, though there was some confusion with the doxology at the end of the Lord's Prayer.

"Thanks for coming, Father Blackie. I'm through being a bastard. It'll be tough, but I'm going to change my life."

"He means it," Regina said firmly. "He really does."

"I'll try," he whispered, "but you gotta help me."

"Count on that," she said firmly. "And thank you, Bishop. Perhaps I could come over to talk to you in a couple of days."

"Surely." I smiled benignly, figuring that once again Herself had called me in to straighten out the minor messes after She had accomplished Her major goals.

Maybe, just maybe it was not too late for Dickie Powers to undergo a metanoia.

John Culhane, trim and fit, as always, silver blue eyes twinkling behind his glasses, met me in the corridor.

"What do you think, Bishop?"

"If I were in your position, Commander, I would arrest Rick Powers immediately and charge him with the attempted murder of his father. I believe that lacking willpower to match his cleverness, he will breakdown and confess at once."

So it went down.

"You had it right, Bishop," he told me while I demolished my pancakes and bacon at the cathedral breakfast table the next morning. "He broke down immediately. Not much guts there."

"Very little, I fear."

"How did you know?"

"I had a visit a couple of Sunday nights ago from a purported professional hit man, who said he was known as the Pro. He told me under the seal of confession that he had killed thirty-two men and that there was a contract to make Dickie Powers number thirty-three. He went through considerable and, on the whole, credible agonizing about the state of his soul, his relationship with God, and his eternal fate, then departed, having argued that his need for money and his obligation to honor his contract forced him to continue with the hit.

"I was intrigued that he would tell me the name of the intended victim. There seemed to be no need to do that. Then he came back a half hour later and released me from the seal on the grounds that maybe God would be more sympathetic with him if he gave Powers a fighting chance by letting him know there was a mob hit man in town.

"That was clearly nonsense. In his first manifestation the hit man did not want to die because of his wife and family. In the second he was putting his life at enhanced risk for no obvious purpose. The devout Catholic he pretended to be would know that from God's point of view, murder is murder whether you put yourself at risk or not.

"The next morning I called a certain source and asked him two questions. He gave me the answers I expected.

"Patently I had been played for the fool by a very clever actor. I was supposed to put out the word that there was a contract on Dickie. Then, when a few weeks had passed and the hit finally went down in Outfit fashion, we were all supposed to figure the hit was a fulfillment of the contract. Rick hired a good actor—probably from out of town—who carried off the scenario to fit his script.

"The scheme was clearly designed to divert suspicion from him. I doubt that it would have worked in any case. But he failed to carry out his part of the scenario when his hand wavered at the end and he didn't kill his father. Hit men may have occasional guilt feelings, but they shoot straight.

"Which turns out to be fortunate for the hit man who couldn't shoot straight. The charge against him will only be attempted murder. When he comes out of prison, I presume he will continue to aspire to make films. Perhaps he will make one about life in prison. Perhaps then his creativity at plot construction may be of some use to him."

"He wanted the money so he could be a film producer," John told me. "He even had a script for a film. He had almost talked his father into financing it. When the old man met Regina, he changed his mind. With Regina in charge, Rick saw his hopes go up in smoke."

"The actor recited his lines well, but finally the script was inadequate and the direction less than convincing," I said, trying to sound like my good friend Roger Ebert. "One and a half stars."

""What were the two questions you asked your source?" The commander rose to leave.

"The first was whether there was a hit man named the Pro. My source, who would know, said he had never heard of him. The second was whether two hundred big ones were out of line for I hit. He whistled and said he had never heard of anything like that. If Rick Powers's script when he emerges from jail is truly about prison life, presumably he will have, courtesy of the state of Illinois, done better research than he did for this script."

THE SWEATING STATUE

EDWARD D. HOCH

IT WAS THE mIRACLE AT Father David Noone's aging inner-city parish that brought Monsignor Thomas Xavier to the city. He'd been sent by the Cardinal himself to investigate the miraculous event, and that impressed Father Noone, even though he might have wished for more run-of-the-mill parish problems now that he'd reached the age of fifty.

Monsignor Xavier was a white-haired man a few years older than Father Noone, with a jolly, outgoing manner that made him seem more like a fund-raiser than the Cardinal's troubleshooter. He shook hands vigorously and said, "We met once years ago when you were at St. Monica's, Father. I accompanied the Cardinal."

"Of course," David Noone replied, bending the truth a little. The Cardinal's visit had been more than a decade earlier, and if he remembered the monsignor at all it was only vaguely.

"Holy Trinity isn't much like St. Monica's, is it?" Monsignor Xavier remarked as he followed David into the sitting room. "These inner-city parishes have changed a great deal."

"Well, we have to scrape a bit to get by. The Sunday collections don't bring in much money, but of course the diocese helps out." He poked his head into the rectory kitchen, "Mrs. Wilkins, could you bring us in some—what will it be, Monsignor, coffee or tea?"

"Tea is fine."

"Some tea, please."

Mrs. Wilkins, the parish housekeeper, turned from the freezer with a carton of ice cream in her hand. "Be right with you. Good of you to visit us, Monsignor."

When they'd settled down in the parlor, the white-haired monsignor asked, "Are you alone at Holy Trinity, Father?"

"I am at present. When I first took over as pastor five years ago I had an assistant, but there just aren't enough priests to go around. He was shifted to a suburban parish two years ago and I've been alone here with Mrs. Wilkins ever since."

Monsignor Xavier opened a briefcase and took out some papers. "The parish is mainly Hispanic now, I believe."

"Pretty much so, though in the past year we've had several Southeast Asian families settle here, mainly in the Market Street area. We're trying to help them as much as we can."

He nodded as if satisfied. "Now tell me about the statue."

Mrs. Wilkins arrived with tea, setting the cups before them and pouring with a steady hand. "I'll bring in a few little cookies too," she said. "You must be hungry after your journey, Monsignor."

"Oh, they gave us a snack on the plane. Don't worry about me."

"We'll have a nice dinner," she promised. "It's not often we have such a distinguished visitor."

When they were alone, Monsignor Xavier said, "You were going to tell me about the statue."

"Of course. That's what you've come about." David Noone took a sip of tea. "It began two weeks ago today. Our custodian, Marcos, had unlocked the church doors for the seven A.M. Mass. There are always a few early arrivals and one of these, Celia Orlando, came up to light a candle before Mass began. She noticed that the wooden statue of the Virgin on the side altar seemed covered with sweat. When she called Marcos's attention to it, he wiped the statue dry with a cloth. But a few moments later the sweating began again."

He paused for some comment, but the monsignor only said, "Interesting, Please continue."

"Marcos showed it to me when I arrived to say the Mass. I didn't think too much of it at first. Perhaps the wood was exuding some sort of sap.

In fact, I thought no more of the incident until later that day when Mrs. Wilkins reported that people were arriving to view the miracle. I went over to the church and found a half-dozen women, friends and neighbors of Celia Orlando."

"Tell me about the woman."

"Celia? Her parents moved here from Mexico City when she was a teenager. She's twenty-eight now, and deeply religious. Attends Mass every morning on her way to work at an insurance company."

A nod. "Go on with your story."

Father Noone shifted in his chair, feeling as if he was being questioned in a courtroom. "Well, I spoke to the women and tried to convince them there was no miracle. I thought things had settled down, but then the following morning the same thing happened. It kept happening, and each morning there's been a bigger crowd at morning Mass. After television covered it on the six o'clock news the church was jammed."

Monsignor Xavier finished the tea and rose to his feet. "Well, I think it's time I saw this remarkable statue."

Father Noone led the way through the rectory kitchen where Mrs. Wilkins was already at work on dinner. "It smells good," the monsignor commented, giving her a smile. They passed through a fire door into a corridor that connected the rectory with the rear of the church.

"It's handy in the winter," David Noone explained.

"Is the church kept locked at night?"

"Oh, yes, all the doors. It's a shame but we have to do it. And not just in the inner city, either. These days they're locked in the suburbs, too."

The two priests crossed in front of the main altar, genuflecting as they did so. The Blessed Virgin's altar was on the far side, and it was there that the wooden statue stood. "There are no people here now," Xavier commented.

"Since we've had all the publicity I've been forced to close the church in the afternoon too, just to get the people out of here. We open again at five for afternoon services."

Monsignor Xavier leaned over for a closer look at the statue. "There is moisture, certainly, but not as much as I'd expected."

"There's more in the morning."

He glanced curiously at Father Noone. "Is that so?"

The statue itself stood only about eighteen inches high and had been carefully carved by a parish craftsman many years before David Noone's arrival. It was a traditional representation of the Blessed Virgin, with the polished unpainted wood adding a certain warmth to the figure. Monsignor Xavier studied it from all angles, then put out a finger to intercept a drop of liquid which had started running down the side of the statue. He placed it to his tongue and said, "It seems to be water."

"That's what we think."

"No noticeable salty taste."

"Why should it be salty?"

"Like tears," the monsignor said. "I'm surprised no one has dubbed the liquid the Virgin's Tears or some such thing."

"That'll be next, I'm sure."

They were joined by a thin balding man who walked with stooped shoulders and wore a pair of faded overalls. David Noone introduced the monsignor to Marcos, the church's custodian. "That means janitor," the balding man said with a smile. I know my place in the world."

"We'd be lost without you," David assured him, "Whatever you're called."

"You unlock the church doors every morning for the early Mass?" Monsignor Xavier asked.

"Sure."

"Ever find signs of robbery or forced entry?"

"No, not in years."

"When I first came here," David Noone explained, "it was customary to leave the side door facing the rectory unlocked all night. But someone stole one of our big gold candlesticks and that put an end to it. With the covered passageway from the rectory we don't really need any unlocked doors. On the rare occasion when someone needed to get into the church at night, they simply came to the rectory and Mrs. Wilkins or I took them over."

"What about this young woman, Celia Orlando?" the monsignor asked Marcos. "Do you know her?"

"Yes, her family has been in the parish many years. She is a good girl, very religious."

"Tell me, Marcos, what do you think causes the statue to sweat?"

The old man shifted his eyes to the wooden Virgin, then back to the monsignor. He seemed to be weighing his answer carefully. "A miracle, I suppose. Isn't that why you came here from the Cardinal?"

"Have you ever seen wood like that sweat before?"

"No."

"Could it be some sort of sap?"

"It has no taste. Sap would be sweet. And there would be no sap after all these years."

"So you think it is a miracle."

"I think whatever you want me to think. I am a good Catholic."

Monsignor Xavier turned away. "We'd best go see this young woman," he said to David Noone. "Celia Orlando."

In the car David tried to explain his people to Monsignor Xavier. "They are deeply religious. You are a stranger from another city, someone sent by the Cardinal himself. Naturally they do not want to offend you in any way."

"That old man does not believe in miracles, David. May I call you David? We might as well be informal about this. I'm Tom." He was relaxing a bit, feeling more at home with the situation, David thought. "Tell me a little about Marcos."

"There's not much to tell. His wife is dead and he lives alone. His children grew up and moved away. His son's a computer programmer."

"A story of our times, I suppose."

David Noone parked the car in front of the neat, freshly painted house where Celia Orlando lived with her brother Adolfo and his wife. It was almost dinner time, and Adolfo came to the door. "Hello, Father. Have you come to see my sister?"

"If she's home. Adolfo, this is Monsignor Thomas Xavier. The Cardinal sent him to look into our strange event."

"You mean the miracle." He ushered them into the living room.

Monsignor Xavier smiled. "That's what I'm here to determine. These things often have a natural explanation, you know."

Celia came into the room to greet them. She was still dressed for work, wearing a neat blue skirt and a white blouse. The presence of the monsignor seemed to impress her, and she hastened to explain that she deserved no special attention. "I attend Mass every morning, Monsignor, but I'm no Bernadette. I saw nothing the others did not see. I was merely the first to notice it."

"And you called it a miracle."

She brushed the black hair back from her wide dark eyes, and Father Noone realized that she was a very pretty young woman. He wondered why he'd never noticed it before. "An act of God," she responded. "That's a miracle isn't it?"

"We believe the wood of the statue is merely exuding moisture."

She shook her head in bewilderment. "Why is the church so reluctant to accept a miracle? What the world needs now are more miracles, not less."

"We must be very careful in matters of this sort," Xavier explained. "Have you ever noticed anything strange about the statue before? Anything unusual?"

"No, nothing."

Her brother interrupted then. "What are you after, Monsignor?"

"Only the facts. I must return home tomorrow and report to the Cardinal."

"I have a boyfriend who thinks I'm crazy. He's not Catholic." The admission seemed to embarrass her. "He says the priests are twisting my mind. He should be here now to see me trying to convince you both of the miracle."

Father Noone glanced at his watch. "I have to get back for the afternoon Mass in fifteen minutes. I hadn't realized it was so late."

She saw them to the door. "Pray for me," she said.

"We should say the same to you," Monsignor Xavier told her.

On the drive back to the parish church he talked little. When he saw the crowds at the five-thirty Mass, filling the small church almost to capacity, he said nothing at all.

✝   ✝   ✝

In the evening they sat in David Noone's small study, enjoying a bit of brandy. They were on a first-name basis now, and it was a time for confidences. "How do you do financially here?" Thomas Xavier asked.

"Poorly," David Noone admitted. "I have to go hat in hand to the bishop a couple of times a year. But he realizes the problems. He helps in every way he can."

"What does he think of the statue?"

"Strictly hands off, Tom. That's why he phoned the Cardinal. It's known as passing the buck."

"I know how he feels. If you think the church was crowded this afternoon, just wait till the national news gets hold of this. You'll have people coming here from all over the country."

"There was a call from the *New York Times* yesterday. They said they might send a reporter out this weekend."

"That's what I mean. We have to be very careful, David—"

He was interrupted by Mrs. Wilkins, who announced, "There's a young man to see you, Father Noone. He says it's very important."

David Noone sighed and got to his feet. "Excuse me, Tom. Duty calls."

He walked down the hall to the parlor where a sandy-haired man in his late twenties was waiting. "You're Father Noone?" the man asked, rising to meet him.

"Yes. What can I do for you?"

"My name is Kevin Frisk. Maybe Celia mentioned me."

"Celia Orlando? No, I don't believe so."

"I'm her boyfriend."

"Oh, yes. I think—"

"I want you to stay away from her."

David could see the anger in his eyes now. "I assure you—"

"You came this afternoon with another priest. She told me about it. I want you to leave her alone, stop filling her head with all these crazy notions of a miracle."

"Actually it's just the opposite. No one is more skeptical than a priest when there's talk of miracles."

"I want to marry her. I want to take her away from your influence."

"We have very little influence over Celia or anyone else. We only try to give a bit of comfort, and a few answers to the questions people ask. Do you work with Celia at the insurance office?"

"Yes. And I'm not Catholic." There was a challenge in his words.

"Celia told me that."

"If you think you can hypnotize me with your crazy notions—"

"Believe me, I'm not trying to hypnotize you or persuade you or convert you."

"Then stay away from Celia. Stop filling her head with statues that sweat. If we're ever married it'll be far from here."

"Mr. Frisk—"

"That's all I have to say. Take it as a warning. The next time I might not be quite so civil."

David watched as he left the room and walked out the front door without looking back. He shook his head sadly and returned to the study where the monsignor was waiting.

"No special problem, I hope," Thomas Xavier said, putting down the magazine he'd been glancing through.

"Not really. It was a young man who's been dating Celia Orlando."

"Ah yes—the non-Catholic one. I caught that point when she made it."

"He thinks we're brainwashing her or something. He seemed a bit angry."

"The statue seems to be having a ripple effect on the lives of a great many people."

The meeting with Kevin Frisk had left David dissatisfied. He felt he'd given the wrong answers to questions that hadn't even been asked. "What will you tell the Cardinal when you go back tomorrow?"

"I want to have another look at our statue in the morning. That may help me decide."

✝ ✝ ✝

It was Father Noone's habit to rise at six-thirty for the seven o'clock Mass, delaying breakfast until after the service. When the alarm woke him he dressed quickly and went downstairs, noting only that the door to the guest room where Monsignor Xavier slept was still closed. Passing through the kitchen he noted that Mrs. Wilkins was not yet up either. The brandy glasses from the previous night sat unwashed on the sideboard, and a carton of ice cream lay melting in the sink. The door to her room, at the rear of the main floor, was also closed.

Through the window he could see a parishioner trying the side door of the church, which was still locked. Had Marcos overslept too? David Noone hurried along the passageway and into the church, switching on lights as he went. It was already ten minutes to seven. He entered the sacristy and was about to open the cabinet where his vestments were hung when something drew him to the stairwell leading to the church basement. There was a light on down there, which seemed odd if Marcos was late arriving.

But Marcus was there, sprawled at the foot of the stairs. David knew before he reached him that the old man was dead.

David knelt by the body for a moment, saying a silent, personal prayer. Then he administered the last rites of the Church. He went back to the rectory and roused Monsignor Xavier, telling him what had happened. "Can you take the Mass for me while I call the police? There are people waiting."

"Certainly, David. Give me five minutes to dress."

He joined David Noone in three minutes and they returned to the

Church together. Staring down at the body, Thomas Xavier said a prayer of his own. "The poor man. It looks as if his neck was broken in the fall."

"He knew these stairs too well to fall on them," David said.

"You think he was pushed? But why, and by whom?"

"I don't know."

"Open the doors of your church. It's after seven and people are waiting. Tell them Mass will begin in a few moments."

"Where are you going now?"

"Just over to see the statue."

David Noone followed him across the sanctuary to the side altar. The Virgin's statue was sweating, perhaps more intensely than before. The monsignor reached out his right hand to touch it, then drew sharply back. "What is it?" David asked.

"The statue is cold, as if it's aware of the presence of death."

† † †

The Mass went on as the police arrived and went through their routine. A detective sergeant named Dominick was in charge. "Anything stolen, Father?" he wanted to know, peering over the rim of his glasses as he took notes.

"Nothing obvious. The chalices are all here. We don't keep any money in the church overnight, except what's in the poor box, and that hasn't been touched."

"Then foul play seems doubtful. He probably just missed his footing in the dark."

"The light was on," David reminded him.

"He was an old man, Father. We got enough crime these days without trying to find it where it doesn't exist."

When they returned to the rectory after Mass, Mrs. Wilkins was busy preparing breakfast. David told her what had happened and she started to cry softly. "He was a good man," she said. "He didn't deserve to die like that."

"The police are convinced it was an accident," David Noone said. "I'm not so sure."

She brought them their breakfast and Monsignor Xavier took a mouthful of scrambled egg. After a moment he said, "This is very good. I wish we had breakfast like this back home."

"What do you think about Marcos?" David Noone asked him.

He considered that for a moment. "I don't know. I did notice that Celia Orlando wasn't at Mass this morning. Didn't you say she comes every day?"

"Yes."

"Perhaps we should see why her routine changed today."

Father Noone had to make some calls at the hospital first, and he was surprised when the monsignor changed his return flight and arranged to stay over an extra day. He wondered what it meant. Then, just before noon, they called on Celia at the insurance office where she was employed.

She was startled to see them enter, and came up to the counter to greet them. "Is something wrong? It's not my brother is it?"

"No, no," Father Noone assured her. "It's just that you weren't at Mass and I wondered if you were ill."

She dropped her eyes. "Kevin—my boyfriend—doesn't want me to go there anymore. He says you're a bad influence on me."

"He certainly can't keep you from practicing your religion."

"He says I should go to another parish. All that business with the statue—"

At that moment one of the office doors opened and Kevin Frisk himself emerged. He hurried over to the counter and confronted the two priests. "Get out of here!" he ordered.

"You can't—"

"I can order you out when you're keeping employees from their jobs, and that's exactly what you're doing. Get out and don't let me see you here again."

David Noone turned to Celia as they departed. "Call me at the rectory. We need to talk."

"Stay away from her!" Frisk warned.

Outside, Monsignor Xavier shook his head. "A hotheaded young man. He could cause trouble."

"If he hasn't already. Maybe he broke into the church and Marcos caught him at it."

"There were no signs of forced entry, David. Perhaps that detective is right about looking for crime where none exists."

"I'm sorry, Tom. I just can't get that old man out of my mind."

As they walked back to the car they saw a headline on the noon edition of the newspaper: MAN FOUND DEAD AT "MIRACLE" CHURCH. Monsignor Xavier said, "I'm afraid this will bring you all the national publicity you've been trying to avoid. It's something more than a miracle now."

"Is that why you're staying over? Did you expect something like this?"

Thomas Xavier hesitated. "Not expect it, exactly. But in a large city we're more in tune with the way the press operates. They couldn't get the right angle on a sweating statue, but now there's a dead old man and they'll have a field day."

"What do you suggest I do?"

"We must have an answer ready when they ask the Church's position on the so-called miracle."

"And what is the Church's position? What will you report to the Cardinal?"

"The answer to that lies back at Holy Trinity."

† † †

There had been no Marcos to lock up the church during the early afternoon, and David Noone realized it had been left open as soon as he drove up to the rectory and saw the streams of people entering and leaving.

"I forgot to lock it," he said sadly.

"I doubt if there's any harm done."

They found Mrs. Wilkins just hanging up the telephone, almost frantic. "It's been like a circus here. Reporters calling from all over the country! The television stations have all been down, filming the statue for the evening news."

"Again? They did that last week."

"There are more people around now. And everyone wants to see where poor Marcos died. I was over there shooing them out of the sacristy myself."

The afternoon Mass was like a bad dream for David. People he'd never seen before filled the church, many with little interest in following the service. Instead they crowded around the side altar where the statue stood. The moisture was not as heavy as it had been that morning, but there was still some to be seen. In his sermon he said a few words about Marcos, then tried to make the point that the phenomenon of the statue was still unexplained. Following the services people lingered around the side altar until finally David had to ask them to leave so he could close the church.

"The only blessing to come out of all this," he told the monsignor over dinner, "is that the crowds, and the collections, have never been better. Still, I'm wondering if I should simply remove the statue temporarily and end all this fuss."

"That would surely bring complaints from some, though it's an option we must consider."

Mrs. Wilkins brought in their coffee. "Sorry there's no dessert tonight. What with all the commotion I didn't get to the store today."

"It'll do us both good," the monsignor assured her.

Later, they walked around the church in the darkness as David Noone checked all the doors to be sure they were locked. "I'll have to find a replacement for Marcos, of course, immediately after the funeral."

Monsignor Xavier stared up at the spire of Holy Trinity Church as it disappeared into the night sky. "I often wish I had a church like this. It would be just the right size for me. In the city, serving the Cardinal, I lose touch with things at times."

"With people?"

"With people, yes, and with their motives."

Later that night, just after eleven, as David was turning out the light and getting into bed, his door opened silently and Thomas Xavier slipped into the room. He held a finger to his lips. "Put on your robe and come with me," he said softly.

"What—"

"Just come, very quietly."

David took his robe and followed Thomas Xavier down the stairs. When they reached the main floor the monsignor headed for the kitchen, then paused as if listening.

"What—"

"Shh!"

He heard a noise from the passageway leading into the church, and then the kitchen door swung open.

It was Mrs. Wilkins, carrying the statue of the Virgin in her arms.

"Let me take that," Monsignor Xavier said with a kindly voice. "We don't want any more accidents, like what happened to poor old Marcos."

† † †

She gave him the statue, and then the will seemed to go out of her. For a long time she cried, and talked irrationally, and it was only the soft words of the monsignor that calmed her at last.

"We know all about it, Mrs. Wilkins. You carried the statue in here each evening, didn't you, and immersed it in water. Then you left it in the freezer overnight, carrying it back into the church each morning before

Mass. Naturally as it thawed it seemed to sweat. That was why there was more moisture in the morning than later in the day, and why it was cold to my touch this morning. I remembered seeing the ice cream melting in the sink when I passed through the kitchen with Father Noone. You took it out of the freezer to make room for the statue, and then forgot to put it back, so there was no dessert for us tonight."

"I only did it so more people would come, so the collections would be bigger and we could help the poor souls in our parish. I never meant to do any harm!"

"Marcos caught you this morning, didn't he? If he was already suspicious, my presence might have prompted him to come in earlier than usual. He hid in the stairwell and turned on the light as you were returning the statue."

"Oh my God, the poor man! He startled me so; he tried to take the statue away and I pushed him. I didn't realize we were so close to the stairs. He just went down, and didn't move. I didn't mean to kill him." Her voice had softened until they could barely hear her.

"Of course you didn't," David Noone said, taking her hand.

"I read about it in a book, about putting the statue in the freezer. I thought it would help the parish. I never meant to hurt anybody."

Monsignor Xavier nodded. "There was something similar down in Nicaragua a few years back. I read about it too. When I saw the ice cream in the sink it reminded me. You see, David, if someone was tampering with the statue overnight it had to be either Marcos or Mrs. Wilkins. The church was locked, with the only entrance from the rectory here. It was locked this morning, when Marcos died. He had a key, and she didn't need one."

"What are they going to do with me?" she asked sadly.

"I don't know," David replied. "We'll have to phone the police. Then I'll go down there with you. I'll stay with you as long as I can. Don't worry."

In the morning Monsignor Xavier departed. He stood for a moment looking up at the church and then shook hands with David Noone. "You have a fine church here. Fine people. I'll tell the Cardinal that."

It was after the morning Mass, and as he watched the monsignor get into his taxi for the airport, Celia Orlando approached him. "The statue is gone, Father. Where is the statue?"

"I didn't expect to see you at Mass, Celia."

"He can't tell me how to pray. I said that to him. But where is the statue?"

"I'm keeping it in the rectory for a few days. It was all a hoax, I'm afraid. There was no miracle. You'll read about it in the papers."

She nodded, but he wondered if she really understood his words. "That's all right," she said. "I managed to wipe a bit of the sweat off one day with a piece of cotton. I carry it with me all the time. I'll never throw it away."

THE STRIPPER

H. H. HOLMES

HE WAS CALLED JACK THE Stripper because the only witness who had seen him and lived (J. F. Flugelbach, 1463 N. Edgemont) had described the glint of moonlight on bare skin. The nickname was inevitable.

Mr. Flugelbach had stumbled upon the fourth of the murders, the one in the grounds of City College. He had not seen enough to be of any help to the police; but at least he had furnished a name for the killer heretofore known by such routine cognomens as "butcher," "werewolf," and "vampire."

The murders in themselves were enough to make a newspaper's fortune. They were frequent, bloody, and pointless, since neither theft nor rape was attempted. The murderer was no specialist, like the original Jack, but rather an eclectic, like Kürten the Düsseldorf Monster, who struck when the mood was on him and disregarded age and sex. This indiscriminate taste made better copy; the menace threatened not merely a certain class of unfortunates but every reader.

It was the nudity, however, and the nickname evolved from it, that made the cause truly celebrated. Feature writers dug up all the legends of naked murderers—Courvoisier of London, Durrant of San Francisco,

Wallace of Liverpool, Borden of Fall River—and printed them as sober fact, explaining at length the advantages of avoiding the evidence of bloodstains.

When he read this explanation, he always smiled. It was plausible, but irrelevant. The real reason for nakedness was simply that it felt better that way. When the color of things began to change, His first impulse was to get rid of his clothing. He supposed that psychoanalysts could find some atavistic reason for that.

He felt the cold air on his naked body. He had never noticed that before. Noiselessly he pushed the door open and tiptoed into the study. His hand did not waver as he raised the knife.

The Stripper case was Lieutenant Marshall's baby, and he was going nuts. His condition was not helped by the constant allusions of his colleagues to the fact that his wife had once been a stripper of a more pleasurable variety. Six murders in three months, without a single profitable lead, had reduced him to a state where a lesser man might have gibbered, and sometimes he thought it would be simpler to be a lesser man.

He barked into phones nowadays. He hardly apologized when he realized that his caller was Sister Ursula, that surprising nun who had once planned to be a policewoman and who had extricated him from several extraordinary cases. But that was just it; those had been extraordinary, freak locked-room problems, while this was the horrible epitome of ordinary, clueless, plotless murder. There was no room in the Stripper case for the talents of Sister Ursula.

He was in a hurry and her sentences hardly penetrated his mind until he caught the word "Stripper." Then he said sharply, "So? Backtrack please, Sister. I'm afraid I wasn't listening."

"He says," her quiet voice repeated, "that he thinks he knows who the Stripper is, but he hasn't enough proof. He'd like to talk to the police about it; and since he knows I know you, he asked me to arrange it, so that you wouldn't think him just a crank."

"Which," said Marshall, "he probably is. But to please you, Sister . . . What did you say his name is?"

"Flecker. Harvey Flecker. Professor of Latin at the University."

Marshall caught his breath. "Coincidence," he said flatly. "I'm on my way to see him now."

"Oh. Then he did get in touch with you himself?"

"Not with me," said Marshall. "With the Stripper."

"God rest his soul . . ." Sister Ursula murmured.

"So. I'm on my way now. If you could meet me there and bring this letter—"

"Lieutenant, I know our order is a singularly liberal one, but still I doubt if Reverend Mother—"

"You're a material witness," Marshall said authoritatively. "I'll send a car for you. And don't forget the letter."

Sister Ursula hung up and sighed. She had liked Professor Flecker, both for his scholarly wit and for his quiet kindliness. He was the only man who could hold his agnostic own with Father Pearson in disputatious sophistry, and he was also the man who had helped keep the Order's soup-kitchen open at the depth of the depression.

She took up her breviary and began to read the office for the dead while she waited for the car.

✝   ✝   ✝

"It is obvious," Professor Lowe enunciated, "that the Stripper is one of the three of us."

Hugo Ellis said, "Speak for yourself." His voice cracked a little, and he seemed even younger than he looked.

Professor de' Cassis said nothing. His huge hunchbacked body crouched in the corner and he mourned his friend.

"So?" said Lieutenant Marshall. "Go on, Professor."

"It was by pure chance," Professor Lowe continued, his lean face alight with logical satisfaction, "that the back door was latched last night. We have been leaving it unfastened for Mrs. Carey since she lost her key; but Flecker must have forgotten that fact and inadvertently reverted to habit. Ingress by the front door was impossible, since it was not only secured by a spring lock but also bolted from within. None of the windows shows any sign of external tampering. The murderer presumably counted upon the back door to make plausible the entrance of an intruder; but Flecker had accidentally secured it, and that accident," he concluded impressively, "will strap the Tripper."

Hugo Ellis laughed, and then looked ashamed of himself.

Marshall laughed too. "Setting aside the Spoonerism, Professor, your statement of the conditions is flawless. This house was locked tight as a drum. Yes, the Stripper is one of the three of you." It wasn't amusing when Marshall said it.

Professor de' Cassis raised his despondent head. "But why?" His voice was guttural. "Why?"

Hugo Ellis said, "Why? With a madman?"

Professor Lowe lifted one finger as though emphasizing a point in a lecture. "Ah, but is this a madman's crime? There is the point. When the Stripper kills a stranger, yes, he is mad. When he kills a man with whom he lives . . . may he not be applying the technique of his madness to the purpose of his sanity?"

"It's an idea," Marshall admitted. "I can see where there's going to be some advantage in having a psychologist among the witnesses. But there's another witness I'm even more anxious to—" His face lit up as Sergeant Raglan came in. "She's here, Rags?"

"Yeah," said Raglan. "It's the sister. Holy smoke, Loot, does this mean this is gonna be another screwy one?"

Marshall had said *she* and Raglan had said *the sister.* These facts may serve as sufficient characterization of Sister Felicitas, who had accompanied her. They were always a pair, yet always spoken of in the singular. Now Sister Felicitas dozed in the corner where the hunchback had crouched, and Marshall read and reread the letter which seemed like the posthumous utterance of the Stripper's latest victim:

My dear Sister:

I have reason to fear that someone close to me is Jack the Stripper.

You know me, I trust, too well to think me a sensationalist striving to be a star witness. I have grounds for what I say. This individual, whom I shall for the moment call "Quasimodo" for reasons that might particularly appeal to you, first betrayed himself when I noticed a fleck of blood behind his ear—a trifle, but suggestive. Since then I have religiously observed his comings and goings, and found curious coincidences between the absence of Quasimodo and the presence elsewhere of the Stripper.

I have not a conclusive body of evidence, but I believe that
I do have sufficient to bring to the attention of the authorities.
I have heard you mention a Lieutenant Marshall who is a close
friend of yours. If you will recommend me to him as a man
whose word is to be taken seriously, I shall be deeply obliged.

I may, of course, be making a fool of myself with my suspicions of Quasimodo, which is why I refrain from giving you
his real name. But every man must do what is possible to rid
this city *a negotio perambulante in tenebris.*

Yours respectfully,
Harvey Flecker

✝   ✝   ✝

"He didn't have much to go on, did he?" Marshall observed. "But he was
right, God help him. And he may have known more than he cared to trust
to a letter. He must have slipped somehow and let Quasimodo see his suspicions. . . . What does that last phrase mean?"

"Lieutenant! And you an Oxford man!" exclaimed Sister Ursula.

"I can translate it. But what's its connotation?"

"It's from St. Jerome's Vulgate of the ninetieth psalm. The Douay version translates it literally: *of the business that walketh about in the dark;* but
that doesn't convey the full horror of that nameless prowling *negotium.* It's
one of the most terrible phrases I know, and perfect for the Stripper."

"Flecker was a Catholic?"

"No, he was a resolute agnostic, though I have always had hopes that
Thomist philosophy would lead him into the Church. I almost think he
refrained because his conversion would have left nothing to argue with
Father Pearson about. But he was an excellent Church Latinist and knew
the liturgy better than most Catholics."

"Do you understand what he means by Quasimodo?"

"I don't know. Allusiveness was typical of Professor Flecker; he
delighted in British crossword puzzles, if you see what I mean. But I think
I could guess more readily if he had not said that it might particularly
appeal to me . . ."

"So? I can see at least two possibilities—"

"But before we try to decode the Professor's message, Lieutenant, tell
me what you have learned here. All I know is that the poor man is dead,
may he rest in peace."

Marshall told her. Four university teachers lived in this ancient (for Southern California) two-story house near the Campus. Mrs. Carey came in every day to clean for them and prepare dinner. When she arrived this morning at nine, Lowe and de' Cassis were eating breakfast and Hugo Ellis, the youngest of the group, was out mowing the lawn. They were not concerned over Flecker's absence. He often worked in the study till all hours and sometimes fell asleep there.

Mrs. Carey went about her work. Today was Tuesday, the day for changing the beds and getting the laundry ready. When she had finished that task, she dusted the living room and went on to the study.

The police did not yet have her story of the discovery. Her scream had summoned the others, who had at once called the police and, sensibly, canceled their classes and waited. When the police arrived, Mrs. Carey was still hysterical. The doctor had quieted her with a hypodermic, from which she had not yet revived.

Professor Flecker had had his throat cut and (Marshall skipped over this hastily) suffered certain other butcheries characteristic of the Stripper. The knife, an ordinary kitchen-knife, had been left by the body as usual. He had died instantly, at approximately one in the morning, when each of the other three men claimed to be asleep.

More evidence than that of the locked doors proved that the Stripper was an inmate of the house. He had kept his feet clear of the blood which bespattered the study, but he had still left a trail of small drops which revealed themselves to the minute police inspection—blood which had bathed his body and dripped off as he left his crime.

This trail led upstairs and into the bathroom, where it stopped. There were traces of watered blood in the bathtub and on one of the towels—Flecker's own.

"Towel?" said Sister Ursula. "But you said Mrs. Carey had made up the laundry bundle."

"She sends out only sheets and such—does the towels herself."

"Oh." The nun sounded disappointed.

"I know how you feel, Sister. You'd welcome a discrepancy anywhere, even in the laundry list. But that's the sum of our evidence. Three suspects, all with opportunity, none with an alibi. Absolutely even distribution of suspicion, and our only guidepost is the word Quasimodo. Do you know any of these three men?"

"I have never met them, Lieutenant, but I feel as though I know them rather well from Professor Flecker's descriptions."

"Good. Let's see what you can reconstruct. First, Ruggiero de' Cassis, professor of mathematics, formerly of the University of Turin, voluntary exile since the early days of Fascism."

Sister Ursula said slowly, "He admired de' Cassis, not only for his first-rate mind, but because he seemed to have adjusted himself so satisfactorily to life despite his deformity. I remember he said once, 'De' Cassis has never known a woman, yet every day he looks on Beauty bare.'"

"On Beauty . . . ? Oh yes. Millay. *Euclid alone* . . . All right. Now Marvin Lowe, professor of psychology, native of Ohio, and from what I've seen of him a prime pedant. According to Flecker . . . ?"

"I think Professor Lowe amused him. He used to tell us the latest Spoonerisms; he swore that flocks of students graduated from the University believing that modern psychology rested on the researches of two men named Frung and Jeud. Once Lowe said that his favorite book was Max Beerbohm's *Happy Hypocrite*; Professor Flecker insisted that was because it was the only one he could be sure of pronouncing correctly."

"But as a man?"

"He never said much about Lowe personally; I don't think they were intimate. But I do recall his saying, 'Lowe, like all psychologists, is the physician of Greek proverb.'"

"Who was told to heal himself? Makes sense. That speech mannerism certainly points to something a psychiatrist could have fun with. All right. How about Hugo Ellis, instructor in mathematics, native of Los Angeles?"

"Mr. Ellis was a child prodigy, you know. Extraordinary mathematical feats. But he outgrew them, I almost think deliberately. He made himself into a normal young man. Now he is, I gather, a reasonably good young instructor—just run of the mill. An adult with the brilliance which he had as a child might be a great man. Professor Flecker turned the French proverb around to fit him: 'If youth could, if age knew . . .'"

"So. There they are. And which," Marshall asked, "is Quasimodo?"

"Quasimodo . . ." Sister Ursula repeated the word, and other words seemed to follow it automatically. "*Quasimodo geniti infantes* . . ." She paused and shuddered.

"What's the matter?"

"I think," she said softly, "I know. But like Professor Flecker, I fear making a fool of myself—and worse, I fear damning an innocent man. . . . Lieutenant, may I look through this house with you?"

He sat there staring at the other two and at the policeman watching them.

*The body was no longer in the next room, but the blood was. He had never
before revisited the scene of the crime; that notion was the nonsense of legend.
For that matter he had never known his victim.*

*He let his mind go back to last night. Only recently had he been willing to
do this. At first it was something that must be kept apart, divided from his normal personality. But he was intelligent enough to realize the danger of that. It
could produce a seriously schizoid personality. He might go mad. Better to
attain complete integration, and that could be accomplished only by frank self-
recognition.*

It must be terrible to be mad.

"Well, where to first?" asked Marshall.

"I want to see the bedrooms," said Sister Ursula. "I want to see if Mrs.
Carey changed the sheets."

"You doubt her story? But she's completely out of the—all right.
Come on."

Lieutenant Marshall identified each room for her as they entered it.
Harvey Flecker's bedroom by no means consorted with the neatness of his
mind. It was a welter of papers and notes and hefty German works on
Latin philology and puzzle books by Torquemada and Caliban and early
missals and codices from the University library. The bed had been
changed and the clean upper sheet was turned back. Harvey Flecker
would never soil it.

Professor de' Cassis's room was in sharp contrast—a chaste monastic
cubicle. His books—chiefly professional works, with a sampling of
Leopardi and Carducci and other Italian poets and an Italian translation
of Thomas à Kempis—were neatly stacked in a case, and his papers were
out of sight. The only ornaments in the room were a crucifix and a framed
picture of a family group, in clothes of 1920.

Hugo Ellis's room was defiantly, almost parodistically the room of a
normal, healthy college man, even to the University banner over the bed.
He had carefully avoided both Flecker's chaos and de' Cassis's austerity;
there was a precisely calculated normal litter of pipes and letters and pulp
magazines. The pin-up girls seemed to be carrying normality too far, and
Sister Ursula averted her eyes.

Each room had a clean upper sheet.

Professor Lowe's room would have seemed as normal as Ellis's, if less
spectacularly so, if it were not for the inordinate quantity of books.
Shelves covered all wall space that was not taken by door, window, or

bed. Psychology, psychiatry, and criminology predominated; but there was a selection of poetry, humor, fiction for any mood.

Marshall took down William Roughead's *Twelve Scots Trials* and said, "Lucky devil! I've never so much as seen a copy of this before." He smiled at the argumentative pencilings in the margins. Then as he went to replace it, he saw through the gap that there was a second row of books behind. Paperbacks. He took one out and put it back hastily. "You wouldn't want to see that, Sister. But it might fit into that case we were proposing about repressions and word-distortions."

Sister Ursula seemed not to heed him. She was standing by the bed and said, "Come here."

Marshal came and looked at the freshly made bed.

Sister Ursula passed her hand over the mended but clean lower sheet. "Do you see?"

"See what?"

"The answer," she said.

Marshall frowned. "Look, Sister—"

"Lieutenant, your wife is one of the most efficient housekeepers I've ever known. I thought she had, to some extent, indoctrinated you. Think. Try to think with Leona's mind."

Marshall thought. Then his eyes narrowed and he said, "So . . ."

"It is fortunate," Sister Ursula said, "that the Order of Martha of Bethany specializes in housework."

Marshall went out and called downstairs. "Raglan! See if the laundry's been picked up from the back porch."

The Sergeant's voice came back. "It's gone, Loot. I thought there wasn't no harm—"

"Then get on the phone quick and tell them to hold it."

"But what laundry, Loot?"

Marshall muttered. Then he turned to Sister Ursula. "The men won't know of course, but we'll find a bill somewhere. Anyway, we won't need that till the preliminary hearing. We've got enough now to settle Quasimodo."

He heard the Lieutenant's question and repressed a startled gesture. He had not thought of that. But even if they traced the laundry, it would be valueless as evidence without Mrs. Carey's testimony . . .

He saw at once what had to be done.

They had taken Mrs. Carey to the guest room, that small downstairs bed-

room near the kitchen which must have been a maid's room when this was a
large family house. There were still police posted outside the house, but only
Raglan and the lieutenant inside.

It was so simple. His mind, he told himself, had never been functioning
more clearly. No nonsense about stripping this time; it was not for pleasure. Just
be careful to avoid those crimson jets. . . .

The Sergeant wanted to know where he thought he was going. He
told him.

Raglan grinned. "You should've raised your hand. A teacher like you
ought to know that."

He went to the back porch toilet, opened and closed its door without
going in. Then he went to the kitchen and took the second best knife. The
best had been used last night.

It would not take a minute Then he would be safe and later when the body
was found what could they prove? The others had been out of the room too.

But as he touched the knife it began to happen. Something came from the
blade up his arm and into his head. He was in a hurry, there was no time—but
holding the knife, the color of things began to change. . . .

He was half naked when Marshall found him.

Sister Ursula leaned against the jamb of the kitchen door. She felt
sick. Marshall and Raglan were both strong men, but they needed help to
subdue him. His face was contorted into an unrecognizable mask like a
demon from a Japanese tragedy. She clutched the crucifix of the rosary
that hung at her waist and murmured a prayer to the Archangel Michael.
For it was not the physical strength of the man that frightened her, not
the glint of his knife, but the pure quality of incarnate evil that radiated
from him and made the doctrine of possession a real terror.

As she finished her prayer, Marshall's fist connected with his jaw and
he crumpled. So did Sister Ursula.

"I don't know what you think of me," Sister Ursula said as Marshall drove
her home. (Sister Felicitas was dozing in the back seat.) "I'm afraid I
couldn't ever have been a policewoman after all."

"You'll do," Marshall said. "And if you feel better now, I'd like to run over it with you. I've got to get my brilliant deductions straight for the press."

"The fresh air feels good. Go ahead."

"I've got the sheet business down pat, I think. In ordinary middle-class households you don't change both sheets every week; Leona never does, I remembered. You put on a clean upper sheet, and the old upper sheet becomes the lower. The other three bedrooms each had one clean sheet—the upper. His had two—upper and lower; therefore his upper sheet had been stained in some unusual way and had to be changed. The hasty bath, probably in the dark, had been careless, and there was some blood left to stain the sheet. Mrs. Carey wouldn't have thought anything of it at the time because she hadn't found the body yet. Right?"

"Perfect, Lieutenant."

"So. But now about Quasimodo . . . I still don't get it. He's the one it *couldn't* apply to. Either of the others—"

"Yes?"

"Well, who is Quasimodo? He's the Hunchback of Notre Dame. So it could mean the deformed de' Cassis. Who wrote Quasimodo? Victor Hugo. So it could be Hugo Ellis. But it wasn't either; and how in heaven's name could it mean Professor Lowe?"

"Remember, Lieutenant: Professor Flecker said this was an allusion that might particularly appeal to me. Now I am hardly noted for my devotion to the anticlerical prejudices of Hugo's *Notre-Dame de Paris*. What is the common meeting-ground of my interests and Professor Flecker's?"

"Church liturgy?" Marshall ventured.

"And why was your Quasimodo so named? Because he was born—or found or christened, I forget which—on the Sunday after Easter. Many Sundays, as you may know, are often referred to by the first work of their introits, the beginning of the proper of the Mass. As the fourth Sunday in Lent is called *Laetare* Sunday, or the third in Advent *Gaudete* Sunday. So the Sunday after Easter is known as *Quasimodo* Sunday, from its introit *Quasimodo geniti infantes* 'As newborn babes.'"

"But I still don't see . . ."

"The Sunday after Easter," said Sister Ursula, "is more usually referred to as *Low* Sunday."

"Oh," said Marshall. After a moment he added reflectively, "*The Happy Hypocrite* . . ."

"You see that too? Beerbohm's story is about a man who assumes a mask of virtue to conceal his depravity. A schizoid allegory. I wonder if

Professor Lowe dreamed that he might find the same happy ending."

Marshall drove on a bit in silence. Then he said, "He said a strange thing while you were out."

"I feel as though he were already dead," said Sister Ursula. "I want to say, 'God rest his soul.' We should have a special office for the souls of the mad."

"That cues into my story. The boys were taking him away and I said to Rags, 'Well, this is once the insanity plea justifies itself. He'll never see the gas chamber.' And he turned on me—he'd quieted down by then— and said, 'Nonsense, sir! Do you think I would cast doubt on my sanity merely to save my life?'"

"Mercy," said Sister Ursula. At first Marshall thought it was just an exclamation. Then he looked at her face and saw that she was not talking to him.

THE BASE OF THE TRIANGLE
A FATHER DOWLING MYSTERY

RALPH MCINERNY

I

WHEN EARL HAVEN SHOWED UP at the rectory door, there was fire in his eye and his manner with Mrs. Murkin would normally have drawn a rebuke from the housekeeper but she brought him to the pastor's study without complaint.

"Father, this is Earl Haven."

"I'm not a Catholic."

"I am. As doubtless the collar tells you."

"She's Catholic. Harriet."

"Ah."

"Harriet Dolan," Mrs Murkin said, and her brows lifted in significance.

"The girl that's getting married?"

A groan escaped Earl and he collapsed into a chair. "She can't marry that idiot, she can't."

The reference would be to Leo Mulcahy with whom Harriet had sat in the front parlor not an hour before, making arrangements for their wedding.

"If it's being Catholic she wants, I'll do it."

"Become a Catholic?"

The man's expression suggested inner anguish. "If she'll marry me, yes I will."

Marie stood in the doorway wringing her apron but her expression was not in every way anguished. The housekeeper had a taste for other people's troubles and she found the various permutations of the relations between man and woman irresistible.

"It will never happen," she had said an hour before after Harriet Dolan and Leo Mulcahy had finished discussing with the pastor their impending nuptials and had left the rectory. Ahead of them lay months of preparation before the big day. Father Dowling conducted a weekly class for couples preparing themselves for marriage. Harriet and Leo would have to attend those classes.

"They seem very attached to one another."

"In love with love."

This was not like Marie, who was one of the last romantics, something she concealed beneath a crusty exterior. Father Dowling wondered if she were seeking to deflect trouble from Harriet and Leo by predicting it; there were depths to Marie's Irish superstitiousness that the pastor did not pretend to fathom. But Marie shook away this explanation, like a pitcher not getting the right signal from his catcher.

"She's taking him on the rebound."

"From what?"

"From whom."

But Marie had intuited little more than this fact. She did not then know who the third party might be, it was simply something that Harriet had said. Now, with Earl Haven collapsed in a chair in the rectory study and unable to suppress his groans, Marie had clearly made an identification.

"Have you proposed to Harriet?" Marie asked.

"She knows."

"But have you asked her?"

"I was going to."

"Apparently Leo Mulcahy got there before you," Father Dowling said.

Marie glared at the pastor and Earl doubled over, as if in pain. Suddenly, he looked up and his expression changed. "He can't afford to marry her!"

"Two can live as cheaply as one," Father Dowling said. Although this was an article in Marie's somewhat plagiarized creed, the housekeeper again glared at him. But then she asked Earl in a soothing voice what he meant.

The question restored Earl to the land of the living. Once his attention had been diverted from his broken heart, he spoke with succinct authority of the business in which both he and Leo Mulcahy were engaged.

There are amazingly inventive ways for people to earn their daily bread and one would have had to lack soul not to respond to the entrepreneurial creativity represented by Boxers Inc. The idea had been Earl's and it involved cutting himself in on the thriving business of the package delivery systems that had proved to be such competition for the U.S. Postal Service. Usually these giants had their own depot, at or near the airport, where the client not large enough to be visited by one of the pick-up trucks might go to send off his packages. Earl had opened a storefront in a mall, the first Boxers Inc, and had served as a clearing house for the various national deliverers—UPS, Federal Express, two or three others—making their services convenient for the occasional non-commercial user. A birthday present, something for a son or daughter at school, the odd item that must be elsewhere in a finite period of time. Boxers provided packaging as well as a clearing house for package delivery. At intervals throughout the day, the packages were taken to the depots of the great delivery systems. Earl had declined the offer to have trucks pick up the packages. It was important for the client to see what Earl was doing for them, thus justifying the modest fee he charged which, added to the payments from the deliverers, made Boxers Inc a money making enterprise. With success came the urge to expand. Earl set Leo Mulcahy up in the business.

"He didn't have a nickel," Earl said, almost with contempt. "I didn't either, when I started, but then I started from scratch. Leo's location in the Naperville mall would be the replica of the original Boxers Inc."

"You lent him the money?"

"Twenty-five thousand dollars."

The whistle came from Marie. "How much does he still owe you?"

"With interest, twenty-seven five. Only Leo could take such a simple idea and mess it up."

"He's in debt $27,500?"

"My accountant could kill me." Earl stood, and there was an unattractive expression on his face. "I am going to collect that money now."

Father Dowling, at his desk, listened to Marie as she accompanied Earl down the hall to the front door. The housekeeper cajoled, threatened, pleaded and, in the end, prophesied.

"Harriet will never forgive you!"
"She would never forgive herself if she married that idiot."

2

Life was full of mystery, Marie Murkin felt, and in this she was certainly
not alone, but she took the common point to uncommon lengths. To
identify the mystery was in some degree to have overcome it. But like
everyone before her, she was utterly baffled by the men to whom some
women were attracted and of course vice versa. The most improbable
combinations formed before one's eyes, defying every law of probability.
Father Dowling often cited a seminary definition of man as a rational animal and of course he did not have to explain to her that the phrase was
meant to cover women as well as men. But the truth was that it applied
to neither men nor women, not when it came to affairs of the heart. Marie
was not being cruel when she thought of Harriet Dolan as, well, what she
was, and how any man, let alone two of them, could make fools of themselves over the girl, Marie did not understand. Nor did she regard this as
merely the limitations of her own abilities. She defied anyone to explain
how a girl hardly more than five and a half feet high, with a round plain
face, abundant if nondescript hair worn in the current bag lady style, narrow little mouth and the body of a boy could turn the heads of both Earl
Haven and Leo Mulcahy. It made no sense, not even when you acknowledged Harriet's smile that transformed her face, crinkled her eyes behind
the lenses of her glasses, and was admittedly infectious.

"I hope I'm doing the right thing," the girl had whispered to Marie,
when Leo was alone with Father Dowling on the occasion of their first
visit.

"How long have you known him?"

"All my life."

"That's good."

"And his whole family," she added significantly.

"Ah. And he is in business for himself?"

"It's his partner who knows things."

Of course a girl was nervous and said odd things when she was on
the brink of marriage but Marie found this particularly enigmatic. Until
Earl Haven showed up at the rectory door. If Leo was a fine specimen of
a man, and he was, Earl Haven was even more so, and his near despair at
the thought of Harriet marrying Leo did nothing to detract from his
attraction. One of the advantages of age was that Marie could deal with

handsome men as she never could have when she was young and they were the same age. All the more did she marvel at the way Harriet had wrapped Leo and Earl around her finger, effortlessly manipulating them. She sent Leo to the rectory as soon as she learned that Earl had been there.

"It's none of his business," Leo almost shouted. His anger added to his imposing presence. He was a larger man than Earl, dark haired, craggy—a term that was much used in the novels Marie read. Earl on the other hand was blonde—golden locked, Marie's author might have said—slim and graceful with the clear blue eyes of a dreamer. Yet he apparently was the business whiz and Leo, in looks the practical man of action, was inept, losing money running a business that, according to Earl, ran itself.

"I understand you and Earl are in business together."

"He leant me some money, Father. Now he wants it back. I don't have it. It's sunk in that lousy business I was talked into starting."

Talked into by whom, Marie wondered. But she did not have to wonder long. Leo's expression had softened.

"I did it for Harriet. I was happy enough working for Midwest Power."

"Why not give up the business and go back to work for Midwest Power?"

Marie could have cheered this suggestion from Father Dowling. She found herself being tugged from side to side in this matter. On the one hand, she did not like to think that a couple would come talk to the priest about getting married, make arrangements for instructions, and then just drop it. On the other hand, if she were Harriet, her choice would certainly have been Earl Haven. But again she was mystified by the fact that little Harriet had her choice of these two paragons.

"I lost my seniority when I quit."

"That could not have been much at your age?" Marie said.

"They gave me a going away party." It seemed clear that Leo had left Midwest Power in such a way that any return would be demeaning. "I can't pay Earl back, not now, I'm losing money."

"He's just bluffing," Marie assured Leo. "Besides, if you don't have it . . ."

"He could take over my business."

Leo's situation was not enviable. He was stuck with a business that was losing money and his partner was demanding repayment of a loan and threatening to take over the business if Leo did not come up with the money. And all this out of spite because Leo had won the hand of the girl Earl loved. Father Dowling would not have thought of Harriet's as a face that would launch a thousand ships. But she was incentive enough for both Leo and Earl.

"I'll talk to Earl," Father Dowling said.

Hope leapt momentarily into Leo's eyes then faded away. "He won't listen to you."

"Let's find out."

3

Peanuts wanted to return some videos he had purchased from a catalog and Tuttle took him to the Boxers Inc store in Naperville to send the merchandise back.

"You know the place?"

"It's just like the ones in Fox River."

Peanuts didn't know them, but how often did he need someone to pack up and return merchandise for him? Tuttle assured him that Boxers Inc was reliable.

"What's wrong with the Post Office?"

"Don't get me started. What's wrong with the videos?"

"I already seen them."

"You're returning them just because you watched them?"

"Not these. I've already seen these. They're not what I ordered."

Peanuts had ordered several dozen old episodes of *The Untouchables.* "I like Frank Nitty."

"Who doesn't?"

Tuttle meant the actor. He wasn't sure what Peanuts meant. No matter, they were at the mall and Tuttle was searching for a parking spot as close as possible to Boxers Inc.

"There's an ambulance," Peanuts observed.

"I noticed the light." Tuttle was also noticing that it seemed to be stopping traffic right in front of Boxers Inc. This could mean anything, of course. It may or not concern Boxers directly, then again it could be a customer fallen ill. Naperville was beyond the jurisdiction in which Peanuts was an officer of the law and a policeman out of his jurisdiction feels like an imposter. But then Peanuts felt like an imposter in Fox River. His sinecure in the local constabulary was due to the influence of his family. When he was on duty he was given tasks of minimal responsibility. This suited Peanuts fine. He was not an ambitious man and was not personally proud, though fiercely loyal to his dubious family.

"I don't have to send these back right now."

"As long as we're here," Tuttle said. He had maneuvered his car through the lot and now drew up to the curb behind the ambulance. "I wish we had a squad car."

If Peanuts had been driving they could have turned on the warning light and given a little goose to the siren, arriving in style and authority. As it was, an overweight cop signaled imperiously for Tuttle to drive on. Tuttle put the car in neutral and hopped out.

"I got here as quick as I could," he said to the cop, silencing the order he was about to bark.

"Who are you?"

Tuttle took off his tweed hat and extracted a calling card from the crown. While the cop was reading it, Tuttle circled him and saw that the commotion was indeed inside the Boxers.

"That's Officer Pianone in the passenger seat."

Tuttle breezed on past then and swept into the door of Boxers Inc. He did not need any explanation of the scene before him. The store was alive with officers and plainclothesmen and paramedics. A young man in a white coat got up from a crouch and looking at a cop crossed his eyes and drew a finger across his throat. The paramedics were prepared to turn matters over to the medical examiner. Tuttle pressed on through to where the body lay on the floor. A man. Leo Mulcahy! Tuttle had the feeling that he had been brought providentially to this scene.

"His name is Leo Mulcahy," Tuttle said in a raised, authoritative voice.

Heads turned to look at him.

"The deceased is a friend of mine. What happened?"

What happened to Tuttle was that he was collared by two officers and hustled outside and into a patrol car. He tried to wave to Peanuts as he was hustled across the walk to the car but the reflection on the windshield made it impossible to see Peanuts. In the back seat of the Naperville squad car, Tuttle was bracketed by a uniformed officer and a plainclothesman.

"Who are you?"

"You're making a great mistake."

"You want to talk to a lawyer?"

"I am a lawyer."

The plainclothesman, who had a face still bearing the traces of teenage acne, narrowed his eyes. Outside the car, the cop to whom he had given his card tapped on the window. It was rolled down and Tuttle's calling card was passed in.

"This you?" the detective asked.

"Tuttle the lawyer."

"You say you know the dead guy?"

"What happened to him?"

Tuttle posed a problem for his captors. His manner disarmed them and yet they were disinclined to admit to having made a mistake. It was easier to act as if they had pressed Tuttle into service as an informant.

"I was afraid something like this would happen," Tuttle said, letting out a little line, getting in deeper. He hoped Peanuts had enough sense to put his car in a parking space. Peanuts could catch a nap in the back seat then and derive some benefit from this failed effort to return the unwanted videos. As for Tuttle, he was asking himself what kind of bill he could send the Naperville police after they solved the murder of Leo Mulcahy.

4

Cy Horvath drove out to the Fox River mall and parked where he could look at the front entrance of Boxers Inc, what was described in the writeup Cy had downloaded from the Web page of the *Tribune* as the flagship of Earl Haven's little empire. This was the first store Haven had opened and which he had used as a model for the others he had then opened in the area. The store in Naperville where the body of Leo Mulcahy had been found was a spin-off that had been jointly owned by Haven and the deceased.

Cy got out of the car and wound his away among parked vehicles, crossed the access road and pulled open the door of Boxers Inc. There were people waiting at the counter, there were customers availing themselves of the pack-it-yourself facilities, there was soothing music oozing through the place. All in all, a picture of pastel prosperity. Cy looked around and then decided that Haven's office would be down the hall past the computers and faxes and copying facilities. A diminutive woman whose blonde hair seemed shaped like a helmet looked up in surprise. The nameplate on her desk said Rose Hanlon. Cy told her he wanted to see Earl Haven.

"Oh he's over in Naperville."

"At the store there?"

"Can I help you?"

"I'm Lieutenant Horvath."

"Lieutenant?"

"Fox River Police."

"Is anything wrong?"

"Do you know Leo Mulcahy?"

Her expression changed. "Why do you ask?"

"Isn't he Earl Haven's partner in the Naperville store?"

She looked at him with growing disapproval. "If that were so, why would it be of interest to the Fox River police? Or are you asking personally?"

"Leo Mulcahy was found dead in the Naperville store an hour ago." No need to tell her that he had been strangled to death with a scarf.

Her gasping intake of air set her chair in motion and she backed away from him. Her eyes were round as dollars and her lips trembled.

"Dead?"

"Yes."

"That's impossible! He was a young man. His health was good."

"How well did you know him?"

"How well did I know him?" she repeated.

"The Naperville police would like some help in their investigation. This looks like something that spans our jurisdictions. When did Mr. Haven go to Naperville."

"He always went over there on Wednesdays."

"A regular visit."

"Yes."

"He hadn't heard of what happened to Mr. Mulcahy?"

"He must have been there already." After she said it, she seemed to regret having said it.

"I understand that there had been a falling out between the two men."

"I'm not sure I should talk about such things."

"Rose, a man has been murdered."

"Murdered! Oh my God." Tears welled into her eyes and then she was sobbing helplessly. Cy took a chair and waited. He let her cry as long as she wanted to and that turned out to be a long time indeed.

"You did know Leo Mulcahy."

"Of course I knew him. We were engaged to be married. Some years ago"

"You and Leo Mulcahy?"

"Yes." Her chin lifted, as if he had doubted her word.

"You broke off with him?"

She thought for a minute. "It wouldn't have worked out."

Phil Keegan had called the St. Hilary rectory while Cy was checking out the *Tribune* Web page. The call from Naperville reminded the captain of something he had heard from Father Dowling. But it was Marie Murkin he talked with. Leo Mulcahy? He was soon to marry Harriet Dolan. Now, talking with Rose Hanlon, Cy wondered if Leo's one time fiancée knew of his marriage plans.

"Do you know Harriet Dolan?"

An angry expression formed on Rose Hanlon's face. "Whatever happened to Leo Mulcahy is her fault."

5

Phil Keegan was in the study with Father Dowling, telling him what he knew of events in Naperville, and Marie was listening in. The picture seemed clear. Earl Haven had been driven half mad by the thought that the woman he loved intended to marry such an idiot as Leo Mulcahy.

"The Wednesday visit to the Naperville store was apparently a regular event," he said.

"Have you talked with him yet?"

"Earl Haven? He can't be found."

"Who has looked for him?"

"Cy."

Phil as much as said that very little mystery remained as to what had happened to Leo Mulcahy. Not only was Earl Haven the prime suspect, he was the only suspect.

"He left a trail as wide as the Interstate. Half a dozen people noticed him arrive at the Naperville store. Two people who were in the store have told us of a fierce argument between two men. The argument was the kind that would almost inevitably lead to blows."

"Did anyone witness a fight?"

"Haven told Mulcahy he was stupid. He told him he could not run a penny lemonade stand. He just threw insults at Mulcahy."

"What was his reaction?"

"He laughed."

"Laughed."

That was when Haven cleared everyone out of the store. "Being laughed at got to him, that was obvious. Mulcahy was hit on the head, probably with a scotch tape holder made of heavy metal. But it was the scarf that did it."

"Scarf."

"He was strangled with a scarf. It was not a pretty sight."

"Did anyone see Earl leave?"

Phil took the cigar from his mouth, studied it, then returned it to his mouth. clamping it between his teeth.

"Of course we're just assuming the man was Earl Haven."

Whatever the ostensible reason for the quarrel, it seemed obvious that Harriet Dolan was the real explanation. Earl's anger was more easily explained by the fact that he had lost Harriet than that he had lost money.

6

Harriet Dolan was unconvincing in the role of tragic woman. Surrounded by the sisters of Leo Mulcahy, she looked around her as if seeking a cue as to how she should behave. Her fiancé was dead and the man who killed him had professed his love for her and was now the object of a police search. Any of Leo's sisters was more attractive than Harriet but none of them had been the cause of such a romantic tragedy. It seemed assumed that Harriet would be brokenhearted by the events and from time to time she dabbed at her dry eyes with a handkerchief. She might have been concealing the little smile that kept forming on her thin lips. Of course it had not really dawned on her that Leo was dead and that Earl had killed him.

"She is in shock," one of the Mulcahy girls said to Marie Murkin.

"Who could blame her?" the housekeeper replied, but her eye was on Harriet and her tone was not as definite as her words. The chair next to Harriet was offered to Marie and she took it. She patted the girl's arm and sighed.

"You have lost them both."

Harriet looked at her.

"Leo and Earl."

"I didn't encourage him," Harriet protested, and rubbed the forming smile from her lips.

"It's not your fault."

But Harriet was distracted by the arrival of a young woman who turned out to be Rose Hanlon, accompanied by her brother. Their arrival created an awkwardness and when Rose approached her, Harriet grew apprehensive, but Rose just took her hand and shook her head in silent disbelief at what had happened. Steve Hanlon stood unobtrusively against a wall. Everyone seemed to be waiting for Rose to say something, but she held her silence. Finally she drifted off to the side of the room and joined her brother.

"She is affected as much as Harriet," a Mulcahy girl whispered to Marie.

"Why would she be?"

"She and Leo were engaged, you know. Informally."

Marie Murkin looked at Rose with new interest. The young woman had begun to weep and was being comforted. The contrast with Harriet was eloquent.

7

Earl Haven was located in a cabin north of town overlooking the Fox River, a summer place that afforded relief from the Midwestern heat. His car had been parked sideways on the narrow gravel drive and he had appeared in the picture window armed with a shotgun. Phil Keegan had prudently decided to address Earl by bull horn from the road. It added to the drama that Earl replied through a bullhorn of his own, one he had made notorious as a fan of the local high school football team.

"Come on out, Earl. We don't want anyone else getting hurt."

"I haven't hurt anyone."

"No reason not to come out then, is there?" Phil looked around, obviously pretty proud of that retort.

When Father Dowling arrived Phil and Earl were still exchanging one liners. Roger Dowling stood beside Cy Horvath.

"What are they talking about, Cy?"

"Football."

"Football!"

"Earl played for the Fox River Reds. His touchdown pass record to Steve Hanlon, who played wide receiver, will never be broken."

"How long has this been going on?"

Cy thought twenty minutes. Phil and Earl were discussing a game against Naperville played in the misty past when Earl had first become the toast of the town.

"Don't spoil it now, Earl. Face up to this."

"Do you think I killed Leo?"

"It doesn't matter what I think, Earl. We've got to straighten it out. Do you have a lawyer?"

Suddenly, through the no man's land between the police cars and the cabin door a short figure, arms raised, one hand waving a greyish handkerchief, waddled toward the door of the cabin.

"It's Tuttle," Father Dowling said.

"Who else?"

A more successful lawyer can wait for clients to come to him. Tuttle was always on the alert for poor devils in need of legal representation and he had been riding in a squad car with Peanuts when he switched the radio dial from Rush Limbaugh and picked up the report of Earl Haven holed up in his riverside summer cottage. Immediately they were on their way to the scene. Tuttle had jumped out of the car, listened for a few minutes and, when his opportunity came, seized it.

His breath came in rapid gasps and he had a stitch in his side before his hand closed over the knob of the front door. He panted for a moment and then lifted his free hand toward the door and knocked. In doing this, his hand turned the knob, the door opened and he tumbled inside, literally sprawling across the uncarpeted floor of the cabin. The windows overlooking the river blinded him with their brightness and he got to his knees and looked blinking about.

"Who are you?"

"Can you pull those blinds?"

"Are you a reporter?"

"No!" Tuttle rose to his feet in indignation. He might be at the bottom rung of his chosen profession but he had not sunk to the level of those purchased pens who hung around the press room of the court house. "I am Tuttle the lawyer." He found his tweed hat and put it on his head. It was like resuming his true persona.

"Oh yeah."

"My advice is that you make no statement whatsoever. We will march out of here, they can book you, but I will do the talking."

"There's nothing to say."

"Exactly."

"I didn't hurt Leo."

Tuttle remembered the scene at the Naperville Boxers Inc. He had not seen Earl there. He could not remember anyone else who had. Rose Hanlon, Earl's secretary, had unwisely told the police that Earl had gone to Naperville.

"That could work."

"What do you mean?"

"Look, I was at the store in Naperville when the cops were investigating. It couldn't have been long after . . ."

Something in Earl's eye caused Tuttle to stop. He did not want to antagonize a potential client.

"What time were you there?"

"I never got there. I got caught in traffic, a jack-knifed semi blocked the road, and finally I just turned around and started back to Fox River. I heard about it on radio, and that I was being sought. I headed here."

"Why?"

"Look out there. I feel like a treed squirrel."

But why would an innocent man run? Tuttle did not ask this question. A lawyer can often represent his client better if he lets innocence remain a presumption. Knowing too much can be a burden.

"Earl, we're going out there. We're going to open that door and march right out to the police, those cameras, everything. You can't stay here forever."

Earl looked as if he wanted to argue about it, but suddenly his shoulders slumped. "You're right. Let's go."

"Let me look at you first."

Tuttle stood in front of Earl and squinted his eyes, imagining what he would look like on television.

"Why don't you take off your cap."

"You going to take off your hat?"

"Okay, leave it on." Tuttle took the door handle, inhaled, and pulled. Silence fell. Tuttle stepped outside first, his eyes shaded by the brim of his hat, and located the television cameras. When Earl came out, Tuttle took his elbow and they walked right at the cameras. Tuttle kept up a non-stop patter as they walked, a lawyer advising his client. Earl looked bewildered but that wasn't bad. It could be mistaken for innocence. All this was being taped. It would be like running a commercial on television. Tuttle moved even closer to his client. He didn't want to be focused out of the picture.

Phil Keegan and Cy Horvath came forward to meet them.

"Remember, Earl," Tuttle said, addressing the media. "You don't have to say a thing."

"I didn't do anything," Earl protested. "I'll say that."

8

There was an unbaptized part of Marie Murkin's soul that took mordant pleasure from the spectacle of Harriet Dolan being deprived of two men, either one of whom had been too good for her. But the fact—or alleged fact, as Tuttle always insisted in speaking to the press—that one of those men had killed the other out of insane desire for Harriet was something it was difficult to accept cheerfully. Harriet rose to her tragic role during the funeral of Leo Mulcahy, sitting in the front pew with the Mulcahy girls, for all the world as if she were a widow. But it soon became clear that Harriet had no intention of going into deep mourning.

"Does she intend to wait for Earl?"

"Ask Phil Keegan about that."

"Does she confide in Phil?"

"She hasn't even been to visit him in jail."

"Well, after all, he is accused of killing her fiancé."

There was no point in trying to explain it to the pastor. One needed a woman's intuition to maneuver through the intricacies of the matter. It was Marie's fear that while she might ignore him while he languished in jail awaiting trial, Harriet would be all too prominent in the court room once proceedings began. What a magnet she would be for the press. The woman whose fiancé the accused had killed because she had spurned him. It was almost too much to bear.

Marie noticed that Harriet came regularly to Mass on Sunday and had to acknowledge that she did nothing to draw attention to herself, not coming late nor leaving early, dressing in a subdued way. Marie was on the verge of thinking that she had misjudged Harriet when she ran into her as she was leaving the mall.

"Hello," Harriet replied warily in response to Marie's greeting.

"I'm Marie Murkin, housekeeper at St. Hilary's."

"Of course I recognize you."

Marie would have liked to chat with the girl but the moment was not propitious. They parted and Marie started for her car. When she got in, she noticed that Harriet was still standing near the door, looking out over the lot. Had she forgotten where she had parked? But then her expression changed as a car drew up to the curb. Harriet, radiant, pulled open the door. Marie had started her engine and managed to drive forward to where she could get a good glimpse of the man behind the wheel of the car that had come for Harriet Dolan. At first she did not recognize him, but then she did.

Steve Hanlon.

9

Earl Haven's trial proceeded with slow inevitability and the apparent fate of the accused could not be ascribed simply to the want of skill on the part of his lawyer. Indeed, when Father Dowling asked Amos Cadbury what he thought of Tuttle's performance, the patrician lawyer, dean of Fox River attorneys, thought for a moment.

"I am only surprised that the prosecution has not called those who said they saw Haven at the Naperville store that morning."

Amos was right. At the time any number of people claimed to have been eye witnesses to a quarrel between Earl and Leo.

"Maybe they don't need that evidence."

"You may be right."

"It looks bad for Earl."

"His chances of acquittal are not good."

"Poor fellow."

"Perhaps he is guilty."

"Perhaps?"

But apparently it was simply the caution of the lawyer. Father Dowling had spoken with Earl Haven and while he was privy to no confidential matters so far as Earl's soul went—as a non-Catholic Earl would not ask to confess his sins—he had the distinct feeling that he was speaking with an innocent man. Or at least with one innocent of the crime of which he was accused. Earl's story about never having gone to the Naperville store on that fateful morning had been difficult to sustain in court. The traffic jam Earl said had decided him to return to Fox River could not be verified. Earl had spoken of a jack-knifed semi, but no police report corroborating the incident had been discovered. Earl said he had never actually seen the semi, but a similar delay three weeks before had been caused by a jack-knifed semi. Tuttle was able to verify that and he produced police reports, subpoenaed half a dozen drivers, proved it beyond the shadow of a doubt. But, as the prosecutor pointed out, that had nothing to do with the traffic on the day Leo was killed. Tuttle then turned to the undisputed negative fact that no one had seen Earl in Naperville that day. The prosecutor did not counter with eyewitnesses. It was soon clear why.

"Ah, but he left proof of his being there," the prosecutor said. A long gray scarf was introduced into evidence. It had been twisted around the neck of the hapless Leo Mulcahy. The scarf was definitely Earl's. It had his name in it.

"I lost that scarf," Earl cried. "I haven't seen it for years."

"Lost it? No, you didn't lose it. But you did leave it behind at the scene where you killed Leo Mulcahy!"

Earl was doomed. The jury withdrew to consider their verdict. Within an hour they were back. They found Earl Haven guilty of causing the death of Leo Mulcahy and with malice aforethought.

"He will be an old man when he gets out," Father Dowling observed to Marie Murkin.

"The poor man."

"There will be no point in the young lady waiting for him."

"There will be no danger of it either."

"Oh?"

Listening to Marie Father Dowling sat very still. It was as if she had suddenly been given the key to recent events. It was unclear that Marie saw the full significance of what she was saying. He said nothing at the time and the housekeeper eventually returned to her kitchen, a little embarrassed at having passed on such gossip. Father Dowling remained at his desk for half an hour, thinking. He got out a piece of paper and prepared to write on it, but did not. He did not need to make a list of what he knew in order to arrive at a conclusion.

He got up and put on a coat and said on his way through the kitchen, "I'm going out, Marie. Would you call Phil Keegan and Cy Horvath to come over tonight?"

"For supper?"

"What a wonderful idea."

✝ ✝ ✝

The one-time wide receiver of the Fox River high school Reds had an office in the same mall in which Earl Haven had opened the original Boxers Inc. Stephen Hanlon was an accountant, a bald man in a blue shirt and striped tie who sat coatless behind his desk, his unblinking eyes concentrating on figures and columns and the quantification of the romance of commerce. He greeted Father Dowling and asked him to be seated. His eyes never left his caller.

"How I marvel at anyone who can do that," Father Dowling exclaimed when Steve Hanlon answered his question as to what he did in this bare and orderly office.

"Who keeps the books at St. Hilary?"

"I keep one set."

The pale brows rose above pale eyes.

"No mortal knows enough to keep a complete account, does he, Steve?"

"There is no mystery about a good set of books."

"Income and outgo, plus and minus, add and subtract?"

Steve Hanlon nodded.

"What sort of balance can there be for taking another life?"

Perhaps if his life had gone differently Steve Hanlon might have become a Trappist. He seemed comfortable with silence. His eyes were all but expressionless as he looked across his neat desk at Father Dowling.

"Was it jealousy, Steve?"

Silence.

"Did it anger you that your old quarterback had teamed up with Leo Mulcahy?"

The fan of Hanlon's computer purred evenly. A digital clock on the wall measured time not quite noiselessly.

"Of course it wasn't that, was it? It was what Leo had done when he jilted Rose."

Steve rose as if he were managed by invisible wires. His hand closed on a large smooth stone that did service as a paperweight.

"You use what's at hand, don't you? How did you happen to be wearing Earl Haven's scarf?"

"You're guessing, I know. But if you can guess, so can others."

"That seems a reason for not compounding your troubles, doesn't it?"

Steve stood there, the rock gripped menacingly in his hand, but he was thinking. What Father Dowling had said was entered into one column, his mind went on to the next. After a moment, he sat down. He put the large stone where it had been and placed his hands on the arms of his chair.

"You're right. It was Rose. She loved him. She still does."

"Does she know?"

"Of course not."

Another item was entered in the ledger in Steve's mind, and Father Dowling feared that he had put himself in danger by the question. But Steve simply looked at him. Finally he said, "What do you want me to do?"

"Come to dinner at the rectory?"

For the first time Steve Hanlon reacted to what Father Dowling had said. His mouth opened in surprise.

10

The drive to and from Joliet was not a long one and Father Dowling did not remain long at the prison. Steve Hanlon seemed to appreciate his visits, but he simply did not have the gift of conversation. Besides, his talents had been put to work in the business office and, while he was no longer a free man, he was free to engage in the accounting that had always made up a large part of his life. Only one thing had truly bothered him. He had kept the books for Boxers Inc and picked a quarrel with Leo Mulcahy over his terrible business sense when he heard that his sister's old fiancé was engaged to marry Harriet Dolan, sacking his old quarterback.

"Please explain to Rose, Father," he had asked when, having dined with Phil Keegan and Cy Horvath at the rectory table, he had told the detectives what he had done in Naperville.

"You invited a murderer to dinner?" Phil asked, after Cy had taken Steve downtown.

"Is this a confession?"

"You know what Captain Keegan means," Marie said, coming in from the kitchen. "When I think that I was urging all that food on someone who had taken a human life."

"He did have a good appetite, didn't he?"

"Second helpings of everything."

"Perhaps he figured out how much he was saving."

But the personality of Steve Hanlon was not known to Marie or Phil Keegan. His matter-of-fact admission that he had strangled Leo Mulcahy, dabbing at his mouth with his napkin as he told of it, had not exactly promoted digestion. Nonetheless, Father Dowling was certain he had been right in following his instinct and asking Steve Hanlon back to the rectory for dinner. The police were already scheduled to be there.

"He ate a hearty meal before he was condemned," Phil said. He seemed to have decided to let Marie carry the complaint alone.

"Well, he certainly won't have to worry about where his next meal is coming from," Marie said.

Phil Keegan sighed. "I can still see him gathering in a pass from Earl Haven."

"That will doubtless be Harriet Dolan's game now," Marie said. She widened her eyes and then turned on her heel and went into her kitchen.

Earl Haven had always attracted Harriet. Nor had his attraction suffered from the accusation that he had strangled Leo Mulcahy rather than let him marry Harriet. When it seemed that this act of gallantry would cause Earl to spend most of the rest of his life in prison, it was only human that Harriet should become susceptible to the charms of Steve Hanlon. Of course she misread his interest. He had been motivated by anger that Leo had dropped his sister Rose for Harriet. But Harriet's fickleness had dissolved the charm she had for Earl.

As he drove back to Fox River from Joliet and his visit with Steve Hanlon, Father Dowling checked his watch. Earl Haven would be coming to the rectory for instructions that evening. He professed to be interested in becoming a Catholic.

"Rose has told me to make up my own mind, of course."

"Of course."

"We would like to be married at St. Hilary's."

Whether the ceremony came before or after Earl's entry into the Church was still undecided. He still seemed to think a Hail Mary was a pass rather than a prayer.

Conventual Spirit

Sharan Newman

June 1137, the convent of the Paraclete, France

"Pride, Catherine! Evil, wicked pride! It will be your damnation, girl!"

Sister Bertrada glared at Catherine, their faces an inch apart. "You'll never be allowed to become one of us unless you learn some humility," the old nun continued. "How dare you try to lecture me on the blessed St. Jerome! Do you think you've received a vision of the Truth?"

Catherine bit her tongue.

"No, Sister," she said.

Even those two words sounded impudent to Sister Bertrada, who considered the student novices under her care to be her own private purgatory. And Catherine LeVendeur, with her ready tongue and sharp mind, was her special bane.

"Abbess Heloise has a soft spot for you, though I can't see why," Bertrada went on. "I don't find your glib attempts at rhetoric endearing at all."

"No, Sister." Catherine tried to back up, but Sister Bertrada had her wedged into a corner of the refectory and there was no farther back to go.

"What you need is some serious manual labor."

Catherine stifled a groan. Sister Bertrada did not consider sitting for hours hunched over a table laboriously copying a Psalter to be real work. Never mind that her fingers cramped, her back ached, and her eyes burned at the end of the day. Now she tried to look meek and obliging as she awaited Sister Bertrada's orders.

She succeeded about as well as most sixteen-year-old girls would.

Sister Bertrada had eyes like the Archangel Michael, which glowed with righteousness and ferreted out the most deeply hidden sins. Her cane tapped the wooden floor with ominous thumps as she considered an appropriate penance.

"Go find Sister Felicitia," she told Catherine at last. "Ask her to give you a bucket and a brush. The transept of the oratory has mud all over the floor. You can easily finish scrubbing it before Vespers, if you give the labor the same passion you use to defy me."

Catherine bowed her head, hopefully in outward submission. Sister Bertrada snorted to show that she wasn't fooled in the least, then turned and marched out, leaving Catherine once again defeated by spiritual superiority.

Outside, she was met by her friend and fellow student, Emilie. Emilie took one look at Catherine's face and started laughing.

"Why in the world did you feel you had to tell Sister Bertrada that St. Jerome nagged poor St. Paula to death?"

Catherine shrugged. "I was only quoting from a letter of St. Ambrose. I thought it was interesting that even the saints had their quarrels."

Emilie shook her head in wonder. "You've been here a year and you still have no sense about when to speak and when to keep silent. Sister Melisande would find it amusing, so would Mother Heloise, but Sister Bertrada. . . !"

"I agree," Catherine said sadly. "And now I'm to pay for it on my knees, as usual."

"And proper." Emilie smiled at her fondly. "Oh, Catherine, you do make lessons interesting, if more volatile. I'm so glad you came here."

Catherine sighed. "So am I. Now if only Sister Bertrada could share our happiness."

If meekness were the only test for judging the worthiness of a soul, then Sister Felicitia should have inherited the earth long ago. She was the only daughter of a noble family, who ought to have had to do nothing more than sing the hours, sew, and copy manuscripts. Her only distinction was that her face was marred by deep scars on both sides, running from temple to jaw. Catherine had never heard how she came by them, but assumed that this disfigurement was the reason she was in the convent instead of married to some lord. Although for the dowry Felicitia commanded, it was surprising that no one was willing to take her, no matter what she looked like.

Felicitia certainly didn't behave like a pampered noblewoman. She always volunteered when the most disagreeable tasks were being assigned. She scrubbed out the reredorter, even leaning into the holes in the seats above the river to scrub the filth from the inside. She hauled wood and dug vegetables. She never lifted her eyes from the job she was doing. She never raised her voice in dispute.

Catherine didn't know what to make of her.

"I'll need the bucket later this evening," Sister Felicitia said when Catherine stated her orders. "I'd help you, of course, but I'm dyeing today."

Catherine had noticed. The woman's hands were stained blue with woad. It would be days before it all washed off. Sister Felicitia didn't appear concerned by this. Nor did she seem aware that the day was soft and bright and that the other women were all sitting in the cloister, sewing and chatting softly while soaking up the June sunshine.

"Sister Bertrada wants me to do this alone, anyway," Catherine said, picking up the bucket and brush. Sister Felicitia nodded without looking up. She did not indulge in unnecessary conversation.

† † †

Catherine spilled half the water tripping over the doorstop to the oratory. Coming in from the sunlight, it seemed to her that there were bright doves fluttering before her eyes. So she missed her step in the darkness, and then mopped up the puddles before spending the better part of the afternoon scrubbing the stone floor. But, true to Sister Bertrada's prediction, she did indeed have the job finished in time for Vespers, although her robes were still damp and stained at the hem, unsuitable attire for the Divine Office.

And that was how she knew that there had been no muddy footprints on the oratory floor when the nuns retired to the dormitory that evening.

Of course, Sister Bertrada didn't believe her.

"This time, do it properly," she told Catherine as she handed her the bucket the next day.

Catherine fervently wanted to protest. She had scrubbed the floor thoroughly, half of it with her own skirts. It had been clean. Perhaps one of the nuns had forgotten and worn her wooden clogs to prayers instead of her slippers. It wasn't her fault.

But Catherine knew that she would never be allowed to remain here at the Paraclete if she contradicted Sister Bertrada every time she opened her mouth, and she wanted to stay at the convent more than anything else in the world. So she took the proffered bucket and returned to the dark oratory.

She propped the door open to let the light in and knelt to begin the task.

"That's odd," she said as she started on the marks.

"That's *very* odd," she added as she went on to the next ones.

These had to have been made recently, after Compline, when all the women had retired for the night. They were in the shape of footprints, starting at the door and running across the transept to the chapter room, stopping at the bottom of the staircase to the nuns' dormitory. The marks were smudged, perhaps by the slippers of the nuns when they came down just before dawn for Vigils and Lauds. But the muddy prints had certainly been made by bare feet. And they were still damp.

Who could have entered the oratory secretly in the middle of the night?

Catherine wondered about it all the while she was scrubbing. When she had finished, she went to the prioress, Astane, for an explanation.

"These footprints," Astane asked. "You already removed them?"

"Sister Bertrada told me to," Catherine explained.

The prioress nodded. "Very good, child. You are learning."

"But I know they weren't there yesterday evening," Catherine insisted. "I did clean the floor carefully the first time. Someone was in the oratory after we went to bed."

"That seems unlikely." Astane did not appear alarmed by Catherine's statement. "The door is barred on the inside, after all."

"Then how did the footprints get there?" Catherine persisted.

The prioress raised her eyebrows. "That is not your concern, my dear."

"It is if I have to wipe them up," Catherine muttered under her breath.

Not far enough under. Astane's hand gripped her chin tightly and tilted her face upward.

"I presume you were praying just then," the prioress said.

Catherine marveled at the strength in these old women. Sister Bertrada, Prioress Astane; they both must be nearly seventy, but with hands as firm and steady as a blacksmith's. And eyes that saw the smallest lie.

"No, Sister," Catherine said. "But I am now. *Domine, noli me arguere in ira tua . . .*"

The prioress's lip twitched and her sharp glance softened. "'Lord, do not rebuke me in your anger. . .'" she translated. "Catherine, dear, I'm not angry with you and I hope and trust that our Lord isn't, either."

She paused. "Sister Bertrada, on the other hand . . ."

Catherine needed no further warning. She resolved not to mention the footprints in the oratory again.

But the next morning, everyone saw them.

The light of early dawn slanted through the narrow windows of the chapter, illuminating the clumps of damp earth, a few fresh stalks still clinging to them, forming a clear trail of footprints across the room.

"How did those get there?" Emilie whispered to Catherine, peering down the stairs over the shoulders of the choir nuns.

"They're exactly the same as yesterday," Catherine whispered back. "But I'm sure I cleaned it all. I know I did."

Sister Bertrada and Sister Felicitia walked through the marks, apparently without noticing, but the other women stopped. They looked at each other in confusion, pointing at the footprints, starting at the barred door to the garden, going through the oratory and ending at the steps to their sleeping room.

Sister Ursula shuddered. "Something is coming for us!" she shrieked. "A wild man of the woods has invaded the convent!"

A few of the others gave startled cries, but Emilie giggled, putting a hand over her mouth to stifle the sound. Behind her, Sister Bietriz bent over her shoulder.

"What is it?" she whispered.

Emilie swallowed her laughter. "'Wild man' indeed!" she whispered back. "Maybe Sister Bertrada has a secret lover!"

Bietriz and Catherine exploded in most unseemly mirth.

"*Quiet!*" The object of their speculation raised her cane in warning.

They composed themselves as quickly as possible, knowing that the matter would not be forgotten, but hoping to alleviate the punishment.

"Catherine," Sister Bertrada continued. "Since you and Emilie find this mess so amusing, you may clean it. Bietriz, you will help them."

Catherine opened her mouth to object that she had already removed the marks twice and it had done no good. Just as she inhaled to speak, Emilie stepped on her toe.

"Yie . . . yes, Sister," Catherine said instead.

Privately, she agreed with both Ursula and Emilie. The marks must have been made by a wild man from the forest. For who else could become enamored of Sister Bertrada?

✝ ✝ ✝

"I agree that there is something very strange about this," Emilie told Catherine as they scrubbed. "Who could be getting in here every night? And why doesn't Mother Heloise say something about it? Do you think she knows who it is?"

Catherine wrung out the washrag. Bietriz, whose family was too exalted for floors, leaned against the wall and pointed out spots they had missed.

"Mother Heloise probably doesn't think this worth commenting on," she said. "Perhaps she thinks someone is playing a trick and doesn't want them encouraged. You don't really believe one of us is letting a man in, do you?"

"Who?" Emilie asked. "Sister Bertrada? She and Sister Felicitia would be the most logical suspects. Since they sleep on either side of the door, they have the best chance of leaving at night without being noticed."

Catherine tried to imagine either woman tiptoeing down the steps to let in a secret lover. In Sister Bertrada's case her imagination didn't stretch far enough.

She laughed. "I would find it easier to believe in a monster."

"It's not so preposterous," Emilie continued. "Sister Felicitia is really quite beautiful, even now. I've heard that she had a number of men eager to marry her, but she refused them all. Her father was furious when she announced that she would only wed Christ."

Catherine leaned back on her heels and considered. "I suppose she might have changed her mind," she said. "Perhaps one of them continued to pursue her even here and convinced her that he wanted her despite her looks and had no interest in her property."

Bietriz shook her head. "I don't think so, Catherine. Felicitia made those scars herself, with the knife she used to cut embroidery thread. She sliced right through her cheeks, purposely, so that no one would desire her. That was how her father was finally convinced to let her come here."

Catherine sat back in shock, knocking over the bucket of soapy water.

"How do you know this?" she asked.

"It was common knowledge at the time," Bietriz answered. "I was about twelve then. I remember how upset my mother was about it. Felicitia threatened to cut off her own nose next. It's dreadful, but I benefited from her example. When I said I wanted to come to the Paraclete, no one dared oppose me. Mother even refused to let me have my sewing basket unless she was present, just in case."

"I see." Catherine was once again reminded that she was only a merchant's daughter, at the Paraclete by virtue of her quick mind and her father's money. Bietriz was from one of the best families in Champagne, related in some way even to the count. Bietriz knew all about the life of a noblewoman and all the gossip she herself would not normally be privy to. At the Paraclete they could be sisters in Christ, but not in the world.

"Very well," Catherine said. "I will accept that Sister Felicitia is not likely to be letting a man in. But I don't see how any of the rest of us could do it without waking someone."

"Nor do I," Emilie agreed. "In which case we might have to consider Ursula's theory."

"That some half-human creature came in from the forest?" Catherine snorted.

Emilie stood, shaking out her skirts. Bietriz picked up the bucket, her contribution to the labor.

"Of course not," Emilie said. "Even a half-human creature would have to unbar the door. But Satan can pass through bars and locks, if someone summons him. And it's said that he often appears as a beautiful young man."

Bietriz was skeptical. "So we should demand to know who has been having dreams of seduction lately? Who will admit to that?"

Catherine felt a chill run down her spine. Was it possible that one of them could be inviting Evil into the convent, perhaps unwittingly? It was well known that the devil used dreams to lure and confuse the innocent into sin. She tried to remember her dreams of the past few nights. The memories were dim, so it was likely that she had only had dreams of *ventris inanitate*, those deriving from an empty stomach and of no relevance.

They walked out into the sunlight and Catherine felt the fear diminish. While it was true that Satan used dreams to tempt weak humans, sin could only occur when one was awake. Tertullian said so. We can no more be condemned for dreaming we are sinners than rewarded for dreaming we are saints.

"And why would the devil leave footprints?" she continued the thought aloud. "That doesn't seem very subtle."

Emilie didn't want to give up her demon lover theory.

"There is a rock near my home with a dent in it that everyone says is the devil's toe print," she told Catherine. "So why not the whole foot? Satan is known to be devious. Perhaps he doesn't just want one soul. He may be trying to cause dissension among us so that he may take us all."

Bietriz had moved on to another worry. "Why is it that the feet are only coming in?" she asked them. "How does this intruder get out?"

"Perhaps he turns into something else," Emilie answered. "Satan can do that, too."

She seemed delighted with her conclusions, and her expression dared them to come up with a refutation.

Catherine looked at her. Was she serious? Did she now believe they were being visited by the devil as shapechanger? Emilie was usually scornful of such tales. Why was she so eager to assign a supernatural explanation to this? An answer leaped unbidden to her mind.

Emilie's bed wasn't that far from the door.

Catherine tried to suppress the thought as unworthy, but it wouldn't be put down. Emilie was blond, beautiful, and also from a noble family. Perhaps she wasn't as happy in the convent as she pretended. It entailed a much smaller stretch of the imagination to see Emilie unbarring the door for a lover than Sister Felicitia.

But that explanation didn't satisfy her, either. It wasn't like Emilie. And Catherine was sure Mother Heloise and Prioress Astane didn't believe that one of the nuns had a secret lover, human or demon. If they did, then Brother Baldwin and the other lay brothers who lived nearby would have been set to guard the oratory entrance.

She was missing something. Catherine hated to leave a puzzle unsolved. She had to find out who was doing this. She sighed. It was either that or spend the rest of her life scrubbing the oratory floor.

It was nearly midsummer. The days were long and busy. Apart from reciting the Divine Office seven times a day, the nuns all performed manual labor. They studied, copied manuscripts for the convent library, sewed both church vestments and their own clothing, as well as doing the daily round of cleaning, cooking, and gardening necessary to keep themselves alive.

Catherine meant to stay awake that night, but after the long day, she fell asleep as soon as she lay down and didn't wake until the bell rang for Vigils.

Even in the dim light of the lamp carried by Sister Felicitia, they could all see the fresh footprints at the bottom of the stairs.

Sister Ursula retreated back up the stairs, whimpering, and had to be ordered to continue to the oratory. The others obeyed as well, but with obvious reluctance.

Mother Heloise and Prioress Astane were already waiting in the chapel. Their presence reassured the women and reminded them of their duty to pray. But Catherine was not the only one who looked to see that the bar was still across the garden door.

"Satan won't distract me," Emilie whispered virtuously as they filed into their places. "He can't get you while you're praying."

Catherine wasn't so confident. Whatever was doing this had thoroughly distracted her. She missed the antiphon more than once and knew that bowing her apology to God would not save her from Sister Bertrada's rebuke.

There was an explanation for this, either natural or supernatural. Catherine didn't care which it was. She only wanted to know the truth.

The next day was the eve of the feast of the Nativity of St. John the Baptist. There would be a special vigil that night. It was also midsummer's eve, a time of spirits crossing between worlds, a fearsome long twilight. A good Christian could be driven mad or worse by the things that walked this night. These beliefs were officially denied and forbidden, but children

learned the folk tales before they were weaned and such stories were hard
to uproot. The shimmering sunlight of the morning was not bright
enough to dispel fear.

Each afternoon while they worked in the cloister, the women were permitted some edifying conversation. Today, the usual gentle murmurs and
soft laughter had become a buzzing of wonderment, anger, and fear.

"What if this thing doesn't stop tonight at the bottom of the stairs?"
Sister Ursula said, her eyes round with terror and anticipation. "What if
it climbs right up and into our beds?"

"All of ours, or just yours?" Bietriz asked.

Ursula reddened with anger. "What are you implying?" she
demanded. "I would never bring scandal upon us. How dare you even
suggest such a thing!"

Bietriz sighed and put down her sewing. She went over to Ursula and
took her gently by the shoulders.

"I apologize," she said. "It was not a kind joke. I make no accusations.
I believe you have become overwrought by these happenings. Perhaps
you could sleep with Sister Melisande in the infirmary tonight."

"Perhaps I will," Ursula muttered. "Better than being slandered by my
sisters or murdered by demons in the dortor."

Sister Felicitia was seated on the grass, her stained hands weaving
softened reeds to mend a basket. She looked up.

"There are no demons here," she said firmly.

They all stared at her. It would have been more surprising if a sheep
in the meadow had spouted philosophy.

"How do you know?" Ursula asked.

"Mother Heloise promised me," Felicitia answered. "The demons
won't come for me here."

She bent again to her work. The others were silent.

"Well," Ursula said finally. "Perhaps I will stay in the dortor. But if
anything attacks me, I'll scream so loud you'll think Judgment Day has
come."

"If you wake me," Emilie warned, "you'll wish it had."

Before Vespers the Abbess Heloise gathered all the women together in
the chapter room. There was a collective sigh of relief as they assembled.
Finally, all would be explained.

The abbess smiled at them all fondly. Her large brown eyes studied them, and Catherine felt that Mother Heloise knew just what each of them was thinking and feeling.

"It has been brought to my attention," she began, "that some of you have been concerned about some mud stains in the oratory and chapel. I fear that you have allowed these queries to go beyond normal curiosity to unwholesome speculation. This saddens me greatly. If something so natural and common as wet earth can cause you to imagine demons and suspect each other of scandalous behavior, then I have not done my duty as your mentor or your mother."

There was a rustle of surprise and denial. Heloise held up her hand for silence. There was silence.

"Therefore," she continued, "I apologize to you all for not providing the proper spiritual guidance. I will endeavor to do so in the future and will ask our founder, Master Abelard, for advice on how this may best be done. I hope you will forgive me."

That was all. Heloise signaled the chantress to lead them in for Vespers.

They followed in bewildered obedience. Catherine and Emilie stared at each other, shaking their heads. As far as Catherine could see, they had just been told that the intruder in the convent was none of their business. It made no sense.

Mindful of her earlier mistakes, Catherine tried desperately to keep her mind on the service for St. John's Eve, despite the turmoil in her mind.

"*Ecce, mitto angelum meum . . .*" Behold, I send my angel, who will prepare the way for you before my coming. "*Vox clamitis in deserto . . .*" A voice crying in the wilderness.

She tried to concentrate on St. John. It was hard to imagine him as a baby, leaping for joy in his mother's womb as they visited the Virgin Mary. She always saw him as the gaunt man of the desert, living naked on a diet of locusts and honey. People must have thought him mad, preaching a savior no one had heard of.

"*Ecce, mitto angelum meum . . .*"

All at once Catherine realized what she had been doing. She had looked at the problem from one direction only. Mother Heloise knew the answer. That was why she wasn't worried. When one turned the proposition around, it made perfect sense. Now, if only she could stay awake tonight to prove her theory.

The night, usually too brief, seemed to stretch on forever. Catherine was beginning to believe that she had made an error in her logic.

There was a rustling from the other end of the room. Someone was getting up. Catherine waited. Whoever it was could be coming this way, to use the reredorter. No one passed her bed. She heard a creak from the end of the room, as if someone else were also awake. She peered over the blanket. It was too dark to tell. There were no more sounds. Perhaps it had only been someone tossing about with a nightmare. Perhaps. But she had to know.

Carefully, Catherine eased out of bed. They all slept fully dressed, even to their slippers, so as to be ready for the Night Office. Catherine looked up and down the rows on either side of the room. In the dim light everyone appeared to be accounted for and asleep. Slowly, fearing even to breathe, Catherine moved down the room to the door. It was open.

All the tales of monsters and demons came rushing suddenly into her mind. Anything could be at the foot of those stairs. Who would protect her if she encountered them against orders, because of her arrogant curiosity?

She said a quick prayer to St. Catherine of Alexandria, who had known what it was to wonder about things, and she started down the stairs.

At the bottom she nearly fainted in terror as she stepped onto a pile of something soft that moved under her foot. She bent down and touched it.

It was clothing just like her own. A shift, a long tunic, a belt, and a pair of slippers. The discovery of something so familiar terrified Catherine even more.

What had happened to the woman who had worn these clothes?

Moonlight shone through the open door of the oratory. Catherine looked down at the floor. In her fear, she had almost forgotten to test her conclusion.

She was right. The floor was clean. So far, nothing had entered. Feeling a little more confident, she stepped out into midsummer night.

The herb garden lay tranquil under the moon. Catherine had been out once before at night, helping Sister Melisande pick the plants that were most potent when gathered at the new moon. This time she was here uninvited.

There was a break in the hedge on the other side of the garden. Catherine thought she saw a flicker of something white in the grove just beyond. Before she could consider the stupidity of her actions, she hurried toward it.

Within the grove there was a small hill that was empty of trees or undergrowth. Sheep grazed there by day, but tonight . . . *"Ecce! Mitto angelum!"*

Catherine stopped at the edge of the trees. There was someone on the hill, pale skin glowing silver in the moonlight, golden curls surrounding her face like a halo. It was Sister Felicitia, naked, dancing in the night, her feet covered with mud. Her arms were raised as she spun, her face to the sky, her back arched, moving to some music that Catherine couldn't hear.

A hand touched her shoulder. Catherine gasped and the hand moved to her mouth.

"Make no sound," Abbess Heloise warned. "You'll wake her."

Catherine nodded and Heloise removed her hand.

"How did you find out?" the abbess whispered.

"It was the footprints," Catherine whispered back, not taking her eyes from Felicitia. "We all thought they were from someone being let in. But it made much more sense if they were made by someone coming back. Then only one person was needed to open the door from the inside. What I didn't understand was the prints of bare feet."

"She always leaves her clothes at the bottom of the stairs and puts them on again before returning to bed," Heloise explained.

"But shouldn't we stop her?" Catherine asked. "She must be possessed to behave like this."

"She might be," Heloise said. "I worried about that, too. But Sister Bertrada convinced me that if she is, it's by nothing evil and we have no right to interfere."

"Sister Bertrada?" Catherine's voice rose in astonishment.

"Hush!" Heloise told her. "Yes, she's on the other side of the grove, watching to be sure no one interrupts. Brother Baldwin is farther on, guarding the gate to the road. Not everyone who saw her would understand. Do you?"

Catherine shook her head. She didn't understand, but it didn't matter. She was only grateful she had been allowed to watch. Felicitia, dancing in the moonlight, wasn't licentious, but sublime. She shone like Eve on the first morning, radiant with delight at the wonder of Eden, in blissful ignorance of sin. The joy of it made Catherine weep in her own knowledge that soon the serpent would come, and with it, sorrow.

Heloise guided Catherine gently away.

"She'll finish soon and go back to bed," the abbess explained. "Sister Bertrada will see that she gets there safely. Come with me. Astane has left some warmed cider for me. You have a cup also, before you go back."

When they were settled in Heloise's room, drinking the herbed cider, Catherine finally asked the question.

"I figured out who and how, Mother," she said. "But I don't understand why."

Heloise looked into her cider bowl for several minutes. Catherine thought that she might not answer. Perhaps she didn't know.

At last she seemed to come to a decision.

"Catherine," she asked, "have you ever believed that you were loved by no one? That you were completely alone?"

Catherine thought. "Well," she answered, "there was about a month when I was thirteen, but . . . no, no. Even then I always knew my family loved me. I know you love me. I know God loves me, unworthy though I am of all of you."

Heloise smiled. "That's right, on all points. But until she came here, Felicitia believed that no one loved her, that God had abandoned her, and she had good reason. That is not a story for you to hear. I only want you to understand that I am sure that Felicitia is not possessed by anything evil."

"I believe you," Catherine said. "But I still don't understand."

"I didn't, either," Heloise admitted. "Until Sister Bertrada explained it to me. Don't make such a face, child. Sister Bertrada sees further into your heart than you know."

"That doesn't comfort me, Mother."

Heloise smiled. "It should. Bertrada told me that Felicitia spent all her life being desired for her beauty, for her wealth, her family connections. In all that desire, there was no love. So she felt she wasn't worthy of love and consented to despair. She endured much to find her way to us. The scars on her face are mild compared to the ones on her soul. She struggles every day with worse demons that any Ursula can imagine. And until a week ago, she had nightmares almost every night."

"And then . . ." Catherine said.

"And then," Heloise smiled, "joy came to her one night, and she danced. It has only been in her sleep so far, but if she is left in peace, we are hoping that soon she will also have joy in the morning, all through the day, and at last be healed."

Catherine sat for a long while, until the cider went cold and the chantress rose to ring the bell for Vigils. Heloise waited patiently.

"Are you satisfied, Catherine?" she asked. "You assembled the evidence, arranged it properly, and solved the mystery. There is no need to tell the others."

"Oh, no, I wouldn't do that," Catherine promised. "I only wanted to know the truth."

"Then why do you look so sad?" Heloise prodded.

"It's only—" Catherine stopped, embarrassed. "I'm so clumsy, Mother. If only I could dance like Felicitia, even in my sleep."

Heloise laughed. "And how do you know that you don't?"

For once in her life, Catherine had no reply.

Miss Butterfingers

Monica Quill

I

By the second day, there was no doubt that the man was following her; he showed up in too many places for it to be a coincidence, but Kim let another day go by before she mentioned it to Joyce and Sister Mary Teresa. "Tell him to knock it off," Joyce said, drawing on pre-convent parlance. "Ignore him," Emtee Dempsey said. But Kim found it impossible to follow either bit of advice. Joyce offered to go with her, but then it was hard to say what Joyce would do for several hours in the Northwestern library. And then suddenly one day there was the man, sitting in the reading room, looking about as comfortable as Joyce would have.

To feel compassion for a pest was not the reaction Kim expected from herself. Now, after days of seeing that oval face, expressionless except for the eyes, whenever she turned around, she felt a little surge of pity.

She settled down to work, driving the man from her mind, and was soon immersed in the research that, God and Sister Mary Teresa permitting, would eventually result in her doctoral dissertation. When she went to consult the card catalogue, she had completely forgotten her pursuer, and when she turned to find herself face to face with him, she let out an involuntary cry.

"Don't be frightened." He looked wildly around.

"I am not frightened. Why are you following me?"

He nodded. "I thought you'd noticed."

"What do you want?"

"I know you're a nun."

Well, that was a relief. The only indication in her dress that she was a religious was the veil she wore in the morning when the three of them went to the cathedral for Mass, but of course Kim didn't wear a veil on campus.

"Why not?" Sister Mary Teresa had asked. As far as the old nun was concerned, the decision taken by the order to permit members either to retain the traditional habit, as Emtee Dempsey herself had done, or to wear such suitable dress as they chose was still in force, no matter that the three of them in the house on Walton Street were all that remained of the Order of Martha and Mary. The old nun was the superior of the house, but would never have dreamt of imposing her personal will on the others. She had subtler ways of getting what she wanted. Of course, when it came to the rule, it was not a matter of imposing her will but that of their founder, Blessed Abigail Keineswegs, the authoress of the particular path to heaven they all had chosen when they were professed as nuns in the order.

"I think it has a negative effect on people."

"Perhaps a dissuasive effect is what a young woman your age might want from the veil, Sister."

"Oh, for heaven's sake."

"Indeed."

The day Emtee Dempsey lost an argument would be entered in the *Guinness Book of Records*. What had been particularly annoying about the young man was the possibility that he did not know she was a nun and would ask for a date, and then the explanation would be embarrassing. What a relief, accordingly, to learn that he knew her state in life.

"What is it you want?" She spoke with less aloofness. If he knew she was a nun, perhaps he was in some trouble and thought she might be of help.

"Oh, I don't want anything."

He looked intelligent enough; he was handsome in a way, dark hair, tall, nice smile lines around his eyes. Still, you never know. People with very low IQs don't always look it.

"You can't just follow people around. Would you want me to call a policeman?" The ragtag band of campus guards would not strike fear in many, but they looked like real policemen and as often as not that was enough.

"I am a policeman."

"You are!" Kim stepped back as if to get a better look at him. "Chicago or Evanston?"

"Chicago."

"I can check up on that, you know. What's your name?"

"Your brother doesn't know I've got this assignment. If you tell him, the whole point of it will be lost."

The allusion to Richard dispelled her scepticism. "What are you talking about?"

"There's been a threat against his family. You're part of his family."

"Who threatened him?"

"Does it matter? We're taking it seriously."

"But his wife and kids are the ones you should be looking after."

"We are."

"Nobody is going to harm me."

"I hope you're right. The reason I've been so obvious about following you is to let anyone who might try anything know that I'm around."

It seemed churlish to object to this and silly to ask how long it would continue.

"You didn't tell me your name."

"That's right." His grin was like a schoolboy's. Well, nuns brought out the boy in men, Kim had long been aware of that. Despite her age, she was often addressed as if she were the nun who had once rapped the knuckles of a now middle-aged man. It wasn't necessary that she know her guardian's name, not if she couldn't call Richard and verify that he was a policeman.

After she knew why he was always around, his presence was more distracting rather than less. She felt self-conscious taking notes, every expression was one that might be observed. Within fifteen minutes, she closed her notebook and gathered up her things. All the way out to the Volkswagen bug and on the drive home to Walton Street, she assumed he was just behind her. Now that she knew he was following her, she couldn't find him. But at least she could tell Emtee Dempsey and Joyce what was going on.

"Oh, that's a relief," Joyce said sarcastically. "There's only a threat on your life and all along we thought it was something serious like a persistent Don Juan."

"He said Richard doesn't know?" Emtee Dempsey asked.

"That's right."

"But why wouldn't he be told? Why don't you call him?"

"What if our phone is tapped?"

Emtee Dempsey tried to look outraged but was actually delighted at the thought of such goings-on. "And if we invite Richard to come over, the young man will of course assume you are going to tell him."

† † †

But Richard stopped by the next day unasked. He was ebullient and cheerful, turned down a beer twice before accepting one, sat in the study and looked around expansively.

"It's nice to stop by here when you're not interfering in my work."

"Richard, I have never interfered in your work," Sister Mary Teresa said primly.

His mouth opened in feigned shock and he looked apprehensively toward the ceiling. "I am waiting for a flash of lightning."

"I do not need dramatic divine confirmations of what I say."

"That isn't what I meant."

"What are you working on now?"

He shook his head. "Nothing important, but I would still rather not let you know."

"Very well. And how is your lovely family?"

"I think Agatha, my oldest, has a vocation."

"Really! What makes you think so?"

"No one can tell her a thing, she already knows it all."

"Richard!" Kim said.

He grinned. "Maybe it's just a stage she's going through."

"It must be very difficult for a child to have a father in the police force," the old nun said.

Richard's smile faded. "Why do you say that?"

"Oh, I don't know. Your work takes you among such unsavory elements. It must sometimes be difficult to protect your family from all that."

Kim gave Sister Mary Teresa a warning glance.

"I never bring my work home."

"Does it ever follow you there?"

"How do you mean?"

"Oh, I think of all the malefactors you have brought to justice. I imagine not all of them are grateful to you."

He laughed. "Sister, there are even some who resent it."

"That's my point."

"What is?"

Sister Mary Teresa hesitated. She had promised Kim she would not tell Richard that he and his family were being provided protection by his colleagues. She had come within an eyelash of saying it already, and she was obviously trying to think what further she could say without breaking her promise.

"Who are some of your victims who might seek revenge?"

"Sister, if I worried about things like that I'd have entered a monastery rather than the department."

"Of course you wouldn't *worry* about it. I don't suggest that for a moment. Certainly not worry about your *own* safety. But just for the sake of conversation, if you had to pick someone who is in jail because of your efforts, blames you, and might want to avenge himself, who would it be?"

Richard adopted the attitude of the man of the world telling a house of recluses what was going on outside their walls. Emtee Dempsey was fully prepared to play the naive innocent in order to keep Richard talking.

"The difficulty would be ruling anyone out," he said. "It's fairly routine for a crook after the verdict is in to turn and threaten any and every cop who was in the investigation. This is especially true if you appear in court during the trial. Some even send letters once they're settled in at Joliet."

"Threats?"

"Kid stuff."

"But that's another crime, isn't it?"

"Sister, if we brought charges for every crime that's committed I wouldn't be able to drop by for a social visit like this."

"You are a very evasive man, Richard."

"Thank you."

"You have managed not to name one single criminal who might actually seek to do you harm because you were instrumental in his arrest."

"I'll give you one.

"Good."

"Regina Fastnekker."

"The terrorist!"

"Miss Butterfingers."

Regina Fastnekker was the youngest daughter of a prominent Winnetka family whose fancy it was to be an anarchist. A modern political theory class at De Paul had convinced her that man and human society are fundamentally corrupt, reform is an illusion, and the only constructive thing is to blow it all up. Something, Regina knew not what, would arise from the ashes, but whatever it was, it could not be worse, than the present situation, and there was at least a chance it might be better. On the basis of a single chemistry class, Regina began to make explosives in the privacy of the apartment she rented in the Loop. Winnetka had become too irredeemable for her to bear to live with her parents anymore. It was when one of her bombs went off, tearing out a wall and catapulting an upstairs neighbor into eternity, that Regina confessed to several bombings, one a public phone booth across the road from the entrance to Great Lakes Naval Base. When she was arrested, Regina's hair was singed nearly completely off and that grim bald likeness of her was something she blamed on Richard. In a corrupt world, Regina nonetheless wanted to look her best.

"You're part of the problem, cop," she shouted at him.

"Sure. That's why you're going to jail and I'm not."

"Someday," she said meaningfully.

"Someday what?"

"POW!"

Emtee Dempsey's eyes rounded, as she listened. "How much longer will she be in jail?"

"How much longer? She was released after two years."

"When was that?"

"I don't know. A couple months ago."

"Richard, won't you have another beer?" Emtee Dempsey asked, pleased as punch. "I myself will have a cup of tea."

"Well, we can't have you drinking alone."

Having found out what she wanted, Emtee Dempsey chattered on about other things. It was Richard who returned to the subject of Miss Butterfingers.

"In court she screamed out her rage, threatening the judge, everyone, but when she pointed her finger at me, looking really demented, and vowed she'd get me, I felt a chill. I did. Nonetheless, she was a model prisoner. Got religion. One of the Watergate penitents spoke at Joliet and she was among those who accepted Jesus as their personal savior."

"Then her punishment served her well."

"Yeah."

"Well, that cancels out Regina Fastnekker," Joyce said when Richard had gone.

"We could make a methodical check," Kim said.

"Or you could insist that your guardian angel tell you who has threatened Richard and his family. I should think you have a right to know if you have to put up with him wherever you go."

"I'll do it."

"I'm surprised you didn't insist on it when you talked with him."

Kim accepted the criticism, particularly since she was kicking herself for not finding out more from . . . But she hadn't even found out his name.

2

The next day two things happened that set the house on Walton Street on its ear, in Emtee Dempsey's phrase. At five in the morning, the house reverberated with a tremendous noise and they emerged from their rooms into the hallway, staring astounded at one another.

"What was that?" Joyce asked, her eyes looking like Orphan Annie's.

"An explosion."

As soon as Emtee Dempsey said it, they realized that was indeed what they had heard. The old nun went back into her room and picked up the phone.

"It works," she said, and put it down again. "Sister Kimberly, call the police."

Joyce said, "I'll check to see . . ."

"No." Emtee Dempsey hesitated. Then she went into Kim's room which looked out over Walton Street. They crowded around her. What looked to be pieces of their Volkswagen lay in the street, atop the roof of a red sedan, and shredded upholstery festooned the powerlines just below their eye level.

"Now you know what to report."

Kim picked up her own phone and made the call.

They were up and dressed when there was a ring at the door. Their call had not been necessary to bring the police. Emtee Dempsey was pensive throughout the preliminary inquiry, letting Kim answer most of the questions. At ten minutes to seven she stood.

"We must be off to Mass."

"Maybe you better not, Sister," one of the policemen, Grimaldi, said. He wore his salt-and-pepper hair cut short and his lids lay in diagonals across his eyes, giving him a sleepy, friendly look.

"It is our practice to attend Mass every morning, Sergeant, and I certainly do not intend to alter it for this."

When he realized she was serious, he offered to drive them to the cathedral and Emtee Dempsey was about to refuse when the drama of arriving at St. Matthew's in a squad car struck her.

"Since we might otherwise be late, I agree. But no sirens."

He promised no sirens, thereby, Kim was sure, disappointing Emtee Dempsey.

It was, to put it mildly, a distracting way to begin the day. As it happened, their emerging from a police car at the cathedral door was witnessed by a derelict or two, but otherwise caused no sensation. Once inside, Emtee Dempsey of course put aside such childishness. It was not until Richard joined Grimaldi later that Emtee Dempsey brought up Miss Butterfingers.

Richard squinted at her. "All right, what's going on? How come you ask me about her yesterday and today your car's blown up?"

"Richard, you introduced her into the conversation. I may have asked a thing or two then, but if I ever heard of the young woman before, I had forgotten it. Are you suggesting that she . . ."

"Aw, come on."

"Sergeant Grimaldi, has the lieutenant been told of the concern about him and his family?"

Grimaldi looked uncomprehending.

"Perhaps you weren't aware of it." She turned to Kim. "I think you will agree, Sister, that I am no longer bound by my promise."

"Of course not."

"Richard, your colleagues have been assigned to look after you and your family. Even Sister Kimberly has had an escort these past days."

Richard glared at Grimaldi, who lifted his shoulders. Richard then got on the phone. Emtee Dempsey's initial attitude was a little smug; clearly she enjoyed knowing something about the police that Richard did not know. But her manner changed as the meaning of Richard's end of the conversation became clear.

"There's been no protective detail assigned to my family. Where in hell did you get such a notion?"

Emtee Dempsey nodded to Kim.

"A man has been following me for several days. Two days ago I had enough and asked him what he was doing. He said he was a policeman."

"A Chicago policeman?"

"Yes."

"What's his name?"

"I don't know."

"Didn't you ask? Didn't you ask for his ID?"

"No, Richard. And I didn't call you up and ask what was going on either. At the time, I was relieved to learn why he was following me."

"Relieved that I was supposedly threatened?"

"Well, I was relieved to think that Mary and the kids . . ."

"I don't suppose he'll be following you around today," Richard broke in, "but I guarantee you a cop we know about will be."

"You want Sister to keep to her regular routine?"

"Sister Mary Teresa, I want all of you to follow your regular routines. And if anything relevant to this happens, I want to know about it pronto."

"An interesting use of the word, Richard. In Italian it means ready. It's how they answer the phone. Pronto," she said, trilling the r. "You, on the other hand, take it in its Spanish meaning."

There was more, much more, until Richard fled the study. At their much delayed breakfast, the conversation was of the car. Joyce thought their insurance covered bombing. "Unless it's considered an act of God."

"Sister, a bombing is always an act of man. Or woman."

The newspaper lay on the table unattended throughout the meal. After all, the news of the day had happened in their street.

"I'll want to speak to Katherine about this. We don't want her to learn of it from someone at the paper. What is in the paper, by the way?"

Joyce had taken the sports page and Kim, standing, was paging through the front section when she stopped and cried out.

"That's him!"

"He," Emtee Dempsey corrected automatically, coming to stand beside her.

The picture was of a young man, smiling, confident, embarking on life. Perhaps a graduation photograph.

His name was Michael Layton. He had been found dead after an explosion in a southside house. He had been missing for five years. He was the man who identified himself as a policeman in the Northwestern library.

3

Katherine Senski caught a cab from her office at the newspaper and was in the house within half an hour of Emtee Dempsey's call, but of course there was far more to discuss now than the mere blowing up of their automobile. The street had been cordoned off, to the enormous aggravation and rage of who knows how many drivers, while special units collected debris and the all but intact rear end of the car, which seemed to have gone straight into the air, done a flipflop, and landed in their customary parking place.

"Dear God," Katherine said. "They might be out there collecting pieces of you three."

"Nonsense," Emtee Dempsey said.

A first discovery was that the device had not been one that would have been triggered by starting the car. This conclusion was reached by noting the intact condition of the rear of the car.

"But aren't such devices hooked up to starters, to motors?"

"The motor was in the rear end," Joyce explained

"Oh," Katherine said, but the three nuns were suddenly struck by that past tense. Their Volkswagen bug was no more.

They had just settled down at the dining room table with a fresh pot of coffee when Benjamin Rush arrived. The elegant lawyer stood in the doorway, taking in the scene, and then resumed his usual savoir faire.

"It is a relief to see you, as the saying goes, in one piece, Sister. Sisters."

They made room for him, but of course he refused coffee. He had had the single cup that must make do until lunchtime. Joyce brought him a glass of mineral water, which he regarded ruefully, not interrupting Emtee Dempsey's colorful account of Kim's being followed, her confronting the man, their attempt to get information from Richard. And then this morning. By the time she got to the actual explosion, it might have been wondered how she could keep the dramatic line of her narrative rising, so exciting the preliminary events were made to sound. Kim found herself wishing she had actually behaved with the forthrightness Emtee Dempsey attributed to her when she confronted her supposed police escort in the Northwestern library. Emtee Dempsey had the folded morning paper safely under one pudgy hand, clearly her prop for the ultimate revelation. But there was so much to be said before she got to it.

"Regina Fastnekker! Do I remember that one," Katherine said. "My pretrial interviews?" She looked around the table. "I was nominated for a Pulitzer, for heaven's sake."

"Do you still have them?"

Katherine smiled sweetly. "My scrapbooks are up to date, thank you."

Benjamin Rush wanted to know where Regina was now. Katherine, to her shame, had not followed further the Fastnekker saga once the girl had been safely put away. Emtee Dempsey told them of the woman's supposed prison conversion.

"'Supposed' in the sense of 'alleged.' I do not mean to express skepticism. Some of the greatest saints got their start in prison."

"I won't ask you how many lawyers have been canonized," Mr. Rush said and sipped his mineral water.

Katherine said, "Conversion isn't a strong enough word for the turnaround that girl would have needed. I have seldom talked with anyone I considered so, well, diabolic. She seemed to have embraced evil."

"'Evil be thou my good,'" murmured Emtee Dempsey.

"Who said that?"

"Milton's Satan, of course, don't tease. I must read every word you wrote about her, Katherine. I suppose the police will know where she now is."

"I suspect they may be talking with her right now."

"The bombing is in her style," Rush said. "Ominously so. It is why I came directly here. Katherine will know better than I that the Fastnekker crowd had a quite unique modus operandi. There was always a series of bombings, the first a kind of announcement, defiant, and then came the big bang. What I am saying is that, far from being out of danger, you may be in far more danger now than before the unfortunate destruction of your means of transportation. If, that is, we are truly dealing with Regina Fastnekker and company."

"Company? How many were there?"

"It's all in my stories," Katherine said. "I wonder why I didn't read of her big conversion."

"If it is genuine, she might not have wanted it to be a media event."

"Well, you have certainly had some morning. But, as Benjamin says, the excitement may be just beginning. I suggest that you go at once to the lake place in Indiana."

"No, no, no," Rush intervened. He thought that for them to be in such a remote place, where the police were, well, local, far from taking the nuns out of danger, might well expose them fatally.

"We have to assume that you are being watched at this very moment."

"Isn't it far more likely that the next attempt will be on Richard's family?"

Katherine said, "I wonder who that phony policeman was?"

That was Emtee Dempsey's cue. "I was coming to that," she said, unfolding the paper. "This is the man."

"But that's Michael Layton," Mr. Rush said in shocked tones.

"Ah, you know him."

"Sister, that boy, that young man, disappeared several years ago. Vanished into thin air."

"That's in the story, Benjamin."

"But I know the Laytons. I knew Michael. I can't tell you what a traumatic experience it was for them."

Emtee Dempsey turned to Katherine. "Was this young man part of Regina Fastnekker's company?"

"That's not possible," said Mr. Rush.

"Why on earth would he impersonate a policeman?"

"Sister Kimberly, please call your brother and tell him that Michael Layton was the one following you around of late."

It was Katherine who summed it all up, despite the evident pain it caused Benjamin Rush. Alerted by what the young man following Sister Kimberly had said, Emtee Dempsey had coaxed from Richard his belief that Regina Fastnekker was more likely than anyone else to seek to do him harm after she was released from jail. She had masked her intention by undergoing a religious conversion while in prison, and some time had elapsed since she had regained her freedom. Richard himself had been lulled into the belief that Miss Butterfingers had gotten over her desire for revenge. She chose to strike where it would be least expected, at Richard's sister. Accordingly, one of the gang followed Kim around and, when confronted, disarmingly claimed to be part of a police effort to protect Richard's family. This morning, their automobile was blown up, a typical first move in the Fastnekker modus operandi.

By this point in Katherine's explanation, Emtee Dempsey had plunged her face into her hands. But Benjamin Rush took it up.

"Michael was then killed for warning Sister Kimberly that she was in danger." The lawyer's spirit rose at the thought of his friends' son exhibiting his natural goodness at such peril to his life.

"What a tissue of conjecture," Emtee Dempsey observed, looking around at her friends. "In the first place, we have no reason at all to think that Michael Layton was connected with this Fastnekker terrorist gang."

"Of course we don't," Benjamin Rush said, switching field.

"Nor do we have any reason to think this is the work of the Fastnekker gang. The idea that her religious conversion was a ploy must deal with the fact that she tried to keep it quiet."

"The sneakiest publicity of all," Joyce said.

"Salinger," Kim agreed.

"What?" Emtee Dempsey looked at her two young colleagues as if they had lost their minds. But she waved away whatever it was they referred to. "We know only two things. First, that a young man named Michael Layton, who had been missing for years, who was lately following Sister Kimberly and claimed to be a policeman when she spoke to him, is dead. Second, we know that our automobile has been destroyed."

"Our insurance company will probably suspect us of that," Joyce said.

Benjamin Rush rose. "You are absolutely right, Sister. I have entered into this speculative conversation, but I must repeat that I cannot believe Michael Layton could possibly be involved in anything wrong or criminal. Let us hope that the police will be able to cast light on what has happened."

4

It was not only those on Walton Street who were reminded of the Fastnekker gang by the exploding Volkswagen. An editorial in the rival of Katherine's paper expressed the hope that Chicago, and indeed the country, was not on the threshold of a renewal of the terrorism of a decade ago. Readers were reminded of the various groups, including that led by Regina Fastnekker, and the fear was stated that the destruction of the car was only a prelude to something worse. How many like the unfortunate Michael Layton, products of good homes, having all the advantages of American society, suddenly dropped from sight only to turn up, incredibly, as terrorists? The editorial immediately added that there was absolutely no evidence of any connection of Layton with any terrorist efforts, though the explanation he had given of following a member of a Chicago policeman's family and the fact that he had been found in a building that had exploded from unknown causes would doubtless prompt some to make that connection. Lieutenant Richard Moriarity had led the investigation that resulted in the successful prosecution of Regina Fastnekker.

Katherine Senski threw the paper down on Emtee Dempsey's desk and fell into a chair. "That is completely and absolutely irresponsible. It is one thing to sit among friends and try to tie things together, but to publish such random thoughts in a supposedly respectable newspaper, well . . ." She threw up her hands, at a loss for words.

But Katherine's reaction was nothing to that of Benjamin Rush. Under his distinguished snow-white hair, his patrician features were rosy with rage.

"It is an outrageous accusation against a man who cannot defend himself."

"Perhaps the Layton family will sue."

"I am on my way there now. That is precisely what they want to do. Alas, I shall advise them not to. The editorial cunningly fends off the accusation of libel by qualifying or seeming to take back what it had just said. When you add the First Amendment, there simply is no case. Legally. Morally, whoever wrote this is a scoundrel. I now understand the feelings of clients who have urged me to embark on a course I knew could end only in failure. One wants to tilt at windmills!"

"You will be talking to the Laytons today?"

An immaculate cuff appeared from the sleeve of Benjamin Rush's navy blue suit as he lifted his arm, and then a watch whose unostentatiousness was in a way ostentatious came into view. "In half an hour. I have come to ask you a favor. Actually, to ask Sister Kimberly."

"Anything," Kim said. No member of the Order of Martha and Mary could be unaware of their debt to Benjamin Rush. He had saved this house at the time of the great dissolution and had insured that an endowment would enable the order to continue, in however reduced a form.

"It would be particularly consoling for the Laytons if they could speak to someone who saw Michael as recently as you have."

The request made Kim uneasy. What if the Laytons wished to derive consolation from the fact that it was a nun who had spoken to their son? Kim herself had wondered if he had not perhaps thought that she could be of help, directly or indirectly, in some difficulty.

"I should tell you that while Melissa Layton is quite devout, her husband Geoffrey is a member of the Humanist Society and regards all religion as a blight."

"Find out which of them the son favored, Sister."

Having already agreed to help Mr. Rush, there was nothing Kim could do, but she was profoundly unwilling to talk to grieving parents about a son they had not seen in years and to whom she had spoken only once, in somewhat odd circumstances. Mr. Rush's car stood at the curb where the Volkswagen had always been, but the contrast could not have been greater. Long and grey with tinted glass, it seemed to require several spaces. Marvin, Mr. Rush's chunky driver, opened the door and Kim got in, and with Mr. Rush at seemingly the opposite end of the sofa, they drove off in comfort to the Laytons.

On the way, Mr. Rush told her a few more things about the Laytons, but nothing could have prepared her adequately for the next several hours. Kim had somehow gotten the impression that the Laytons would be Mr. Rush's age, which was foolish when she considered that the son had been closer to her age, but Mrs. Layton was a shock. She was beautiful, her auburn hair worn shoulder length, her face as smooth as a girl's, and the black and silver housecoat, floor length, billowed about her, heightening the effect she made as she crossed the room to them. Kim felt dowdy in her sensible suit, white blouse, and veil, and it didn't help to remind herself that her costume befitted her vocation. Melissa Layton tipped her cheek for Mr. Rush's kiss and extended a much braceleted arm to Kim.

"Sister." Both hands enclosed Kim's and her violet eyes scanned Kim's face. "Ben assured us that you would come."

Geoffrey Layton rose from his chair, nodded to Rush, and gave a little bow to Kim, but his eyes were fastened on her veil.

"Come," Mrs. Layton said. She had not released Kim's hand and led her to a settee where they could sit side by side. "Tell me of your meeting with Michael." And suddenly the beauty was wrenched into sorrow and the woman began to sob helplessly. Now Kim held her hand. Mrs. Layton's tears made Kim feel a good deal more comfortable in this vast room with its period furniture, large framed pictures, and magnificent view.

Mrs. Layton emerged from her bout of grief even more beautiful than before, teardrops glistening in her eyes, but composed. Mr. Layton and Mr. Rush stood in front of the seated women while Kim told her story.

"How long had he been following you around?"

"For several days."

"That you know of," Mrs. Layton said.

"Yes. I spoke of it with the other sisters. At first it was just a nuisance, but then it became disturbing. We decided that I should talk to him. On Wednesday morning . . ."

"Wednesday," Mrs. Layton repeated, and her expression suggested she was trying to remember what she had been doing at the time this young woman beside her had actually spoken to her long lost son.

"He said he knew I was a nun."

"Of course," said Mr. Layton.

"I do not wear my veil when I go to Northwestern."

"Why not?"

"I just don't."

"Could he have seen you with it on?"

"I suppose."

"But what did he say?" Mrs. Layton asked. Kim was aware that another woman had come into the room, her hair and coloring the same as Mrs. Layton's, though without the dramatic beauty. Mrs. Layton turned to see what Kim was looking at. "Janet, come here. This is Sister Kimberly who talked with your brother Michael."

The daughter halved the distance between them, but as Kim talked on, answering questions that became more and more impossible, about the Layton son, Janet came closer. The parents wanted to know what he looked like, how he acted, did she think he was suffering from amnesia, on and on, and from time to time when Kim glanced at Janet she got a look of sympathy. Finally the younger woman stepped past Mr. Rush.

"Thank you so much for telling us about your meeting with Michael." Comparing the two women, Kim could now see that, youthful as Mrs. Layton looked, she looked clearly older than her daughter, who made no effort to be attractive.

The Laytons now turned to Mr. Rush to insist that he bring suit against the editorialist who had slandered their son. Janet led Kim away.

"There's coffee in the kitchen."

"Oh good."

"You realize that all this is to put off the evil day. We have not seen Michael's body. It is a question whether we will. As a family. I certainly intend to."

There was both strength and genuineness in Janet Layton, and Kim could see, when they were sitting on stools in the kitchen, sipping coffee, that with the least of efforts Janet could rival her mother in beauty. If she didn't, it was because she felt no desire to conceal her mourning.

"You're a nun?"

"Yes.

"I wanted to be a nun once. I suppose most girls think of it."

"Very briefly."

"What's it like?"

"Come visit us. We have a house on Walton Street."

"Near the Newberry?"

"Just blocks away. Do you go there?"

She nodded. "What is so weird is that I also use the Northwestern library. What if I had gone there Wednesday?"

"I hope I made it clear that your brother seemed perfectly all right to me. But then I thought he was the policeman he said he was and that changed everything. He looked the part."

"It's cruel after years of thinking him dead to find out he was alive on Wednesday, in a place I go to, but now is truly dead." Her lip trembled and she looked away.

"He just disappeared?"

She nodded, not trusting herself to speak for a moment. "One day he left the house for school and never came back. No note, no indication he was going. He took nothing with him. He just ceased to exist, or so it seemed. The police searched, my parents hired private investigators. My father, taking the worst thing he could think of, suspected the Moonies. But not one single trace was found."

"On his way to school?"

"Chicago. He was an economics major."

"How awful."

"I don't know how my parents bore up under this. My mother of course never lets herself go physically, but inside she has been devastated. It is the first time my father confronted something couldn't do anything effective about. That shook him almost as much as the loss of Michael."

"Mr. Rush says your mother is very devout."

"Let me show you something."

They went rapidly through the house, which was far larger than Kim's first impression of it. On an upper floor as they came down a hallway stood a small altar. There was a statue of perhaps three feet in height of Our Blessed Lady and a very large candle in a wrought-iron holder burning before it. Janet turned and widened her eyes significantly as she indicated the shrine.

"Mother's. For the return of her lost son."

There was nothing to say to that. Janet went into a room and waited for Kim to join her.

"This is just the way it was when he disappeared. Michael's room. Maybe now Mother will agree to . . ."

No need to develop the thought. No doubt Mrs. Layton would consider it an irreverence to get rid of her son's clothes and other effects, even though she knew now he was dead. A computer stood on the desk, covered with a clear plastic hood. A bookshelf the top row of which contained works in or related to economics. The other shelves were a hodgepodge, largely paperbacks—mysteries, westerns, science fiction, classics. Michael Layton had either unsettled literary tastes or universal interests.

"The police checked over this room and the private investigators Daddy hired also looked it over. They found no indication Mike intended to leave, and of course that introduced a note of hope. That he'd been kidnapped, for instance. But no demands were made. Every investigation left us where we'd been—with something that made utterly no sense."

"It must have been awful."

"I am glad the waiting is over, after all these years. Does that sound terrible?"

"No."

"I wanted you to see this. I wanted you to know that there are no clues here."

Kim smiled. "You've heard of Sister Mary Teresa?"

Janet nodded.

As they went downstairs, Kim reflected that if Janet was right, and why wouldn't she be, the explanation for Michael Layton's murder would have to be sought in what he had been doing in the years since he left his home for the last time. And no one seemed to know where on earth he had been.

5

"Miss Butterfingers is going to call on us," Joyce whispered when Kim returned to Walton Street.

"Wow."

"Just what I said to Emtee Dempsey."

"Yes," Sister Mary Teresa said, when Kim went into the study and asked about the impending visit. "Miss Fastnekker called half an hour ago and asked if she might come by. I am trying to read these articles of Katherine's before our visitor arrives. Here are the ones I've read."

Kim took the photocopies and began to read them as she crossed to a chair. What a delight they were. This was Katherine at the height of her powers, the woman who had been the queen of Chicago journalism longer than it was polite to mention. Reading those old stories acquainted Kim with the kind of person she preferred not to know. The Regina Fastnekker Katherine had interviewed intensively and written about with rare evocative power was a prophet of doom, an angel of destruction, a righteous scourge of mankind. At twenty-two years old, she had concluded that human beings are hopelessly corrupt, there is nothing to redeem what is laughingly called civilization. Any judgment that what she had done was illegal or immoral proceeded from a system so corrupt as to render the charges comic. Katherine described Regina as a nihilist, one who preferred nothing to everything that was. It was not that the world had this or that flaw, the world was the flaw.

"I am glad you don't have possession of hydrogen weapons," Katherine had observed.

"Atomic destruction is the solution. Inevitably one day it will arrive. I have been anticipating that awful self-judgment of mankind on itself by the actions I have taken."

"Who appointed you to this destructive task?"

"I did."

"Have you ever doubted your judgment?"

"Not on these matters."

"From the point of view of society, it makes sense to lock you up, wouldn't you say?"

"Society will regret what has been done to me."

Katherine had clearly been as awed as Kim was now that a woman who had done such deeds, who had killed by accident rather than design, should continue to speak with such conviction that she was somehow not implicated in the universal guilt of the race to which she belonged.

"You are employing a corrupt logic," Miss Butterfingers had replied.

Katherine had concluded that the only meaning "corrupt" seemed to have was "differing from Regina Fastnekker."

"What a sweetheart," Kim commented when she had finished.

"We must not forget that this was the Regina of some years ago. On the phone she seemed very nice."

"Did you tell her the police would know if she visited us?"

"I saw no reason to say such a thing."

Emtee Dempsey had invited Regina to come to Walton Street on the assumption that she was now a changed woman, radically different from the terrorist so graphically portrayed by Katherine Senski in her newspaper stories. If she was wrong, if Regina had been behind the blowing up of the Volkswagen and if her custom was to announce a serious deed by a lesser one, Emtee Dempsey could be inviting their assassin to visit. She did not have to wonder what Richard would say if asked about the advisability of admitting Regina to their home.

The woman who stood at the door when Kim went to answer the bell wore a denim skirt that reached her ankles and an oversize cableknit sweater; her hair was pulled back severely on her head and held with a rubber band. Pale blue eyes stared unblinkingly at Kim.

"I have come to see Sister Dempsey."

There was no mistaking that this was Regina Fastnekker, despite the changes that had occurred in her since the photos that accompanied Katherine's stories. Kim opened the door and took Regina down the hall to the study. Her back tingled as she walked, as if she awaited some unexpected blow to fall. But she made it to the study door without incident.

"Sister Mary Teresa, this is Regina Fastnekker."

The old nun did not rise but watched closely as her guest came to the desk. Regina put out her hand and the old nun stood as she took it.

"Welcome to our home."

"I must tell you that I consider the Catholic Church to be the corruption of Christianity and that it is only by a return to the gospels that we can be saved. One person at a time."

"*Ecclesia semper reformanda.*"

"I don't understand."

"You express a sentiment as old as Christianity itself. Do you know the story of the order St. Francis founded?"

"St. Francis is someone I admire."

"I was sure you would. Francis preached holy poverty, personifying it, calling it Lady Poverty, his beloved. After his death, his followers disputed what this meant. Could they, for example, own a house and live in it, or did poverty require them to own absolutely nothing and rely each day on the Lord to provide? Did they own the clothes they wore, since of course each one wore his own clothes?"

"Why are you telling me this?"

"It is possible to make Christianity so pure that it ceases to be."

"It is also possible to falsify it so much that it ceases to be."

"Of course."

"You sound as if you had won an argument."

"I wasn't sure we were having one. I am told that you have become a Christian."

"That makes it sound like something I did. It was done to me. It is a grace of which I am entirely unworthy."

"Do you know Michael Layton?"

The sudden switch seemed to surprise Regina. She rearranged her skirt and pushed up the sleeve of her sweater.

"I knew him."

"Before your conversion?"

"Before I went to prison, yes."

"Have you any idea who killed him?"

"I came here to tell you that I have not."

"Have you seen him since you were released?"

"That is the question the police put to me in a dozen different ways."

"And how did you answer?"

"Yes and no."

"How yes?"

"I saw his photograph in the paper."

"Ah."

"It is my intention always to tell the truth, even when it seems trivial."

"An admirable ideal. It is one I share."

There was not a trace of irony in Emtee Dempsey's tone, doubtless because she felt none. Her ability so to speak that she did not technically tell a lie, however much others might mislead themselves when listening to her, was something Kim tried not to be shocked at. Whenever they discussed the matter, the old nun's defense—if it could be called a defense—was unanswerable, but Kim in her heart of hearts felt that Emtee Dempsey should be a good deal more candid than she was.

"The truth, the whole truth, and nothing but the truth," she had reminded the old nun.

"A noble if empty phrase."

"Empty?"

"What is the whole truth about the present moment? Only God knows. I use the phrase literally. Since we cannot know the whole truth we cannot speak it."

"We can speak the whole truth that we know."

"Alas, that too is beyond our powers. Even as we speak, what we know expands and increases and we shall never catch up with it."

"You know what I mean."

"Only by what you say, my dear, and I am afraid that does not make much sense."

"I didn't invent the phrase."

"You have at least that defense."

But now, speaking to Regina Fastnekker, Emtee Dempsey seemed to be suggesting that she herself sought always to tell the whole truth. If they were alone, Kim might have called her on this. But at the moment, she watched with fascination the alertness with which Regina listened to the old nun. In her articles, Katherine had described the ingénue expression Regina wore when she pronounced her nihilistic doctrines. Her beliefs might have changed, but her expression had not. Now she looked out at the world with the innocence of one who had been saved by religious conversion, but nonetheless, however much she had changed, Regina Fastnekker was still on the side of the saved.

"What I have come to tell you is that I did not blow up your car, and I have no intention to harm you."

"I am glad to hear that."

"I tell you because it would be reasonable to think I had, given my sinful past. I am still a sinner, of course, but I have chosen Jesus for my personal savior and have with the help of His grace put behind me such deeds."

"You have been blessed."

"So have you. If I had not been converted I might very well have conceived such a scheme and put it into operation."

"And killed me?"

"The loved ones of those who put me in prison."

"A dreadful thought."

Regina said nothing for a moment, and when she spoke it was with great deliberateness. "I have never killed anyone. I do not say this to make myself seem less terrible than I was. But I never took another's life."

"I had thought someone died when an explosion occurred in your apartment."

"That is true."

"And you were the cause of that explosion."

"No. It was an accident."

"You express yourself with a great deal of precision."

"Praise the Lord."

Seldom had the phrase been spoken with less intonation. Regina put her hands on her knees and then rose in an almost stately manner.

"I challenge you to accept the Lord as your savior."

"My dear young lady, I took the vows of religion nearly fifty years ago. I took Jesus as my spiritual spouse, promising poverty, chastity, and obedience. But I take your suggestion in good grace and shall endeavor to follow your advice."

Regina Fastnekker, apparently having no truth, however trivial, to utter, said nothing. She bowed and Kim took her to the door.

"Thank you for visiting us."

"Did you too take those vows?"

"Yes. But not fifty years ago."

Regina Fastnekker's smile was all the more brilliant for being so rare. Her laughter had a pure soprano quality. Lithe, long-limbed, her full skirt lending a peculiar dignity to her passage, she went across the porch, descended the steps, and disappeared up the walk.

6

Two days later, in the Northwestern University library, Kim looked up from the book she was reading to find Janet Layton smiling down on her.

"Can we talk?" she whispered.

Kim, startled to see the sister where she had had such a dramatic encounter with the brother, got up immediately. Outside, Janet lit up a cigarette.

"There is something I should have told you the other day and didn't. In fact I lied to you. I have known all along that Mike was still alive."

"You did!"

"He telephoned me in my dorm room, within a month of his disappearance. The first thing he said was that he did not want my parents to know of the call."

"And you agreed?"

"I didn't tell them. I don't think I would have in any case. You would have to know how terribly they took Mike's disappearance, particularly at the beginning. If I had told them, they would have wanted proof. There was none I could give. And of course I had no idea then that it would turn into a permanent disappearance. I don't know that he himself thought so at the time."

"What did he want?"

"He wanted some computer disks from his room."

She had complied, putting the disks in a plastic bag and the bag in a trash container on a downtown Chicago corner. She walked away, as she had been instructed, but with the idea of hiding and watching the container. She took up her station inside a bookstore and watched the container. Clerks asked if they could be of help and she shook her head, her eyes never leaving the container. After an hour, the manager came and she moved to a drugstore, certain her eyes had never left the container. After four hours of vigil, she was out of patience. She decided to take the disks from the container and wait for another phone call from her brother. The plastic bag containing the disks was gone.

"I felt like a bag lady, rummaging around in that trash, people turning to look at me. But it was definitely gone. Someone must have taken it within minutes of my putting it there, while I was walking away."

"And your brother called again?"

"Months later. I asked him if he got the disks. He said yes. That was all. His manner made me glad I'd done what I had."

Before leaving the disks in the container, Janet had made copies of them. She opened her purse and took out a package.

"Would you give these to Sister Mary Teresa?"

"You should give them to the police."

"I will leave that up to her. If that's what she thinks should be done with them, all right."

"Did you read the disks?"

"I tried to once. I don't know what program they're written on, but I typed them out at the DOS prompt. They looked like notes on reading to me. The fact that Mike wanted them means only that they were important to him. Frankly, I'd rather not admit that I've heard from Mike over the years. My parents would never understand my silence."

Kim had difficulty understanding it herself, Emtee Dempsey, on the other hand, found it unsurprising.

"But of course it would have been unsurprising if she told them too. Singular choices do not always have moral necessity. There were doubtless good reasons for either course of action and she chose the one she did."

"What will you do with them?"

"What the young lady suggested. Study their contents. Can you print them out for me?"

Before she did anything with the disks, Kim took the same precaution Janet had and made copies of them. There were three disks, of the five-and-a-half-inch size, but only two were full, the third had only twelve thousand bytes saved on it. Running a directory on them, Kim jotted down the file names.

> BG&E.one
> BG&E.two
> TSZ.one
> TSZ.two
> TSZ.tre

That was the contents of the first disk. The second was similarly uninformative.

> PENSEES.UNO
> PENSEES.DOS
> PENSEES.TRE

The third disk had one file, AAV.

The files had not been written on Notabene, the program Kim preferred, nor on either Word or WordPerfect. Kim printed them from ASCI and began reading eagerly as they emerged from the printer but quickly found, as Janet had, her interest flagging. Michael Layton seemed to have devised a very personal kind of shorthand "Para fn eth no es vrd, Pero an attmpt Para vanqr los grnds."

Let Emtee Dempsey decipher that if she could. The fact that Michael Layton wrote in a way difficult, if not impossible, to follow suggested that the disks contained information of interest. The old nun spread the sheets before her, smoothing them out, a look of anticipation on her pudgy face. Kim left her to her task.

The old nun was preoccupied at table and after night prayers returned to her study. At one in the morning, Kim came downstairs to find Emtee Dempsey brooding over the printout. She looked up at Kim and blinked.

"Any luck?"

"You are right to think that decoding always depends on finding one little key. Whether it is a matter of luck, I do not know."

"Have you found the key?"

"No."

"I couldn't make head nor tails of it."

"Oh, the first two disks present no problem. They are paraphrases of Nietzsche."

"You mean you can understand those pages?"

"Only to the degree that Nietzsche himself is intelligible. The young man paraphrased passages from the mad philosopher and interspersed his own comments, most, of them jejune."

"How did you know it was Nietzsche?"

"*Beyond Good and Evil. Thus Spake Zarathustra.*"

"And the second is Pascal?"

"Unfortunately no. The thoughts are young Layton's, thoughts of unrelieved tedium and banality. Do you know the *Pensieri* of Leopardi? Giacomo Leopardi?"

"I don't even know who he is."

"Was. His work of that name is a collection of pessimistic and misanthropic jottings, puerile, adolescent. If a poet of genius, however troubled, was capable of writing such silliness, we should not perhaps be too harsh with young Layton."

"What is on the third disk?"

She shook her head. "Those few pages are written in a bad imitation of *Finnegan's Wake,* a kind of macaronic relying on a variety of languages imperfectly understood. I had hoped that the first disks would provide me with the clue needed to understand the third, but so far this is . . ."

An explosion shook the house, bringing Emtee Dempsey to her feet. But Kim was down the hall ahead of her and dashed upstairs. As she came into the upstairs hall, she saw that a portion of the left wall as well as her door had been blown away. The startled face of Joyce appeared through plaster cloud.

"Strike two," she said.

7

Sister Mary Teresa wanted to take a good look around Kim's room before calling the police, although why the neighborhood had failed to be shaken awake by the explosion was explained by the incessant street racket that did not really cease until three or sometimes four in the morning. The explosion of Kim's computer would have been only one noise among many to those outside, however it had filled the house. The wall that had been blown into the hall was the one against which Kim's computer had stood.

"Why would it do a thing like that?" the old nun asked.

"I've never heard of it before."

"Was it on?"

"I never turn it off." Kim explained the theory behind this.

They puzzled over the event for perhaps fifteen minutes before Kim called Richard, relying on him to alert the appropriate experts. They came immediately, a tall woman with flying straight hair and her companion whose thick glasses seemed to have become part of his face. They picked around among the debris, eyes bright with interest. This was something new to them as well.

"Computers don't blow up," the girl said.

"There had to be a bomb." Behind the thick lenses her companion's eyes widened.

"When did you last use the machine?"

"I printed out some disks."

"Any sign of them?"

They were in the plastic box that had bounced off the far wall and landed on her bed. She opened it and showed them the five disks it contained.

"Five!" she exclaimed. "There are only five."

"Only?"

She showed them the three copies she had made, and two of the disks she had been given by Janet Layton, And then she remembered.

"I left the third in the drive."

"Can a computer disk be a bomb?" Emtee Dempsey asked.

Her question brought amused smiles to the two experts. The girl said, "Anything can be a bomb."

"Michael Layton delivered his second bomb," Emtee Dempsey said. "Posthumously."

"Janet Layton gave them to me," Kim reminded her.

"Yes. Yes, she did."

Richard came and kept them up until three going over what had happened. Kim let Emtee Dempsey tell the story she herself had heard from Janet Layton. She went over in her mind the conversation she had had with Janet at the Layton home and then what she had said at Northwestern that afternoon. If Janet had told her the truth, the disks she had given Kim were copies of those her brother made, rather than his originals. If one of those disks had been made into a bomb, it had to have been by Janet. But why?

"I'll ask her why. And I don't intend to wait for daylight either."

The next time Kim saw Janet Layton was under police auspices. The violet eyes widened when Kim came in.

"Oh."

"I'm alive."

"Thank God."

She, rose and reached a hand across the table. Mastering her aversion, Kim took the hand. Janet turned to Richard.

"Why didn't you tell me she was unharmed?"

"I don't talk to people who don't talk to me."

Janet talked now. What she had told Kim was true as far as it went; well, almost. She had not, years ago, made copies of the disks her brother asked her to bring, but everything else had happened as she had said.

"Regina told me to tell you what I did."

"Regina Fastnekker!"

Janet nodded. "After Michael's death, she called me. She asked me if I remembered delivering some computer disks to Michael long ago. Of course I did. She said she had them and felt they might help solve the mystery of Michael's death. She asked if I would pass them on to you with just the message I gave you. You could decide, or Sister Mary Teresa could decide, what to do with them."

Richard made a face. "She knew she could rely on the nosiness of you know who."

But he was on his feet and heading out of the room. "I'm going to let you go," he said to Janet.

"Come with me," Kim said. There was no substitute for Emtee Dempsey's hearing this story from Janet herself.

† † †

But the old nun merely nodded impatiently as Janet spoke. Her interest was entirely in Regina Fastnekker. Katherine, having heard of the second explosion on Walton Street, hurried over, but Janet stayed on, far from being the center of attention. Katherine was almost triumphant when she heard the news that the supposedly converted Regina Fastnekker had used Janet to deliver a second bomb to Walton Street.

"The brazen thing," she fumed, a grim smile on her face.

"You think she blew up our car?"

"Of course. Your car, Michael Layton, and very nearly Sister Kimberly.

Oh, I never believe these stories of radical conversion. People just don't change character that easily."

"She denied it, Katherine."

"It's part of her new persona. But the gall of the woman, to use the same pattern she always used before."

"As if she were drawing attention to herself."

"More insolence," Katherine said.

Regina Fastnekker denied quite calmly through hours of interrogation that she had killed anybody. Richard, when he brought this news to Walton Street, regarded it as just what one would expect.

"But she does talk to you?"

"Talk?" He shook his head. "She goes on and on, like a TV preacher. How she has promised the Lord to tell the truth and that is what she is doing."

"I suppose you have gone over the place where Regina lives?"

Richard nodded. "Nothing."

"And this does not shake your confidence that she is responsible for these bombings?"

"You know what I think? I think she sat in prison all those years and planned this down to the minute. But she wasn't going to risk being sent to prison again. She would do it and do it in a way that I would know she had done it and yet would not be able to prove she had."

"Can you?"

"We will. We will."

Katherine wrote a feature on the Backsliding Miss Butterfingers, in the words of the header. The veteran reporter permitted herself some uncharacteristic forays into what made someone like Regina Fastnekker tick. Prison may not breed criminals, her argument ran, but it receives a criminal and releases him or her worse than he or she was before.

"Wouldn't 'he' be sufficient?"

"I've told you of our manual of style?"

"Style is the man," Emtee Dempsey purred. "Would you be allowed to write that?"

Katherine seemed to be blushing beneath her powdered cheeks. "'Style is the woman' is the way it will appear in my tomorrow's article."

"*Et tu,* Katherine? Didn't Regina take credit for what she had done when she was arrested before?"

"She did."

"And now she continues to deny what she is accused of?"

"'I have not touched a bomb since I left prison.' That's it verbatim."

"Gloves?"

"I thought of that. Something in the careful way she speaks suggested that I do. 'As far as I know I have never been in the vicinity of an explosive device since leaving prison.'"

"What does she say about what Janet Layton told us?"

"She denies it."

"How?"

"She says it is a lie."

"Verbatim?"

"Verbatim."

"Hmmm."

The following morning when they were returning from St. Matthews on foot, creating a sensation, Emtee Dempsey suddenly stopped and clapped her hands.

"Of course!" she cried, and began to laugh. When she set off again, it was almost skippingly, and her great starched headdress waggled and shook. Joyce and Kim exchanged a look. The mind is a delicate thing.

Emtee Dempsey bounded up the porch steps and inside removed the shawl from her shoulders.

"First breakfast, then call Richard."

"Why not ask him for breakfast?" Joyce said facetiously.

"No. Afterward. Let's try for ten o'clock, and we want everyone here. The Laytons, Katherine, Regina Fastnekker, and of course Richard."

"Regina Fastnekker is under arrest."

"That is why we must convey the invitation through Richard."

"He is not going to bring a mad bomber to the scene of the crime."

"Nonsense. I'll talk to him if necessary."

"I'll talk to her," Richard said, "but it's not necessary, it's impossible, as in it necessarily can't happen. I am not going to help her put on one of her amateur theatricals."

"You have every reason to object," Emtee Dempsey said, already on the phone in her study. "But wouldn't you like to clear this matter up?"

"Only what is obscure can be cleared up. This is simple as sin. We have the one responsible for those bombings."

"There's where you're wrong, Richard."

"How in hell can you know that?"

"The provenance of my knowledge is elsewhere. I realized what had happened when we were returning from Mass less than an hour ago."

"Not on your life, Sister Mary Teresa. And I mean it."

With that outburst, Kim was sure the old nun had won. Richard had to bluster and fulminate but it was not in his nature to deny such a request. Too often in the past, as he would never admit, such a gathering at Walton Street had proved a breakthrough. When he did agree, it was on his own terms.

"I will be bringing her by," he said, as if changing the subject. "I want her to see that upstairs bedroom and what's left of the computer."

"That's a splendid idea. Ten o'clock would be best for us."

Mr. Rush agreed to bring the Laytons, and wild horses could not have kept Katherine away.

8

Benjamin Rush introduced the Laytons to Sister Mary Teresa, who squeezed the grieving mother's hand while Geoffrey Layton tried not to stare at the old nun's habit. He looked around the room as if fearful of what signs of superstition he might find, but a man who could get used to the shrine in the hallway of his own house had little to fear on Walton Street. Katherine swept in, a glint in her eye. At the street door she'd whispered that she couldn't wait to see how Emtee Dempsey broke the shell of Miss Butterfingers.

Kim said nothing. It was unnervingly clear that Emtee Dempsey meant to exonerate the convicted terrorist. Katherine might soon be witnessing the first public embarrassment of her old friend, rather than another triumph. Janet was in the kitchen talking with Joyce, so Kim answered the door when Richard arrived. Regina Fastnekker stood beside him, hands joined in front of her, linked with cuffs, but her expression was serene. Behind them were two of Richard's colleagues, Gleason and O'Connell, shifting their weight and looking up and down the street. Kim stepped aside and they trooped in.

"Okay if we just go upstairs?"

"The others are in the living room."

Richard ignored that and proceeded up the stairs with his prisoner. O'Connell leaned close to Kim. "Who's here?"

"I'll introduce you."

Gleason tugged O'Connell's arm and shook his head warningly. They would stay right where they were.

When Richard came into the living room, one hand on Regina's elbow, he feigned surprise at the people gathered there.

"I'm here for an on-site inspection of the bombing," he announced to the far wall.

Mrs. Layton was staring with horror at Regina Fastnekker and her husband looked murderously at the expressionless terrorist. Regina had an announcement of her own.

"Your automobile was blown up by Michael Layton," she said to Sister Mary Teresa.

"Get her out of here!" Geoffrey Layton cried. "Better yet, we'll go."

"Wait," Emtee Dempsey said. "Let us hear what Regina has to say."

She repeated, "Michael Layton blew up your car. I called him as soon as I heard of it on the news." She moved closer to the old nun. "He despised me for being born-again. He meant to force my hand."

Geoffrey Layton sneered. "He blew up their car and then blew up himself and then blew up the sisters' computer? Is that your story?"

"Did you kill Michael Layton?" Sister Mary Teresa asked Regina.

"No."

The old nun shifted her hands on the arms of the chair. "Did you do anything that resulted in the death of Michael Layton?"

Regina started. But she did not answer. She looked warily, almost fearfully at the old nun.

"I know you express yourself with great precision," Emtee Dempsey said. "One who has vowed always to tell the truth must be most precise in what he says. I ask you again. Did you do anything that . . ."

"Yes!'

A smile broke out on Richard's face and he looked as if he might actually hug Emtee Dempsey.

"But you didn't murder him?"

"No."

"Richard, let our guest sit down so that she can speak at her leisure."

But Regina shook her head. She preferred to speak standing. "Michael blew up your car, using skills we had learned together. This consisted in planting the device and from a distance activating it. After Michael's phone call, I drove past his house with a transceiver set at the appropriate frequency."

"And there was an explosion."

"Yes."

"So you killed him!" Richard said.

"No. He killed himself. That radio signal could only harm him if he intended to harm someone else. If a man fires at another and his gun backfires and kills him, has his intended victim killed him or has he killed himself?"

It was a discussion that went on for some time. The general consensus in the room was that Regina was lying, blaming a dead man.

"That's how she planned it," Geoffrey Layton said with disgust.

Benjamin Rush sat sunk into himself. Nothing Geoffrey Layton could say would restore his son's honor.

Emtee Dempsey rose and went to Mrs. Layton who was looking around almost wildly, as if she could not at all understand what was going on. Kim felt much the same way. Her eye met Janet's and she went to her. How awful this must be for her. But Janet did not want to be consoled.

"I'm leaving," she said, and started for the kitchen door.

"Wait, my dear." Surprisingly, Emtee Dempsey was at Kim's side. She took Janet's hand authoritatively and led her to Regina.

"Regina Fastnekker," she said, "did you give this girl computer disks to pass on to me?"

Regina looked surprised for the second time.

"No."

"You are not dissembling, are you?"

Regina peered at Janet. "Is that how it was done?"

Janet lunged at Regina, who lifted her manacled hands and staved off the blow. By then Emtee Dempsey had again grasped Janet's wrist and Richard had come to her assistance.

"We're talking about the device that blew up the computer?"

"She's the one," Janet screamed, trying to free herself. "She ruined Michael's life and he waited for her while she was in jail and out she comes a religious freak. No more terrorism for Miss Butterfingers."

Janet threw back her head and began to howl in frustration. Her father seemed to age before their eyes and Mrs. Layton recoiled from the spectacle of her out-of-control daughter. Benjamin Rush tried to calm Janet, but she lowered her shoulder and bumped him away, very nearly sending him to the floor. That's when O'Connell and Gleason came in and subdued her. It seemed a good idea to unshackle Regina and put the cuffs on Janet. Katherine Senski stood, looked around the room, and asked if she could use the study. She had a story to write.

But her story was incomplete until two days later when a defiant but subdued Janet told of rigging the disks in order to turn suspicion firmly on
Regina. The woman had ruined Michael's life and Janet was sure she had
killed him as well. By continuing with her brother's plan, she hoped to
send Regina Fastnekker back to prison.

That, as it turned out, was her own destination, however postponed
it would be, given the legal counsel her parents hired for her defense. She
released a statement saying that she regretted that anything she might
have done had threatened the nuns on Walton Street. But by then she had
reverted to her story that Regina Fastnekker had persuaded her to deliver
the disks.

Questioned about this at the mall where she was urging shoppers to
repent and be saved, Regina would say only, "When I was a child I spoke
as a child, but now that I have become a man I have put away the things
of a child."

Emtee Dempsey asked Katherine if her paper's policy would necessi-
tate altering the scriptural passage cited by Miss Butterfingers, but her old
friend pretended not to hear.

In the Confessional

Alice Scanlan Reach

Blue slipped in through the side door of St. Brigid's and stood motionless in the shadow of the confessional. Opposite him loomed the statue of the Blessed Virgin treading gently on a rising bank of vigil lights. Blue's eyes, darting to the ruby fingers of flame flickering around the marble feet, saw that the metal box nearby with the sign *Candles—10¢* had not yet been replenished. Only a few wax molds remained. Had the box been full, Blue would have known he was too late—that Father Crumlish, on depositing a fresh supply, had opened the drawer attached to the candle container and emptied it of the past week's silver offerings.

So all was well! Once again, all unknowingly, the house of God would furnish Blue with the price of a jug of wine.

Now, from his position in the shadow, Blue's red-rimmed eyes shifted to the altar where Father Crumlish had just turned the lock in the sacristy door, signaling the start of his nightly nine-o'clock lock-up routine.

Blue knew it by heart.

First, the closing and locking of the weather-weary stained-glass windows. Next, the bolting of the heavy oaken doors in the rear of the church. Then came the dreaded moment. Tonight, as every night, listening to Father Crumlish make fast the last window and then approach the confessional, Blue fought the panic pushing against his lungs—the fear that the priest would give the musty interior of the confessional more than a quick, casual glance.

Suppose tonight it occurred to Father Crumlish to peer into the confessional's shadow to see if someone were lurking—

Blue permitted himself a soft sigh of blessed relief. He was safe! The slow footsteps were retreating up the aisle. To be sure, there were torturing hours ahead, but that was the price he had to pay. Already he could almost feel his arms cradling the beloved bottle, his fingers caressing the gracefully curved neck. He could almost taste the soothing, healing sweetness.

It was almost too much to bear.

Now came what Blue, chuckling to himself, called "the floor show."

Extinguishing the lights in the rear of the church and thus leaving it, except for candlelight, in total darkness, Father Crumlish, limping a little from the arthritis buried deep in his ancient roots, climbed the narrow winding stairway to the choir loft.

Blue, hearing the first creaking stair, moved noiselessly and swiftly. In the space of one deep breath he flickered out of the shadow, entered the nearest "sinner's" door of the confessional, and silently closed it behind him. Then he knelt in cramped darkness, seeing nothing before him but the small closed window separating him from the confessor's sanctuary.

By now Father Crumlish had reached the choir loft and the "show" began. Believing himself alone—with his God and Maker, the descendant of a long line of shillelagh wielders ran his arthritic fingers over the organ's keys and poured out his soul in song. Presently the church rafters rang with his versions of "When Irish Eyes Are Smiling," "Come Back to Erin," and "The Rose of Tralee."

It was very pleasant and Blue didn't mind too much that his knee joints ached painfully from their forced kneeling position. As a matter of fact, he rather enjoyed this interlude in the evening's adventure. It gave him time to think, a process which usually eluded him in the shadowy, unreal world where he existed. And what better place to think than this very church where he had served as an altar boy forty—fifty?—how many years ago?

That was another reason he never had the slightest qualm about filching the price of a bottle from the Blessed Virgin's vigil-light offering box. "Borrowing," Blue called it. And who had a better right? Hadn't he dropped his nickels and dimes in the collection basket every Sunday and Holy Day of Obligation from the time he was a tot until—?

The Blessed Virgin and Father Crumlish and the parishioners of St. Brigid's were never going to miss a few measly dimes. Besides, he was only "borrowing" until something turned up. And someday, wait and see, he'd walk down the center aisle of the church, dressed fit to kill, proud as a peacock, and put a $100 bill in the basket for the whole church to see, just as easy as you please!

A small smile brushed against Blue's thin lips, struggled to reach the dull sunken eyes, gave up in despair, and disappeared. Blue dozed a little.

He might more appropriately have been called Gray. For there was a bleak grayness about him that bore the stamp of fog and dust, of the gray pinched mask of death and destruction. His withered bones seemed to be shoved indifferently into threadbare coat and trousers; and from a disjointed blob of cap a few sad straggles of hair hung listlessly about his destroyed face. Time had long ceased to mean anything to Blue—and he to time.

All that mattered now was the warm, lovely, loving liquid and the occasional bite of biscuit to go with it. And thanks to St. Brigid's parishioners, thanks to his knowledge of Father Crumlish's unfailing nightly routine, Blue didn't have to worry about where the next bottle was coming from. The job was easy. And afterward he could doze in peace in the last pew of the church until it came time to mingle with the faithful as they arrived for six o'clock morning Mass, and then slip unnoticed out the door.

Now, kneeling in the confines of the confessional, Blue jerked his head up from his wasted chest and stiffened. Sudden silence roared in his ears. For some unseen reason Father Crumlish had broken off in the middle of the third bar of "Tralee."

Then, in the deathly pale quiet, the priest's voice rang out.

"Who's there?"

Sweet Jesus! thought Blue. Did I snore?

"Answer me!" More insistent now. "Who's there?"

Blue, his hand on the confessional doorknob, had all but risen when the answer came.

"It's me, Father—Johnny Sheehan."

Sinking back to his knees, Blue could hear every word in the choir loft clear as a bell, resounding in the shuttered, hollow church.

"What's on your mind, Johnny?"

Blue caught the small note of irritation in the priest's voice and knew it was because Father Crumlish treasured his few unguarded moments with "The Rose of Tralee."

"I—I want to go to confession, Father."

A long pause and then Blue could almost hear the sigh of resignation to duty and to God's will.

"Then come along, lad."

Now how do you like that for all the lousy luck, Blue thought, exasperated. Some young punk can't sleep in his nice warm beddybye until he confesses.

Confesses!

Blue felt the ice in his veins jam up against his heart. Father Crumlish would most certainly bring the repentant sinner to *this* confessional since it was next to the side-door entrance. Even now Blue could hear the oncoming footsteps. Suppose he opens *my* door instead of the other one? Dear God, please let him open the first door!

Trembling, Blue all but collapsed with relief as he heard the other door open and close, heard the settling of knees on the bench, and lastly, the faint whisper of cloth as Father Crumlish entered the priest's enclosure that separated himself from Blue on one side and from Johnny Sheehan on the other by thin screened windows.

Now Blue heard the far wooden window slide back and knew that Johnny Sheehan was bowing his head to the screen, fixing his eyes on the crucifix clasped in the confessor's hands.

"Bless me, Father, for I have sinned. . ."

The voice pulled taut, strained, and snapped.

"Don't be afraid to tell God, son. You know about the Seal of Confession—anything you tell here you confess to God and it remains sealed with Him forever."

Confess you stole a bunch of sugar beets and get it over with, Blue thought angrily. He was getting terribly tired and the pain in his knees was almost more than he could bear.

"I—she—"

She! Well, what do you know? Blue blinked his watery eyes in a small show of surprise. So the young buck's got a girl in trouble. Serves him right. Stick to the warmer embrace of the bottle, my lad. It'll keep you out of mischief.

"I heard your first confession when you were seven, Johnny. How old are you now? Sixteen?"

"Y—yes, Father."

"This girl. What about her?"

"I—I killed her!"

In the rigid silence Blue heard the boy's body sag against the wooden partition and was conscious of a sharp intake of breath from the priest. Blue was as alert now as he ever was these soft, slow days and nights, but he knew that sometimes he just thought he heard words when actually he'd only dreamed them. Yet—Blue eased one hurting kneecap and leaned closer to the dividing wood.

Father Crumlish shifted his weight in his enclosure.

"Killed?"

Only retching sobs.

"Tell me, Johnny." Father Crumlish's voice was ever so gentle now.

Then the words came in a torrent.

"She laughed at me—said I wasn't a man—and I couldn't stand it, Father. When Vera May laughed—"

"Vera May!" the priest broke in. "Vera May Barton?"

Even in the shifting mists and fog of his tired memory, Blue recognized that name. Who didn't these past few weeks? Who didn't know that every cop in the city was hunting Vera May Barton's murderer? Why, even some of Blue's best pals had been questioned. Al was ready to hang a rap on some poor innocent.

Blue rarely read newspapers, but he listened to lots of talk. And most of the talk in the wine-shrouded gloom of his haunts these past weeks had been about the slaying of sixteen-year-old Vera May Barton, a choir singer at St. Brigid's. Someone had shown Blue her picture on the front page of a newspaper. A beautiful girl, blonde and soft and smiling. But someone—someone with frantic, desperate hands—had strangled the blonde softness and choked off the smile.

Blue was suddenly conscious once more of the jagged voice.

"She wasn't really like they say, Father. Vera May wasn't really good. She just wanted you to think so. But sometimes, when I'd deliver my newspapers in the morning, sometimes she'd come to the door with hardly any clothes. And when I'd ask her to go to a show or something, she'd only laugh and say I wasn't a man."

"Go on," Father Crumlish said softly.

"I—she told me she was staying after choir practice that night to collect the hymnals—"

The priest sighed. "I blame myself for that. For letting her stay in the church alone—even for those few moments—while I went over to the rectory."

"And then—then when she left," the halting words went on, "I followed her out in the alley—"

Blue's pals had told him about that—how one of St. Brigid's early morning Mass parishioners found Vera May lying like a broken figurine in the dim alley leading from the church to the rectory. She wasn't carrying a purse, the newspapers said. And she hadn't been molested. But her strangler, tearing at her throat, had broken the thin chain of the St. Christopher's medal around her neck. It had her initials on the back but the medal had never been found.

"What did you do with the medal, Johnny?" Father Crumlish asked quietly.

"I—I was afraid to keep it, Father." The agonized voice broke again. "The river—"

The weight of the night pressed heavily on Blue and he sighed deeply. But the sigh was lost in the low murmuring of the priest to the boy—too low for Blue to catch the words—and perhaps, against all his instincts, he dozed. Then there was a sudden stirring in the adjoining cubicles.

Blue knelt rigid and breathless while the doors opened, and without turning his head toward the faint candlelight shimmering through the cracks in the door of his enclosure, he knew that Father Crumlish had opened the side entrance and released Johnny Sheehan to the gaunt and starless dark.

Slowly the priest moved toward the first pew before the center altar. And now Blue risked glancing through the sliver of light in his door. Father Crumlish knelt, face buried in his hands.

A wisp of thought drifted into the wine-eroded soil of Blue's mind. Was the priest weeping?

But Blue was too engrossed in his own discomfort, too aware of the aching, ever-increasing, burning dryness of his breath and bones. If only the priest would go and leave Blue to his business and his sleep!

After a long time he heard the footsteps move toward the side door. Now it closed. Now the key turned in the lock.

Now!

Blue stumbled from the confessional and collapsed in the nearest pew. Stretched full length, he let his weary body and mind sag in relief. Perhaps he slept; he only knew that he returned, as if from a long journey.

Sitting upright, he brought out the tools of his trade from somewhere within the tired wrappings that held him together.

First the chewing gum—two sticks, purchased tonight.

Blue munched them slowly, carefully bringing them to the proper consistency. Then, rising, he fingered a small length of wire and, leaving the pew, shuffled toward the offering box beneath the Blessed Virgin's troubled feet.

Taking the moist gum from his mouth, Blue attached it to the wire and inserted it carefully into the slot of the box. A gentle twist and he extracted the wire. Clinging to the gummed end were two coins, a nickel and a dime.

Blue went through this procedure again and again until he had collected the price of a bottle. Then he lowered himself into the nearest pew and rested a bit.

He began to think of what had happened in the confessional. But it had been so long since Blue had made himself concentrate on anything but his constant, thirsting need that it took a while for the rusted wheels to move, for the pretty colored lights to cease their small whirlings and form a single brightness illuminating the makings of his mind.

Finally he gave up. The burning dryness had gripped him again and he began to yearn for the long night to be over so that he could spend, in the best way he knew, the money he held right in his hand this minute.

Two bottles! I should have two bottles for all the trouble I've been through tonight, Blue thought. They owe it to me for making me kneel there so long and robbing me of my sleep. Yes, they owe it to me!

And so thinking, he took out the gum once more and, bringing it to his mouth, chewed it again into pliable moistness.

The first try at the offering box brought him only a dime, but the second try—God was good—another dime, a nickel, and a dollar bill!

Too exhausted to drag himself to his customary last-pew bed, Blue stretched out once more on the nearest wood plank and slept.

✝   ✝   ✝

Some time later, the unrelenting dryness wakened him. This "in between" period was the only time Blue ever approached sobriety. And in the sobering, everything seemed terribly, painfully clear. He began to relive the events of the night, hearing the voices again with frightening clarity. Father Crumlish's and then the kid's—

Blue's own voice screamed in his ears.

"Out! I've got to get out of here! Nobody knows but me—nobody knows about the murder but me. I've got to tell. But first I'll have to have a little sip. I need a little sip. And then I'll tell—"

In a flurry of cloth and dust Blue rushed to the side door. He had never before tried to let himself out this way and had no idea if the door was locked. But the knob gave easily, and in an instant he had closed the door behind him and, leaning heavily against it, was breathing the night's whispering wind.

It had been a long time since Blue had been out alone in the deep dark, and suddenly, with the night's dreadful knowledge inside him, it was overpowering. Shadows rushed at him, clawed at his face and fingers, and crushed him so bindingly that he could scarcely breathe.

In an agony to get away, he plunged into the blackness and began to run.

And in his urgency Blue never heard the shout behind him, the pounding feet on the pavement. He never heard the cry to halt or risk a bullet. He only knew that he was flying, faster and faster, yet not fast enough, soaring higher and higher, until a surprisingly small jagged thrust of sidewalk clawed at him and brought him to his knees.

The bullet from his pursuer, meant to pierce his worn and weary legs, pierced his back.

Suddenly it was calm and quiet and there was no longer any need for speed. He lay on his side, crumpled and useless, like a discarded bundle of rags.

A wave, a wine-red wave, swept over him and Blue let himself rock and toss for a moment in its comforting warmth. Then he opened his eyes and, dimly, in the fast-gathering darkness, recognized Father Crumlish bending over him.

"Poor devil," Blue heard the priest say. "But don't blame yourself, officer. The fellow probably just didn't know you'd be suspicious of his running away like that. Particularly around here, now, after the Barton girl. The poor devil probably just didn't know."

Didn't know? Blue didn't know? He knew, all right! And he had to tell.

"Father!"

Quickly the priest bent his ear to Blue's quivering lips. "I'm listening," he said.

"I—was in the confessional too."

"The confessional?"

The wave rushed to envelop him again. Before he could speak the urgent words, he heard the officer's voice.

"He came out of the church door, Father. I saw him."

"I don't see how that's possible," the priest said bewilderedly.

Blue forced the breath from his aching lungs.

"I heard—the kid confess. I have to tell—"

"Wait!" Father Crumlish said sharply, cutting Blue off. "You have nothing to tell. Maybe you heard. But you don't know about that boy. The poor confused lad's come to me to confess to every robbery and murder in this parish for years. You have nothing to tell, do you hear me?"

"Nothing?"

Blue almost laughed a little. For the pain was gone now and he felt as if—as if he were walking down St. Brigid's center aisle, dressed fit to kill, proud as a peacock, and putting a $100 bill in the collection basket for the whole church to see just as easy as you please.

"There's something—"

His voice was strong and clear as he brought his fumbling fingers from within the moldy rags and stretched out his hand to the priest.

"I was 'borrowing' from the Blessed Virgin, Father. Just enough for a bottle, though. I need it, Father. All the time. Bad! She caught me at it. And she was running to tell you. But if she did, where in the world would I ever get another bottle, Father? Where? So I had to stop her!"

Fighting the final warm, wine-red wave that was washing over him, Blue thrust into Father Crumlish's hand a St. Christopher's medal dangling from a broken chain and initialed V.M.B.

"I've been saving it, Father. In a pinch, I thought it might be worth a bottle."

AUTHOR BIOGRAPHIES

CHARLOTTE ARMSTRONG (1905–1969) was a "modern witch" according to the late and esteemed writer-critic Anthony Boucher. She took common, everyday situations and found the danger and menace in them. Her short novel *Mischief* is a perfect example: Husband and wife going on a business trip to New York hire a babysitter for their young daughter. The trouble is, the sitter is dangerously ill mentally and resents the life the little child leads. Only by the skin of their teeth are they able to rescue their daughter. A truly harrowing novel. Armstrong was one of the leading suspense novelists of her time and died far too young, in her early sixties.

"Among the writers I admire most are Christie, Allingham, Rendell, and Margaret Millar," **ROBERT BARNARD** once noted. Perhaps this is why his own voice is that of a "pure" detective writer. Whatever else a given Barnard novel may offer (humor, keen social observation, place description that is genuinely poetic) his novels and stories always remain focused on the mystery. While one hates to speculate on which writers of our time will be read by future generations, Barnard, with his grace, his intelligence, and his enormous range of skills, is certainly a likely contender. *Death of an Old Goat* (1977), *Bodies* (1986), and *A City of Strangers* are among his many worthwhile novels, with his latest including *The Lost Boy* and *A Murder in Mayfair.*

Not many writers can sell a manuscript from the slush pile that goes on to be nominated for both the Agatha and Anthony mystery awards. But **Jan Burke** did just that. And, in a handful of novels about her newspaper protagonist Irene Kelly, Burke has found an ever-expanding audience eager for her next book. She is also a fine short story writer, her story "Unharmed" winning both the Ellery Queen Mystery Readers Award and the Macavity award. Her most recent novels include *Bones* and *Flight*.

G. K. Chesterton (1874–1936) was so well known for his Father Brown detective stories that he sometimes grew resentful, feeling that the press tended to overlook his "serious" writings. Good as some of that writing undoubtedly was, it is largely for the Father Brown stories—and one extraordinary novel, *The Man Who Was Thursday*—that we remember him today (Chesterton scholars to the contrary not withstanding). The Browns are some of the best pure detective stories of all times, and deliciously, delightfully British. They influenced, among many others, everybody from Julian Symons to Agatha Christie.

Born in New York, **Richard Connell** (1893–1949) claimed to be the world's youngest professional author. He covered baseball games at the age of six with his father, who was then editor of the *New York News Press*. He attended Georgetown College for a year, but graduated from Harvard in 1915, after which he served as a reporter for the *New York American*. When World War I broke out, he served with the Twenty-Seventh Division in France. After the war he became a freelance writer, turning out more than three hundred short stories, novels, and scripts. He is best remembered for the classic adventure story "The Most Dangerous Game," which was filmed three times.

P. C. Doherty is the prolific author of more than three dozen novels featuring three different characters, all set at different times in the Middle Ages. He has written under several pseudonyms, including Michael Clynes, Ann Dukthas, C. L. Grace, and Paul Harding. His research is always authentic, mostly due to his doctorate in history from Oxford University. His most recent novel is *The Horus Killings*.

Kathleen Dougherty's story "When Your Breath Freezes" was one of the seven finalist stories for the Mystery Writers of America's fiftieth anniversary contest. Her novels have been described as "explorations of the dark underbelly of the mind." She has worked as a sales manager for an artificial intelligence company and as a research associate in pharmacology.

Westerns, gangster novels, private eyes, historical novels, Victorian gothics starring Jack the Ripper and assorted other monsters (including the sometimes monstrous Holmes himself), **LOREN D. ESTLEMAN** has had one of those enviable careers filled with kudos and commercial success. His work, mystery and non-mystery alike, constantly appears on annual year's best lists, and his list of admiring critics grows increasingly longer. Here he is working the shadowy streets of crime fiction, where a down-on-his-luck private eye stumbles into a case of a high-ranking member of the Catholic church gone wrong.

LADY ANTONIA FRASER is not only a mystery writer but also a serious student of history, having earned her B.A. and M.A. at Lady Margaret Hall, Oxford. Her father is Lord Langford, a man who writes; and her husband the famous playwright Harold Pinter. She edits *The Kings and Queens of England* books while finding time to write her internationally renowned mystery novels, including the recent *Oxford Blood*. She recently edited the nonfiction book *The Lives of the Kings and Queens of England*.

MARGARET FRAZER is the pseudonym of Gail Frazer, who has been writing mystery novels for years, formerly as the partner of Mary Kuhfield. She has since taken the pseudonym and continued the medieval murder mystery series featuring Sister Frevisse, a great-niece of Geoffrey Chaucer. The series currently spans nine novels, with *The Maiden's Tale* and *The Prioress's Tale* being the most recent. She lives in Minnesota, where she is hard at work on future Sister Frevisse novels.

NEIL GAIMAN is a world-class fantasist. Whether in his graphic novels of *The Sandman* or in his many novels or story collections, Gaiman has elected to show us—and the world around us—in the slightly skewed perspective that writers from Lord Dunsany to Ray Bradbury to Clive Barker to Terry Prachett favor—and, in truth, Gaiman's unique voices manage to incorporate just about every major strain of traditional and modern fantasy—and yet remain just that, unique, and unlike anyone else's. Recent books include *The Day I Swapped my Dad for Two Goldfish, Stardust,* and *American Gods*.

Who says a priest can't have a second career as a bestselling author? Father **ANDREW GREELEY** has done just that. In addition to his excellent mainstream novels (*Irish Gold, Irish Lace, Irish Whiskey, Fall from Grace*), he has also graced the mystery field with his Father "Blackie" Ryan series. Greeley is never better than when he gives us a behind-the-scenes look at Church politics and brinksmanship. He couples his priestly devotion with his very real concerns for how the Church conducts itself in this most trying of times. His fiction, in whatever form he chooses to use, is always a pleasure to read.

EDWARD HOCH is probably the only man in the world who supports himself exclusively by writing short stories. He has appeared in every issue of *Ellery Queen Mystery Magazine* since the late 1970s, and manages to write for several other markets as well. He has probably created more short story series characters than anybody who ever worked in the crime fiction field. And what great characters, too—Michael Vlado, a Gypsy detective; Dr. Sam Hawthorne, a small-town GP of the 1920s who solves impossible crimes while dispensing good health; and, among many others, his outre and bedazzling Simon Ark, who claims, in the proper mood, to be two thousand years old. Locked room, espionage, cozy, hard-boiled, suspense, Ed Hoch has done it all and done it well.

In his all too brief life, Anthony Boucher (1911–1968), who wrote under several pseudonyms, **H. H. HOLMES** being just one of them, managed to be a seminal editor, reviewer, publisher, and writer in not one but two genres: mystery and science fiction. He was the founder and long-time co-editor of *The Magazine of Fantasy & Science Fiction* and the mystery reviewer for the *New York Times* for many years. He was also a writer of great wit, subtlety, and skill—again in both genres—and whether in fantasy or mystery fiction, he showed himself to be a devout and serious Catholic scholar. His short stories of Sister Ursula are especially good. No one has come close to replacing him since his death in 1968. The largest annual mystery convention in the United States—the Bouchercon—is named for him.

RALPH MCINERNY has long been acknowledged as one of the most vital voices in lay Catholic activities in America. He is co-founder and co-publisher of CRISIS, a widely read journal of Catholic opinion, while finding time to teach Medieval Studies at Notre Dame University and write several series of mystery novels, one of which, *The Father Dowling Mysteries*, ran on network television for several seasons, and can now be seen on cable. Scholars are rarely entertainers. Ralph McInerny, both as himself and under his pseudonym Monica Quill, has been both for many, many years.

Just in case you don't think anything exciting happened in twelfth-century France, just consult **SHARAN NEWMAN**'s excellent, lively novels in her Catherine LeVendeur mystery series. A genuine medievalist, Newman won the Macavity with her first novel *Death Comes as Epiphany*, which was also nominated for the Agatha and Anthony awards. The books have continued to grow in popularity and the demands of writing them ever more difficult. But even so, and despite her workload, she is finishing her Ph.D in history at the University of California. Her latest novel is *To Wear the White Cloak*.

ALICE SCANLAN REACH is the creator of Irish priest Father Xavier Crumlish, who made more than a dozen appearances in the pages of *Ellery Queen's Mystery Magazine* and *Alfred Hitchcock's Mystery Magazine* in the 1960s. Her work is characterized by wry insight into the workings—and failings—of the human heart. Unfortunately, the good Father has never appeared in a novel-length work, but there is always hope that that situation might change.

COPYRIGHTS AND PERMISSIONS